MIDWIFE

SUE MACKAY

HIS BEST FRIEND'S BABY

BY

SUSAN CARLISLE

MILLS & BOON

MIDWIVES ON-CALL

Welcome to Melbourne Victoria Hospital—
and to the exceptional midwives
who make up the Melbourne Maternity Unit!

These midwives in a million work miracles on a daily basis, delivering tiny bundles of joy into the arms of their brand-new mums!

Amidst the drama and emotion of babies arriving at all hours of the day and night, when the shifts are over, somehow there's still time for some sizzling out-of-hours romance…

Whilst these caring professionals might come face-to-face with a whole lot of love in their line of work, now it's their turn to find a happy-ever-after of their own!

Midwives On-Call

Midwives, mothers and babies—
lives changing for ever…!

Eight special stories to collect and treasure:

Just One Night? by Carol Marinelli
Meant-to-Be Family by Marion Lennox
Always the Midwife by Alison Roberts
Midwife's Baby Bump by Susanne Hampton
Midwife…to Mum! by Sue MacKay
His Best Friend's Baby by Susan Carlisle
Unlocking Her Surgeon's Heart by Fiona Lowe
Her Playboy's Secret by Tina Beckett

MIDWIFE...TO MUM!

BY
SUE MACKAY

Published in Great Britain 2015
by Mills & Boon, an imprint of Harlequin (UK) Limited,
Eton House, 18-24 Paradise Road, Richmond, Surrey, TW9 1SR

Special thanks and acknowledgement are given to Sue MacKay
for her contribution to the *Midwives On-Call* series

ISBN: 978-0-263-24711-4

Harlequin (UK) Limited's policy is to use papers that are natural, renewable and recyclable products and made from wood grown in sustainable forests. The logging and manufacturing processes conform to the legal environmental regulations of the country of origin.

Printed and bound in Spain
by CPI, Barcelona

Dear Reader,

I'm so excited to have written one of the ***Midwives On-Call*** continuity stories set in Melbourne.

When Kiwis visit Australia we call it hopping across the ditch. In this case my story has hopped over there. It's fun to write a story set in a very different location from my usual haunts.

Flynn and Ally are made for each other—it just takes them time to work that out. But who could go wrong with love on the beautiful Phillip Island, which sits just below Melbourne and the Victoria coastline? Throw in the cutest little boy and a big friendly dog and life's a beach.

I hope you enjoy reading Flynn and Ally's story, and seeing how it ties in with the other stories in this series.

Drop by my website, suemackay.co.nz, or send me an email at sue.mackay56@yahoo.com

Cheers!

Sue MacKay

With a background of working in medical laboratories, and a love of the romance genre, it is no surprise that **Sue MacKay** writes Mills & Boon® Medical Romance™ stories. An avid reader all her life, she wrote her first story at age eight—about a prince, of course. She lives with her own hero in the beautiful Marlborough Sounds, at the top of New Zealand's South Island, where she indulges her passions for the outdoors, the sea and cycling.

Books by Sue MacKay

Mills & Boon® Medical Romance™

Doctors to Daddies

A Father for Her Baby
The Midwife's Son

The Family She Needs
A Family This Christmas
From Duty to Daddy
The Gift of a Child
You, Me and a Family
Christmas with Dr Delicious
Every Boy's Dream Dad
The Dangers of Dating Your Boss
Surgeon in a Wedding Dress

Visit the author profile page at millsandboon.co.uk for more titles

Praise for Sue MacKay

'A deeply emotional, heart-rending story that will make you smile and make you cry. I truly recommend it—and don't miss the second book: the story about Max.'

—*HarlequinJunkie* on *The Gift of a Child*

'What a great book. I loved it. I did not want it to end. This is one book not to miss.'

—*GoodReads* on *The Gift of a Child*

CHAPTER ONE

ALYSSA PARKER DROPPED her bags in the middle of the lounge and stared around what would be her next temporary living quarters. She could pretty much see it all from where she stood. Dusting and vacuuming weren't going to take up her spare time, like it had at the last place. She'd have to find something else to keep her busy after work. Take up knitting? Or hire a dog to walk every day?

Her phone rang. Tugging it from her jacket pocket, she read the name on the screen and punched the 'talk' button. 'Hey, boss, I've arrived on Phillip Island.' The bus trip down from Melbourne city had been interminable as she'd kept dozing off. It had taken the ferry crossing and lots of fresh air to clear her head.

'How's the head?' Lucas Elliot, her senior midwife, asked.

'It's good now. Who have you been talking to?' She and some of the crew from the Melbourne Midwifery Unit had gone out for drinks, which had extended to a meal and more drinks.

'My lips are sealed,' Lucas quipped. 'So, Phillip Island—another place for you to tick off on the map.'

'Yep.' Her life was all about new destinations and

experiences. Certainly not the regular nine to five in the same place, year in, year out, that most people preferred.

'How's the flat?'

'About the size of a dog kennel.' Stepping sideways, Ally peered into what looked like an overgrown cupboard. 'It's an exaggeration to call this a kitchen. But, hey, that's part of the adventure.' Like she needed a kitchen when she favoured takeout food anyway.

'Ally, I forgot to tell you where the key to the flat would be, but it seems you've taken up breaking and entering on the side.'

She was Ally to everyone except the taxman and her lawyer. And the social welfare system. 'It was under the pot plant on the top step.' The first place she'd looked.

'Why do people do that? It's so obvious.' Lucas sounded genuinely perplexed.

Still looking around, she muttered, 'I doubt there's much worth stealing in here.' Kat, the midwife she was replacing temporarily, certainly didn't spend her pay packet on home comforts.

'Are you happy with the arrangements? I know you enjoy everywhere we send you, but this should be the best yet as far as location goes. All those beaches to play on.'

'It's winter, or haven't you noticed?' Ally shook her head. 'But so far the island's looking beautiful.'

His chuckle was infectious. 'I'll leave you to unpack and find your way around. You're expected at the medical centre at eight thirty tomorrow. Dr Reynolds wants to run through a few details with you before you get started with the Monday morning antenatal list.'

'Same as any locum job I do, then?' She couldn't help the jibe. She'd been doing this relief work for two years now. It suited her roving lifestyle perfectly and was the only reason she remained with the Melbourne Midwifery Unit. They'd offered her fixed positions time and again. She'd turned them all down. Fixed meant working continuously at the midwifery unit, which in turn meant getting too close to those people she'd work with every day.

The days when she set herself up to get dumped by anyone—friends, colleagues or lovers—were long over. Had been from the monumental day she'd turned sixteen and taken control of her life. She'd walked out of the social welfare building for the very last time. It hadn't mattered that she'd had little money or knowledge on how to survive. She'd known a sense of wonder at being in charge of herself. Since then no one had screwed up her expectations because she'd been in charge of her own destiny. Because she hadn't allowed herself to hope for family or love again.

'I'm being pedantic.' Lucas was still on the other end of the line. 'I wanted to make sure everything's okay.'

Why wouldn't it be? She didn't need him fussing about her. She didn't like it. It spoke of care and concern. But Lucas did care about the people he worked with, which, despite trying not to let it, had always warmed her and given her a sense of belonging to the unit. Since she didn't do belonging, it showed how good Lucas was with his staff.

She told him, 'I'll take a walk to get my bearings and suss out where the medical centre is as soon as I've unpacked.' Tomorrow she'd collect the car provided for the job.

'Even your map-reading skills might just about manage that.' He laughed at his own joke. 'I'll leave you to get settled. Catch you in four weeks, unless there's a problem.'

Stuffing the phone back in her pocket, she headed into the bedroom and dumped a bag on the bed. At least it was a double. Not that she had any man to share the other half with. Not yet. *Who knows? There might be a hot guy at the surf beach who'd like a short fling, no strings.* Her mouth watered at the thought of all those muscles surfers must have. Winter wouldn't stop those dudes getting on their boards. There were such things as wetsuits.

After dropping her second, smaller bag full of books and DVDs out of the way in the corner of the lounge, she slapped her hands on her hips and stared around. Four o'clock in the afternoon and nothing to do. Once she started on the job she'd be fine, but these first hours when she arrived in a new place and moved into someone else's home always made her feel antsy. It wasn't her space, didn't hold her favourite possessions.

Except… Unzipping the bag, she placed two small silver statues on the only shelf. 'Hey, guys, welcome to Cowes.' Her finger traced the outlines of her pets. If she ever got to own a pet it would be a springer spaniel like these. Make that two spaniels. One on its own would be lonely.

She hadn't forgiven the Bartlett family who'd given her these on the day they'd broken her heart, along with their promise they'd love her for ever. She'd wrapped the statues in an empty chocolate box and tied it with a yellow ribbon, before burying them in the Bartletts' garden. The gift had been a consolation prize for abandoning her, but one dark day when she'd felt unable to carry on, she'd remembered the dogs *she'd* abandoned and had sneaked back to retrieve them. They'd gone everywhere with her ever since, a talisman to her stronger self.

Having the statues in place didn't make the flat hers,

though. Again Ally stared around. She could do a lap of the cupboards and shelves, learning where everything was kept. By then it'd be five past four and she'd still not know what to do with herself.

This moment was the only time she ever allowed that her life wasn't normal. *Define normal.* Doing what other people did.

Standing in the middle of a home she'd never been in before, didn't know the owner of, always brought up the question of what would it be like to settle down for ever in her own place.

As if she'd ever do that.

What if it was with a man who loved me regardless?

The answer never changed. That person didn't exist.

She followed her established routine for first days in new towns. First, off came her new and amazing knee-high black boots, then she pulled on her top-of-the-line walking shoes.

Sliding on her sunglasses, she snatched up the house key and stuffed it and her wallet into her pocket and headed out. There had to be a decent coffee shop somewhere. Might as well check out the options for takeout dinners, too. Then she'd head to the nearest beach to do some exploring.

The coffee turned out to be better than good. Ally drained the paper mug of every last drop and tossed it into the next rubbish bin she came across. The beach stretched ahead as she kicked up sand and watched the sea relentlessly rolling in. Kids chased balls and each other, couples strolled hand in hand, one grown-up idiot raced into the freezing water and straight back out, shouting his head off in shock.

Ally pulled out her phone and called the midwifery

centre back in the city, sighing happily when Darcie answered. 'Hey, how's the head?'

'Nothing wrong with mine, but, then, I was on orange juice all night.'

'You shouldn't be so quick to put your hand up for call.'

Darcie grumped, 'Says the woman who works more hours than the rest of us.' Then she cheered Ally up with, 'You can move into my spare room when you get back to town. As of this morning it's empty, my flatmate having found her own place.'

'Great, that's cool.' Darcie was fast becoming a good friend, which did bother her when she thought about it. But right this moment it felt good to have a friend onside when she was feeling more unsettled than usual at the start of a new assignment. Today she sensed she might be missing out on the bigger picture. This was the loneliness she'd learned to cope with whenever she'd been shuffled off to yet another foster home full of well-meaning people who'd always eventually packed her bags and sent her away.

'You still there?' Darcie asked.

'Did you get called in today?'

'I've just finished an urgent caesarean, and I'm about to get something to eat.'

'I'll leave you to it, then. Thanks for the bed. I'll definitely take you up on that.' After saying goodbye, she shoved her hands deep into her jacket pockets and began striding to the farthest end of the beach, feeling better already. Being alone wasn't so bad when there were people at the end of a phone. At least this way she got to choose which side of the bed she slept on, what she had for dinner, and when to move on to the next stop.

A ball came straight for her and she lined it up, kicked it back hard, aiming for the boys running after it. One of them swung a foot at it and missed, much to his mates' mirth at a girl kicking it better.

'Girls can do anything better.' She grinned and continued walking a few metres above the water's edge, feeling happier by the minute. How could she remain gloomy out here? The beach was beautiful, the air fresh, and she had a new job in the morning. What else could she possibly need?

The sun began dropping fast and Ally stopped to watch the amazing reds and yellows spreading, blending the sky and water into one molten colour block, like a young child's painting. Her throat ached with the beauty of it.

Thud. Something solid slammed into her. For a moment, as she teetered on her feet, she thought she'd keep her balance. But another shove and she toppled into an ungainly heap on the sand with the heavy weight on top of her. A moving, panting, licking heavy weight. A dog of no mean proportions with gross doggy breath sprawled across her.

'Hey, get off me.' She squirmed between paws and tried to push upright onto her backside.

One paw shoved her back down, and the dark, furry head blocked out all vision of the sunset. The rear end of the animal was wriggling back and forth as its tail whipped through the air.

'Sheba, come here.' A male voice came from somewhere above them. 'Get off now.'

Sheba—if that was the name of her assailant—gave Ally's chin a final lick and leapt sideways, avoiding an outstretched hand that must've been aiming for her collar.

'Phew.'

Her relief was premature. The dog lay down beside her as close as possible, and farthest away from the man trying to catch her. One paw banged down on her stomach, forcing all the air out of her lungs.

Somewhere behind her a young child started laughing. 'Sheba, you're funny.'

The sweet childish sound of pure enjoyment had Ally carefully pushing the paw aside and sitting up to look round for the source. A cute little boy was leaping up and down, giggling fit to bust.

'Sheba. Sit now.' The man wasn't nearly as thrilled about his dog's behaviour.

Ally stared up at the guy looming above her. 'It's all right. I'm fine, really.' She even smiled to prove her point.

'I'm very sorry Sheba bowled you over. She doesn't understand her own strength.' As he glanced across at the child his annoyance was quickly replaced by something soft she couldn't read. 'Adam, don't encourage her.'

'But it's funny, Dad.' The boy folded in half, still giggling.

Ally clambered to her feet, dusting sand off her jeans, and grinned. 'What is it about kids and giggling? They don't seem to know how to stop.' Just watching the boy made her happy—especially now that the dog had loped across to bunt him in the bottom, which only made the giggles louder. Laughter threatened to bubble up from deep inside her stomach.

The guy was shaking his head, looking bemused. 'Beats me how he keeps going so long.'

Ally winced. Slapping the sand off her left hip just made it sore. Sheba must've bruised her.

'Are you all right?' the man asked, worry darkening

his expression. 'Look, I apologise again. I hope you haven't been hurt.'

'Look,' she used his word back at him. 'I'm fine. Seriously. Sheba was being playful and if I hadn't been staring at the sunset I'd have seen her coming.' She stuck her hand out. 'I'm Ally. That's Sheba, and your boy's called Adam. You are?'

'Flynn. We've been visiting friends all day and needed some fresh air before settling down for the night.' He looked at her properly, finally letting go the need to watch his boy and dog. 'What about you?'

'Much the same. The beach is hard to resist when the weather's so balmy.' He didn't need to know she'd only just arrived. Running her hands over the sleeves of her jacket, she smoothed off the remaining sand, trying to refrain from staring at him. But it was impossible to look away.

Despite the sadness in his eyes, or because of it, she was taking more notice of him than a casual meeting on the beach usually entailed. The stubble darkening his chin was downright sexy, while that tousled hair brought heat to her cold cheeks. If she played her cards right, could this be the man she had her next fling with?

She glanced downward, taking in his athletic build, his fitted jeans that defined many of his muscles. The sun glinted off something on the guy's hand and she had her answer. A band of gold. Said it all, really.

'Can I call you Ally?' Adam bounced up in front of her.

Blink, blink. Refocus on the younger version now that the older one was out of bounds. 'Of course you can.' As if they were going to see each other again. Though they might, she realised, if Flynn brought his son to the beach often. She'd be walking along here most days that she wasn't caught up with delivering babies and talking to pregnant mums.

Hopefully, if they ran into each other again, Flynn would have his wife with him. A wife would certainly dampen the flare of attraction that had snagged her, and which should've evaporated the moment she'd seen that ring. Flings were the way to go, but never, ever with a man already involved with someone else. She didn't do hurting for the sake of it, or for any reason at all, come to think of it.

Guess she'd have to keep looking for someone to warm the other half of that bed. *Whoa, Ally, you haven't been here more than an hour. What's the hurry?*

The thing was, if she was playing bed games there wouldn't be long, empty nights that had her dreaming of the impossible. She could shove the overpowering sense of unworthiness aside as she and a man made each other happy for a short while, and then bury her face in the pillow while he left. Every parting, even as casual as her relationships were, was touched with a longing for the life she craved, had never known, and was too afraid to try for.

Flynn Reynolds dragged his gaze away from the most attractive woman he'd met in a long while and focused on his son. Except Adam stood directly in front of her, talking nonstop, and Flynn's gaze easily moved across the tiny gap to a stunning pair of legs clad in skin-tight jeans. His breathing hitched in his throat. Oh, wow. Gorgeous.

The woman—*Ally, she has a name*—laughed at something Adam said, a deep, pure laugh that spoke of enjoyment with no hidden agenda. Very refreshing, considering most women he met these days seemed intent on luring him into their clutches with false concern about him and Adam. He hated it that many women believed the way to attract him was by being overfriendly to his son. What they didn't get was that Adam saw through them almost as quickly as he did.

What they also didn't get was that Flynn wasn't interested. Not at all. So why was his gaze cruising over the length of this curvy woman with a smile that had him smiling back immediately, even when it wasn't directed at him? Especially since he apparently didn't do smiling very much these days.

He looked directly at his son. 'Time we made tracks for home. The sun's nearly gone and it will be cold soon.' Any excuse to cut this short and put some space between him and Ally before his brain started thinking along the lines of wanting to get to know her better. He wasn't ready for another woman in his life. Certainly wouldn't have time for years to come, either.

'Do we have to?'

'Yes, I'm afraid so.'

What I'm really afraid of is staying to talk to Ally too long and ending up inviting her home to share dinner with us. If she's free and available. As if a woman as attractive as her would be seriously single. The absence of rings on her fingers didn't mean a thing.

He looked around and groaned. 'Sheba,' he yelled. 'Come here.'

Too late. The mutt was belly deep in the sea, leaping and splashing without any concern for how cold the water had to be.

Adam ran down to the water's edge and stood with his

hands on his skinny hips. 'Sheba, Dad says we're going home. You want your dinner?'

Beside Flynn, Ally chuckled. 'Good luck with that.'

Glancing at her, he drew a deep breath. Her cheeks had flushed deep pink when the mutt had dumped her on the sand, and the colour still remained, becoming rosier every time she laughed. Which was often.

He noticed her rubbing her hip. 'You did hurt yourself.'

She jammed her hand in her pocket. 'Just a hard landing, nothing to worry about.'

'You're sure?' He'd hate it if Sheba had caused some damage.

'Absolutely.'

Adam and Sheba romped up to him. Then the dog did what wet dogs did—shook herself hard, sending salty spray over everyone. Now Ally would complain and walk away. But no. Her laughter filled the air and warmed the permanent chill in his soul. It would be unbelievably easy to get entangled with someone like her. Make that with this woman in particular.

He sighed his disappointment. There was no room in his life for a woman, no matter how beautiful. Not even for a short time. Adam and work demanded all his attention. Besides, how did a guy go about dating? He hadn't been in that market for so long he wouldn't know where to start. Was there a dating book for dummies? *I don't need one. It's not happening.* He gave himself a mental slap. All these questions and doubts because of a woman he'd met five minutes ago. He was in need of a break. That was his real problem. Solo parenting and work gobbled up all his time and energy.

'Let's go.' He grabbed Sheba's collar and turned in the direction of their street. 'Nice meeting you.' He nodded abruptly at the woman who'd been the first one to catch his interest since Anna had died two years ago. It had to be a fleeting interest; one that would've disappeared by the time he reached home and became immersed in preparing dinner, folding washing and getting ready for work tomorrow. Damn it all. It could've been fun getting to know her.

'Bye, Ally,' Adam called, as they started walking up the beach.

She stood watching them, both hands in her jacket pockets. 'See you around.' Was that a hint of wistfulness in her voice?

'Okay,' Adam answered, apparently reluctant to leave her. 'Tomorrow?'

'Adam,' Flynn growled. 'Come on.' He aimed for the road, deliberately stamping down on the urge to invite the woman home to share dinner. He did not need anyone else's problems. He did not need anyone else, full stop.

Anyway, she probably wouldn't like baked beans on toast.

Baked beans. He only had to close his eyes to hear Anna saying how unhealthy they were. They'd eaten lots of vegetables for lunch so he could relax the rules tonight. Beans once in a while wouldn't hurt Adam, and would save *him* some time. Who knew? He might get to watch the late news. Life was really looking up.

CHAPTER TWO

PLASTERING ON HER best smiley face the next morning, Ally stepped inside the medical centre, unzipping her jacket as she crossed to the reception desk. 'Hi, I'm Alyssa Parker.' Lucas always wrote her full name on her credentials when sending them to medical centres. It was a technicality he adhered to, and she hated it. 'Ally for short. I'm covering for Kat while she's away.'

A man straightened from the file he was reading and she gasped as the piercing blue eyes that had followed her into sleep last night now scanned her. Her smile widened. 'Flynn.' The buzz she'd felt standing by this man yesterday returned in full force, fizzing through her veins, heating her in places she definitely didn't need warmed by a married man. He was still as sexy, despite the stubble having been shaved off. *Stop it.* But she'd have to be six feet under not to react to him.

'Ally. Or do you prefer Alyssa?'

'Definitely Ally. Never Alyssa. So you're Dr Reynolds?' They hadn't swapped surnames the previous day. Hardly been any point when the chances of meeting again had seemed remote. Neither had she learned his first name when she was told about this job. She became aware of the receptionist glancing from her to Flynn, eyebrows high and a calculating look in her eyes.

Fortunately Flynn must've seen her, too. 'Megan's our office lady and general everything girl. She'll help you find files and stock lists and anything else you want.'

'You two know each other?' Megan asked her burning question.

Ally left that to Flynn to deal with and took a quick look around the office, but listened in as Flynn told the receptionist, 'We met briefly yesterday. Can you tell the others as they arrive that we're in the tearoom and can they come along to meet Ally?' Then he joined her on the other side of the counter. 'I'll show you around. You've got a busy clinic this morning. Three near full-term mums and four who are in their second trimester.'

'Three close to full term? Was there a party on the island eight months back that everyone went to?' She grinned.

'You'd be surprised how many pregnant ladies we see. Phillip Island's population isn't as small as people think. One of the women, Marie Canton, is Adam's daytime caregiver when he's not at preschool.'

So Adam's mum worked, too. Ally wondered what she did. A doctor, like her husband? 'Will Marie be bringing Adam with her?'

'I'm not sure.'

'What time's my first appointment?' she asked, suddenly needing to stay on track and be professional.

But Flynn smiled, and instantly ramped up that heat circulating her body, defying her professionalism. 'Nine. Was it explained to you that Kat also does high school visits to talk to the teenagers about contraception?' Flynn stood back and indicated with a wave of his hand for her to precede him into a kitchen-cum-meeting-room. 'You've got one on Thursday afternoon.'

'I didn't know, but not a problem.' What was that aftershave? She sniffed a second time, savouring the tangy scent that reminded her of the outdoors and sun and…? And hot male. She tripped over her size sevens and grabbed the back of a chair to regain her balance. 'I'm still breaking these boots in,' she explained quickly, hoping Flynn wouldn't notice the sudden glow in her cheeks. He mustn't think she was clumsy but, worse, he mustn't guess what had nearly sent her crashing face first onto the floor.

But when she glanced at him she relaxed. His gaze was firmly fixed on the boots she'd blamed. Her awesome new boots that had cost nearly a week's pay. His eyes widened, then cruised slowly, too slowly, up her thighs to her hips, up, up, up, until he finally locked gazes with her. So much for relaxing. Now she felt as though she was in a sauna and there was no way out. The heat just kept getting steamier. Her tongue felt too big for her mouth. Her eyes must look like bug's eyes; they certainly felt as though they were out on stalks.

Flynn was one sexy unit. The air between them sparked like electricity. His hair was as tousled as it had been yesterday and just as tempting. Her fingers curled into her palms, her false nails digging deep into her skin as she fought not to reach out and finger-comb those thick waves.

'You must be the midwife.' A woman in her midforties suddenly appeared before her. 'Faye Bellamy, part-time GP for my sins.'

Ally took a step back to put space between her and Flynn, and reached for Faye's proffered hand. 'That's me. Ally Parker. Pleased to meet you.'

'Pleasure's all ours. Darned nuisance Kat wanting time off, but I've read your résumé and it seems you'll be a perfect fit for her job.' Bang, mugs hit the benchtop. 'Coffee, everyone?'

Kat wasn't meant to take holidays? Or just this one? 'Yes, thanks. Where's Kat gone?'

Flynn was quick to answer. 'To Holland for her great-grandmother's ninetieth birthday. She's been saving her leave for this trip.' He flicked a glance at Faye's back, then looked at Ally. 'She could've taken two months and still not used up what she's owed,' he added.

'Europe's a long way to go for any less time.' Not that it had anything to do with her, except she would have been signed on here for longer and that meant more weeks—okay, hours—in Flynn's company. Already that looked like being a problem. His marital status wasn't having any effect on curtailing the reaction her body had to him.

She took the mug being handed to her and was surprised to see her hand shaking. She searched her head for something ordinary to focus on, and came back to Kat. 'Bet the trip's another reason why there isn't much furniture or clutter in the flat.' A girl after her own heart, though for a different reason.

'Morning, everyone.' A man strolled in. 'Coffee smells good.' Then he saw Ally. 'Hi, I'm Jerome, GP extraordinaire, working with this motley lot.'

Amidst laughter and banter Ally sat back and listened as the nurses joined them and began discussing patients and the two emergencies that had happened over the weekend. She felt right at home. This was the same Monday-morning scenario she'd sat through in most of the clinics she'd worked at ever since qualifying. Same cases, different names. Same egos, different names. Soon her gaze wandered to the man sitting opposite her, and she felt that hitch in her breathing again.

Flynn was watching her from under hooded eyes, his chin low, his arms folded across his chest as he leaned as far back in his chair as possible without spilling over backwards.

Ally's breathing became shallow and fast, like it did after a particularly hard run. The man had no right to make her feel like this. Who did he think he was? The sooner this meeting was finished the better. She could go and play with patients and hide from him until all her body parts returned to their normal functions. At the rate she was going, that'd be some time around midnight.

The sound of scraping chairs on the floor dragged her attention back to the other people in the room and gave her the escape she desperately needed.

But fifteen minutes after the meeting ended, Flynn was entering her room with a frightened young girl in tow. 'Ally, I'd like you to meet Chrissie Gordon.' He ushered the girl, dressed in school uniform, to a chair.

'Hi, Chrissie. Love your nail colour. It's like hot pink and fiery red all mixed up.' It would have lit up a dark room.

'It's called Monster Red.' Chrissie shrugged at her, as if to say, Who gives a rat's tail? Something serious was definitely on this young lady's mind.

Given that Flynn had brought Chrissie to see *her*, they must be about to talk about protection during sex or STDs. Or pregnancy. The girl looked stumped, as if her worst possible nightmare had just become real. Ally wanted to scoop her up into her arms and ward off whatever was about to be revealed. Instead, she looked at Flynn and raised an eyebrow.

'Chrissie's done several dip-stick tests for pregnancy and they all showed positive.' Flynn's face held nothing but sympathy for his patient's predicament. 'I'd like you to take a blood sample for an HCG test to confirm that, and then we'll also know how far along she is if the result's positive.'

It wasn't going to be negative with all those stick tests showing otherwise. 'No problem.'

Ally took the lab form he handed her and glancing down saw requests for WR and VDRL to check for STDs, antibodies and a blood group. She noted the girl's date of birth. Chrissie was fifteen. Too young to be dealing with this. Ally's heart went out to the frightened child as she thought back to when she'd been that age. She'd barely been coping with her own life, let alone be able to manage looking after a baby. Face it, she doubted her ability to do that *now*. Locking eyes with Flynn, she said, 'Leave it to me.'

His nod was sharp. 'Right, Chrissie, I'll call you on your cell when the lab results come back.'

'Thanks, Dr Reynolds,' Chrissie whispered, as her fingers picked at the edge of her jersey, beginning to unravel a thread. 'You won't tell Mum, will you?'

'Of course not. You know even if I wanted to—which I don't—I'm not allowed to disclose your confidential information. It's up to you to decide when to talk to your mother, but let's wait until we get these tests done and you can come and see me again first, if that'll make it easier for you.' Flynn drew a breath and added, 'You won't be able to hide the pregnancy for ever.'

'I know. But not yet, okay?' The girl's head bowed

over her almost flat chest. 'I'm afraid. It hurts to have a baby, doesn't it?'

Ally placed a hand over Chrissie's and squeezed gently. 'You're getting way ahead of yourself. Let's do those tests and find out how far along you are. After I've taken your blood I'll explain a few things about early-stage pregnancy if you like.'

'Yes, please. I think.' Fat tears oozed out of Chrissie's eyes and slid down her cheeks to drip onto her jersey. 'Mum's going to kill me.'

'No, she won't,' Flynn said. About to leave the room, he turned back to hunker down in front of Chrissie and said emphatically, 'Angela will be very supportive of you. You're her daughter. That's what mothers do.'

Yeah, right, you don't know a thing, buster, if that's what you believe. Did you grow up in la-la land? Ally clamped her lips shut for fear of spilling the truth. *Some mothers couldn't care two drops of nothing about their daughters. Some dump their babies on strangers' doorsteps.*

But when she glanced at Flynn, he shook his head and mouthed, 'It's true of Angela.'

Had he known what she'd been thinking? The tension that had been tightening her shoulders left off as she conceded silently that if he was right then Chrissie was luckier than some. A big positive in what must feel like a very negative morning for the girl. 'Good,' she acknowledged with a nod at Flynn. As for his mind-reading, did that mean he'd known exactly what she'd been thinking about him back there in the staffroom?

'Have you had a blood test before?' she asked Chrissie. She'd wasted enough time thinking about Dr Reynolds.

Flynn disappeared quietly, closing the door behind him.

'Yeah, three times. I hate them. I fainted every time.'

'You can lie on the bed, then. No way do I want to be picking you off the floor, now, do I?'

She was rewarded with a glimmer of a smile. 'I don't weigh too much. You'd manage.'

It was the first time anyone had suggested she looked tough and strong. 'I might manage, but me and weight-lifting don't get along. How heavy are you anyway?'

'Forty-eight k. I'm lucky, I can eat and eat and I stay thin. My mum's jealous.' At the mention of her mum her face fell and her mouth puckered. 'I can't tell her. She'll be really angry. She had me when she was seventeen. All my life she's told me not to play around with boys. She wants me to go to university and be educated, unlike her. She missed out because she had me.'

Handing Chrissie a cup of cold water and a box of tissues, Ally sat down to talk. Her first booked appointment would have to wait. 'I won't deny your mother's going to be disappointed, even upset, but she'll come round because she loves you.' Flynn had better have got that right because she didn't believe in giving false hope. It just hurt more in the long run.

'You think? You don't even know her.'

'True. But I see a young woman who someone's been making sure had everything that's important in life. You look healthy, which means she's fed you well and kept you warm and clothed. Your uniform's in good condition, not an op-shop one. You're obviously up to speed with your education.' She daren't ask about her father. It didn't sound like he factored into Chrissie's current situation so maybe he didn't exist, or wasn't close enough for it to matter. 'I'm new here. Where do you live?'

'Round in San Remo. It's nice there. Granddad was

a fisherman and had a house so Mum and I stayed with him. He's gone now and there's just us. I miss him. He always had a hug and a smile for me.'

'Then you've been very lucky. Not everyone gets those as they're growing up.' She sure as heck hadn't. 'Let's get those blood samples done.'

Chrissie paled but climbed onto the bed and tugged one arm free of her jersey and shirt. Lying down, she found a small scared smile. 'Be nice to me.'

Ally smiled. 'If I have to.' She could get to really like this girl. Pointless when she'd be gone in a month. Despite Chrissie's fear of what the future had in store for her, she managed to be friendly and not sulky, as most teens she'd met in this situation had been.

Ally found the needle and tubes for the blood in the top drawer of the cabinet beside the bed. 'Do you play any sport at school?' She swabbed the skin where she would insert the needle.

'I'm in the school rep basketball team and play soccer at the club. I get knocked about a bit in basketball because I'm so light, but my elbows are sharp.' The needle slid in and the tube began to fill. 'I'm fast on my feet. Learnt how to get out of the way when I was a kid and played rough games with the boys next door.'

Ally swapped the full tube for another one, this time for haematology tests. Flynn was checking Chrissie's haemoglobin in case she had anaemia. 'I see one of the beaches is popular for surfing. You ever given that a try?' All done.

'Everyone surfs around here. Sort of, anyway. Like belly-surfing and stuff.'

'You can sit up now.' Ally began labelling the tubes.

'What? Have you finished? I didn't feel a thing.'

'Of course you didn't.' She smiled at the girl, stopped when she saw the moment Chrissie's thoughts returned to why she was there, saw the tears building up again. 'You're doing fine.'

'I'm not going to play sport for a while, am I?'

'Maybe not competitively, but keeping fit is good for you and your baby.'

Chrissie blew hard into a handful of tissues. 'You haven't told me I'm stupid for getting caught out. Or asked who the father is, or anything like that.'

'That's irrelevant. I'm more concerned about making sure you do the right things to stay healthy and have an easy pregnancy. Have you got any questions for me?'

Chrissie swung her legs over the side of the bed and stared at the floor. 'Lots, but not yet. But can I come see you later? After school? You'll have the tests back by then, right?'

'The important one, anyway. But won't you want to see Dr Reynolds about that?' She was more than happy to tell Chrissie the result, but she had no idea how Flynn might feel if she did.

'He's going to phone me, but I might need to see someone and I don't want to talk to a man. It would be embarrassing. I'd prefer it's you.'

'That's okay.' Ally scribbled her cell number on a scrap of paper. 'Here, call me. Leave a message if I don't answer and I'll get back to you as soon as I'm free. Okay?'

'Thanks.' Sniff. 'I didn't sleep all night, hoping Dr Reynolds would tell me I'd got it wrong, that I wasn't having a baby. But I used up all my pocket money on testing kits and every one of them gave me the same answer so I was just being dumb.'

'Chrissie, listen to me. You are not dumb. Many women

I've been midwife to have told me the same thing. Some of them because they couldn't believe their luck, others because, just like you, they were crossing their fingers and toes they'd got it wrong.' Ally drew a long breath. 'Chrissie, I have to ask, have you considered an abortion? Or adoption?'

The girl's head shot up, defiance spitting out of her eyes. 'No. Never.' Her hands went to her belly. 'This is my baby. No one else's. I might be young and dependent on Mum, but I am keeping it.'

In that moment Ally loved Chrissie. She reached over to hug her. 'Attagirl. You're awesome.' It would be the hardest thing Chrissie ever did, and right now she had no idea what she'd let herself in for, but that baby would love her for it.

'Have you ever had a baby?' Chrissie pulled back, flushing pink. 'Sorry, I guess I'm not supposed to want to know.'

'Of course it's all right to ask. The answer's no, I haven't.'

An image of a blue-eyed youngster bent over double and giggling like his life depended on it flicked up in her mind. *Go away, Adam. You've got a mother, and anyway I'd be a bad substitute.*

'So while I will tell you lots of things over the weeks I'm here, I only know them from working with other mums-to-be and not from any first-hand experience.' She would never have that accreditation on her CV. She would not raise a child on her own, and she wouldn't be trusting any man to hang around long enough to see a baby grow to adulthood with her.

Flynn appeared in the doorway so fast after Chrissie left that she wondered if he'd been lurking. She said,

'She's only fifteen and is terrified, and yet she's coping amazingly well, given the shock of it all.'

'You must've cheered her up a little at least. I got the glimmer of a smile when she came out of here.' He leaned one shoulder against the doorframe. 'I meant what I said about her mother. Angela is going to be gutted, but she'll stand by Chrissie all the way. From what I've been told, Angela's always been strong, and refused to marry Chrissie's dad just because people thought it was the done thing. Her father supported them all the way.'

Another baby with only one parent. But one decent parent was a hundred percent better than none. 'Aren't you jumping the gun? Chrissie didn't mention the father of her baby, but that could be because she's protecting him. They might want to stick together.'

'They might.' Flynn nodded, his eyes fixed on her. Again.

When he did that, her stomach tightened in a very needy way. Heat sizzled along her veins, warming every cell of her body. *Damn him. Why does he have to be married?*

'Right, I'd better see my first patient. First booked-in one, that is. I told Chrissie I'll talk to her later today. Is that all right with you?'

'Go for it. As long as she's talking with someone, I'm happy. You did well with her.' There was something like admiration in his voice.

She didn't know whether to be pleased, or annoyed that he might be surprised. 'Just doing my job.'

'Sure.'

The way he enunciated that one word had her wondering if he had issues with Kat and her work. But that didn't make sense after he'd been fighting the other woman's corner about using her holiday time. 'Being a filler-in person, I don't have the luxury of knowing the patients I see. Neither do I have a lot of time with them so I work hard to put them at ease with me as quickly as possible.'

'So why aren't you employed at a medical practice on a permanent basis? Wouldn't you prefer getting to know your mums, rather than moving on all the time?'

If he hadn't sounded so genuinely interested she'd have made a joke about being a wandering witch in a previous life and ignored the real question. But for some inexplicable reason she couldn't go past that sincerity. 'I get offers all the time from my bosses to base myself back at the midwifery unit, but I don't do settled in one spot very well. Yes, I miss out on seeing mothers going the distance. I'm only ever there for the beginning of some babies and the arrival of others, but I like it that way. Keeps me on my toes.'

'Fly in, do the job and fly out.' Was that a dash of hope in his eyes? Did he think she might be footloose and fancy-free enough to have a quick fling with him and then move on? Because she'd seen the same sizzle in his eyes that buzzed along her veins.

Then reality hit. Cold water being tipped over her wouldn't have chilled her as much. *Sorry, buster, but you're married and, worse, you're not even ashamed to show it.*

She spun around to stare at the screen in front of her. What was the name of her next patient?

'Ally, I've upset you.'

Of course he had. He only had to look at her to upset her—her hormones anyway. Flicking him a brief smile, she continued staring at the computer. 'Holly Sargent, thirty-five weeks. Anything I need to know about her that's not on here?'

When Flynn didn't answer, she had to lift her head and seek him out. That steady blue gaze was firmly fixed on her. It held far too many questions, and she didn't answer other people's enquiries about anything personal. 'Flynn? Holly Sargent?'

'Third pregnancy, the last two were straightforward. She's had the usual colds and flu, a broken wrist and stitches in her brow from when she walked through a closed glass slider. Full-time mum.'

Ally looked at her patient list. 'Brenda Lewis?'

'First pregnancy, took six months to conceive, family history of hypertension but so far she's shown no signs of it, twenty-five years old, runs a local day care centre for under-fives.'

Her anger deflated and laughter bubbled up to spill between them as she stared at this man who had her all in a dither with very little effort. 'That's amazing. Do you know all your patients as thoroughly?'

'How long have you got?' He grinned. 'Makes for scintillating conversations.'

Deliberately rolling her eyes at him, she said, 'Remind me not to get stuck with you at the workplace Friday night drinkies.'

'Shucks, and I was about to ask you on a date,' he quipped, in a tone that said he meant no such thing.

So he was as confused as she was. That didn't stop a quick shiver running down her spine. She'd love to go out with this man. *But hello. If that isn't a wedding ring, then what is it? He's obviously a flagrant playboy.* 'Sorry, doing my hair that night.'

'Me, too,' he muttered, and left her to stare at his retreating back view.

A very delectable view at that. Those butt muscles moved smoothly under his trousers as he strode down the hall, those shoulders filled the top of his shirt to perfection. A sigh trickled over her bottom lip. He would've been the perfect candidate for her next affair. *Flynn might be the one you can't easily walk away from.*

'Get a grip, man,' Flynn growled under his breath. How? Ally was hot. Certain parts of his anatomy might've been in hibernation for the past couple of years, but they weren't dead. How did any sane, red-blooded male ignore Ally without going bonkers?

'Flynn.' Megan beckoned from the office. 'Can you explain to this caller why she should have a flu jab?'

'Can't Toby do that?' The practice nurse was more than capable of handling it.

'Busy with a patient and…' Megan put her hand over the phone's mouthpiece '…this one won't go away.'

'Put her through.' He spun around to head to his consulting room. *See? You're at work, not on the beach with nothing more important to think about than getting laid.* Forget all things Alyssa. *Alyssa.* Such a pretty name, but it had been blatantly obvious no one was allowed to use it when talking to their temporary midwife.

'Dr Reynolds.' Mrs Augusta's big voice boomed down the line, causing him to pull the phone away from his ear. 'I've been told I have to have a flu injection. I don't see why as I never get sick.'

Except for two hits with cancer that had nearly stolen her life. 'Mrs Augusta, it's your decision entirely but there are certain conditions whereby we recommend to a patient they have the vaccination. Your recent cancer puts you in the category for this. It's a preventative measure, that's all.'

'Why didn't Megan just tell me that?'

'Because she's our receptionist, not a qualified medical person. It's not her role to advise patients.'

'All right, can you put me back to her so I can book a time? Sorry to have been a nuisance.' Mrs Augusta suddenly sounded deflated, all the boom and bluster gone.

'Pat, is there something else that's bothering you?'

'No, I'm good as gold, Doctor. Don't you go worrying about me.'

'How about you make an appointment with me when you come for your jab?'

'I don't want to be a problem, Doctor.'

That exact attitude had almost cost her life. By the time the bowel cancer had been discovered it had nearly been too late and now she wore a bag permanently. 'I'll put you back to Megan and you make a time to see me.' When he got the receptionist on the line he told her, 'Book Mrs Augusta in with me at the first opening, and don't let her talk you out of it.'

A glance at his watch on his way out to the waiting room told him he was now behind the ball as far as keeping on time with appointments. 'Jane, come through.' As he led the woman down the hall, laughter came from the midwife's room. Sounded like Ally and Holly were getting along fine. A smile hovered on his mouth, gave him the warm fuzzies. Everyone got along with their temp midwife.

Jane limped into his room on her walking cane and sat down heavily. 'I'm up the duff again, Flynn.'

Not even ten o'clock and his second pregnant patient

of the morning. What had the council put in the water? 'You're sure?' he asked with a smile. Nothing ever fazed this woman, certainly not her gammy leg, not a diabetic three-year-old, not a drunk for a husband.

'Yep, got all the usual signs. Thought I'd better let you know so I can get registered with Kat.'

Now, there was something that did tend to wind Jane up. Kat's attitude to her husband. Kat had tried to intervene one night at the pub when he'd been about to swing a fist at Jane. Something Flynn would've tried to prevent, too, if he'd been there. 'Kat's away at the moment so you'll get to meet Ally.' Of course, there were nine months to a pregnancy, and Kat was only away for one, but hopefully Ally could settle Jane into things so that she'd be happier with Kat this time round.

'Is she nice?' Jane's eyes lit up.

More than. 'You'll get along great guns. Now, I'm surmising that we need to discuss your arthritis meds for the duration of your pregnancy.'

The light in those eyes faded. She accepted her painful condition without a complaint, but she knew how hard the next few months were going to be. 'I've cut back already to what you've recommended before. There's no way I'm risking hurting junior in there.' Her hand did a circuit of her belly. 'Can't say I'm happy with the extra pain, but I want this wee one. Think I'll make it the last, though. Get my bits chopped out afterwards.'

As he made a note to that effect in her computer file, Flynn tried not to smile. Her bits. He got to hear all sorts of names for vaginas and Fallopian tubes in this job. 'How far along do you think you are?'

'I've missed two periods. Should've come to see you sooner, I know, but that family of mine keeps me busy.'

Jane wasn't mentioning the lack of money, but he knew about it. 'Anyway, it's not like I don't know what to expect. They haven't changed the way it's done in the last three years, have they?'

'Not that anyone's told me.'

After writing out prescriptions, ordering blood tests, including an HCG for confirmation of the pregnancy, and taking Jane's blood pressure, he took her along to meet Ally.

It wasn't until he was returning to his room and he passed Faye, who rolled her eyes at him, that he realised he was walking with a bounce in his stride and a smile on his face. All due to a certain midwife.

What was it about her that had him sitting up and taking notice? It had happened instantly. Right from that moment when Sheba had knocked her down and he'd reached out a hand to haul the dog off, only to be sidetracked by the most startling pair of hazel eyes he'd ever seen.

Whatever it was, he'd better put a lid on the sizzle before anyone else in the clinic started noticing. That was the last thing he needed, and no doubt Ally felt the same.

CHAPTER THREE

'FLYNN,' MEGAN CALLED from her office as he was shrugging into his jacket. 'The path lab's on line one.'

'Put them through.' Damn, he'd just seen Ally head out the front door for home. He'd intended talking to her before she left, maybe even walk with her as far as Kat's flat, then backtrack to home. Which, given he lived on the opposite side of town, showed how fried his brain had become in the last twenty-four hours.

For an instant he resented being a GP. There were never any moments just for him. Like it had been any different working as an emergency specialist. Yeah, but he'd chosen that career pathway, not had it forced on him. So he'd give up trying to raise Adam properly, hand him over to spend even more hours with day carers? No, he wouldn't. The disgruntled feeling disappeared in a flash, replaced with love. His little guy meant everything to him.

'Flynn?' Megan yelled. 'Get that, will you?'

He kicked the door shut and grabbed the persistently ringing phone from his desk. 'Flynn Reynolds. How can I help?' *Could you hurry up? I'm on a mission.*

'Doctor, this is Andrew from the lab. I'm calling about some biochemistry results on William Foster.'

William Foster, fifty-six and heading down the overweight path through too much alcohol and fatty food since his wife had died twelve months back. He'd complained of shoulder pain and general malaise so he'd ordered urgent tests to check what his heart might be up to. 'I'm listening.'

'His troponin's raised. As are his glucose and cholesterol. But it's the troponin I'm ringing about.'

He took down details of the abnormal results, even though Andrew would email them through within the next five minutes. Finding William's phone number, he was about to dial but thought better of it. Instead, he phoned Marie on the run. 'I'm going to be late.'

'I'll feed Adam dinner, then.'

Flynn sighed. 'I owe you. Again.'

Marie chuckled. 'Get over yourself. I love having him.'

Yeah, she did, but that didn't make everything right. For Adam. Or for him.

William lived ten minutes away and halfway there Flynn decided he should've rung first to make sure the man was at home and not at the club, enjoying a beer. William didn't know it yet, but beer would be off the menu for a while.

William opened his front door on the third knock, and appeared taken aback to find Flynn on his doorstep after dark. 'Doc, what's up?'

'Can I come in for a minute?'

William's eyes shifted sideways. 'What you want to tell me?'

The man was ominously pale. He hadn't been like that earlier. 'Let me in and we'll discuss it.' From the state of William's breathing and speech, Flynn knew there'd be a bottle of whisky on the bench. That wouldn't be helping the situation. 'It's important.'

With a sigh the older man stepped back, hauling the door wide at the same time. 'I haven't done the housework this week, Doc, so mind where you step.'

This week? Flynn tried not to breathe too deeply, and didn't bother looking into the rooms they passed. It was all too obvious the man was living in squalor. He wasn't coping with Edna's passing, hadn't since day one, and nothing Flynn or William's daughter had done or said made the slightest bit of difference. The man had given up, hence Flynn's visit. A phone call would never have worked. Besides, he needed to be with William as he absorbed the news.

In the kitchen William's shaky hands fidgeted with an empty glass he'd lifted from the table. He didn't look directly at Flynn, not even for a moment, but every few seconds his eyes darted sideways across the kitchen. Sure enough, an almost full whisky bottle was on the bench, as were three empty ones. How long had it taken for him to drink his way through those?

It would be too easy to tell the man some cold hard facts about his living conditions and his drinking, but Flynn couldn't do it. He understood totally what it was like to lose the woman he loved more than life. He suspected if it hadn't been for Adam and having to put on a brave face every single day, he might've made as big a mess of his own life after Anna had been killed. He still struggled with the sense of living a life mapped out by fate, one that held none of his choices.

Pulling out a chair, he indicated William should sit down. Then he straddled another one, not looking at the condition of the once beautiful brocade on the seat.

'William, your test results have come back. They're not good, I'm afraid.'

'Figured that'd be why you're here.'

'The major concern is that you've had a cardiac incident. A heart attack, William.'

Rheumy eyes lifted to stare at him, but William said nothing, just shrugged.

'You need to go to hospital tonight. They'll run more tests and keep an eye on you until they find the cause of the attack.'

'What else?' William wheezed the question.

'They'll give you advice on diet and exercise.' Things he'd have no inclination to follow. The same as with any advice he had given him.

'I meant what other tests were bad?'

He was about to add to the man's gloomy outlook, but couldn't see a way around it. All he could hope for was that he shocked his patient into doing something about his lifestyle before it was too late. 'Your cholesterol's high, which probably explains your cardiac arrest. You've got diabetes and your liver's not in good nick.'

'I hit the jackpot, didn't I?' The sadness in William's voice told how much he didn't care any more. 'I don't suppose you went on a bender when you lost your wife, Doc.'

Yeah, he had. Just one huge bender, when he'd almost killed himself. Big enough and frightening enough to put him off ever doing it again. But he knew he still might've if it hadn't been for Adam. 'I couldn't afford to, William.'

'I get it. Your boy.'

'You've got family who care about you, too.' Flynn tried to think of something that might interest William in getting his act together, but nothing came to mind, apart from his daughter and grandkids. That had been tried before and William hadn't run with it. 'Now, don't get upset, but I've ordered the ambulance to transfer you to hospital. It should be here any minute.'

'I don't need that. I can drive myself there.'

'What if you have another heart attack and cause an accident that hurts someone?'

There was silence in the kitchen. Not a lot William could say to that. He was a decent man, unable to cope with a tragedy. He wasn't reckless with other people.

'I'll wait here until you're on your way. Want me to talk to your daughter?' Working in the ED, he'd have phoned the cardiologist and had William wheeled to the ward, no argument. Patients were in the ED because someone recognised the urgency of their situation. Urgent meant urgent—not talking and cajoling. He missed that fast pace at times, but if he got William under way to getting well then he'd feel deep satisfaction.

'After I've left. Don't want her telling me off tonight.' William stared around the kitchen, brought his gaze back to Flynn. 'Don't suppose I can have a whisky for the road.'

By the time Flynn finally made it home Adam was in his pyjamas and glued to the TV. 'Hiya, Dad.'

'Hello, my man.' Tonight he couldn't find it in him to make Adam stop watching—an Anna rule or not. Instead, he turned to Marie. 'I appreciate you bringing him home.'

Marie was already buttoning up her coat, the gaps between the buttons splayed wide over her baby bulge. 'Have you decided who's going to look after Adam when my little one arrives?' Marie was determined to look after Adam right up to the last minute. She'd also sorted through the numerous girls wanting to take her place until she was ready to take Adam back under her wing and had decided on two likely applicants.

'Caught. I'll get onto it.' He pushed his fingers through his hair. 'Tonight?'

'Whenever.' She laughed. 'It's not as though you'll be left high and dry. Half the island would love to look after Dr Reynolds's boy. Not just because he's such a cute little blighter either. There's a family likeness between father and son.'

'Haven't you got a husband waiting at home for his dinner?' He wasn't keen on dating any of the island's females. Too close to home and work. Anyway, no one had caught his interest in the last two years. Not until Ally had got knocked over by Sheba, that was.

Ally wasn't answering when he phoned after putting Adam to bed. She wasn't answering her phone when he called at nine, after giving in to the tiredness dragging at his bones and sitting down to watch a crime programme on TV. She might've answered if he'd rung as he was going to bed at ten thirty, but he didn't want her to think he was stalking her.

But she sure as hell stalked him right into bed. As he sprawled out under the covers he missed her not being there beside him, even though she'd never seen his bed, let alone lain in it. He stretched his legs wide to each side and got the same old empty spaces, only tonight they felt cold and lonely. Make that colder and lonelier. In his head, hot and sexy Ally with those brilliant hazel eyes was watching and laughing, teasing, playing with him. How was he supposed to remain aloof, for pity's sake? He was only human—last time he looked.

Was this what happened when he hadn't had sex for so long? Should he have been making an effort to find an obliging woman for a bit of relaxation and fun? He yawned.

Did Ally know she'd cranked up his libido? Yeah, it was quite possible she did, if the way the air crackled between them whenever they came within touching distance was any indication.

So follow up on it. Have some fun. Have sex. Have an affair with her. It would only be four weeks before Ally moved on. He wouldn't disrupt Adam's routine too much or for too long.

Flynn rolled over to punch his pillow and instead squashed his awakening reaction to the woman in his head. The air hissed out of his lungs as he grinned. That had to be a good sign for the future, didn't it?

'Morning, Ally,' Megan called as she stepped through the front door of the clinic on Tuesday. 'I see you've found the best coffee on the island already.'

'First thing I do on any job.' She sniffed the air appreciatively just to wind Megan up.

Scowling happily at her, Megan lifted her own container then asked, 'What did you think of the movie?'

'It was great. Nothing like a few vampires to fill in the evening.' She'd bumped into the receptionist and her boyfriend as they'd been walking into the theatre. 'Seeing you there made me feel I'd been living here for a while.'

Megan laughed. 'Small towns are like that. Believe me, people around here will know what you had for dinner last night.'

'Then they'll be giving me lectures on healthy eating. Fried chicken and chips from Mrs Chook's.' It had been delicious, even if she should've been looking for a salad bar. In winter? Hey, being good about food could sometimes be highly overrated. Anyway, she'd wanted comfort food because when she had gone back to the flat after work she'd felt unusually out of sorts. Arrival day in a new place, yes, that was normal; every other day thereafter, never.

This nomadic life had been one of her goals ever since she'd left school and become independent of the welfare system. Those goals had been simple—earn the money to put herself through a nursing degree then support herself entirely with a job that she could give everything to but which wouldn't tie her to one place. Along with that went to establish a life where she didn't depend on anyone for anything, including friendship or love.

So far it had worked out fine. Sure, there were the days when she wondered if she could risk getting close to someone. She had no experience of being loved, unconditionally or any other way, so the risks would be huge for everyone involved. She had enough painful memories of being moved on from one family to the next to prove how unworthy of being loved she was. At unsettled moments like this those memories underlined why she never intended taking a chance on finding someone to trust with her heart. Sometimes she wondered if her heart really was only there to pump blood.

In the midwife's room she dumped her bag and jacket, then wandered into the staffroom, surreptitiously on a mission to scope out Flynn, if he'd arrived. He must've, because suddenly her skin was warming up. Looking around the room, her eyes snagged with his where he sat on a chair balanced on two legs. She'd known he was there without seeing him. She'd felt an instant attraction before setting eyes on him. What was going on? Hadn't she just been remembering why she wasn't interested?

She took a gulp of coffee and spluttered as she burned her tongue. 'That's boiling.'

Concern replaced the heat in Flynn's gaze and the front legs of the chair banged onto the tiled floor as he came up onto his feet. 'You all right?' He snatched a paper towel off the roll on the wall. 'Here, spit it out.'

Taking the towel to wipe the dribble off her lips before he could, she muttered, 'Too late, I swallowed it instantly.' And could now feel it heating a track down her throat. 'I forget to take the lid off every time.' But usually she wasn't distracted enough to forget to sip first. 'Black coffee takes for ever to cool in these cardboard cups.'

'Slow learner, eh?' That smile should be banned. Or bottled. Or kissed.

It sent waves of heat expanding throughout her body, unfurling a need so great she felt a tug of fear. What if she did give in to this almost overwhelming attraction? Could she walk away from it unscathed? Like she always did? This thing with Flynn didn't feel the same as her usual trysts. There was something between them she couldn't explain. But they wouldn't be getting started. Staying remote would keep things on an even keel. *You're not lovable. Forget that and you're toast.*

'I called you last night to ask how you felt about your first day here.'

So much for remote. He wasn't supposed to play friendly after hours. 'That explains one of two missed calls. I went to a movie and switched it off for the duration.'

Flynn looked awkward. 'I rang twice.'

'Did I miss something?' Had one of her patients gone into labour? Or developed problems? Had Chrissie wanted to talk to her again? This wouldn't look good for her if she had.

'Relax. They were purely social calls.'

The way he drawled his words did everything but relax her. She managed through a dry mouth, 'That's all right, then.' Highly intelligent conversation going on here, but she was incapable of much more right now. He shouldn't be phoning her.

'Ally, I was wondering—'

'Morning, everyone.' Jerome strolled in. 'You came back for more, then, Ally?'

'Yes.' She shook her head to clear the heat haze. 'Missed the ferry back to the mainland so thought I'd fill in my day looking after your pregnant patients,' she joked pathetically.

Then Flynn asked, 'How was Chrissie when you talked to her after school?'

She wondered what he'd been going to ask before Jerome had interrupted. 'Resigned would best describe her attitude. But today might be a whole different story after a night thinking about it all.' Ally dropped onto a chair and stared her coffee. 'I hope she's going to be all right.' Chrissie still had to tell her mother. That'd be the toughest conversation of her young life.

'Like I said, Angela will be very supportive.' Flynn returned to his seat. 'Marie was happy with her new midwife, by the way.'

Marie was happy with her boss and his boy, with the impending birth of her baby, with her husband, with the whole world. 'I saw Adam for a few minutes when she came in. At least he'd stopped giggling.'

'Ah, you missed the standing in the dog's water bowl

giggles, and the dollop of peanut butter on the floor right by Sheba's nose giggles.'

She could picture Adam now, bent over, howling with laughter. 'He's one very happy little boy, isn't he?'

Flynn's smile slipped. Oops. What had she gone and done? Sadness filtered into his eyes and she wanted to apologise with a hug for whatever she'd managed to stir up, but she didn't. Of course she didn't. Hugging a man she'd only met two days ago and who was one of her bosses wasn't the best idea she'd ever had. She sipped coffee instead—which perversely had turned lukewarm—and waited for the meeting to get under way.

'I see you had William admitted last night,' Faye said as she joined them.

Flynn looked relieved he'd been diverted from answering what she'd thought had been a harmless question. He hurried to explain. 'He'd had a cardiac event. Hardly surprising, given the way he's been living.'

'He'll be seen by a counsellor while in hospital. Maybe they can make him see reason,' Faye said. 'Not that we all haven't tried, I know.'

Flynn grimaced, his eyes still sad. 'I'm hoping this is the wake-up shock required to get him back on track.' He turned to Ally. 'William's wife succumbed to cancer last year.'

'That's terrible.' She shuddered. *See? Even if you got a good one, someone who never betrayed your trust, they still left you hurt and miserable.* No wonder Flynn looked sad. He seemed to hold all his patients dear.

Jerome spoke up. 'Ally, I believe you're doing house calls today. One of your patients is Matilda Livingstone. This is her first pregnancy. Be warned she's paranoid about something going wrong and will give you a million symptoms to sort through.'

Ally's interest perked up. 'Any particular reason for this behaviour?'

'She has a paranoid mother who suffered three miscarriages in her time and only carried one baby full term. She's fixated with making sure Matilda checks everything again and again. It's almost as though she doesn't want her daughter to have a stress-free pregnancy.' Jerome shook his head, looking very puzzled.

'Mothers, eh?' She smiled, knowing her real thoughts about some mothers weren't showing. Ironic, considering she spent her days working with mums—the loving kind. 'Thanks for the nod. I'll tread carefully.'

'You know you've got the use of the clinic's car for your rounds, don't you?' Flynn asked.

'Sure do. I'm hoping it's a V8 supercharged car with wide tyres and a triple exhaust.'

'Red, of course.' Flynn grinned.

Faye stood up. 'Time to get the day cranking up. There seems to be a kindergarten lot of small children creating havoc in the waiting room.'

'Toby's doing vaccinations. For some reason, the mothers thought it better if they had them all done at the same time,' Jerome explained. 'Seems a bit much, considering that if one cries, they'll all cry.'

Flynn stood up. 'Who's going to cry when they've got Toby? That man's magic when it comes to jabbing a child.' He turned to Ally. 'I heard that you're also no slug when it comes to drawing bloods. Chrissie was seriously impressed, even told Toby that he needs practice.'

'So Toby's magic doesn't extend to older children?' Chrissie was still a child in many ways, baby on the way or not. When they'd talked about her HCG result yesterday afternoon it had been difficult. One minute Chrissie had acted all grown up and the next Ally could picture her tucked up with her teddy and a thumb in her mouth as she watched cartoons on TV.

'Sure it does, just not Chrissie. Has she mentioned when she might apprise her mother of the situation?'

'I think never would be her preferred approach. But realistically she's preparing herself. She did ask if I'd be present.'

'How do you feel about that?' Flynn asked.

'Of course I'll do it if that's what she wants, but I'd have thought you, as the family doctor, should be the one to talk to Angela with her.'

Flynn didn't look fazed. 'If she's relaxed with you then that's good. I'm not getting on my high horse because she's my patient. What works for her works for me. Or we can both be there.'

'Thanks.' Why was she thanking him? Shrugging, she added, 'Guess I'd better get on the road. My first appointment's at nine and I haven't looked at the map yet.'

Flynn gave her that devastating smile of his. 'You're not in Melbourne now. Come here and tell me who you're visiting.' He closed the door behind Jerome and Ally felt as though the air had been sucked out of the room.

What was he doing? Here? At work? Any minute someone could walk in for a coffee.

'Here's the clinic.' Flynn tapped his finger on the back of the door. 'Who's first on your list?'

Ally's face reddened as her gaze took in the map pinned to the door. 'Um.' Think, damn it, peanut brain. 'Erika Teale.'

She watched in fascination as Flynn's finger swept across the map and stopped to tap at some point that made no sense whatsoever. Running her tongue over her lips, she tried to sound sane and sensible. 'That's next to the golf ranch.' Too squeaky, but at least she'd got something out.

He turned to stare at her. 'Are you all right? Is map-reading not your forte?'

'I'm better with drawing bloods.' No one could read a map when Flynn was less than two feet away. Even a simple map like this one suddenly became too complex. Taking a step closer to the map—and Flynn—she leaned forwards to study the roads leading to Erika's house. Truth was, despite moving from town to town every few weeks she'd never got the hang of maps. 'So which side of the golf place is she on?' Why did he have to smell so yummy?

'What are you doing tonight?'

Gulp. Nothing. Why? 'Eating food and washing dirty clothes.' Like there was a lot of those, but she had to sound busy. Saying 'Nothing' was pathetic.

'Have dinner with me. We could go to the Italian café. It's simple but the food's delicious.'

She gasped. *Yes*, her head screamed. *I'd love to. Yes, yes, yes.* 'No, thanks,' came from her mouth. Sanity had prevailed. Just. 'You're married.'

Flynn's mouth flattened, and his thumb on his right hand flicked the tell-tale gold band round and round on his finger. The light went out in his eyes. 'I'm a widower. My wife died two years back.'

Her shoulders dropped their indignant stance as his words sank in. 'Oh.' She was getting good at these inane comments. 'I'm so sorry. That must be difficult for you and Adam. But he seems so happy, you must be a great father.'

Shut up, dribble mouth.

But he's free, available.

Yeah. I'm a cow.

Guilt followed and she reached a hand to his arm, touched him lightly. 'I don't know what else to say. How do you manage?' The way he looked at that moment, he'd be retracting his invitation any second.

'Adam keeps me sane and on the straight and narrow. If it wasn't for him, who knows what I might've done at the time?' Sadness flicked across his face and then he looked directly at her and banished it with a smile. 'For the record, you're the first woman I've asked on a date in the last two years. The only woman I've looked at twice and even considered taking out.' Then his smile faltered. 'I guess it's not much of an offer, going to the Italian café, considering what you must be used to in the city.'

'Flynn, it's not about where I go but who I go with. I'd love to try the local Italian with you.' She meant every word. A wave of excitement rolled through her. A date—with this man—who set her trembling just by looking at her. What more could she want? Bring it on.

'Then I'll pick you up after I've put Adam to bed and got the babysitter settled. Probably near eight, if that's all right?' There was relief and excitement mingling in his expression, in those cobalt eyes locked on her, in the way he stood tall.

She was struggling to keep up with all his emotions. 'Perfect.' She'd have time for a shower, to wash and blow-dry her hair, apply new make-up and generally tart herself up. Bring it on, she repeated silently.

CHAPTER FOUR

SOMEONE SHOULD'VE TOLD the pregnancy gods that Ally had a date and needed at the minimum an hour to get ready. Seems that memo had never gone out.

As she slammed through the front door of the flat at seven forty-five, Ally was cursing, fit to turn the air blue. 'Babies, love their wee souls, need to learn right from the get-go to hold off interrupting the well-laid plans of their midwife.'

Baby Hill thought cranking up his mum's blood pressure and making her ankles swell was a fun thing to do a couple of weeks out from his arrival. Pre-eclampsia ran through Vicky Hill's family but she'd been distressed about having to go to hospital for an evaluation, and it had taken a while to calm her down. Jerome had finally talked to his patient and managed to get her on her way with her thankfully calm husband.

Ally suspected some of Vicky's worry was because she was dealing with a new midwife right on the day she needed Kat to be there for her. Ally had no problem with that. Being a midwife had a lot to do with good relationships and they weren't formed easily with her, due to the come-and-go nature of her locum job.

The shower hadn't even fully warmed up when Ally

leapt under the water. Goose bumps rose on her skin. Washing her hair was off the list. A hard brush to remove the kinks from the tie that kept it back all day would suffice. If there was time. She'd make time. After slipping on a black G-string, she snatched up a pair of black, body-hugging jeans to wriggle her way into. The lace push-up bra did wonders for her breasts and gave a great line to the red merino top she tugged over her head.

The doorbell rang as she picked up the mascara wand. Flick, flick. Then a faster-than-planned brush of her hair and she was as ready as she was ever going to be.

She might not have had all the time she'd wanted, but by the look on Flynn's face she hadn't done too badly. His Adam's apple bobbed as his gaze cruised the length of her, making her feel happy with the hurried result.

'Let's go,' he croaked.

We could stay here and not bother with dinner. Or we can do both.

She slammed the front door shut behind her and stepped down the path. 'I'm starving.' For food. For man. For fun.

Flynn knew he should look away. Now. But how? His head had locked into place so that he stared at this amazing woman seated opposite him in the small cubicle they'd been shown to by the waiter. He hadn't seen her with her hair down before. Shining light brown hair gleaming in the light from wall sconces beside their table and setting his body on fire. He desperately wanted to run his hands through those silky layers, and over it, and underneath at the back of her neck.

'Excuse me, Dr Reynolds. Would you like to order wine with your meal?'

Caught. Staring at his lady friend. Reluctantly looking up, he saw one of his young patients holding out the wine menu. 'Hello, Jordan. How's the rugby going? Got a game this weekend?' He glanced down the blurred list of wines.

'It's high school reps this weekend. We're going up to Melbourne on Thursday.'

After checking with Ally about what she preferred, he ordered a bottle of Merlot, and told Jordan what meals they'd chosen. Then he leaned back and returned his attention to Ally, finding her watching him with a little smile curving that inviting mouth.

'How often do you get out like this?' she asked.

'Never. When I go out it's usually with people from work.' Comfortable but not exhilarating.

'Who's looking after Adam tonight? Not Marie?'

'No, she needs her baby sleep. Jerome's daughter came round, bringing her homework with her.' Better than having a boyfriend tag along, like the last girl he'd used when he'd had a meeting to attend. He'd sacked her because of that boyfriend distracting her so she hadn't heard Adam crying.

'So they know at work that you and I are out together?' Her eyes widened with caution.

'There's no point trying to be discreet on Phillip Island. Everyone knows everyone's business all too quickly, even if you try to hide it.'

The tip of her tongue licked the centre point of her top lip. In, out, in, out.

Flynn suppressed a groan and tried to ignore the flare of need unfurling low down. What was it about this woman compared to any of the other hundreds he'd crossed paths with over the last two years that had him wanting her so much? Admittedly, for a good part of those years he'd been wound up in grief and guilt so, of course, he hadn't been the slightest bit interested. His libido hadn't been tweaked once. Yet in walks Ally Parker and, slam-bang, he could no longer think straight.

The owner of the café brought their wine over and with a flourish poured a glass for Ally. '*Signorina*, welcome to the island. I am Giuseppe and this is my café. I am glad our favourite doctor has brought you here to enjoy our food.'

Ally raised her glass to Giuseppe. 'Thank you for your welcome. Is everyone on Phillip Island as kind as you and the medical centre staff?'

'*Si*, everyone. You've come at the right time of year when there are very few tourists. Summer is much busier and no time for the small chat.'

Finally Giuseppe got around to filling Flynn's glass, and gave him a surreptitious wink as he set the bottle on the table. 'Enjoy your evening, Doctor.'

Cheeky old man. Flynn grinned despite himself. 'I intend to.'

Ally watched him walk away, a smile lighting her pretty face. 'I could get to like this.' Then the smile slipped. 'But only for a month. Then I'll have somewhere else nice and friendly to visit while I relieve yet another midwife.'

He wanted to ask what compelled her to only take short-term contracts, but as he opened his mouth the thought of possibly spoiling what was potentially going to be a wonderful evening had him shutting up fast. Then their meals arrived and all questions evaporated in the hot scent of garlic and cream and tomatoes wafting between them.

Ally sighed as she gazed at her dish. 'Now, that looks like the perfect carbonara.' This time her tongue slid across first her bottom lip and then the top one. What else could she do with that tongue? Lifting her eyes, she studied his pizza. 'That looks delicious, too.'

'I know it will be.' The best pizzas he'd ever tasted had been made right here. 'One day I'll get to trying a pasta dish, but I can't get past the pizzas.'

Sipping her wine, Ally smiled directly at him. 'Thank you for bringing me here.'

'It's the best idea I've had in a long time.' Had he really just said that? Yes, and why not? It was only the truth. Picking up a wedge of pizza, he held it out to her. 'Try that.'

Her teeth were white and perfect. She bit into the wedge and sat back to savour the flavours of tomato and basil that would be exploding in her mouth. As he watched her enjoyment, he took a bite. Ally closed her eyes and smiled as she chewed. 'How do you do that?' he asked.

She swallowed and her eyelids lifted. 'Here, you must try this.' She twirled her fork in her pasta and leaned close to place it in his mouth.

The scent of hot food and Ally mingled, teasing him as he took her offering. The tastes of bacon and cream burst across his tongue. 'Divine.' Though he suspected cardboard would taste just as good right now.

They shared another wedge of pizza. Then Ally put her hands around her plate. 'Not sharing any more.'

Moments later she raised her glass to smile over the rim at him and let those sultry eyes study him.

Flynn sneaked his fork onto her plate and helped himself. 'You think you're keeping this to yourself?' Not that his stomach was in the mood for more food while she was looking at him like he was sexy. He felt alive and on top of his game, very different from his usual sad and exhausted state.

Her tongue ran around the edge of her glass, sending desire firing through his body heading straight for his manhood. *Pow.* 'You're flirting with me, Miss Ally.'

'Yes.' Her tongue lapped at her wine, sending his hormones into overdrive.

He placed the fork, still laden with carbonara, on his plate. 'Come here,' he growled. 'I've wanted to do this for two whole days.'

He placed his fingers on her cheeks to draw her closer. Pressing his mouth to her lips, all he was aware of was this amazing woman and the taste, the feel, the heat of her.

Finally, some time later—minutes or hours?—Flynn led Ally outside, only vaguely aware they'd eaten tiramisu for dessert, and hoped he'd had enough smarts to pay the bill before leaving. No worry, Giuseppe knew where to find him. In one hand he held the wine bottle, still half-full, while his other arm wrapped around Ally's waist as she leaned in close, her head on his shoulder, her arm around him with her hand in his pocket, stroking his hip, stroking, stroking.

Forget the car. He led her across the road and down to the beach. It was cold, but he was hot. They didn't talk, and the moment they were out of sight of the few people out on the road, Ally turned into him, pressing her body hard against his. Her hands linked at the back of his neck and she tugged his mouth down to hers.

The bottle dropped to the sand as he slid his hands under her top. Her skin was satin, hot satin. Splaying his fingers, he smoothed his hands back and forth, touching more of her, while his mouth tasted her, his tongue dancing around hers. He wanted her. Now.

'Ally?' he managed to groan out between kisses.

Between their crushed-together bodies she slipped a hand to his trousers, tugged his zip down. The breath caught in his throat as her fingers wrapped around him.

'Ally.' This time there was no question in his mind.

She rubbed him, up, down. Up, down.

Reaching for her jeans, he pushed and pulled until he had access to her, trying—and nearly failing—to remain focused on giving her pleasure. She was wet to his touch, moaning as his fingers touched her, and she came almost instantly, crying out as she rocked against his hand. Her hand squeezed him, eased, squeezed again, and his release came quickly.

Too quickly. 'Can we do that again?' he murmured against that soft hair.

Ally had wrapped herself against him, her arms under his jacket, her breaths sharp against his chest. Her head moved up and down. 'Definitely.'

'Come on, we'll go home.'

Her head lifted. 'You've got a babysitter. We could go to the flat.'

His lips traced a kiss across her forehead and down her cheek. 'Are you always so sensible?' He'd fried any brain matter he had. 'Good thinking.'

'What are we waiting for?' Ally spun around and took his hand to drag him back up the beach to his car.

The flat was less than five minutes away. Thank goodness. He didn't know how he'd manage to keep two hands on the steering wheel for that long, let alone actually function well enough to drive.

* * *

The moment she shut the front door behind them Ally grabbed Flynn's hand and almost ran to the bedroom. That had been amazing on the beach, but it was only a taste of what she knew they could have. It had been nowhere near enough.

She laughed out loud. 'I want to wrap myself around you.' She began tearing clothes off. Flynn's and hers. 'I want to get naked and up close with you.'

'Stop.' It was a command.

And she obeyed. 'Yes?'

'Those knickers. Don't take them off. Not yet.'

So he was into G-strings. She turned and saucily moved her derrière, then slowly lifted her top up to her breasts, oh, so slowly over them, and finally above her head, tossing it into the corner.

Then turned around, reaching behind her to unclasp her bra. Flynn's eyes followed every move. When she shrugged out of the lace creation, his hands rose to her breasts, ever so lightly brushing across her nipples and sending swirls of need zipping through her. Once had definitely not been enough with this man.

Twice probably wouldn't be, either. This was already cranking up to be a fling of monumental proportions. Her time on Phillip Island had just got a whole lot more interesting and exciting. 'Flynn.' His name fell as a groan between them.

As he leaned over to take her nipple in his mouth he smiled. A smile full of wonder and longing. A smile that wound around her heart.

Back off. Now. Your heart never gets involved. Back off. Remember who, what you are. A nomad, soon to be on the road again. Remember. You take no passengers.

Flynn softly bit her breast, sending rationale out the window. Her hands gripped his head to keep his mouth exactly where it was. His hands cupped her backside. Tipping her head back so her hair fell down her back, Ally went with the overwhelming need crawling through her, filling every place, warming every muscle until she quivered with such desire she thought she'd explode.

Flynn's mouth traced kisses up her throat, then began a long, exploratory trip downward. Back to her breasts, then her stomach and beyond. It was impossible to keep up with him, to savour each and every stroke. They all melted into one, and when her legs trembled so much she could barely stand, Flynn gently guided her onto the bed, where he joined her, his erection throbbing when she placed her hand around him and brought him to where she throbbed for him.

Ally rolled over and groaned. *Is there any part of me that doesn't ache?* A delicious, morning-after-mind-blowing-sex ache that pulled the energy out of her and left her feeling relaxed and unwilling to get up to face the day.

She was expected at work by eight thirty. *Yeah, tell that to someone who cares.* But she dragged herself upright and stared around. The bed was a shambles, with the sheets twisted, the cover skew-whiff and the pillows on the floor.

What a night. Really only for an hour, but for once she doubted she could've gone all night. Not with Flynn. He took it out of her, he was so good.

The phone rang. It wasn't on her bedside table or on the floor next to the bed. But it did sound as though it was in this room. She tossed the cover aside, shivering as winter air hit her bare skin. Lifting the sheets and pillows, she found her jeans, but not what she was looking for. 'Don't hang up.' What if it was one of her mothers having contractions? 'Where is the blasted phone?'

Picking up her top from the corner where she'd thrown it last night, she pounced, pressed the phone's green button. 'Morning, Ally Parker speaking.'

'Morning, gorgeous,' Flynn's voice drawled in her ear. 'Thought I'd make sure you're wide-awake.'

'And if I hadn't been?' The concern backed off a notch at the sound of his warm tone. 'You'd have come around and hauled me out of bed?'

'My oath I would.'

'That does it. I'm sound asleep.' What was wrong with her? Encouraging Flynn was not the way to go.

His laugh filled her with happiness. 'Unfortunately I have a certain small individual with me this morning and I know he'd love nothing better than to try and pull you out of bed.'

'So not a good look, considering I'm naked.' She'd left her brain on the beach. Had to have.

Flynn growled. 'I certainly wouldn't be able to fault that.'

Then she saw the time. 'Is it really eight o'clock? It can't be. Got to go. I'm going to be late.' She hung up before he could say anything else and ran for the bathroom. The left side of her left brain argued with the right side about what she was doing with Flynn.

'Only five minutes late,' she gasped, as she charged into the staffroom. A large coffee in a takeout mug stood on the table at the spot where she usually sat. 'Black and strong,' Flynn muttered, as he joined her.

'You're wonderful.' She popped the lid off.

Jerome and Toby sauntered in. 'What did you think of our local Italian?' Jerome asked with a twinkle in his eye.

'I'm hooked. Definitely going back there again.' Her knee nudged Flynn's under the table.

He pushed back as he continued to stare across at the other men. 'She's got Giuseppe eating out of her hand.'

I thought that was your hand. 'He's a sweetheart.'

'Ally.' Megan popped her head around the door. 'You've got visitors. Chrissie and her mum.'

Back to earth with a thud. Reality kicked in. 'Show-time.' Ally stood up, sipped her coffee, found it cool enough to gulp some down. No way could she start her day without her fix, especially not this morning. Her stomach was complaining about the lack of breakfast, but it'd have to make do with caffeine. 'Is it okay if I go and see Chrissie? Or would you prefer I stay for the meeting?'

'Don't worry about the meeting. One of us can fill you in later if there's anything you need to know,' Toby told her.

Flynn spoke up. 'If you need me, just call. But I'm sure you'll be fine.'

'Chrissie's mum would have to be dense not to know why her daughter has requested an appointment with a midwife, wouldn't she?'

Flynn nodded. 'And dense is not a word I'd use to describe Angela. She's probably cottoned on but could be denying it.'

Angela didn't deny it for any longer than it took for the three of them to be seated in Ally's room with the door firmly shut. 'You're going to tell me Chrissie's pregnant, aren't you?'

'Actually, I was hoping Chrissie might've told you.' She looked at the girl and found nothing but despair blinking out at her. Dark shadows lined the skin beneath her sad eyes and her mouth was turned downwards, while her hands fidgeted on her thighs. 'Chrissie, did you get any sleep last night?'

She shook her head. 'I was thinking, you know? About everything.' Her shoulders dropped even lower. 'I'm sorry, Mum. I didn't mean it to happen.'

'Now, that I can understand.' Angela might have been expecting the news but she still looked shocked. 'All too well.' She breathed deeply, her chest rising. 'How far along are you, do you know?' Her gaze shifted from her daughter to Ally and then back to Chrissie.

'Nearly twelve weeks.' Chrissie's voice was little more than a whisper. 'You're disappointed in me, aren't you?'

Angela sat ramrod straight. Her hands were clenched together, but her eyes were soft and there was gentleness in her next words. 'No, sweetheart, I think you're the one who's going to be disappointed. You had so many plans for your future and none of them included a baby.'

'But you managed. You've got a good job. You're the best mum ever.'

'Chrissie, love.' Angela sniffed, and reached for one of her daughter's hands. 'A good job, yes, but not the career I'd planned on.'

Ally stood up and crossed to the window to give them some space. They didn't need her there. Yet. Flynn had been right. This woman was a good mum. *Why didn't I have one like her? Why didn't I have one at all? One who loved me from the day I was born?*

Behind her the conversation became erratic as Chrissie and Angela worked their way through the minefield they were facing. At least they were facing it together.

'Do you regret having me?' Chrissie squeaked.

'Never.' A chair scratched over the surface of the floor and when Ally took a quick peek she saw Angela holding her daughter in her arms. 'Never, ever. Not for one minute.'

'I'm keeping my baby, Mum.'

Ally held her breath. This was the moment when Angela might finally crack. She fully understood the pitfalls of single parenthood. And the joys. But she'd want more for Chrissie.

Angela was strong. 'I thought you'd say that. I hope your child will love its grandmother as much as you loved your grandfather, my girl, because we're in this together. Understand?'

As Chrissie burst into long-overdue tears, Ally sneaked out the door, closing it softly behind her. In the storeroom she wiped her own eyes. Did that girl understand how loved she was? How lucky?

'Hey, don't tell me it was that bad in there.' Flynn stood before her, holding the box of tissues she'd been groping for.

'It was beautiful.' Blow. 'What an amazing mother Angela is. Chrissie will be, too, if that's the example she's got to follow.'

'Told you.' Did he have to sound so pleased with himself? His finger tipped her chin up so she had to meet his kind gaze. 'Come and finish that coffee I bought you. We can zap it in the microwave.'

He'd be thinking she was a right idiot, hiding in the cupboard, crying, because her patient had just told her mother she was pregnant. 'I'll give them five minutes and then go and discuss pregnancy care and health.'

'Make it ten. You'll be feeling better and they'll have run out of things to say to each other for a while.' His hand on her elbow felt so right. And for the first time it wasn't about heat and desire but warmth and care.

More stupid tears spurted from her eyes. Her third day here and he was being gentle and kind to her. Right now she liked this new scenario. Thank goodness Flynn would think these fresh tears were more of the same—all about Chrissie and her mother, not about him. And her.

CHAPTER FIVE

THE MOMENT FLYNN saw the clinic's car turn into the parking lot on Friday night he couldn't hold back a smile. A smile for no other reason than he was glad to see Ally. Her image was pinned up in his skull like a photo on a noticeboard. More than one photo. There was the one of Ally in those leg-hugging, butt-defining jeans and the red jersey that accentuated her breasts. Then the other: a naked version showing those shapely legs, slim hips and delicious breasts.

There was a third: tearful Ally, hiding away and looking lost and lonely. What was that about?

The front door crashed against the wall as she elbowed it wide and carried her bag in. 'Hi, Flynn, you're working late. Had an emergency?'

Yep, two hours without laying eyes on you definitely constitutes an emergency. 'Do you want to join Adam and me for dinner? There's a chicken casserole cooking as we speak. Nothing flash, but it should be tasty.'

'A casserole's not flash?' Her smile warmed him right down to his toes. 'My mouth's watering already.'

'Is that a yes, then?' His lungs stopped functioning as he waited for her reply.

'Are you sure there'll be enough?' As he was about

to answer in the affirmative, she asked, 'Shall I stop in at the supermarket and get some garlic bread to go with the meal? Some wine?'

'Good idea. I left the Merlot behind the other night. On the beach,' he added with a grin.

'You're too easily distracted, that's your problem.' Her mouth stretched into a return smile. 'Someone probably got lucky when they went for a walk that morning.'

A devilish look crossed his face and his eyes widened. 'I got lucky that night.'

'A dinner invitation will get me every time.' She swatted his arm. 'What's your address? Better give me precise directions if you really want me to join you.'

'The island's not too large and most people know where to find me.' Glancing at his watch, he added, 'I'll get home so Marie can leave.'

Flynn hummed all the way home, something he hadn't done in for ever. Even without Tuesday night's sexual encounters, the fact that Ally was coming to his place for a meal made him feel good. Mealtimes weren't lonely because Adam was there, but sometimes he wished for adult conversation while he enjoyed his dinner. He'd also like an occasional break from Adam's usual grizzles about what he was being made to eat. His boy was a picky eater. Just because his mother had wanted him to eat well, it didn't mean Adam agreed.

Flynn shook his head. Where did Adam come into this? This hyper mood had nothing to do with him. Try Ally. And himself. *Be honest, admit you want a repeat of Tuesday night's sex.*

Guilt hit hard and fast.

What was he thinking? How could he be having fun when Anna was gone? He didn't deserve to. It had been his fault she hadn't been happy with her life. He should've taken the time to listen to her when she'd tried to explain why it was so important to her to leave the city behind.

He'd loved his life in Melbourne, had thought he was well on the way to making a big name for himself in emergency medicine. Sure, he hadn't always been there for Anna and Adam, had missed meals and some firsts, like Adam saying 'Hello, Mummy', but they'd agreed before Adam had been conceived that he'd be working long hours, getting established, and that it would take a few years before he backed off so they could enjoy the lifestyle they both had wanted.

Anna had quickly forgotten their agreement once Adam had arrived, instead becoming more demanding for him to give up his aspirations and move to family-orientated Phillip Island. What he hadn't told Anna before she'd died was that he'd begun talks with the head of the ED to cut down his hours. It would've been a compromise. Too late. Anna had driven into an oncoming tram, and he and Adam had moved to her island full-time. Sometimes he had regrets about that—regrets that filled him with guilt. This was right for Adam. He should've done it for Anna while he could.

Turning into his drive, he automatically pressed the garage door opener and drove in, hauled on the handbrake and switched off the engine. He tipped his head back against the headrest. 'Anna, I miss you.'

A lone tear tracked down his cheek.

Is it wrong to want to have some fun? To want to move on and forge a new life for me and our boy? Adam misses his mummy so much I'm afraid I'm getting it all wrong. I try to do things as you'd want, but sometimes I feel I'm living your life, not mine.

The engine creaked as it began cooling down. Sheba nudged her wet nose against his window and Flynn dragged himself out of the car. He didn't have time to sit around feeling sorry for himself. Rightly or wrongly, Ally was coming to dinner.

After stopping off at the supermarket, Ally went back to the flat and had a quick shower, before changing into jeans and a clean shirt. She took a moment to brush her ponytail out, letting it fall onto her shoulders. If the way Flynn kept running his hands through it the other night was an indicator, he obviously liked her hair.

She checked her phone for texts. Nothing. Not even from Darcie. She quickly texted.

How's things?

The reply was instant.

The usual. What r u doing 2night?

Having dinner with hot man.

You're not wasting time.

Did I mention his 4-yr-old son?

Ally? That's different for you.

Ally slipped her phone into her pocket without answering. What could she say? In one short message Darcie had underlined her unease.

Swiping mascara over her lashes, she stared at her reflection in the mirror. Most of the day, even when busy with patients, a sense of restlessness had dogged her. Strange. Her first-day nerves weren't going away.

Get over it. Coming to a new job's nothing like starting over with a new family when you're scared and wondering if they'll love you enough to keep you past the end of the first week. Don't let the worry bugs tip you off track. You're in control these days.

She twisted the mascara stick into its holder so hard it snapped.

Thank goodness she had something to do tonight other than sit alone in that pokey lounge, eating takeaways and watching something boring on TV. She'd be with Flynn and his boy, and be able to have a conversation. What about didn't matter, as long as she had company for a few hours. It would be an added bonus if she and Flynn ended up in bed. But she wasn't sure if it would happen, with Adam being in the house, Flynn rightly being super-protective of him.

Then she laughed at herself. Since when did she put sex second to conversation? After one night with Flynn she hadn't stopped wondering where he'd been all her life. What was happening? Had her regular hormones packed their bags and taken a hike, only to be replaced with a needier version?

She froze, stared into the mirror, found only the same face she'd been covering with make-up for years. No drastic changes had occurred. The same old wariness mixed with a don't-mess-with-me glint blinked out of her eyes. And behind that the one emotion she hoped no one ever saw—her need to be loved.

Dropping her head, she planted her hands wide on the

bathroom counter, stared into the basin and concentrated on forcing that old, childish yearning away.

Sex with Flynn and now this? Why now? Here? What was it about him that had the locks turning on her tightly sealed box of needs and longings?

She couldn't visit him. Throwing the mascara wand at the bin, she grimaced. She had to, then she'd see that he was just an everyday man working to raise his son and not someone to get in a stew over. If he was wise he'd never want a woman as mixed up as her in Adam's life.

A quick glance in the mirror and she dredged up a smile.

Attagirl. You're doing good. She kissed her fingertips and waved them at her image. But right now she'd love a hug.

Ally got her hug within seconds of stepping inside Flynn's house.

'Hey, there.' His eyes were sombre and his mouth not smiling as he wrapped her in his arms. Her cheek automatically nestled against his chest. Her determination to be Ally the aloof midwife wobbled. *Should've stayed away. At least until this weird phase passes.*

Then Adam leapt at her, nearly knocking her off her feet and winding his arms around her waist.

'Is this a family thing?' she asked, as she staggered back against the wall. She dredged up a smile for Adam.

'Easy, Adam, not so hard. You're hurting Ally.'

'No, I'm not,' he answered. Then he was racing down the hall to where light spilled from a room. 'Now we can eat.'

'There's an honest welcome.' Kind of heart-warming. 'I'm sorry if I've kept you waiting.'

Flynn shook his head. 'You're not late. You could've

got here by midday and Adam would've been waiting for dinner. He's a bottomless pit when it comes to his favourite food.'

'I bought him a wee treat at the supermarket. I hope that's all right.' The house was abnormally quiet. No blaring TV, she realised.

'The occasional one's fine, but I try not to spoil him with too much sugar and fatty foods. His mother held strong beliefs about giving children the right foods early on to establish a good lifestyle for growing up healthy. Healthy body, healthy mind was a saying close to her heart.'

He was trying to implement his late wife's beliefs. 'Fair enough.' Ally had no idea what it must be like to be suddenly left as a solo parent to a two-year-old, especially while juggling a demanding career. 'Have you always worked on Phillip Island?'

'Only since Anna died.' Flynn found matching glasses and poured the Chardonnay she'd brought. 'I was an emergency consultant in Melbourne. Being a GP is relatively new for me, and vastly different from my previous life.'

'So you had to re-specialise?' Why the drastic change?

'It was a formality really as my specialty leant itself to general practice.' He lifted his glass and tapped the rim to hers. 'Cheers. Thanks for this.'

The wine was delicious, and from the way Flynn's mouth finally tipped up into a smile after he'd tasted it, he thought so, too.

'Thanks for feeding me.' She pulled out a bar stool from under the bench and arranged herself on it to watch Flynn put the finishing touches to dinner. *Looking for the everyday man?*

As he chopped parsley he continued the conversation in a more relaxed tone. 'Anna grew up here and it had always been her intention to return once she had a family.' His finger slid along the flat of the knife to remove tiny pieces of the herb and add them to the small pile he'd created. 'I wasn't ready to give up my career in the city. I was doing well, making a name for myself, working every hour available and more. We lived in a big house in the right suburb, had Adam registered for the best schools before he was born. It was the life *I'd* dreamed of having.'

She sensed a deep well of sadness in Flynn as he sprinkled the parsley on the casserole and rinsed his hands under the tap. *Not quite the definition of an everyday man.* Hadn't he and Anna discussed where they wanted to live and work before they'd married? Before they'd started a family? 'Yet here you are, everyone's favourite GP, living in a quiet suburban neighbourhood, seemingly quite happy with it all. Apart from what happened to your wife, of course,' she added hurriedly.

She wanted to know more about him, his past, his plans for the future. She craved more than to share some nights in bed with him. *Leave. Now.* But her butt remained firmly on the seat and her feet tucked under the stool. She'd have to stay and work through whatever was ailing her.

Flynn's smile was wry. 'Odd how it turned out. It took Anna's death for me to wake up to what was important. Family is everything, and Adam is my family, so here we are.' He held cutlery out for her to take across to the table.

Did he add under his breath, 'Living the life Anna wanted for all of us?' If he did, then he'd pull the shutters down on any kind of relationship other than a fling.

His late wife wouldn't be wanting him to have a woman flitting in and out of his life, and definitely not Adam's.

Relief was instant. She didn't have to fight this sense of wanting more from him. There wasn't going to be anything other than sex and a meal or two. *You're jumping the gun. He mightn't even want the sex part any more.* Except when she glanced across to where he was dishing up the meal, she knew he did. It was there in the way he watched her, not taking a blind bit of notice where he spooned chicken and gravy. When their gazes locked she was instantly transported back to the moment they'd come together on the beach. Oh, yes, there were going to be more bed games.

Games that didn't involve her heart and soul, just her hormones and body.

'What is there to do on the island during winter?' Apart from going to bed with sexy doctors. 'I read somewhere about a racetrack, but there's not going to be a race meeting this month.'

'Do you like watching cars going round and round for hours on end?' He looked bored just thinking about it.

'I've never been, but I'm always looking for new adventures.'

'So what do you do with your spare time?'

Not a lot. Her standard time-fillers were, 'Shopping, movies, sunbathing on the beach, swimming, listening to music.'

'That's it?' His eyebrows lifted. 'Seriously?'

'What's wrong with that? It's plenty.' *I don't have a child to look after. Or a house to clean and maintain. Or a partner who wants me to follow him around.*

Flynn shook his head. 'Don't tell me your life is all work and no play?'

She locked her eyes on him. 'No play? Care to rephrase that?' She'd done playing the other night—with him.

He grinned. 'How about we take you to see the penguins this weekend? It's something I can take Adam to with us.'

'Penguins?' Adam's head swivelled round so fast he should've got an instant headache.

'Big Ears always hears certain words.' Flynn shrugged.

'Can we really go, Dad? They're funny, Ally.' Adam leapt up from the table to do his best impersonation of a penguin, and Sheba got up to run circles around him. Next Adam was having a fit of giggles.

Ally chuckled. 'I love it when he does that. Okay, yes, let's go and see these creatures.' It would be something to look forward to. Going out with an everyday man and his child. Different from her usual pursuits. She bobbed her head at Adam and held her arms tightly by her sides as she shuffled across the floor.

Adam rewarded her with more giggles as they returned to the table.

'That's enough, you two.' Flynn looked so much better when he laughed. 'Sorry we're eating early, but Adam needs to have his bath and get to bed.' Flynn didn't look sorry at all.

'I understand you must have a routine. Don't ever think you have to change it for me. I'm more than happy being fed,' she said, before forking up a mouthful of chicken. 'This is better than anything I'd make, believe me.'

Adam pushed his plate aside. 'Are we having pudding, Dad?'

'I've chopped up some oranges and kiwi fruit. Just need to add the banana when we're ready.'

'Can I get the ice cream out of the freezer?'

'Yes, you can tonight since we've got a visitor.' Flynn winked at her. 'You'll get an invitation every day now.'

I wish. 'I'll clean up the kitchen after dinner.' A small price for a home-cooked meal.

While Flynn was putting Adam to bed, Ally cleared away the plates. Once she'd put the last pot into the dishwasher and wiped down the benches she approached the coffee machine and began preparing two cappuccinos. 'These things make decent frothy milk,' she commented as Flynn joined her. 'How's Adam?'

'Asleep, thank goodness.' He took the coffees over to the lounge.

Following, she asked, 'This your quiet time?'

'Definitely. Don't get me wrong, I love my boy, but to have a couple of hours to unwind from the day before I go to bed is bliss.'

Bed. There it was. The place she wanted to be with Flynn right now. But he'd sat down and was stretching his legs out in front of him. She remembered those legs with no clothing to hide the muscles or keep her hands off his skin. Skin that covered more muscle and hot body the farther up she trailed her gaze. *Stop it.* She sipped the coffee, gasped as it burned her tongue. 'I'm such a slow learner.'

He stood up to take the mug out of her hand and place it on a small table beside the chair. Then he reached for her hands and pulled her to her feet. His mouth was on hers in an instant; his kiss as hot, as sexy, as overwhelming as she remembered from the previous night. She hadn't been embellishing the details.

His arms held her close to his yummy body, his need as apparent to her as the need pulsing along her veins.

When he lifted his mouth away she put her hands up and brought his head back to hers. She liked him kissing her. More than any man before. *Scary. Don't think about what that means right now. Don't think at all. Enjoy the moment.* Her tongue slipped across his bottom lip, tasting him, sending enough heat to her legs to make them momentarily incapable of holding her upright without holding on to Flynn tighter.

'Ally, you're doing it to me again. Sending me over the edge so quickly I can't keep up.' Thankfully he returned to kissing as soon as he stopped talking.

So not the moment for talking. This was when mouths had other, better, things to do. Since when had kissing got to be so wonderful anyway? Or was it just Flynn's kisses that turned her on so rapidly? Before Flynn she'd thought they were just a prelude to bedroom gymnastics, but now she could honestly spend the whole evening just kissing.

Then his hands slid under her top to touch her skin and she knew she'd been fooling herself. She had to have him, skin to skin, hips to hips. Hands touching, teasing, caressing. Now. Pulling her mouth free, she growled, 'The couch or your bedroom?'

His eyes widened, then he shook his head. 'Bedroom. There's a lock on the door.'

She hadn't had to think about children barging in before. But why did Flynn have a lock on his bedroom door? Did he do this often? No, he'd told her she was the first since Anna died. Somehow she knew he hadn't lied to her. Whatever the reason it was there, she was grateful or Flynn wouldn't have continued with this even with Adam sound asleep.

He said, 'I'm hoping you've got more of those condoms in your bag.'

'That's what the pharmacy's handy for. Called in at the one farthest from the clinic on my way back from visiting a patient.' No point in creating gossip if she didn't have to.

Flynn laughed. 'You don't honestly think they won't know who you are already?'

Her fingers caught his chin and pulled that talkative mouth down for another kiss. 'Let's get back to where we were.'

'Now who's talking too much?'

They both shut up from then on, too busy touching and stroking, kissing, undressing one another as their desire coiled tighter and tighter. And tighter.

The phone woke Ally. It was a local number, though not one she knew. Seven o'clock on a Saturday morning. She might not know many people on this island, but it seemed someone always wanted to get her out of bed before she was ready. Or in bed, as with Flynn.

'Ally, is that you? It's Chrissie.'

'Hey, Chrissie, what's up?" Ally pushed up the bed to lean back against her pillow.

'I'm bleeding. I'm not losing the baby, am I?' Her voice rose.

'First of all, take a deep breath and try to calm down. I'll have to examine you to know the answer to that, but you're not necessarily having a miscarriage. Sometimes women do have some spotting and it's fine.'

'But what if I am miscarrying?' There were tears in Chrissie's voice. 'I don't want to lose it.'

Ally felt her heart squeeze for this brave young woman. 'How heavy is the bleeding?' Wrong question. To every pregnant mother it would be a flood.

'Not lots. Nothing like my period or anything.'

Got that wrong, then, didn't I? 'I'll come and see you this morning. Try to relax until I get there. This could just be due to hormonal changes or an irritation to your cervix after sex.' Had Chrissie been seeing the boy who'd had a part in this pregnancy? There'd still been no mention of the father and she was reluctant to ask. It wasn't any of her business, unless Chrissie was under undue pressure from him about the pregnancy and so far that didn't seem to be the case.

'Really?' Chrissie's indrawn breath was audible on the phone. Girls of this age didn't usually like talking about their sexual relations to the midwife. It was *embarrassing*. 'But that didn't happen before when I wasn't pregnant.'

'Your body is changing all the time now, and especially your cervix.' It sounded like they might have the cause of the spotting, but she needed to make absolutely sure. Ally got up and stretched, her body aware of last night's lovemaking with Flynn. Easing the kinks out of her neck and back, she used one hand to pull on a thick jersey and trackpants before making her way to the kettle for a revitalising coffee. 'Have you told your mum what's happening?'

'Yes. She said to ring you or Dr Reynolds.'

And I got the vote. Warmth surged through her. 'If I'm at all worried after the exam, you'll still need to see Dr Reynolds. He might want you to have an ultrasound. But first things first. I'll be at your house soon. Is that all right?' She wouldn't mention the blood tests she'd need samples for. Chrissie might've sailed through the last lot without a flinch, but she didn't need to be stressed over today's until the last minute.

'Thank you, Ally. That's cool. I'm sorry to spoil your day off.'

'Hey, you haven't. This is what being a midwife's about. You wait until junior is ready to come out. He or she won't care what day of the week it is, or even if it's day or night.'

'I'm going to find out if it's a boy or girl. I want time to think of a name and to get some nice things for it. I feel weird, calling the baby "it". Like I don't care or something.'

Talking about the scan was more positive than worrying she might be losing the baby. Ally sighed with relief. 'Catch you shortly.'

Four hours later Ally parked outside Flynn's house and rubbed her eyes. She was unusually tired. Her head felt weighed down—with what, she had no idea. Maybe the slower pace of the island did this to people. She'd noticed not everyone hurried from place to place, or with whatever they were doing. Certainly not the checkout operator at the supermarket, where she'd just been to stock up on a few essentials. The girl had been too busy talking to her pal she'd previously served to get on with the next load of groceries stacked on her conveyor belt.

Tap-tap on her window. Flynn opened her door. 'Hey, you coming in or going to sit out here for the rest of the day? Adam could run errands for you, bring you a coffee or a sandwich.'

'That sounds tempting.' The heaviness lifted a little and she swung out of the car. 'How's things in your house this morning?'

He ignored her question. 'You look exhausted. All that sexercise catching up with you?' He suddenly appeared genuinely concerned. 'You're not coming down with anything, are you?'

'Relax, I'm good. Just tired. I've spent most of this morning with Matilda Livingstone, trying to calm her down and make her understand that her pregnancy is going well, that she doesn't need to worry about eclampsia at this early stage, if at all.'

'Her mother's been bleating in her ear again, I take it?'

'Unfortunately, yes. Such a different outlook from Angela and Chrissie. I had an hour with Chrissie, as well. She had some mild spotting this morning, but hopefully I've allayed her concerns. We talked a lot about the trimesters and what's ahead for her and the baby. I'm amazed at how much detail she wanted to know.'

'Could be her way of keeping on top of the overwhelming fact that she's pregnant and still at school and hoping to go to university.'

Ally nodded. 'Yes, well, that plan of becoming a lawyer is on hold for a little while, but I bet she will do her degree. Maybe not in the next couple of years, but some time. There's a fierce determination building up in her that she'll not let baby change her life completely, that she's going to embrace the situation and make the most of everything.'

'That's fine until her friends leave the island to study and she's at home with a crying infant. That's the day she'll need all the strength she can muster.'

Ally shook her head at him. 'She'll love her precious baby so much she'll be fine.'

'Spoken like someone who hasn't had a major disappointment in her life.'

Spoken like a woman who's had more than her fair share of those, and has learned to try and see only the best in life by not involving herself with people so they can't hurt her.

'That's me—Pollyanna's cousin.' It shouldn't hurt that Flynn didn't see more to her than her cheery facade, didn't see how forced that sometimes was, but it did. Even if she cut him some slack because it had barely been a week since they'd met and outside work they'd only had fun times, she felt a twinge of regret.

What would it be like to have someone in her life who truly knew her? Where she'd come from. Why she kept moving from one clinic to the next, one temporary house to another. She'd thought she'd won the lottery with the Bartletts. She had come so close to belonging, had been promised love and everything, even adoption, so when it hadn't eventuated, the pain of being rejected for a cute three-year-old had underscored what she'd always known. She was unlovable. Letting people into her heart was foolish, and to have risked it to the Bartletts because they'd made promises of something she'd only ever dreamed of having had been the biggest mistake of her young life. So big she'd never contemplated it again.

Oh, they'd explained as kindly as they could how their own two children, younger than her, hadn't wanted a big sister. Being mindful of their children's needs made Mr and Mrs Bartlett good parents, but they should never have promised her the earth. She'd loved them with such devotion it had taken months to fully understand what had happened. They'd said she was always welcome at their home. Of course, she hadn't visited.

As she locked the car she watched Flynn with her bags of goodies striding up the path to his front door. Why did she feel differently about Flynn? Whatever the answer, it was all the more reason to remain indifferent.

Did his confidence come from having loved and been loved so well that despite his loss he knew who he was and why he was here? He wasn't going to share his life with her or another woman. It was so obvious in the way he looked out for Adam, in the balancing act he already had with his career and his son. She'd been aware right from the get-go that there would be no future for her here.

That's how she liked it, remember?

As Flynn stopped to look back at her she knew an almost overwhelming desire to run up to him and throw herself into his arms. So strong was this feeling that she unlocked the car. She had to drive away, go walk the beach or take a visit to the mainland.

'Ally? You gone to sleep on your feet?' The concern was genuine. 'I think you should see a doctor.' Then he smiled that stomach-tightening smile straight at her. 'This doctor.'

How could she refuse that invitation? There was friendship in that smile. There was mischief, as in sex, in that smile. That was more than enough. That's all she ever wanted.

She locked the car again and headed inside.

Flynn watched Ally with Adam. She didn't appear to be overly tired, more distracted. By what? Was she about to tell him thanks, she'd had a blast, but it was over? Already?

He wasn't ready to hear that news. Not yet. They'd just got started. It had come as a surprise to find he wanted her so much, needed to get to know her intimately. He understood it had to be a short-term affair. Ally would leave at the end of her contract in three weeks—no doubt about that. For that he should be grateful. There wasn't room in his life for anyone else. Adam came first, second, and took anything left over from the demands of the clinic.

Anyway, he doubted whether Ally had room for him or any man in her life. She was so intent on moving on, only touching down briefly in places chosen for her by her bosses and circumstances, doing her job with absolute dedication and then taking flight again.

'Hey, Adam, what've you been doing this morning?' The woman dominating his thoughts was talking to his boy and scratching Sheba's ears.

'We went to the beach to throw sticks for Sheba. I chucked them in the water. That's why she's all wet.' Mischief lightened that deep shade of blue radiating out of Adam's eyes. *Here we go, another round of giggles coming up.*

'The water must've been freezing.' Ally smiled softly and ruffled his hair, which Adam seemed to like. And that simple show of affection put the kibosh on the giggles as he stepped close to Ally and patted the top of Sheba's head, too.

'Sheba likes swimming.' Adam looked up at Ally, hope in his eyes. 'Are you still coming to see the penguins with us?'

'That's why I'm here. You and I can do the funny walk on the beach, see if they want to be our friends.' She was good with him, no doubt about that.

Which set Flynn to more worrying. That look Adam had given her showed how much his boy already felt comfortable with Ally. Though, to be fair, he was comfortable with just about everybody. But was this a good idea, having Ally drop by for lunch and a drive around the island? His boy didn't need to lose anyone else in his life. It was only recently that he'd got past that debilitating grief after Anna's death. *He must not get close to Ally. He could not.*

'Flynn, you've caught the sleeping-on-your-feet bug.' Ally had crossed to his side and was nudging him none too gently in the ribs with her elbow. 'You with us?'

He relaxed. Let the sudden fire in his belly rule his head. 'You bet. Do you want to come back for dinner tonight?' *Afterwards we could have some more of that bedroom exercise.*

'Did you have anything else in mind for the evening? There's a wicked glint in your baby blues.'

'Dessert maybe.'

'With whipped cream?' Her tongue slid across her lips and sent heat to every corner of his body.

So this was what it was like to wake up after a long hibernation. Not slowly, but full-on wide-awake and ready to go. Making love with this woman had been like a promise come true. Exciting and beautiful. He wanted to do it again and again. *Making love as against having sex? Now, there's something to think about.*

'Can I have ice cream, too?' Adam asked, bringing them back to earth with a thud.

'We can get cones when we're out this afternoon.' How many hours before Adam was tucked up in bed fast asleep? How long until he could kiss Ally until she melted against him?

'Flynn,' she mock growled. 'We have plans for this afternoon. Let's get them under way, starting with lunch. My shout at a café or wherever you recommend near this penguin colony. The busier we are, the quicker the day will go by.'

'Can't argue with that.' She was so right he had to drop a kiss on her cheek as a reward. It would've been too easy to move slightly and cover her mouth with his. Thank goodness common sense prevailed just in time and he stepped back to come up with, 'I'm thinking of getting our flippers out of the cupboard in the garage so that you two human penguins can flip-flop along the beach.'

'Can we, Dad? Ally, want to?' Adam yelled, as he ran in the direction of the garage internal door.

Flynn waved a hand after him. 'Go easy on that cupboard door. You know what happened last time you opened it.'

'I'll help him.' Ally was already moving in the same direction, her fingers tracing the spot on her cheek he'd just kissed.

'Good idea. Things tend to spill all over the place when he starts poking through the junk on the shelves.' He relaxed. Adam was excited, and Ally was just being a part of that, helping make his day more fun. It wasn't like she'd moved in or would see him every day of the week. She'd be gone soon enough, and Adam would still have all his playmates and the many adults on the island who enjoyed spoiling and looking out for him. He'd be safe. He wasn't in danger of getting hurt.

Flynn paused. Neither was he. Despite being equally excited as his boy. Ally hadn't said anything about calling their affair—if that's what it was—quits yet, so he'd carry on for three more weeks and make the most of her company. It wasn't as though he'd be broken-hearted when she went, mad, crazy attraction for her and all. He'd miss her for sure. She was the woman who'd woken him up, but that didn't mean he had to have her in his life permanently.

CHAPTER SIX

'WHERE'S DAD?' ADAM bounced into the bedroom and jumped up on the bed, effectively ending any pretence of Ally sleeping.

Groaning, she rolled over to stare up at this little guy. Something warm and damp nudged her arm. Turning her head, she came eye to eye with Sheba. Another groan escaped her. So this was what it was like to wake up in a family-orientated house. Kind of cosy, though it would've been better if Flynn were here.

'Why are you here?' Adam asked, looking around as though he might find his father in the wardrobe or on the floor beside the bed.

'Dad had to go to work so I stayed to look after you.'

'Did someone have a crash?' No four-year-old should look so knowledgeable about his father's work.

'Yes, during the night.' The call had come through requesting Flynn's presence as Ally had been about to walk out the door to return to the flat. They'd agreed she shouldn't be there in the morning with him when Adam woke up. But when the call came Flynn had been quick to accept her offer to stay, so apparently he could break his own rules.

Jerome had picked up Flynn ten minutes later. Teens

had been racing on the bridge in the wee hours of the morning after too much alcohol. Two cars had hit side on and spun, slamming into the side of the bridge, injuring four lads. Carnage, Flynn had told her when he'd phoned to explain he wouldn't be back until early morning as he was accompanying one of the boys to the Royal Melbourne Hospital.

'He doesn't like going to crashes. They're yucky.' Adam patted the bed and the next thing Ally felt the bed dipping as Sheba heaved herself up to join them.

'Is she allowed on the bed?' Ally shuffled sideways to avoid being squashed by half a ton of Labrador.

'Sometimes.'

'Right, and today's one of those times. Why did I not see that coming?' She chucked him under the chin. About to sit up, she stopped. Under the covers she wore only underwear. Definitely not the kind that decently covered all the girl bits. 'Adam, do you think you could take Sheba out to the kitchen while I get up?' Her clothes were in a tangled heap on the floor where she'd dropped them before climbing back into bed after Flynn had left.

'Do you want Dad's dressing gown? It's in the wardrobe. He never uses it.' Adam leapt off the bed, obviously unperturbed that she was there. Maybe he could explain that to his father. 'He walks around with no clothes on when he gets up in the morning.'

Too much information. At least while Flynn wasn't there and this little guy was. But she could picture Flynn buck naked as he strolled out to put the kettle on. Seriously sexy. 'I'd love the dressing gown.'

Adam had just dumped the robe on the bed when they both heard the front door opening. 'Dad's back.' He raced through the house, Sheba lumbering along behind him.

Making the most of the opportunity Ally slipped out of bed and into the dressing gown, tying the belt tightly around her waist. A glance in the mirror told her that as a fashion statement, an awful lot was lacking. Her face could do with a scrub, too. All that mascara had worked its way off her lashes and smudged her upper cheeks.

In the kitchen she plugged in the coffee maker and leaned her hip against the bench, waiting for the males of this house to join her.

Flynn sloped into the kitchen, with Adam hanging off his back like a monkey. Sheba brought up the rear. 'Morning, Ally. Sleep well?'

Huh?

Then he winked and she grinned. 'Like a lizard.'

'Like your outfit,' he tossed her way.

'I'm not sure about the colour. Brown has never been my favourite shade of anything. Want a coffee?'

'I'd kill for one, but can you give me five? I want to leap under a very hot shower.' His face dropped and his eyes saddened. 'It was messy out there,' he said quietly.

She nodded, wanting to ask more but reluctant to do so in front of Adam. Instead, she reached a hand to his cheek, cupped his face. 'Go and scrub up. I'll have the coffee waiting.' *Cosy, cosy.*

'Ta. You're a treasure.' For a moment she thought he was going to kiss her. His eyes locked on hers and he leaned closer. Then he must've remembered Adam on his back because he pulled away. 'I won't take long.'

He returned in jeans and a polo-neck black jersey that showed off his physique to perfection. His feet were bare, his hair a damp mess. He couldn't have looked more sexy if he'd tried. It came naturally.

Passing over a mug of strong coffee, she picked up

the container she'd found in the pantry. 'Feel like croissants for breakfast?'

'Croissants it is. I'll heat them while you have a shower if you like.' He didn't like her lounging around in his dressing gown? Then his eyes widened and she realised he was staring at her cleavage. An exposed cleavage.

Grabbing the edges of the robe, she tugged them closed. 'As soon as I've finished my coffee I'll get cleaned up.' Then what? Did she head home after breakfast? It would be fun to hang out with these two for a while. Talk about getting used to this cosy stuff all too quickly. Today she was simply ignoring the lessons learned and taking a chance. At what?

'We always go for a walk on the beach after breakfast in the weekends. You coming?' Flynn asked.

'Love to. Were you having a late breakfast when Sheba bowled me over last Sunday?' she asked around a smile, suddenly feeling good about herself. A chance at some normal, everyday fun that families all over the country would be doing. She wouldn't think about how often she'd stared through the proverbial window, longing for exactly this. She wouldn't contemplate next Sunday or the one three weeks away when she was back in Melbourne. Instead, she'd enjoy the day and keep the brakes on her emotions.

'No, two walks in one day. Makes up for the weekdays when she gets short-changed. I don't like dragging Adam out of bed too early. Marie walks her occasionally, but I think she's worried about being knocked over in her pregnant state.'

'Have you known Marie long?'

He nodded. 'Anna and Marie were school friends. They went their separate ways but kept in touch and Anna always talked about when they'd both be living back here with their families.' That sadness was back, this time for himself and his family.

Great. It was hard to compete with a woman who held all the aces and wasn't around any more to make mistakes. *You're competing now? What happened to your fixed-in-concrete motto—Have Fun and Move On?* That was exactly what she was doing. Having fun. And…in three weeks she'd be moving on. So none of this mattered. *Really?* Really. She tried for a neutral tone even when she felt completely mixed up. 'Marie must miss her, too.'

'She does, especially now her first baby's due.'

'What would Marie have to say if she knew about us?' Would she stick up for Anna or accept that Flynn was entitled to get on with his life? *Hello? What does any of that matter? You're out of here soon enough.*

'I have no idea.' Flynn looked taken aback. 'It's nothing to do with her.' But now that Ally had put the question out there he seemed busy trying to figure out the answer.

Am I trying to wreck this fling early? Because Flynn is sure to pull the plug now.

Placing her empty mug in the sink, she headed for the bathroom. The hot water could ease the kinks in her body, but it was unlikely to quieten the unease weaving through her enjoyment of being with Flynn. It was ingrained in her to protect her heart, but already she understood this wasn't a fling she'd walk away from as easily as any other. What worried her was not understanding why. She already knew she was going to miss Flynn.

But she would go. That was non-negotiable.

Sheba and Adam raced ahead of them, one barking and one shouting as they kicked up sand and left huge footprints. Flynn stifled a yawn and muttered, 'Where do they get their energy?'

'Perhaps you should try dry dog pellets for breakfast instead of hot, butter-soaked croissants,' a certain cheeky midwife answered from beside him.

'You're telling me Adam didn't eat a croissant with a banana and half a bottle of maple syrup poured on top? That was all for show and he actually scoffed down dog food?' Breakfast hadn't stacked up against Anna's ideas of healthy eating, but sometimes his boy was allowed to break the rules. Or *he* broke the rules and Adam enjoyed the result.

Ally's shoulder bumped his upper arm as she slewed sideways to avoid stepping on a fish carcass that had washed up on the tide. 'Yuk. That stinks.'

His hand found hers, their fingers interlaced, and he swung their arms between them. For a moment everything bothering him simply disappeared in this simple gesture. How much more relaxed could life get? He and Ally walking along the beach, hand in hand, watching Adam and the dog playing. Right now this was all he needed from life.

Then his phone broke the magic. 'Hello? Flynn Reynolds speaking.'

'This is William Foster's sister, Maisey. He's having chest pains again and refusing to go in the ambulance I called. Can you talk some sense into that stubborn head of his?'

'On my way. Can you hold on a moment?' He didn't wait for her reply. 'Ally, I've got to see a patient urgently. Can you take Adam home for me when you've finished your walk?' Asking for help twice in less than twenty-four hours didn't look like he managed very well. She'd probably be running away fast.

'No problem. Key to the house?'

'I'll need it to get my car out so I'll leave it in the letterbox.' He waved Adam over. 'I've got to see a patient. Ally's going to stay with you, okay?'

'Can we get an ice cream, Ally?' Hope lightened his face.

'No, you can't.' He wiped that expectancy away. 'Not after that enormous breakfast.' Bending down, he dropped a quick kiss on Adam's forehead. 'See you in a bit, mate.'

'You haven't said goodbye to Sheba.'

'I'm sure she won't mind.' Straightening up, Flynn looked at Ally, leaned in and kissed her cheek. 'Thanks, I owe you.'

Then he started to jog the way they'd come and got back to talking to Maisey. 'I didn't know William had been discharged.'

'He wasn't.'

So the old boy had taken it in his own hands to get out of hospital. 'He definitely needs that talking to, but I have to say I've already tried on more than one occasion and he's never been very receptive to anything I've said.'

'He's lost the will to live.'

That was it in a nutshell. 'I'll talk to his daughter again.' Not that he held out any hope. She'd had no more luck than anyone else.

Glancing over his shoulder, he saw Adam throwing a stick for Sheba, laughing and shouting like only four-year-olds could. *When he's older, will he fight for me if the need arose? I hope I am such a good parent that he will.* Ally drifted into his vision as she chased another stick Adam had thrown, and he felt a frisson of longing touch him. Longing that followed him up and across the road and all the way home.

Longing that wasn't only sexual; longing that reminded him of lazy days with Anna and Adam, of friendship and love. Longing he had no right to explore. He'd been married to the love of his life. No one got a second whack at that. Anyway, as Anna had told him on the day she'd died, he hadn't been the perfect husband. He'd worked too many hours, putting his career before his family apparently. It hadn't mattered that the career had given them the lifestyle they'd had. Yeah, the one Anna apparently hadn't wanted. Not in the middle of Melbourne anyway. *Damn it, Anna, I'm so sorry we were always arguing. I'm sorry about so many things.*

He needed to scrub that from his mind and concentrate. William needed him urgently. Hitting the gas accelerator, he drove as fast as the law allowed—actually, a little faster.

Sure enough, the ambulance was parked in William's driveway. Maisey led him inside, where the paramedics had the heart monitor attached to William's chest. The reading they passed him was abnormal. He inclined his head towards the door, indicating everyone should leave him with his patient for a few minutes.

'Don't even start, Doc,' William wheezed the moment they were alone.

'You think you have the right to decide when you should clock out, do you?'

William blinked. 'It's my life.'

'From the moment you're born, it's not just yours. You have family, friends, colleagues. They all have a part of you, whether you care or not. Whether you love them or not.'

'I've lost interest in everything since Edna died. You know how it is, Doc.'

Yes, he sure did, but, 'Don't play that card with me, William. Look me in the eye and tell me Edna would want you ignoring your daughter's love? What about your grandchildren, for goodness' sake? What sort of example are you setting them with this attitude? You think teaching them to give up when the going gets tough is good for them?' Flynn sat down and waited. He wouldn't belabour the points he'd made. There was such a thing as overdoing it.

Silence fell between them. The house creaked as the sun warmed it. Somewhere inside he heard Maisey and the paramedics talking. He continued to wait.

William crossed his legs, uncrossed them. His hands smoothed his trousers. He stared around the room, his gaze stopping on a photograph of his family taken when Edna had still been alive.

Flynn held his breath.

William's gaze shifted, focused on a painting of a farmhouse somewhere on the mainland, then moved on to another of a rural scene. Paintings Edna had done.

Flynn breathed long and slow, hoping like hell his patient didn't have another cardiac incident in the next few minutes. What if he'd done the wrong thing? But he'd tried the soft approach. It was time to be blunt. They had to get William aboard that ambulance and manhandling him when he refused to go wasn't the answer—or legal. He had every right to say no. But he'd better not arrest, at least not until he was in hospital.

William had returned to that family photo, his gaze

softening, his shoulders dropping a little from their indignant stance. Then one tear slipped from his right eye and slowly rolled down his cheek. He nodded once. 'I'll go. For my Edna.'

Good for you. 'I'll tell the paramedics.' And Maisey, who'd no doubt be phoning her niece the moment William had been driven away.

After Flynn had filled in some paperwork to go with his patient, he talked briefly to Maisey and then headed for his car. He was going home to Adam and Ally. They'd go for a jaunt round to San Remo. If only he didn't feel so drained of energy. Already tired after last night's emergency call-out, talking with William had taken more out of him than he'd have expected. He understood all too well how the other man felt; he also knew William was wrong. Hopefully, one day the old guy would acknowledge that, at least to himself if no one else.

The sunny winter's day had brought everyone out to San Remo to stroll along the wharves and look at the fishing boats tied up. The restaurants and bars were humming as the locals made the most of fewer tourists.

'What's your preference for lunch?' Flynn asked Ally, after they'd walked the length of the township's main street and had bumped into almost the entire register of his patients at the clinic.

'Fish and chips on the beach.' Then she smiled at him.

Her smiles had been slow in coming since he'd returned home, making him wonder if she felt he'd been using her. Which, he supposed, he had, but not as a planned thing. She'd been there when he'd got both calls and he hadn't hesitated to ask her. She could've said no.

'Good answer. There's a rug in the boot of my car we can spread on the sand.'

Had he used Ally by putting his work before what she might've wanted? *Just like old times.* But asking Ally to stay was putting Adam first, just not her. Turning, he touched a finger to her lips. 'Thank you.'

'What for?'

'Being you. I'm going to get lunch.'

'Adam and I will be over on that monster slide.'

'He's conned you into going down that?' Flynn grinned. 'Don't get stuck in the tube section.'

Yep, this felt like a regular family outing. Dad ordering the food, Adam wanting to play with Mum. Except Ally wasn't Mum, and never would be.

Which part of having a short affair had he forgotten? As much as Ally turned him on with the briefest of looks or lightest of touches, no matter how often they fell into bed together, this was only an affair with a limited number of days to run. When was that going to sink in?

While he waited for his order he watched the woman causing him sleepless nights. She smiled sweetly at his son bouncing alongside her, said something that made him giggle. Then she rubbed her hand over his head, as she often did. How come Adam didn't duck out the way as he did with other people who went to touch him?

Flynn sighed. Should he be getting worried here? How would his boy react when Ally left them? Yes, he'd asked himself this already, and would probably keep doing so until he knew what to do about it. He'd have the answer on the day Ally left.

The real problem was that he didn't want to stop what he and Ally had going on. It was for such a short time, couldn't he make the most of it? Wasn't he entitled to some fun? If only that's all it was, and the fun didn't come with these conflicting emotions.

The fish and chips were the best he'd ever had, the batter crisp, the fish so fresh it could've still been flapping. The company was perfect.

Ally rolled her eyes as her teeth bit into a piece of fish. 'This is awesome. I'm going to have to starve all week to make up for it.'

As if she needed to watch her perfect figure. 'We'll eat salads every day till next Sunday.'

Surprise widened those beautiful eyes. 'Something you haven't talked to me about yet?'

It had only occurred to him at that moment. 'You might as well join us for dinner every night. I like cooking while you obviously have an aversion to it. Next Saturday we can visit the wildlife centre.' Once he got started, his plan just grew and grew. 'Fancy a return visit to Giuseppe's on Saturday night? It's band night.'

'Don't tell me. The old two-step brigade.' She grinned to take the sting out of her words.

'Way better than that. The college has a rock band that's soon going to compete in a talent show. Giuseppe's way of supporting them is to hire them on Saturday nights. He says the music is crazy.'

'We can crazy dance, then. Yes to all those invitations. Thank you. You've saved me having to stock up on instant meals.' She wrapped up the paper their meal had come in and stood to take it across to a rubbish bin.

'Can we go to the wildlife park now, Dad?'

'Not today, Adam. You've already had a busy weekend, going places that you don't usually visit.'

'But, Dad, why can't I go? Now?'

'Don't push it, son. We're going home. I've got things

to do around the house.' Flynn could feel that tiredness settling over him again, stronger this time. He yawned just as Ally sat down on the sand again.

'Can't hack the pace, eh, old boy?'

'I don't know anyone who can run a marathon first up after no practice for years.' Not that making out with Ally felt as difficult as running a marathon. It all came too naturally.

'So that's why we do sprints.' Her grin turned wicked and the glint in her eyes arrowed him right in his solar plexus.

It also tightened his groin and reminded him of the intensity of her attraction. They'd be waiting hours before they could act on the heat firing up between them. Adam did put a dampener on the desire running amok in his veins.

'Dad, we're going to the school tomorrow.'

'What school? What are you talking about?' First he'd heard of it.

'Where the big kids go. Marie's taking me with the play group to see what it's like.'

He'd phone Marie when they got home. 'Are you sure?' This sounded like something he should be doing. 'That's my job, taking you there. I'm your parent, not Marie.'

Ally put a hand on his forearm. 'Wait till you've talked to her. Adam might've got it wrong.' The voice of reason was irritating.

'I doubt it. Marie should've mentioned it. She knows that when it comes to the major parenting roles I'll do them. Not her or anyone else.' Now he sounded peevish, but he *was* peeved. 'I'm doing what Anna would've wanted. What I want. I'm not a surface parent, supplying warmth and shelter and avoiding everything else going on in Adam's life. No, thank you.'

She pulled her hand away, shoved it under her thigh. 'Has anyone suggested otherwise?' An edge had crept into her tone.

Had he come across too sharply? Probably. 'Sorry, but you don't understand.' Had she just ground her teeth? 'When Anna was alive she did most things with Adam. We agreed she'd be a stay-at-home mother, and when she died I wanted nothing more than to stay at home with him, but of course that's impossible.'

'How can you say I don't understand? What do you know about me? I might have ten kids back in Melbourne.'

'Perhaps you should try telling me something.' He drew a calming breath. This was crazy, arguing because Adam might be going to school with Marie tomorrow. It wasn't Ally's fault he hadn't known or that he felt left out. 'Have you had a child?' he asked softly after a few minutes. Had she been a teenage mother who'd had her baby adopted?

'No,' she muttered, then again, a lot louder. 'No. Never.'

'Got younger brothers and sisters, then?'

Now her hands fisted on her thighs. 'No.'

He backed off a bit, changed direction with his quest for knowledge about her. 'Why did you choose midwifery as your specialty?' Was that neutral enough? Or was her reason for becoming a midwife something to do with her past? A baby she wasn't admitting to?

'I wanted to be a midwife after helping deliver my foster-mother's baby at home when I was fifteen. The whole birthing process touched something in me. I'd never seen a newborn before and I knew immediately I wanted to be a part of the process.'

Flynn wanted to know how Ally had found herself in that situation, but he didn't dare ask. Instead, he said, 'Birth is pretty awe-inspiring.'

'You're saying that from a parent's perspective.' She stared out beyond the beach at who knew what. 'My foster-mother let me hold the baby and when she asked for him back I struggled to let him go. He was beautiful and perfect and tiny. And vulnerable.'

Flynn sat quietly, afraid to say anything in case she closed down.

'For the first time in my life I'd experienced something so amazing that I wanted to do it again and again.' Her fingers trailed through the sand. 'I felt a connection—something I'd never known in my life.'

The eyes that finally locked onto his knocked the air out of his lungs. The pain and loneliness had him reaching for her, but she put a hand on his chest to stay him, saying, 'Until that moment I'd supposed birth and babies were things to be avoided at all cost. My own mother abandoned me when I was only days old.'

He swore. Short and sharp but full of anger for an unknown woman. How could anyone do that? How could Ally's mother not have wanted her? But, then again, as a doctor he'd seen plenty of people who just couldn't cope. Drug problems, mental illness, abusive partners—sometimes bringing up a baby was beyond people when they couldn't even take care of themselves.

She continued as though she hadn't uttered such a horrific thing. 'There was something so special about witnessing a new life. New beginnings and hope, that instant love from the mother to her baby.' Ally blinked but didn't cry. No doubt she'd used up more than her share of tears over the years. 'It doesn't matter how many births I've attended, each one rips me up while also giving me hope for the future.'

'Yet you don't stay around long enough to get involved with your mums and their babies.'

'No.'

So Ally didn't believe in a happy future for herself.

Her laugh was brittle as she shifted the direction of the conversation. 'I had one goal—to become a midwife. Shortly after my foster-mother's baby arrived, I went back into a group home, but I enrolled for night lessons at high school and worked my backside off during the day. Finally I made it to nursing school and then did the midwifery course and here I am.' The words spilled out as though she wanted this finished. But she couldn't hide her pride.

'It must've been darned hard work.' Lots of questions popped into his head, questions he doubted she'd answer. Ally looked exhausted after revealing that much about herself. It obviously wasn't something she did often—or at all.

The drive home was quiet. Flynn's forefingers drummed a rhythm on the steering wheel as his frustration grew. He'd learnt something very important about Ally that had briefly touched on who she was, and yet it wasn't enough. There had to be so much behind what he'd heard, things she obviously kept locked up, and he needed to hear them. How else could he help her?

'Dad, stop. You're going past our house.'

Flynn braked, looked around. 'Just checking to see if you were awake.'

Ally stared at him like he'd grown another nose. 'It's dangerous not to concentrate when you're driving.'

Because she was right and he didn't want to tell her what had distracted him, he ignored her and pressed the automatic garage door opener.

Inside the house, Flynn reached for the kettle. 'What would you like to do now, Ally?'

She tensed briefly then shook her head. 'You know what? I'm going to head back to the flat. I've got a few chores that need doing.'

His heart lurched. 'Thank you for sharing some of your story.'

Her deliberate shrug closed him off from her. 'I'm just your regular girl. And this regular girl needs to do some washing and answer some emails before work tomorrow.'

He wanted to insist she stay and share a light dinner, watch a movie on TV with him, but for once he knew when to shut up. 'Okay. I'll see you in the morning, then.'

CHAPTER SEVEN

ALLY DROPPED HER keys on the bench and stared around Kat's flat. Not grand on any scale, but a cosy and comfortable bolthole for Kat at the end of her day, a place to kick off her shoes and be herself. A place to face the world from.

What had possessed her to spill her guts to Flynn? At least he'd understand why she wasn't mother material. But it was Adam's laughing face cruising through her mind, teasing her with hope when in reality she wasn't ready for a child, would never be. Ally caressed her two ornamental dogs, her mouth twisted in sadness. Real-life pets required stability in their lives. The idea of owning a home hadn't made it onto her list of goals for the next ten years. She faced everything the world threw her way by digging deep and putting on a mask. She didn't need bricks and mortar to hide behind. Honestly, she had no idea about setting up a home that she could feel comfortable in.

Would I feel more content, less alone, if I had a place I could call home? A place—the same place—to live in between jobs, instead of bunking with whoever has a spare bed?

Sweat broke out on her upper lip. Her stomach rolled

with a sickening sensation. Thirty-one and she'd never had a home, not even as a child. Those foster-homes she'd lived in had been about survival, not about getting settled. She'd always tried so hard to please her foster-parents in the desperate hope they'd fall in love with her and adopt her, but that had never happened. The only time she'd believed she might be there long term had ended in tears and her packing her few possessions to take to the next stop in her life. She'd finally wised up to the fact—starting with her own mother—that no one cared for her enough to give her what she craved.

Don't go there. You've been over and over and over trying to understand why she left you on a stranger's doorstep. There is no answer.

Poking around in her bag, she found her music player, put the earbuds in and turned the volume up loud. Music helped to blot out the memories. Sometimes.

Then her phone vibrated against her hip and broke through her unease. Removing the earbuds, she answered the phone. 'Hey, Lilia, glad you rang.' Curling up on the settee she sighed with relief. A bit of girl talk would send those other thoughts away. 'What have you been up to?'

Lilia had refused to be pushed away while she'd been on a job in Lilia's home town, and they'd become friends despite her wariness.

'Just the usual. What about you? Having a blast on the island?'

'Yep, it's great.'

'Try to sound like you mean that,' Lilia said. 'Not like you've been sent to the middle of nowhere with no man in sight.'

That might've been boring, but it would've been safer. Flynn was sneaking in under her radar. She drew a breath and found some enthusiasm. 'Oh, there are men here. Even downright drop-dead sexy ones.'

'Ones, as in many? Or one? As in you're having fun?'

'One. Dr Flynn Reynolds. Do you know him? He used to work at one of Melbourne's hospitals, left about two years ago.'

'The name doesn't ring any bells, and I can't picture him. Is he a GP?'

'A GP, a widower and father of one. Perfect for a short fling.'

'Why do I hear a note of uncertainty?' Lilia suddenly laughed. 'Oh, my God, don't tell me you've gone and fallen for him? You? Miss Staying Single For Absolutely Ever? I don't believe it.'

'That's good because it's not true.' Not true. Not true. Her heart thudded so loudly Lilia probably heard it. Her fingers gripped the phone. 'We've been doing the leg-over thing, even taken the dog and kid for a walk, but that's as far as it's going.'

'Taken the kid and dog for a walk?' Lilia shrieked. 'That's Domesticity 101. You are *so* toasted.'

Panic began clawing through Ally, chilling her, cranking her heart rate up. 'Seriously.' She breathed deeply. 'Seriously, it's all about the sex. Nothing else.'

Lilia was still laughing. 'Go on, tell me some more. Is this Flynn gorgeous?'

'Yes, damn it, he is.'

'Good. Is he a great dad?'

'What's that got to do with anything?' The panic elbowed her. Adam was happy, but even if he wasn't, that had nothing to do with her. Unless she was contemplating having babies with the man. The phone hit the floor with a crash.

Slowly bending to retrieve the phone, she couldn't think of what to say to Lilia. She didn't know what to think, full stop.

Fortunately, Lilia had no such difficulty. 'What happened? You okay? I'm sorry if I've upset you. You know I mean nothing when I say these things.'

Swallow. 'Sure. I dropped the phone, that's all.' Another swallow. 'Lilia, what if I did like Flynn? I can't do anything about it. I know nothing about families or looking after kids or playing house.'

'Hey, girlfriend, go easy on yourself. You're so much better than you think. You're capable of anything you set your mind to. I know you haven't told me everything, but how you handled putting yourself through school and getting a degree shows that in bucketloads. Do you really like him?'

Unfortunately, it could be shaping up that way. It would explain her unease and sudden need to re-evaluate her life. But it was early days. She'd soon be out of here and so would whatever feelings she was dealing with. She'd settle back to her normal, solo life and forget Flynn. Easy. 'He's okay. So how's it going in Turraburra? Any interesting men coming your way?'

'That's why I rang.' Lilia got a giant-sized hint without having to be bashed over the head. 'You know Noah Jackson, don't you?'

'Enough to say hello to and swap a sentence or two about our weekends whenever I bump into him, which isn't often as I rarely see the surgical teams. Seems an okay guy, though.' She turned the tables. 'You interested in him?'

'I've heard he's starting here in a month or so, apparently.'

'He can't be. You've got the wrong guy. Noah doesn't do general practice. He's a senior surgical registrar, not a GP. Great guy he may be, but he's very determined to get to the top of his career—and that does not include sitting and talking to mothers and their colicky babies in a small town.'

Lilia sniffed. 'Nothing wrong with general practice.'

'I know that. But I can't see Noah fitting into it. Nah, you've got the wrong guy. The Noah I know wouldn't be seen dead in a place like Turraburra.'

'Well, I heard he'll be with us for four weeks. Perhaps it's a mistake.'

'Well, if he does turn up, the good news is he's a seriously good-looking dude and definitely sexy.' Didn't set her hormones dancing but plenty of women drooled over him.

No, her hormones got a kick out of a certain doctor living here on the island. She had to get a grip, put any stupid concerns behind her and get the job done. Three weeks to go. Twenty-one days. Couldn't be too hard to have some fun and not get involved with the source of that fun. Face it, Flynn no more wanted or needed anything more connected than she did. He definitely wouldn't want Adam getting too attached to her, and she felt exactly the same. More than anything, she couldn't abide hurting that cute wee boy because she understood more than most what it was like to be left behind or shunted on. And she certainly would never be moving into their home and becoming super-mum.

'You still with me?' Lilia interrupted her musings.

'All ears. When are you coming down to Melbourne next?'

After Lilia hung up, Ally went to tug on her running

shoes and shorts. A good hard pounding of the pavement would help what ailed her and put everything back into perspective.

'You've got a busy morning stacked up,' Flynn greeted her the moment she walked into the medical centre the next morning. 'Seems word's out that we've got a great new midwife and everyone who's pregnant wants to meet you.' His smile was friendly, but there was caution in his eyes. Did he think she might start considering staying on?

Returning his smile, she shrugged. 'I won't be delivering most of them. Kat will be back before long.'

His smile dipped. 'The islanders are friendly, that's all it's about. Bet you get an invitation or two for a meal before the morning's out.'

'Cool. But I'm all booked up—most nights anyway.' She locked eyes with Flynn. He hadn't changed his mind on her joining him and Adam for dinners, had he? Of course, she should be backing off a little, but how when right this moment her body was bending in his direction in anticipation of being woken up again? *Back off.* Easy to say, hard to do.

'So you'll come to dinner tonight. I'm glad.' At last the caution disappeared. His smile widened, brought a different kind of warmth to her.

A warmth that touched her deep inside in that place she went when alone. A warmth she hadn't realised she'd needed until she'd walked in and seen him. She'd missed him overnight. Had reached out to hug him and come up empty-handed—empty-hearted as well. 'Babies withstanding, I'll be there at six. Is that okay?'

He leaned close, whispered, 'Bring your toothbrush.'

That warmth turned to heat, firing colour into her

chilled cheeks and tightening her stomach. 'Think I'll buy a spare,' she whispered back, before entering the office to collect the notes in her tray.

Megan winked at her. 'Have a good weekend?'

How much had she heard? Ally bit back a retort. She and Flynn would have to learn to be far more careful. 'I went to San Remo.'

Megan laughed. 'Was that you I saw out running late yesterday?'

'Running?' Flynn looked surprised.

'As in putting one foot in front of the other at a fast pace.'

'That explains...' He spluttered to a stop as Megan's eyes widened. 'A lot,' he added lamely. 'Come on, meeting time.'

As she led the way to the staffroom, she wanted to turn around and wrap her arms around him. She wanted to feel his body against hers, his chest against her cheek, his shoulder muscles under her palms. She kept walking, facing directly ahead. She wouldn't be distracted by Flynn at work. She wouldn't. It was all very well for the others to know they'd had a meal out together, might even be aware they'd spent hours doing things over the weekend, but she couldn't show how her body craved his.

'Meeting's cancelled.' Faye barrelled out of her office. 'Flynn, we're needed at the school. Two kids on bikes have been hit by a car. Where's Toby?'

'Do you need me to come along?' Ally asked.

'No, we're sorted.' Faye sped to the back door and the car park, her medical bag in one hand.

Flynn glanced around, quickly dropped a kiss on Ally's mouth. 'See you later.' And he was gone.

Leaving her with her finger pressing her lips, holding that kiss in place. Yeah, she really had missed him all night. But she'd be seeing him tonight. The knot in her tummy loosened as she headed to her room and prepared for her first mum of the day.

Her relaxed mood stayed in place all day, and when she knocked on Flynn's door that night, she didn't hold back on her smiles.

'Ally, you came,' Adam swung the door wide, inadvertently letting Sheba out.

'Sheba, no,' Ally made a grab for her collar. 'Inside, you big lump.'

Sheba replied with a tongue swipe on her hand.

'Now the woman insults my dog.' Flynn stood behind Adam, grinning at her.

Were they both as happy to see her as she was them? Stepping inside, she closed the door behind her, shutting off the world and entering the cosy cocoon that was the Reynolds home. 'Sheba knows I think she's awesome.' Then she had a brainwave. 'I could take her with me when I go running.'

Flynn's eyebrows rose. 'She'd probably have a heart attack. Walks are one thing, but a run?'

'I'm not very quick. More of a snail.' She followed Flynn and Adam into the kitchen, suddenly very aware that by making that suggestion she'd committed herself to this little family for the rest of her stay. As she had that morning when she'd said she would be here for dinners. Nothing wrong with that, as long as she kept everything in perspective. As long as Adam didn't get too close and miss her when she left.

Flynn said, 'See how you go. You might find you just want to get on the beat and not have to swing by to collect her.'

Was he having second thoughts, too?

'Can I run, too?' Adam asked hopefully.

'No,' Flynn said emphatically.

As his little face began to crumple, Ally explained. 'It's usually very early when I go.'

'It's not fair.'

'Adam, you can't do everything just because you want to. Ally's told you why you can't go with her so leave it at that.' Worry filtered into Flynn's eyes as he watched his son stomp away. When Adam turned on the TV, Flynn growled. 'Turn it off, please.'

Ally glanced from Flynn to his boy's sulky face. 'Has he been naughty?'

'He's not allowed to watch TV often. Anna was against it.'

Ah, Anna's rules. 'Surely a little time watching kids' programmes can't hurt?' *Mind your own business.* 'Other kids don't turn out as delinquents because of it.' *Shut up.*

Flynn stared at Adam, not her. 'It's hard to let go. You know?'

No, she didn't. 'Fair enough. But Adam needs to fit in with his peers at times.'

'You have a point, I guess.' Then he changed the subject. 'How was your day? Angela called me, full of praise for the way you've handled Chrissie's crisis. She doesn't want you leaving before the baby's born.'

Sliding onto a stool and propping her elbows on the bench, she shook her head. 'Chrissie will be fine with Kat.'

Flynn nodded. 'Sure she will. It's just that with Chrissie being so young and this not being a planned pregnancy, she's taken a shine to you and won't be keen to start over. But it'll work out.'

'It has to.'

'It does, doesn't it?'

Ally stared at him. What did that mean exactly? 'I was never going to be here any longer than the month Kat's away.'

He locked his eyes with hers. 'I know. But sometimes I find myself wishing you were.'

Pow. That hit right in the solar plexus, and knocked her heart. Never in a million years would she have thought he'd say something like that. 'A month's long enough for a fling. Any longer and we'd have to start wondering just what we were doing.'

'You ever had a long-term relationship?' He picked up a wooden spoon and stirred the gravy so hard a glob flicked out onto the stovetop.

'No.' She reached for a cloth to wipe up the gravy.

'Never?'

'Never. I go for short flings. Makes leaving the job easier.' *Don't ask me any more.*

'Surely you haven't always moved around as much as you currently seem to do?' He'd stopped stirring, instead studying her as though she was an alien.

Compared to him and his normal family life, she probably was different to the point of being weird. 'I spent two years in Sydney while I went to school, then moved to Melbourne for the years it took to get my degree.' Which had seemed like for ever at the time. She wouldn't mention how often she'd moved flats during those years.

Reaching across to put her hand on his, she pushed the spoon around the pot. 'You're burning the gravy.' His hand was warm under hers, and she squeezed it gently. This was so intimate—in a way she'd never known before—that tears threatened. Tugging her hand away, she stood up and went to set the table.

Flynn watched Ally banging down cutlery on the table. She was hiding something. The answer hit him hard. *More of her past.* What was so bad that she couldn't talk about it? He wouldn't judge her, but maybe he could help her. From what little she'd disclosed about being abandoned, he'd surmised that she'd grown up in the welfare system. Had she gone off the rails as a teen? Asking her outright wouldn't get him any answers, more likely her usual blunt response of no or yes. Those tight shoulders showed the chance of learning anything tonight was less than winning the lottery and he never bought tickets.

He'd told her about Anna. *You call all of about five sentences spilling your guts?* He hadn't said he and Anna had been in love from the first day they'd met at university or all the promises he'd made about Adam at her funeral.

'When's dinner? I'm hungry.'

'Now, there's a surprise.' He saw Ally wink at his son and then Adam started showing off to her.

Yeah, Adam definitely liked her a lot. So did he. Enough to want more than this affair she was adamant was going nowhere? He began dishing up, thinking how he'd never once considered he might feel something for another woman. Anna had been his everything. Hard to believe he might want a second chance at love.

The pot banged onto the stove top. Love? Get outta here. No way. Too soon, too involved, too impossible.

'You all right?' Ally stood in front of him, studying him carefully.

Swallowing hard, he nodded. 'Of course. Here…' He handed her a plate and was shocked to see his hand shaking.

'You sure?' Her gaze had dropped to his hand. 'Flynn?'

'It's nothing,' he growled. 'Adam, sit up.'

Ally did that irritating shrug of hers and picked up Adam's plate just as he reached for it. Rather than play tug of war, Flynn backed off and headed for his seat at the table. As he gulped his water he struggled to calm down. It wasn't Ally's fault he'd just had a brain melt. But love? Not likely. He needed some space to think about this. How soon could he ask her to go home for the night? Guess she'd want to eat dinner first, though the way she was pushing the food around with her fork she wasn't so keen any more. 'Chicken not your favourite food?'

'I eat more chicken than anything.' She finally took a mouthful, but instead of her eyes lighting up she was thoughtful as she chewed. Swallowing, she asked, 'Do we have a problem? Would you like me to leave?'

Yes. No. 'Not really.' Damn it. 'Sorry. Please stay. For a while at least. I'd like to get to know you better and I can't do that if you're back at Kat's flat.' He'd taken a risk, but he had to learn more about her. Had to.

Her smile was wobbly. 'You want to know more about me? You are hard up for entertainment.'

Another diverting answer, but he wasn't going to be fobbed off any more. He'd start with something innocuous. 'What sort of books do you read?'

'Suspense and thrillers. The darker the better. You?'

'I'm more into autobiographies, especially of people who battle the odds to achieve their goals. Solo round-the-world sailors, mountain climbers, those kinds of people.' Definitely not dark, but it was staggering what a person could achieve if he was determined enough.

Her mouth curved deliciously. 'You're not a suppressed endurance man who wants to battle the odds, are you?'

He shuddered. 'Definitely not. I've got too much respect for my limbs to go off doing something that crazy. Quite happy to read about others' exploits, but that's as far as I go.'

'That's a relief. For a moment there I got worried. Think of that guy who recently tried to kayak from Australia to New Zealand. It must've been incredibly hard for his wife to have to wait for him to make it safe and sound.'

But you're not my partner, so why would you be worried? 'That's why I won't be letting Adam do anything remotely dangerous until he's old and decrepit.'

He leaned back in his chair as the tension eased out of him. They were back on safe ground and suddenly he didn't want to ask even about the weather in case he put her on edge again. He enjoyed her company too much to chance her leaving early.

'Good luck with that.' She chuckled.

Unfortunately, Ally was referring to Adam. Or so he thought until Ally came around to stand by him, putting a finger on his chin, pressuring him to look at her. She bent to kiss him, softly, sweetly, and still the passion came through fiery and urgent.

At last they'd moved past that earlier little conundrum. The last thing he wanted was to watch Ally walk out the front door tonight. The only place he wanted to be with her was in his bed, making love, tangling the sheets around their legs and holding her so close they'd be as one. He returned her kiss, hard and fierce, trying to convey his need for her.

When she stepped back her eyes were slumberous and that hazel colour had darkened. How soon could he insist Adam go to bed? Because they'd be heading down the hall the moment his son closed his eyes.

Tonight he'd make up for sleeping alone last night. He'd pleasure Ally so much she'd never contemplate a night without him again while she was on the island. Hopefully then this crazy, wonderful desire for her might calm down enough for him to make rational decisions about where they were going with their fling. Ally's word, not his.

Though maybe a fling was still all he needed, and the fact that sex had become alien to him over the last two years could be the answer to why he was reacting like a teenager who'd finally discovered sex.

Ally nudged him in his side. 'Can I read Adam's stories tonight?'

Adam shrieked, 'Yes.'

Flynn spanked her gently on the bottom. 'Anything to get out of doing the dishes.'

She wriggled her butt under his hand. 'Just speeding up the process.'

Of course, Adam had no intention of settling down and going to sleep after only one story. He must've caught the vibes playing between Flynn and Ally because he was wide-awake. 'He's hyper. Unusual for him,' Flynn muttered to Ally when he looked in to see what the delay was.

'It's all right. We're having fun.'

'I'll make coffee, then.' *Go to sleep, Adam. Please, please. Oh, damn it, just go to sleep. I'm going to explode with need any minute.*

He listened as Ally read on, and on, and on. And told himself off for wanting to deny Adam his time with her. Adam came first. First.

Finally, an hour later than he'd hoped, Flynn swung Ally up into his arms and carried her to his bedroom, locking the door behind them. He stood her on her feet and leaned in to kiss that mouth that had been teasing him all night. 'At last.'

Ally already had her shirt over her head, and was pushing those magnificent breasts into his hands. 'You talk too much.'

So he shut up and showed her how much he wanted her, and gave her everything he had.

CHAPTER EIGHT

THE DAYS FLEW by but the nights went even faster. Ally had never known a placement to be so engaging. Was that entirely down to Flynn? Yes, if she was being honest, Flynn owned it—made her dizzy with excitement, warmed her with everyday fun and laughter, distracted her to the point she caught herself wondering how hard it would be to stop in one place for ever.

These heady days hinted at what her childhood dreams had been made of—someone to love her unconditionally for the rest of her life, someone she could give her heart to and not have it returned when the gloss rubbed off. But reality had taught her differently. The only difference now was that she chose where she moved to, and not some overworked, underpaid bleeding heart sitting behind a desk in a dimly lit welfare office. She was no longer a charity case.

Unfortunately, a reality check didn't slow her enthusiasm for all things Flynn. Her body ached in every muscle, her lips were sore from smiling too much, her eyes were heavy from lack of sleep. But would she wish for quiet nights at Kat's flat with only her music and a book for company? No. Not even knowing that the day of reckoning was approaching made her want to change a thing. The complete opposite, in fact. She found herself needing to grab at more and more time with Flynn.

'Hey,' Flynn called as he walked past the medical storeroom. Then he was in there with her, sucking up all the oxygen and leaving her light-headed. When he traced her chin with his forefinger she caught it and licked the tip, delighting in the sound of his quickly indrawn breath. 'This room's never been so exciting.'

'Are we all set for tonight?' she asked.

'The table's booked at the restaurant. The babysitter's organised. The warning's gone out that no one on Phillip Island is to have an accident.' He ticked the points off his fingers. 'I've put clean sheets on the bed and bought more condoms since we must've used up your supply.'

Her giggle was immature, but that's how she reacted these days. She was always laughing or coming out with mixed-up, stupid things. 'I go to the supermarket on a regular basis.'

'I was beginning to wonder why you had so many.' He grinned, looking as loony as she felt.

'Everyone on the island must be talking about us by now. In fact, the women are probably giving their men a hard time about how many condoms we're getting through.' She didn't care at all. Every night she raced home to change into something relaxed and less midwife-like, touch up her make-up and put the washing on, then drove around to Flynn's house. She wasn't tired of him at all.

Flynn grinned. 'I'm sure they've all got better things to do than talk about their GP and the midwife.'

'I hope so.' Her heart lurched. That grin always got her behind the knees, making her nearly pitch forward onto her face. For a casual fling Flynn was breaking all the rules and turning her to mush, making her heart skip when no one had done that to her before. 'Does Giuseppe know we're returning to his restaurant?'

'I spoke to him earlier. He's planning a special meal for us. Unless there's something you don't like to eat, we are to sit back and let the courses come.'

'Sounds wonderful.' She planned on wearing a dress tonight, a short black number that she'd found in one of the local shops during her lunch break yesterday. It looked fantastic with her knee-high boots and black patterned stockings. She wouldn't be wearing anything else, bras and knickers being expendable.

'Are you two going to spend the day in that room?' Faye muttered loudly as she stomped past the door. 'There are patients waiting for both of you.'

Guilt had Ally leaping back from Flynn. 'Onto it,' she called out. 'Seriously, Doctor, you should know better than to kiss the nurse at work.'

'I'll do it out in the open next time.' His finger flicked her chin lightly. 'I'll pick you up at seven thirty.'

'I can't wait.' It was true. She'd see him on and off all day and yet she felt desperate to be with him, just the two of them sharing a meal in a restaurant, no interruptions from Adam or the phone or Sheba.

Uh-oh. What was happening? This was starting to feel way wrong. Keep this up and she'd have difficulty leaving at the end of her contract.

'Ally,' Megan called urgently from the office. 'Ally, you're needed. Lisa Shaw's on the line, her waters have broken.'

Now, that was reality. 'Coming.' She picked up her

medical bag and dashed to the office, Flynn sent to the back of her mind only to be brought back out when she wasn't helping a baby into the world. This was the real stuff her life was about. The grounded, helping-others kind of thing that gave her the warm fuzzies without asking anything of her heart.

'I'm going to be late.' Ally phoned Flynn at five o'clock when it became obvious Baby Shaw had no intention of hurrying up for anyone, least of all so his mother's midwife could go out to dinner with the local GP. 'I have no idea when Ashton will make his entry. Lisa's contractions slowed nearly two hours ago and so far don't look like speeding up.' Not very medically technical terminology, but he'd get the gist.

'You can't hurry babies.' Disappointment laced Flynn's words. 'Is it selfish to wish Lisa hadn't wanted a home birth?'

'Yes, it is. I'd better go. I'll call you when I know if we're still on for our date.'

An image of that black dress hanging on the wardrobe door flicked across her mind, and she had to suppress a groan.

Lisa was the only person allowed to groan around here, which she was doing with deep intensity right this moment. Scott held her as she draped her pain-ridden body against him and gritted her teeth.

Ally rubbed Lisa's back. 'You're doing great. Seriously.'

'I have no choice, do I?' Lisa snapped. 'Next time I have a dumb idea that having a baby would be wonderful, tell me to take a hike.' She glared at Scott. 'Or you have it.'

Scott kissed her forehead and wisely refrained from commenting.

Ally went for diversion. 'How long have you been married?'

'Two years,' Lisa ground out.

'We've been wanting a baby right from the beginning.' Scott grinned. 'Couldn't get it right.'

Ally chuckled. 'Babies are control freaks. They get conceived when it suits them, arrive when they choose, and they've hardly started. But you know what? They're wonderful.'

Under her hand Lisa's shoulders tensed as she yelled out in the pain of the next contraction.

'Lisa, breathe that gas in. You're doing brilliantly.'

The next hour passed slowly. Ally took observations regularly, noting them on Lisa's chart, occasionally going for a walk to the letterbox and back to give the couple a few moments alone, then returning to give Lisa more encouragement. Six o'clock clicked over on her watch. *There goes dinner with Flynn.* Even if Baby Ashton miraculously popped out right then, she'd be needed for a time. Guilt hovered in her head. Never before had she cared how long the birthing process took, she just loved being there with the mums, dads and their babies. But now she loved being with Flynn, too.

Her head jerked up. Loved being with him? Or loved Flynn, full stop?

'Ally, come quick. Lisa's pushing,' Scott called down the hall.

Good, focus on what's important. 'That's good, but we

could be a while yet.' Though for Lisa's sake she hoped not. She was exhausted.

Examining her, Ally was happy to announce, 'Baby's crowning. When the urge to push comes, go with it. Don't try to hold back.'

'It's too damn painful to push,' Lisa yelled.

'Come on, Lisa. He's got to come out of there.' Scott reached for Lisa's hand and grimaced as she gripped him.

'Easy for you to say,' his wife snarled.

Ally had heard it all before. 'As soon as Ashton makes his appearance, you two will forget everything but your beautiful little boy.' This parenthood thing was awesome. Babies were amazing, so cute and vulnerable and yet bonding their parents in a way nothing else could.

Why hadn't her mother felt like that about her? Was her mother a freak? She was definitely the reason Ally would never have her own baby. What if the don't-love-your-own-baby gene was hereditary? There was no way on earth she'd chance having a child, only to dump her into the welfare system and disappear. And even if she did love her baby—which she was sure she would despite her past—she didn't know the first about raising one, about providing all the things a child needed, including loads of love. Her experience of babies stopped once she knew they were able to feed from mum's breast.

'Ally, I think he's coming,' Lisa broke into her thoughts, brought her back to the here and now, away from the daydreams of someone who should know better.

When Ashton slid into her hands, Ally felt tears prick her eyelids. 'Wow, look, Scott, he's lovely.' She lifted him to meet his parents. Her knees were shaky and her heartbeat erratic. 'He's the most beautiful baby I've seen.'

'Of course he is,' Scott whispered.

All babies were. She'd reacted the same way at that very first birth that had started her on the path to becoming a midwife. *Thank you, wee Lloyd, wherever you are now. Not so wee any more, I guess.* Mopping her eyes with her arm, she cleaned the mucus from Ashton and placed him on Lisa's breast.

Flynn picked her up a little after eight. She was tired and exultant. 'Another little baby safely delivered and in good hands.' She clicked her seat belt into place. 'Do you remember when you first held Adam?' That hadn't exactly changed the subject, had it? Darn.

'Everything about him—his scrunched-up face, his red skin, spiky black hair and ear-shattering cry. He hasn't changed much.' Flynn smiled with a far-away look in his eye.

'His face isn't red.' The love in Flynn's voice brought tears to her eyes and she had to look out the window at the houses they were passing until she got herself back under control. It was too easy to picture Flynn carefully cradling Adam wrapped in a blanket, like he was made of something so fragile he'd break at the slightest pressure. *I want that. No. I don't. I can't have it. It would be wrong for everyone.*

'Ally? Where've you gone?'

Suck it up, play the game. You know how to. 'I'm thinking pasta and garlic and tomatoes. It's been a long day and I forgot to buy my lunch on the way to work so missed out what with Baby Ashton stealing the show.'

'I'm sure Giuseppe will fix what's ailing you.' Flynn pulled up outside the restaurant.

'Good.' Pity there was no cure for what really troubled her. She could not, would not get too involved. Flynn had been hurt badly with Anna's death. So had Adam. She couldn't risk hurting them again. Forget involvement being a risk; hurting them would be a certainty. She was clueless in the happy-families stakes, and they so didn't deserve or need to be hurt by her. She shoved the door wide before Flynn had a chance to come round to open it for her. 'Let's go and have the night of our lives.'

'Ally.' Flynn's hand on her arm stayed her. 'You look absolutely beautiful tonight. More beautiful, I mean.'

'Thank you.' Her heart rolled. Talk about making everything harder. 'I went shopping yesterday.'

'I'm not talking about the dress, though you look stunning in it. It fits you like a second skin, accentuates all those curves I love touching.' He hesitated, breathed deep. 'But it's you that's beautiful—from the inside out.'

Nothing could've made her move at that moment if she'd tried. His words had stolen the breath out of her, liquefied her muscles, making them soft and useless. She was supposed to be having dinner with Flynn and then going back to his house and bed. He was not meant to be saying things that undermined her determination to stick to her rules—no deep, attaching involvement.

'Ally? Did I go too far?'

Yes, you did. Way too far. You're frightening me. Forcing a smile, she laid her hand over his. 'Thank you. That was a lovely compliment.'

'A heartfelt one. Now, let's enjoy ourselves and I'll stop the sentimental stuff since it seems to be upsetting you.' He hopped out of the car and strode around the front to her side.

She'd let him down. But what was a girl supposed to do? She couldn't take in what he'd said and start believing. That would be dangerous, but at the same time she couldn't walk away from Flynn tonight, or tomorrow, or any time during the next two weeks. No, she couldn't. Pushing out of the car, she laced her fingers through his and walked up the path to the welcoming door of the restaurant. 'I see the tide's farther in tonight. We won't be having our wicked way on the beach.'

Grinning, Flynn held the door wide and ushered her inside, whispering as she passed, 'You give up too easily.'

Did she? 'I'm not going to ask what's on your mind. I want to eat first.' She ran a hand over his delectable butt before turning to follow the same young waiter they'd had last week.

Giuseppe was there before they'd sat down. 'Welcome back, Ally. I'm glad you enjoyed our food enough to return.'

'Come on, Giuseppe, how could I not?' She kissed her fingertips. 'That carbonara was superb.'

'The carbonara or the company you were keeping?' the older man asked with a twinkle in his eye. 'By the way, you might be wanting this.' He held up the half-full bottle of Merlot they'd left on the beach.

Flynn laughed loudly. 'You old rascal. Who found that?'

'I go for a walk along the beach every night after I close the door for the last time.' Giuseppe kept the bottle in his hand.

Uh-oh. What time had he closed the restaurant last Friday? Ally glanced across at Flynn, saw the same question register in his eyes. Had Giuseppe seen them making out? She croaked out, 'Thank you. It seemed a waste not to have finished a good wine.'

Giuseppe nodded, his eyes still twinkling, leaving her still wondering what he'd seen, as he said, 'Tonight you will try something different. Something I recommend to match the meal I have arranged. This half-finished one you can take with you when you leave.'

Ally watched as he walked away, pausing at other tables to have a word with his guests. 'Do you think he knows?'

'That we made love on the beach? Yes, I suspect he does.' Flynn reached across and took her hand in both his. 'You know what? I couldn't care less.'

'Then neither do I.' And she wouldn't worry about anything else tonight either.

The meal was beyond superb and the wine excellent. The company even better. Flynn made her laugh with stories from his training days and she told him about going to school as an adult. It was a night she'd remember for a long time. It was intimate, almost as though they had a future, and she refused to let those bleak thoughts refuting that spoil anything.

'Here.' She twined her arm around Flynn's, their glasses in their hands. 'To a hot night under the stars. Tide in or out.'

Flynn smiled, a deep smile that turned her stomach to mush and her heart to squeezing. 'To a wonderful night under the bright stars with a special lady.'

But when they stepped outside there were no stars. A heavy drizzle had dampened everything and was getting heavier by the minute. 'You forgot to order the weather.' Ally nudged Flynn as they hurried to the car.

'Never said I was perfect.' He held the car door while she bundled inside.

No, but he wasn't far off. Leaning over, she opened his door to save him a moment in the rain. 'How long will it take you to drop off the babysitter?'

'Ten minutes.'

'That long?'

'You can warm the bed while I'm away.' Flynn laid a hand on her thigh. 'Believe me, I'll be going as fast as allowed.'

Heat raced up her thigh to swirl around the apex between her legs, melting her. 'Pull over.'

'What? Now? Here?' The car was already slowing.

'Right now and here.' She was tugging at his zip. Under her palm his reaction to her move was more than obvious.

'I haven't done it in a car since I was at high school.'

'Hope you can still move your bones, you old man.'

He growled as he nibbled the skin at her cleavage. 'Just wait and learn.' His hand covered her centre, his fingers did things that blanked out all the doubts and yearnings in her mind and made her cry with need, followed with release.

Flynn rolled onto his side, his arm under his head and his gaze fixed on the beautiful woman sleeping beside him. He was addicted to Ally Parker. There was no other word for what he felt. Addiction. He'd never known such craving before. The more he had of her, the more he wanted. His need was insatiable. If it wasn't so damned exciting it would be frightening. Frightening because it was filled with pitfalls.

He'd loved Anna beyond reason and had still failed her. If he hadn't been so damned determined to follow his career the way he'd wanted it she wouldn't have been in Melbourne that day and the accident wouldn't have happened. If he'd listened to her wishes, instead paying them lip service, his boy would still have his mother. That, more than anything, he could never forgive himself for. Every child deserved two parents, and especially their mother, to nurture them as they grew up.

And this had what to do with Ally? Ally already enjoyed being with Adam, didn't treat him as a pawn to get to his father but rather as an individual in his own right. She'd nurture and mother Adam if they got together.

A chill lifted goose bumps on his skin. He withdrew his arm and rolled onto his back to stare at the ceiling. They could not get together. Firstly, Ally didn't do settling down. That was so clear he'd be a fool not to acknowledge it.

He glanced across at her sleeping form. 'What happened that you can't stop in one place for more than a few weeks? Who hurt you so badly that you're prepared to miss out on what life's all about?' he whispered. 'Someone other than your mother?' That would be enough to knock anyone sideways for ever. But he had this niggling feeling he hadn't heard it all.

As the chill lifted and his skin warmed back to normal he ran a hand over her hair, rubbed a strand between his fingers. 'I would never hurt you, let you down.'

Huh? Hadn't he just reminded himself of how badly he'd let Anna down? Yep. And Adam. Adam. The crux of the matter. He'd do anything for his son. Anything. Which meant not getting too close to Ally, not seeking the answers to those questions in case they drove him on to making her happy, not sharing his life with her.

Ally rolled over, blinked open her eyes and smiled in a just woken up and still sleepy way. 'Hi,' she whispered.

'Hi, yourself.' He leaned in to place a light kiss on her brow, then her cheek, her chin, her lips. Two weeks. *Make the most of them. Stop analysing the situation and enjoy what's left.*

As he reached for her, the door flew open.

'Dad. Why was the door shut?' Adam shouted, loud enough for the whole island to hear as he pushed it wide.

'Good morning to you, too.' Flynn smiled and pulled the bedcovers up to Ally's chin. 'Hope you're okay with this,' he whispered to her. 'I forgot to relock the door after I went to the bathroom.'

'Not a problem, unless he wants to get in here with us,' she whispered back. 'Hello, Adam. How long have you been awake?'

'A long time. I've been watching cartoons.' Adam started to climb onto the bed.

Hell, Ally was buck naked. Adam was used to seeing him in the nude, but not a woman. 'Adam, can you pass Ally my robe? She's getting cold.'

'She should wear pyjamas to bed.'

How did Adam know she hadn't? Distraction needed. 'Let's have pancakes for breakfast.' That'd get his attention, pancakes being his all-time favourite breakfast food. *Unhealthy. Tough.*

'Ally, are you coming for a sleepover every night now?'

Flynn mentally threw his hands into the air. If pancakes didn't work, then he had to get serious. 'Adam, go out to the lounge while we get up.'

Ally shook her head as though trying to make sense of everything. 'Sometimes when it's late I don't go home, but not every night. I've got my own place to go to.'

Adam nodded. 'I thought so. But if you want to stay every night we don't mind, do we, Dad?'

Which part of 'Go out to the lounge' hadn't he got? 'I guess not. Adam, we want to get up.'

'Okay. Are we having maple syrup and bacon on the

pancakes?' Adam didn't look like he had any intention of moving this side of Christmas.

'We won't be having pancakes at all if you don't leave us.'

Under the covers Ally touched his thigh and squeezed it. 'Bacon, syrup *and* bananas. But I want to shower first and the longer we lie around, talking, the longer we're going to wait for our yummy breakfast.'

Adam nodded again. Where had this new habit come from? 'I'll get everything ready.'

'Great. See you out there soon.' Ally nodded back with a smile. 'But promise me you won't start cooking anything.'

'I don't know how to mix the flour and stuff.'

As Adam ran out of the room Flynn stared after him. 'He listens to you.'

'I'm a novelty. You're Dad.' Her hand stroked where a moment ago it had been squeezing.

'Keep that up and breakfast will be postponed for hours.'

She instantly removed her hand. Damn it. 'Hours? Talk about bragging.' She grinned at him. Then slid out of bed and wrapped herself in the too-large robe. 'I'm going to look so good sitting down to breakfast in my little black dress. Why didn't I think to bring a change of clothes?'

'You should leave a set here for the morning after.'

'If I did that, I wouldn't have many clothes left at the flat.'

She travelled light. Very light. 'Go shopping. Get some gear to keep here. In the meantime…' he swung his legs over the side of the bed, dug into his drawers for a sweat-shirt and pair of trackpants '…try these for size.'

'I already know they'll be too long and loose around

the waist, but my hips might hold them up.' She took the clothes and hugged them to her breasts. 'Who's first in the shower?'

'You go. I'll keep an eye on proceedings in the kitchen. Today could be the day Adam decides to try mixing the batter and that would be messy, not to mention uncookable.'

'You're not fair. He's got to have a go at these things. How else is he going to learn to look out for himself?'

'But it's so much quicker to do everything myself.'

Her face tightened and her chin lifted. 'In the long run you'll save heaps of time because Adam will be able to do these things for both of you.'

Ouch. She'd gone from Fun Ally to Serious Ally in an instant. She'd also had the nerve to tell him how his parenting sucked. 'Go and have that shower,' he ground out through clenched teeth.

He didn't want to start an argument by saying she should leave this to him, but it had nothing to do with her. Even if she might be right, Ally wasn't the one constantly working with a time deficit.

For a moment she stood there, staring at him. Was she holding back a retort, too? Or formulating a whole load more criticisms? Or, heaven forbid, was she about to explain why she felt so strongly about his son learning to cook?

Not likely. She'd never do that. Ally was a closed book when it came to herself. Except for that one time of sharing her past hurts, what drove her, and what held her back, her past was still blurred. He needed to remember that—all the time. But right this minute he had to get back onside with her. They were spoiling what had been a wonderful night and should be a great day ahead. 'Ally, please, go and get cleaned up. Let's not waste the morning arguing.'

Her eyes widened. Then her stance softened, her shoulders relaxed. 'You're right. We've got pancakes and a morning at the wildlife centre to enjoy. And we'll need to stop at the flat on the way so I can put on some proper clothes.'

He'd dodged a slam dunk. 'Proper clothes? Since when weren't trackies and a sweatshirt proper?'

'Since fashion became important. In other words, since the first time a woman put on an animal hide.' She grinned and his world returned to normal.

His new normal. The one with Ally Parker in it. The normal that would expire in two weeks' time.

CHAPTER NINE

TUESDAY, AND ALLY parked outside the bakery just as her phone vibrated in her pocket. 'Hello?'

'It's Marie. I'm in labour.'

Her due date was in three weeks, but technically speaking Marie wasn't having her baby too early. Two weeks before due date was considered normal and nothing to be concerned about. 'I'm on my way. After I examine you we'll arrange to get you over to the mainland and hospital.'

'I doubt I'm going anywhere. The contractions are already coming fast.' Marie's voice rose with every word. 'Hurry, will you?'

'On my way. Try to relax. I know, easy for me to say, but concentrate on your breathing and time the contractions.' Great. The last thing Marie had said to her was that she never wanted to have a home birth. A friend of hers had had one last year and there'd been complications that had nearly cost the baby her life.

With a wistful glance at the bakery she jammed the gearshift in Reverse and backed out into the street.

Adam opened the door the moment she parked in Marie's driveway. 'Ally, Marie's got a tummyache. She's holding it tight.'

Adam was there. Of course he was. It was a weekday. He wasn't going to be anywhere else in the afternoon. 'Does Flynn know you've gone into labour?' she asked Marie the moment she stepped inside.

'No. I needed a midwife, not a doctor.' Marie glanced in the direction Ally was looking. 'Oh, Adam. He'll be fine. Anyway, what can Flynn do? Take Adam to the surgery for the rest of the day?'

'Surely Flynn's got someone he can ask to look after him?'

Marie's face contorted as a contraction gripped her. She held on to the back of a chair and screwed her eyes shut.

'Breathe deep. That's it. You're doing good.' Ally stepped close to rub her back and mutter inane comments until the contraction passed. Then she got down to business. 'Let's go to your bedroom so I can examine you. Adam, sweetheart, Marie is having her baby so I want you to be very good for her. Okay?'

'She's having a baby? Really? Why does it hurt her?' His little eyes were wide.

'It's baby's way of letting everyone know it's coming.'

'Can I tell Dad?'

'Soon. I'm going with Marie to her bedroom.' His eyes filled with expectancy and she quickly stomped on those ideas. 'I want you to help me by getting things I need, like water or cushions or towels. But not until I ask you, all right?'

'Yes, I'll be good. Can I bring them into the bedroom?'

'No, leave them outside the door.' Hopefully Marie was wrong about her baby coming quickly and she'd soon be on her way to hospital. 'Why don't you watch TV until I call you?'

'I want to help.'

'I know, but first I have to check the baby, then I'll know what you can do for us.' If Marie was heading to hospital she'd drop Adam off at the medical centre. Flynn would sort out childminding. He must have made alternative arrangements for this eventuality.

Adam's mouth did a downturn, but he trotted off to the lounge and flicked on the TV.

'Thank you, Adam,' she called, before hurrying to Marie's bedroom and closing the door behind her. 'Have you called your husband?'

Tears welled up in Marie's eyes. 'My call went straight to voice mail. He's at sea on the fishing boat. This wasn't supposed to happen. He's booked leave for when the baby's due. He can't get here for days,' she wailed.

Ally gave her a hug and a smile. 'Well, in the meantime it's you and me. Unless you've got a close friend you'd like here, or family?' Someone familiar would make things work more smoothly.

'My family all live on the mainland and my girlfriend would be hopeless. Faints if there's the hint of blood or anyone's in pain.' Marie sank onto the bed as another contraction gripped her. 'I don't think I'm going anywhere. These contractions are coming too fast. I seriously doubt I've got time to get to the hospital.' Her voice was strained.

Ally glanced at her watch. She'd already begun timing the contractions. 'Four minutes. You're right, they're close.' She held Marie's hand until the current contraction passed. 'If you lie down I'll see what's going on.'

Marie flopped back onto the bed. 'I feel this pushing sensation, but I don't want a home birth. What if something goes wrong?'

'We have doctors only five minutes away. But you're jumping the gun. Baby might just pop out.' Ally mentally crossed her fingers as she snapped on vinyl gloves and helped Marie out of her panties. She wasn't surprised at the measurement she obtained. 'You're ten centimetres, fully dilated, so, yes, baby's on its way.' She calmly told her patient, 'Sorry, Marie, but hospital's definitely out. There isn't time.'

Marie's face paled and her teeth dug deep into her bottom lip. The eyes she lifted to Ally were dark with worry.

'Hey.' Ally wrapped an arm around her shoulders. 'You're going to be fine. I'll phone the surgery to tell them what's going on.' One of the doctors would be on notice to drop everything and rush here if anything went wrong.

'Sorry, I'm not good at this.' A flood of tears wet her cheeks.

'Find me a mother who is. This is all new to you. Believe me, no one pops their baby out and carries on as though nothing has happened. It's an emotional time, for one. And tiring, for another.' She sat beside Marie. 'Take it one contraction at a time. You've done really well so far. I mean it.'

Marie gripped Ally's hands and crushed her fingers as another contraction ripped through her.

'Breathe, one, two, three.' Finally getting her hands back and able to flex her fingers to bring the circulation back, Ally said, 'I'll get the gas for you to suck on. It'll help with the pain.'

'That sounds good. But I do need to push.'

'Try to hold off until I'm back. Promise I'll hurry.' She dashed out of the room and nearly ran Adam down in the hallway. 'Oops, sorry, sweetheart, I didn't see you there.'

'Is the baby here yet?'

'No.' But it wasn't too far away. 'Can you fill two beakers with water and leave them outside the door?' She had no idea if Marie wanted one, but giving Adam something to do was important.

His little shoulders pulled back as pride filtered through his eyes. 'I'll put them on a tray, like Dad does sometimes.'

'Good boy.' Out at the car she dug her phone out of her pocket and called the medical centre. 'Megan, it's Ally. Can you put me through to Flynn?'

'He's with a very distressed patient and said not to be interrupted unless it was an emergency.'

Define emergency. She guessed a baby arriving early didn't quite fit. 'When it's possible, will you let him know that I'm with Marie and she's having her baby at home? There isn't time to transfer her to hospital. Also mention it to Faye and Jerome in case I need help.'

'That's early. Tell her good luck from me. When Flynn's free I'll talk to him, but I suspect he's going to be a while. His patient is really on the edge.'

'Thanks, Megan, that'd be great.' She cut the receptionist off. Marie needed her. She gathered up the nitrous oxide tank, a bag of towels and another bag full of things she'd need.

'I'm still getting the water,' Adam called as she closed the front door.

'Good boy.' Back in the bedroom the temperature had dropped a degree or two. Sundown was hours away, but outside she'd noticed clouds gathering on the horizon. 'Marie, how are you doing?'

'Okay, I guess.'

'Here, suck on this whenever the pain gets bad.' Ally handed over the tube leading from the nitrous oxide tank.

'Have you got a heater we could use? I don't want baby arriving into a cold room, and I'd prefer to warm these towels as well.'

'There's an oil column one in the laundry. Adam knows where it is and can push it along on its wheels. It'll be perfect for what you're wanting.'

'Onto it.'

Outside the door Adam was placing the beakers ever so carefully on a tray he'd put on the floor earlier. 'Can you bring me the heater out of the laundry? Or do you want me to help?'

'I can do it. Do I have to leave it out here?'

'Yes, please.'

His little shoulders slumped. 'Why can't I see Marie?'

Ally knelt down and took his small hands in hers. 'When women have babies they don't like lots of people with them, watching what's happening. They get shy.'

'Why?'

'Because having a baby is private, and sometimes it hurts, and Marie wouldn't want you to see her upset.' *Sometimes it hurts?* Understatement of the century.

'No, she only likes me to see her laughing. I'll knock when I've got the heater.'

For a four-year-old, Adam was amazingly together about things. Nothing fazed him. But then he had lost his mother so he wasn't immune to distress, had probably learned a lot in his short life. He coped better than she did. He did have a great dad onside. 'Then you can play with all those toys I saw in a big box in the lounge.'

'But I like playing outside. Marie always lets me.'

'Today's different. I need you to play inside today, Adam.' She held up a finger. 'Promise me you won't go outside at all.'

'Promise, Ally.'

Her heartstrings tugged. What a guy. As she gave him a hug a groan sounded from inside the bedroom. 'You're a champ, you know that?' Now, please go away.

'What's a champ?' Adam didn't seem to have heard Marie.

'The best person there is.' The groan was going on and on. 'I've got to see Marie.' *Please, go away so you don't hear this.* Nothing was wrong but that deep, growling groan might frighten him, or at least upset him.

Thankfully Adam had his father's sensitivity and recognised a hint when it came. He raced down the hall towards the laundry and Ally let herself back into the bedroom.

'Hey, how's it going?' The pain on Marie's scrunched-up face was all the answer she needed. 'Feel like pushing some more, I take it.'

'How can you be so cheerful?'

So they were at the yell-at-anyone stage. 'Because you're having a baby and soon you'll forget all this as you hold him for the first time. Can you lie back so I can examine you again?'

'Examine, examine—that's all you do.' But Marie did as asked.

Kneeling on the floor, she gently lifted Marie's robe. 'The crown's further exposed. Baby's definitely on its way.' She stood up and dropped the gloves into a waste bag. 'Have you tried to get hold of your husband again?'

'His name's Mark and, no, I haven't. He's not going to answer if he's on deck, hauling in nets. They don't have time.' Tears tracked down her face. 'Anyway, I want him here, not on the end of a phone.'

Ally picked up Marie's phone. 'How do we get hold of him? Can we talk to his captain?'

Marie stared at her like she'd gone completely nuts. Then she muttered, 'Why didn't I think of that?'

'Because you're having a baby, that's why.' Ally handed her the phone. 'Go on. Try every contact you've got.'

Just then another contraction struck and Marie began pushing like her life depended on it, all thoughts of phone calls gone.

'That's it. You're doing well.' Ally again knelt at the end of the bed, watching the crown of the baby as it slipped a little farther out into the world.

Knock-knock. 'I got the heater,' Adam called.

'Thank you. Now you can play with those toys.' She gave him a minute to walk away before opening the door and bringing the heater in. Plugging it in, she switched it on and laid two towels on top of the columns to warm for baby.

'Hello?' Marie yelled at someone on her phone. 'It's Marie, Mark's wife. I can't get hold of him and I'm having our baby. I need to talk to him.'

Ally held her hand up, whispered, 'Slow down, give the guy a chance to say something.'

Marie glared at her but stopped shouting long enough to hear a reply. 'Thank you so much. Can you hurry? Tell Mark to phone back on the landline so I can put him on speaker.' A moment later she tossed the phone aside, grabbed the edges of the bed and pushed again.

The phone rang almost immediately. Ally answered, 'Hey, is that Mark? This is Ally, Marie's midwife.'

'Hello, yes, this is Mark. What's up? Is she all right? The baby's not due for weeks.'

'Marie's fine. You can be proud of how she's handling this. Baby has decided today's as good as any to arrive.'

Marie snatched the phone out of her hand and yelled, 'Why aren't you here with me? I need you right now.' Then she had to drop it and clutch her belly.

Ally pressed the speaker button and Mark's voice filled the room. 'Hey, babe, you know I'd be there if I'd thought this would happen. How're you doing? Come on, babe, talk to me, tell me what's going on.'

'I'm having a baby, and it hurts like hell. It's nearly here and I can't talk any more. I've got to push.'

'Babe, I'm listening. Imagine me holding you against my chest like I did when you dislocated your shoulder. Feel my hands on your back, rubbing soft circles, whispering how much I love you in your cute little ear. Can you feel me there with you?'

Ally tried to block out this very personal conversation, pretend she was deaf, but those words of love touched her, taunted her. These two had a beautiful relationship. If Mark was a deep-sea fisherman, he was no softy, would definitely be a tough guy, and yet here he was speaking his heart to his wife when she needed him so much.

Marie cried out with pain, and pushed and pushed.

'Hey, babe, you're doing great. I know you are. You're a star. I'm not going anywhere until you have our little nipper in your arms, okay?'

Ally blinked back a tear and slipped out the door for a moment to get herself sorted. It wouldn't do for the midwife to have a meltdown in the middle of a birth. Not that that had ever happened but Marie's birth was affecting her deeply, more so than any other she'd attended. Leaning back against the wall, she took deep breaths to get her heart and head under control. *What was it like to have a man love you that much?* She could take a chance with a man like that. Even if she screwed up he'd be there to help her back onto her feet.

I want what Marie's got. Shivers ran through her and her skin lifted in goose-bumps. *No. I can't, don't, won't.*

Straightening up, she slapped away the tears and returned to her patient. Marie was still talking to Mark and didn't seem to notice her return. Had she seen her leave?

Then Marie was pushing again and this time there was no relief. Baby was coming and Ally prepared for it. 'The head's out. Here come the shoulders. That's it. Nice and gentle now.' She spoke louder so Mark could hear everything. Her hands were under the baby's head, ready for any sudden rush as the baby slid out into its new world. And then, 'Here he is, a beautiful boy. Oh, he's a sweetheart.'

Her heart stuttered. She'd called Adam a sweetheart earlier. It was one thing to say that about a baby she wouldn't be seeing much of, but Adam? He was wriggling into her heart without trying and soon she'd have to say goodbye.

'Can I hold him?' Marie asked impatiently, reaching out.

'In a moment. The APGAR score's normal.' Ally gently wiped away vernix, mucus and blood spots from his sweet little face.

'Give him to me, give him to me. Mark, we've got a boy. He's gorgeous. Looks like his dad.'

Ally rolled her eyes as she placed the baby on Marie's swollen breasts. 'I need him back in a moment to weigh him.'

Mark was yelling out to his crewmates, 'It's a boy. I'm a dad.' And then he was crying. 'Wish I was with you, babe. Tell me everything, every last detail. Are we still going to name him Jacob?'

'Well, I can't name him after our midwife so I guess so. I think it suits him.' Marie was laughing and crying and drinking in the sight of her son lying over her breast.

'Here comes the placenta.' Ally clamped it and cut the cord. 'I need to examine you once more, then I'll cover you up and let you talk to Mark alone for a bit.' Adam would be getting lonely out in the lounge. She'd make him a bite to eat, poor kid.

Her examination showed a small tear. 'You need a couple of stitches. Nothing major,' she added when worry entered Marie's eyes. 'It often happens in fast deliveries.'

'Right.' Marie went back to talking to Mark, the worry gone already.

Ally quietly went about retaking Jacob's APGAR score. His appearance and complexion were good. Counting his pulse, she tried not to listen in to the conversation going on between Jacob's parents, concentrating on the sweet bundle of new life. Her heart swelled even as a snag of envy caught her again. She could have it all if only she found the right man. Flynn instantly popped up in her head. Losing count, she started taking Jacob's pulse again, this time totally concentrating and pushing a certain someone out of her skull.

'Pulse one hundred and ten. Good.' She flicked lightly on Jacob's fingers, watched as he immediately curled them tight. 'Reflex good, as is his activity.' His little legs were moving slowly against his mother's skin, and she couldn't resist running a finger down one leg. He hadn't done more than give a low gasp but his chest was rising and falling softly. So his respiratory effort was okay. Ally wrote down her obs and then dealt with the tear while Marie carried on talking.

She found Adam in the lounge, despondently pushing a wooden bulldozer around the floor. He leapt up the instant he saw her with the rubbish bag. 'Ally, has the baby come?'

'Yes, and it's a little boy.'

Adam stared up at her. 'Can I see him now?'

'I can't see why not.' She took his hand and walked down to Marie's room, saying to the new mum, 'You've got your first visitor.' And then her heart squeezed.

Marie was cuddling her precious bundle and trying to put him on the breast. 'I hope Jacob takes to this easily.'

'Don't rush. It takes time to get the hang of it.' She went to help position Jacob.

Marie smiled down at her boy. Then looked up. 'Hello, Adam, want to see Jacob? Come round the bed so you can see his face. Isn't he beautiful?'

'Can I hold him?' Adam hopped from foot to foot and Ally saw the hesitancy in Marie's expression.

'Not today. He's all soft and needs careful holding. But tomorrow you can. He'll be stronger then.'

Adam stood close to Marie and stared at the baby. Slowly he placed one hand very carefully on his tiny arm and stroked it. His mouth widened into a smile. 'Hello, baby.'

Ally's eyes watered up. She'd never forget this moment. Adam's amazement, Marie's love, Jacob so tiny and cute. She'd seen it before, often, but today it was definitely different. Not because she'd begun to see herself in Marie's place, holding her own precious bundle of joy. Definitely not because of that.

She stood there, unable to take her gaze away from the

scene, unable to move across to the towels that needed to be put into a bag for the laundry company. Just absorbing everything, as though it was her first delivery. The incredible sense of having been a part of a miracle swamped her. *Could I do this? Give birth myself?* Having a baby wasn't the issue. She'd be fine with that. But everything after the moment she held that baby in her arms—that was the problem. Did she have mothering instincts? Or had she inherited her mother's total lack of interest when it came to her own child, her own flesh and blood?

She couldn't afford to find out. It wouldn't be fair on her baby if she got it wrong.

'Marie, you certainly don't waste time when you decide you're ready to have your baby.' Flynn strode into the room and came to an abrupt halt. 'Adam, what are you doing in here?'

CHAPTER TEN

'Dad!' Adam jumped up and down. 'Marie's got a new baby. I think it hurt her.'

'What?' Flynn spun around, his face horrified, and demanded, 'How does he know that?'

Ally stepped up to him. 'Adam did not see the birth, if that's what you're thinking.'

'Then explain his comment.'

Ally backed away from the anger glittering at her. 'He asked why he couldn't come in here and I said that having a baby is private and sometimes it hurts a little.' She had not done anything wrong.

Marie was staring at Flynn like she'd never met him before. 'For goodness' sake. Do you think either of us would've allowed him in here while I was giving birth? Seriously?'

Flynn shoved a hand through his hair, mussing it up, except this time that didn't turn Ally on one little bit. 'I guess not.'

'Dad, I helped Ally. I got water and the heater.'

Flynn's mouth tightened.

Ally told him, 'Adam left everything outside the door. The closed door.' Why can't he see the pride shining in his son's eyes? She ran a hand over Adam's head. 'My little helper.'

Flynn flinched. 'Sorry for jumping to conclusions, everyone.' He was starting to look a little guilty. 'I never did do anything about making alternative arrangements for this eventuality.' He gave Marie a rueful smile. 'Now can I meet Jacob?'

Reluctantly Marie handed the baby over. 'Only for a minute. I don't like letting him out of my arms.'

Ally watched Flynn's face soften as he peered into the soft blue blanket with its precious bundle, and felt her heart lurch so hard it hurt. There was so much love and wonder in his expression she knew he was seeing Adam the day he'd been born. It was a timely reminder that she didn't have a place in his life.

Spinning around, she shoved the baby's notes at Marie. 'I'll make that coffee I promised.' Like when?

Marie was quick, grabbing her hand to stop her tearing out of the room. Her eyes were full of understanding. 'White with two sugars.' She nodded and let Ally go.

Thank you for not outing me.

Flynn was oblivious anyway, so engrossed in Jacob that it was as though no one else was in the room.

When she returned with three coffees he was reading the notes and only grunted, 'Thanks,' at her. Guess he'd finally worked out where his loyalties truly lay, and they weren't with her.

Ally asked Marie, 'Is there anything you want me to do? Washing? Get some groceries in?'

Flynn answered before Marie could open her mouth. 'No need. Marie's mother will be here soon.'

Marie gaped at him. 'Tell me you didn't phone her.'

Colour crept into Flynn's cheeks and another dash of

guilt lowered his eyebrows and darkened his eyes. He was having a bad afternoon. 'With Mark at sea for another week, you need someone here. Who better than your mother?'

'You know the answer to that,' Marie growled. 'Ring her back and tell her to turn around.'

'You don't think this is an opportune time to kiss and make up?' Flynn asked. 'Estelle sounded very excited about the new baby.'

Ally looked from Marie to Flynn. What was going on here? They knew each other well, but for Flynn to be telling Marie to sort her apparent problem with her mother could be stretching things too far. Time for a break from him. Taking Adam's hand, she said, 'Come on, let's get you some food. I bet your tummy's hungry.'

'It's always hungry.'

She glanced at Flynn as she reached the door and tripped. He was staring at her with disappointment in his eyes. 'What?' she demanded in a high-pitched voice.

He shook his head. 'Nothing.'

Hadn't she been telling herself what she and Flynn had going was only a short-term fling? If she needed proof, here it was.

In the kitchen Ally put together enough sandwiches for everyone. She got out plates and placed the food on them. Next she put the kettle on to make hot drinks all round. All the while she was trying to ignore that look she'd seen in Flynn's eyes.

Adam chomped through two sandwiches in record time.

'Slow down or you'll get a tummyache.'

'No, I won't. My tummy's strong.' He banged his glass on the table.

Ally smiled tiredly at the ring of milk around his mouth and ignored the tug at her heart. 'Wipe your face, you grub.'

Flynn strode into the kitchen and picked up one of the sandwiches, munched thoughtfully.

'Dad, can I see the baby again?'

'Of course you can. But be very careful if you touch him. He's only little.' Flynn watched his son run down the hall, a distant gleam in his eyes making Ally wonder what he was thinking. When Adam disappeared into Marie's room he closed the kitchen door and she found out. 'Marie's very happy with how you handled the birth. Said you were calm and reassuring all the time.'

'I'm a midwife, that's what we do. It's in the job description.'

'What I don't condone is my son's presence in the house at the time. He shouldn't have been with Marie from the moment she went into labour. Why couldn't you have gone next door to see if Mrs James could look after him?'

'One, there wasn't a lot of time. Two, as I don't know Mrs James, I'm hardly going to leave a small boy with her. Your small boy at that. You could've arranged for someone to come and collect him. You did get my message?' Two could play this game.

'Why didn't you get Megan to arrange someone?'

'It's not my place to make demands of your receptionist.'

Flynn didn't flinch. 'What was Adam doing while you were occupied with Marie? You weren't keeping a proper eye on him, were you?'

'You know what? Adam isn't my responsibility.' She was repeating herself, but somehow she had to get through that thick skull. Except she suspected she was wasting her time. Maybe shouting at him might make him listen. But as she opened her mouth her annoyance faded. She didn't want to fight with him.

'But you were here. You could've taken a few moments to find a solution. Marie's baby wasn't going to arrive that quickly.'

Maybe he had a point, and she had made a mistake. 'I'm sorry. I got here as soon as I could after Marie phoned to say she'd gone into labour. Everything was hectic and Adam was happy watching TV.' But she should've thought more about Adam. Just went to show how unmotherly her instincts were. 'I did my best in the situation. I explained to Adam what was happening and he was happy to bring towels and water to leave outside the bedroom door. Not once did he see anything he shouldn't.'

'He's a little boy.' Flynn wasn't accepting her explanation. 'He'd have heard her cries and groans. It's not a massive house.'

'He was safe. I didn't put him in a position where he'd be scared, and I honestly don't think he was.' Her guilt increased. She should've thought more about Adam's age, should've tried harder to find a solution. He might've heard things a young child was better off not hearing. What if he had nightmares about it? But he'd been excited to see Jacob, not frightened of the baby or Marie. But there was no denying she'd got it wrong. Apparently she should've seen to Adam before Marie.

Ally shivered. Forget thinking she might have her own baby. She wasn't mother material. Having never had the parental guidance that would've made her see how she should've cared for Adam had shown through this afternoon. One thing was for sure, she wouldn't be any better with her own.

At least she could be thankful that she'd had a reminder of that now and not after she'd given in to the yearning for her own baby that had begun growing inside her. She would not have her own children. That was final. She squashed that hope back where it belonged—in the dark, deep recesses of her mind, hopefully to stay there until she was too old to conceive.

Flynn waited until Marie's mother arrived before he took Adam home. *Talk about being a spare wheel.* Ally and Marie talked and laughed a lot, getting on so well it reminded him of Anna with Marie. Ally had fussed over the baby while his mum had taken a shower, but handed Jacob back the moment Marie returned to her bedroom. She hadn't been able to entirely hide the longing in her eyes.

Flynn had tried to deny the distress he'd seen in Ally's face earlier. The distress that had changed to bewilderment and lastly guilt—brought on by him. The guilt had still been there whenever she'd looked at him, which was probably why she'd kept her head turned away as much as possible. He'd become the outsider in that house. Marie and Jacob and Adam had got all her attention. And he'd hated that. So he'd taken Adam and left. *Like a spoilt child.*

Now at home he swore—silently so Adam didn't pick up any words he'd then be told off for using. Then he deliberately focused on his son and not the woman who had his gut in a knot and his head spinning. He really tried. *Adam, my boy. I love you so much I'm being overprotective. But that's better than not caring.*

If ever there was a woman he could've expected to

look out for Adam it was Ally. Not to mention Marie. He'd seen that stunned look on Marie's face when he'd given Ally a hard time. Of course Marie would know how unusual it was for him to lose his cool.

He cracked an egg and broke the yolk. 'Guess that means scrambled eggs and not poached.' He found a glass jug and put the pan away. Broke in some more eggs, whisked them into a froth and added a dash of milk. 'Adam, want to put the toast on?'

'Okay, Dad.' His boy stood on tiptoe at the pantry, reaching for the bread. 'Why isn't Ally sleeping over?'

Because your father's been a fool. 'She's tired after helping Jacob be born.'

'I like Jacob.'

Adam sounded perfectly happy, as if being around while a birth was going on was normal. And why wouldn't it be? Ally had made sure Adam wasn't affected by seeing anything untoward.

Flynn put the eggs into the microwave. *Ally, I'm so sorry for my rant. It was my responsibility to look out for my son, not yours, or anyone else's.* Ever since Anna's death he'd been determined to be the best dad he could to make up for Adam not having a mother. Hell, that's why they lived on the island and he did the job he did. Yet today he'd been quick to lay the blame right at Ally's feet for something that bothered him.

Sheba rubbed her nose against his thigh and he reached down to scratch behind her ears. 'Hey, girl, I've made a mess of things.' Picking up his phone, he punched in Ally's number. His call went straight to voice mail. 'Ally, it's Flynn. I'd like to talk to you tonight if you have a moment.'

But he knew that unless she was more forgiving than he deserved, she wouldn't call. Action was required.

'Adam, want to go and see Ally?'

The shout of 'Yes!' had him turning the microwave off and picking up his keys. 'Let's go.'

Despite the absence of the car in Kat's drive, Flynn still knocked on the front door and called out. 'Ally? Open up.'

Adam hopped out and added his entreaties but Ally wasn't answering.

Flynn doubted she'd be hiding behind the curtains. That wasn't her style. Ally wasn't at home.

Back on the road Flynn headed to town to cruise past the restaurants and cafés. 'There.' He pointed to a car parked outside the Chinese takeaway and diner.

'Yippee, we found her.' Adam was out of the car before Flynn had the handbrake on.

'Wait, Adam.' Though Ally was less likely to turn away from his son, he had to do this right or there'd be no more nights with her in his bed, or meals at Giuseppe's, or walks on the beach. *There aren't going to be many more anyway. She leaves at the end of next week.* He wouldn't think about that.

She sat in a corner, looking glum as she nodded her head to whatever music was playing through her earphones.

'Ally, we came to see you.'

Her head shot up when Adam tapped her hand. 'Hey.' She smiled directly at his son. 'Are you here for dinner?' Did she have to look as though she really hoped they weren't?

Flynn answered, 'Only if it's all right with you.'

Her eyes met his. No smile for him as she shrugged. 'I only need one table.'

'We'd like to share this one with you.' He held his breath.

Adam wasn't into finesse. He pulled out a chair and sat down. 'What can I have to eat, Dad?'

Flynn didn't take his gaze off Ally, saw her mouth soften as she glanced at his son. He said, 'I apologise for earlier. I was completely out of line.'

She didn't come close to smiling. 'Really?' Her gaze returned to him.

He took a chance and pulled out another chair. 'Really. I should've had something in place for today—for whatever day Marie had her baby. Adam is my responsibility, no one else's. It's been on my list to arrange another sitter but I never got around to it.' Much to his chagrin. He twisted the salt shaker back and forth between his fingers. 'I was angry for stuffing up, and I took it out on you. I apologise for everything I said.'

Ally pushed the menu across the table, a glimmer of a smile on her lips. 'I only ordered five minutes ago.'

That meant she accepted his apology, right? 'Adam, do you want fried rice with chicken?'

'Yes. Ally, are you coming for another sleepover tonight?'

Flynn's stomach tightened. *Too soon, my boy. Too soon. We need to have dinner and talk a bit before asking that.*

Ally shook her head. 'Not tonight. I need to do some washing and stuff.' She was looking at Adam, but Flynn knew she was talking to him.

Two steps forward, one back.

She hadn't finished. 'Besides, I'm always extra-tired

after a delivery and need to spend time thinking about it all.' Her voice became melancholy, like she was unhappy about a bigger issue and not just about what he'd dumped on her earlier.

He gave the order to the woman hovering at his elbow and turned to lock eyes with Ally. 'What's up?' How could he have been so stupid as to rant at her? Now she wasn't staying the night, and who knew when she'd be back at his house, in his bed? Actually, he'd love nothing more than to sit down with a coffee or wine and try some plain old talking, getting to know each other better stuff. When she didn't answer he continued, 'What does a birth make you think about?'

'Everything and nothing. That whole wonderful process and a beautiful baby at the end of it. Like I told you the other day, I find it breathtakingly magical.' Her finger was picking at a spot on the tabletop. 'Yet I'm the observer, always wondering what's ahead for this new little person.'

'Do you want to have children someday?' Didn't most people?

The finger stopped. Ally lifted her head and looked around the diner, finally bringing her gaze back to him. 'No.'

'You'd be a great mother.'

Silence fell between them, broken only when Ally's meal arrived. But she didn't get stuck in, instead played with the rice, stirring and pushing it around the plate with her fork.

Adam asked, 'Where's my dinner?'

Flynn dragged his eyes away from Ally and answered. 'We ordered after Ally so it will be a few more minutes.'

Ally slid her plate across to Adam. 'Here, you have this one. It's the same as what you ordered.'

'You sound very certain—about no children of your own,' Flynn ventured.

'I am.'

'That's sad.'

'Believe me, it's not. If I'd had a child, that would be sad. Bad. Horrible.' The words fell off her trembling lips.

He couldn't help himself. He took her hand in his and was astonished to feel her skin so cold. 'Tell me.'

'I already did.' She'd found a point beyond his shoulder to focus on.

While he wished they were at home in the comfort and privacy of his lounge, he kept rubbing her hand with his thumb, urging her silently to enlighten him, let out what seemed to be chewing her up from the inside. 'Only that you were abandoned. Doesn't that make you determined to show yourself how good you'd be?'

Their meals arrived and they both ignored them.

'My mother didn't want me. I grew up in the welfare system. Moved from house to house, family to family, until I was old enough to go it alone.' Her flat monotone told him more than the words, though they were horrifying enough.

'Your father?'

'Probably never learned of my existence—if my mother even knew who he was.'

'You know,' Flynn said gently, 'your mother may have done what she did because she *did* love you. If she wasn't in a safe situation, or wasn't able to cope, it might have been that giving you up was her way of protecting you. Haven't you ever worked with women in that position?'

'Yes,' Ally admitted slowly. 'But if it was love, it didn't feel much like it to me.'

Flynn hated to think of Ally as a kid, adrift in the foster-care system without a steady and loving upbringing. It wasn't like that in all cases, he reminded himself. Anna's brother and sister-in-law had two foster-children that they loved as much as their own three. But look at Ally. Adorable, gorgeous, kind and caring. What's not to love about her? Was that his problem? Had he fallen for her? Nah, couldn't have. They'd only known each other a little more than two weeks. Hardly time to fall in love, especially when they knew nothing about each other. Except now he did know more about Ally than he would ever have guessed. And he wanted more. He could help her, bring her true potential to the fore.

Ally tugged her hand free, picked up her fork. 'See? You're speechless. It's shocking, but that's who I am, where I come from, what I'll always be. Now you know. You were right. I shouldn't have been in charge of Adam, even if by proxy. I know nothing about parenting.'

No. No way. Flynn grabbed both her hands, fork and all. 'Don't say that. I'd leave Adam with you any day or night. Today was me being precious. Since Marie and I are friends, I felt a little left out. Plain stupid, really.'

Ally tried to pull free, but he tightened his grip.

Finally she locked the saddest eyes he'd ever seen on him. 'Are we a messed-up pair, or what?' she whispered.

I'm not messed up. I get stuff wrong, but I think I've done well in moving on from Anna's death and raising our son.

'I am determined to do my absolute best for Adam, in everything.'

'You're doing that in spades.'

'So why do I feel guilty all the time?'

Her brow furrowed. 'About what?'

About Adam not having his mother in his life. 'I try to raise him as his mother wanted.' This was getting too deep. He aimed for a lighter tone. 'Eating raw vegetables every day and never having a sweet treat is too hard even for me, and I'm supposed to make Adam stick to that.' *But it isn't always what I want, or how I'd bring my boy up.*

Her fingers curled around his hands. 'That's not realistic. Even if you succeed at home, the world is full of people eating lollies and ice cream, roast vegetables and cheese sauces.' At last her eyes lightened and her mouth finally curved into a delicious smile that melted the cold inside him.

The smile he looked for every day at work, at night in his house. 'Like Danish pastries, you mean.'

'You've got it.' Her shoulders lifted as she straightened her back. Digging her fork into her rice, she hesitated. 'I haven't known you very long, but it's obvious how committed you are to your son, and how much you love him. Believe me, those are the most important things you can give him.'

Said someone who knew what it was like to grow up without either of those important things. He answered around a blockage in his throat, 'Thank you. Being a solo dad isn't always a level road. Scary at times.'

'It's probably like that when there are two parents. Come on, let's eat. I'm suddenly very hungry.'

'Something you and Adam have in common. You're always hungry.' The last hour being the exception.

She grinned around a mouthful of chicken and rice.

His stomach knotted. He loved that grin. It was warm and funny. But now he understood she used it to hide a lot of hurt. Hard to imagine her childhood when he'd grown up in what he'd always thought of as a normal family. Mum, Dad and his brothers. No one deliberately hurt anyone or was ungrateful for anything. Everyone backed each other in any endeavours. When Anna had died he'd been swamped with his family and their loving support to the point he'd finally had to ask them to get back to their own lives and let him try to work out his new one.

'Dad, can I have ice cream for pudding?'

Ally smirked around her mouthful.

'Gloating doesn't suit you.' He laughed. 'Yes, Adam, you can. Ask that lady behind the counter for some while Ally and I finish our dinner.'

As Adam sped across the diner, probably afraid he'd be called back and told to forget that idea, Flynn watched him with a hitch in his chest and a sense that maybe he was getting this parenting stuff right after all.

'Good answer,' said Ally.

'Would you change your mind about a sleepover?' Might as well go for broke. After being so angry with Ally, then getting the guilts, all he wanted now was some cuddle time. Yeah, okay, and maybe something hotter later. But seriously? He wanted to be with Ally, sex or no sex.

Her smile stayed in place. 'I meant it when I said I get exhausted after a delivery. And I do like to think it all through, go over everything again.'

Huge disappointment clenched his gut but he wouldn't pressure her. 'Fair enough. But if you decide you need a shoulder to put your head on during the night, you know where to find me.' Huh? What happened to no pressure? 'If you want company without the perks, I mean.' He smiled to show he meant exactly what he'd said, and got a big one in return.

'You have no idea how much that means to me. But this is how I deal with my work. I'm not used to dumping my thoughts on anyone else.'

'You should try it. You might find it cathartic.' Next he'd be begging. 'Tell me to shut up if you like.'

She took his hands in hers, and this time her skin was warm. Comfort warm, friendly warm. 'I'm not used to being with a man every night of the week. I'm used to my own company and like my own space. Don't take it personally, it's just the way I am.'

Sounded awfully lonely to him. 'I'll cook you dinner tomorrow night.' When would he learn to zip his mouth shut? 'If you'd like that.'

'It's a date. I'll bring dessert. Something Adam will love.'

'You're corrupting my kid now?'

'You'd better believe it.'

CHAPTER ELEVEN

'YOU LOOK WORSE than the chewed-up mess my cat dragged in this morning,' Megan greeted Ally the next morning when she walked into the surgery. 'Not a lot of sleep going on in your bed?'

'No. I tossed and turned for hours.'

'Haven't heard it called tossing and turning before, though I see the resemblance.' Megan laughed.

'Trust me, I was very much alone. Is everyone here yet?' Was Flynn here? He mightn't have kept her awake in the flesh, but she'd spent hours thinking about him. Hours and hours. Nothing like her usual night after a birth.

'I think they're all in the tearoom.'

Ally looked at the list of her appointments for the morning. 'At least there's no chance of falling asleep at my desk with all these women to visit.'

In the tearoom a large coffee from her favourite coffee shop was set at what had become her place. 'Thanks,' she muttered, as Flynn nodded to her. He was the only one in there.

'I was out early visiting Marie and Jacob so Adam and I had breakfast at the café.'

Ally chuckled. 'Now who's spoiling him?' Then wished

the words back as his smile dipped. 'Spoiling's good. Who's looking after Adam today?'

'A friend on the other side of the island. She's had him before when Marie needed to go somewhere little boys weren't welcome.' Flynn pulled her chair out.

Sinking onto it, she lifted the lid on her coffee and tentatively sipped the steaming liquid. 'That's so good. Caffeine's just what I need. If I hadn't been running late I'd have stopped for one myself.' So Flynn had lots of friends he could call on. Lucky man. But friends also meant staying in touch, being there when needed, opening up about things best left shut off. *Has he changed how he feels about me now that he knows the truth?* 'Is Adam happy to go to this lady?'

'Absolutely. He gets to take Sheba so they can go for walks in the park with Gina's two spaniels.'

Cosy. Did the woman have a husband? *Down, green monster, down. You have no right poking your head up.* So far her night-time lectures to herself about falling in love with a man who was out of reach didn't seem to have sunk in. Slow learner. *Flynn is totally committed to Adam and his job. There is no room for you in his life.* She repeated what she'd said over and over throughout the night. And again it didn't make a blind bit of difference. Try, *There's no room for Flynn and Adam in your life. They live in the same place every day of the year. You move somewhere new so often you're like a spinning top.*

'Morning, Ally.' Faye strolled into the room. 'I hear Marie's baby arrived in a bit of a hurry.'

'He sure did. And he's absolutely gorgeous.' She couldn't wait to visit this morning.

'Humph. Babies are all the same to me. Cry and poo in their nappies a lot. Very uninteresting at that age.'

Ally blinked. Had she heard right? 'You haven't had your own children?' All babies were beautiful, even if some were more so than others.

'Got three of the blighters. Love each and every one, but that doesn't mean I thought they were cute when they arrived.'

What a strange lady. But at least she was there for her kids and probably did a lot with them. 'How was Marie this morning?' She looked at Flynn.

'Arguing with her mother about who was bathing Jacob.' He grinned like he'd been naughty. Which he had. If not for him Marie's mother wouldn't be there. 'But at least they're talking, which is a vast improvement.'

Jerome joined them and the meeting got under way. Thankfully it was short as Ally was itching to get on the road and go visiting patients, to get away from that distracting smile of Flynn's. As she headed to the door and her car, he called, 'You still on for tonight?'

'I'm buying the dessert after my house calls.' She shouldn't join him for the whole night, but she couldn't resist. This had been a fling like no other she'd ever had. This time she dreaded finishing it and heading away. Not that she wanted to stay put on Phillip Island for however long the fling took to run its course either. But there was this feeling of so much more to be done, to share with Flynn, to enjoy with his son.

For the first time in her adult life she didn't want to move on. For the first time ever a person had got under her skin, warmed her heart in a way it had never been warmed. It made her long for the impossible—a family she could truly call her own.

She should've said no, that she'd be staying home to wash her hair.

But there was no denying the liquid heat pouring through her body just at the thought of a night with Flynn. So—how could she leave next week without shattering her heart?

It's too late. Might as well grab every moment going. It'd be silly to go through the rest of my time here staying in the flat, being miserable. Miserable would come—later, back on the mainland.

'Chocolate Bavarian pie.' Ally placed the box she'd bought in the supermarket on Flynn's bench. 'It's defrosted and ready to go.' She bent down to scratch Sheba's ears. 'Hey, girl, how're you doing? Recovered from that run yet?'

Lick, lick. Yes or no? Sheba had struggled a bit as they'd loped along the beach early yesterday morning.

Flynn slid a glass of red wine in her direction. 'Merlot tonight. Goes with the sausages I'm cooking.' He grinned that cheeky grin that got to her every time. 'They're beef.'

'Beef and red wine. A perfect combination,' she said with her tongue firmly in her cheek. That navy striped shirt he wore with the top button open to show a delectable V of chest was also perfect. Just enough visible chest to tantalise and heat her up in places that only Flynn seemed able to scorch. She winked. 'What time does Adam go to bed on Fridays?'

'Half past nine,' Flynn told her, straight-faced.

She spluttered into her glass. 'Half past nine? You've got to be kidding me.' Three hours before she could get her hands on the skin under that shirt? She'd combust with heat.

'Yep, I am.' Then he grinned again. 'You're so easy to wind up.'

'Phew. For a moment there I thought I'd have to lock

him in the lounge with Sheba and race you down the hall for a quickie.'

Desire matching hers flicked into his eyes. 'Now, there's a thought.'

This banter she could do. It was easy and fun and how flings were run. 'Guess I'd better stick to wine for now.'

'We're invited to Jerome's tomorrow night for an indoor barbecue, along with the rest of the staff. But he specifically asked us as a couple.'

The air leaked out of her lungs. This might be something she couldn't do. It hinted at something more than a casual relationship, like a date involving his colleagues and friends. Colleagues and friends who'd read more into the situation than was there. Was Jerome playing matchmaker? 'That's nice.' Well, it would be under other circumstances.

'You're not happy?'

She shrugged. 'I'm sure it will be fun, but maybe I'll give it a miss.'

A furrow appeared between his eyes. 'I accepted for both of us.'

'Then you'll have to *un*accept.' What had happened to consulting her first?

'Why? You've been working with everyone for three weeks so what's the big deal?' Then that furrow softened. 'I get it. The *couple* word. That's what's got your knickers in a twist, isn't it?'

'So what if it has? We're not a couple. Not in the true sense. We're having an affair. Next weekend it will be over. How do you face your colleagues then, if they're thinking we've got something more serious going on?'

How do I look Megan in the eye next week and say of course we're only friends. Even friends with benefits doesn't cover it. I'm falling for you and I need to be pulling back, not stepping into a deeper mire.

'Ally, relax. Everyone's aware you're moving on and I'm staying put. Jerome thought it would be more comfortable for you to go with me as there will be others there you haven't met. That's all there is to it.'

'You're ignoring that *couple* word.' Didn't it bother him? Because he was so comfortable in his life that he thought it ludicrous to even consider he was in a relationship?

Flynn set his glass carefully on the bench and ran his fingertip over her lips. 'Sure I am. It was the wrong word to use. We've spent a lot of time together since you turned up on the beach that first day. You've given me something special, and I'm going to miss you, but we've both known right from that first kiss that whatever we have between us would never be long-term. I don't care what anyone else thinks. It's no one's business.'

Where was the relief when she needed it? Flynn had saved her a lot of hassle by saying what they had going was a short-term thing. But the reality hurt. A lot. In her tummy, especially in her heart. Her head said the best thing for everyone was that she'd be leaving. Her heart said she should stay and see if she could make a go of a relationship with Flynn and his son.

'Ally? Would you please come to the barbecue with me as my partner for the night?' When she didn't answer he added, 'People know we've been seeing each other—going out for meals, taking Adam to the beach and other places. It's not as though this is going to be a shock for them or the source of any gossip.' He drew a breath and continued. 'I want this last week with you.' His smile was soft and yet determined. It arrowed right into her chest, stabbed her heart.

And made everything even more complicated.

How could she say no when she wanted it, too? In the end it was Flynn who'd be left to face any gossip. In the end it would be agony to leave him whether she went out with him again or not. She had to grab whatever she could and stack up the memories for later. 'I'd love to go with you,' she said quietly.

The days were flying by and Ally was withdrawing from him. Flynn hated it. Sure, she still came home with him for the night, but there seemed to be a barrier growing up between her and them as a twosome. She'd already begun moving on in her mind. There, he'd said it. He'd started denying the fact she would be leaving soon, even when it was there in black and white on the noticeboard in this office. Kat would return home on Friday—tomorrow. She'd take over the reins on Saturday and Ally would leave the island and head for her next job. He knew all that. He'd signed the contract with Ally's employers.

But knowing and facing up to what her leaving truly meant were entirely different. He refused to admit the other half of his bed would be cold and empty again. Wouldn't contemplate sitting down to an evening meal with only Adam for company. Daren't think how he'd fill in the weekends without her laughter and eagerness for fun pulling him along.

'That needs photocopying so the hospital in Melbourne have records.' Ally dropped a file beside Megan. 'Hey, Flynn, got a minute?'

'Of course.' *Always got hours for you.* Had he been

hasty in thinking she was putting space between them? Did she have a plan for what they might do on her last nights?

'I'm concerned about Chrissie.'

So much for plans and hot farewells. 'Come into my office.' He nodded at the patients sitting in the waiting room.

Ally got the message. 'Sure.' The moment she stepped inside his room she spun to face him. 'Chrissie's doing great physically. But she's got attached to me already and that's not good. She says she doesn't want to see Kat.'

'Strange. Kat gets on with everyone.' Like Ally. 'Did she give a reason?'

'Something about Kat's sister and Chrissie being rivals at school.' Ally shrugged those shoulders he'd spent a long time kissing last night. 'I was wondering if you could see her, maybe talk sense into her. I've explained that Kat would never tell her sister a single thing about the pregnancy, but Chrissie's not wearing it.'

'I'll talk to Chrissie, maybe with Angela there.' But he wondered how much of this had to do with Kat and how much was due to the way Chrissie had taken to Ally. 'You handled the situation very tactfully and sympathetically at a time when Chrissie was beside herself with worry. This could be about her not wanting you to leave.' He didn't want her going. Adam wouldn't, either.

A soft sigh crossed Ally's lips. 'There's not much I can do about that. I am going.'

'I know.' All too well. 'Do you ever get tired of moving on?'

Her eyes met his and she seemed to draw a breath before answering. 'No. It's how I live and there's a certain simplicity to not owning a house or a truckload of furniture or even a carful of clothes.' She looked away.

Flynn couldn't read her. He wanted to know if she felt sad about leaving him, or happy about another job done and their affair coming to an end. But as he started to ask his heart knocked so hard against his ribs he gasped. *I love her. I love Ally Parker. I'm not wondering any more. I know.* Asking her about her feelings just became impossible. She might ask some questions in return, questions he still wasn't ready to answer.

So he continued to study her while not being able to lock gazes with her, and he thought he saw no regret in her stance, her face or her big eyes. So Ally hadn't come to love him in the way he had her. Pain filled him, blurred his vision for a moment. Rocked him to the core. How could he have fallen in love with Ally? He'd never believed he'd love again, and yet it only taken a few short weeks. Had it happened that first day when Sheba had dumped her on the beach?

Ally's soft voice cut through his mind like a well-honed blade. 'I'd better get a move on. I'm going to weigh Jacob this morning.'

He watched her retreating back, his hands curled into fists to stop from reaching after her. So much for thinking she might reciprocate his feelings. It wasn't going to be at all difficult for her to walk away.

Ally stayed in the shower until she heard Flynn and Adam leave for their walk on the beach with Sheba. She'd cried off, saying she had a headache. That was no lie. Behind her eyes her skull pounded like a bongo drum. Her hands trembled as she towelled herself dry. Her knees knocked as she tried to haul her jeans up her legs. It was Saturday.

'Goodbye, Flynn.' She hiccupped around the solid

lump of pain in her throat. 'Bye-bye, Adam. Be a good boy for your dad.' *I will not cry. I don't cry. Ever.*

Reaching out blindly, she snatched a handful of tissues and blew her nose hard, scrubbed at her eyes. One glance at her hands and she knew it'd be a waste of time trying to apply make-up. 'Go plain Jane today.' What did it matter anyway? It wasn't as though she'd be seeing Flynn.

Tears threatened and she took as deep a breath as possible. 'Suck it up, be tough, get through the day. Tomorrow will look a whole heap better.'

Now she'd taken to lying to herself. But if it got her out of the house and on the road before Flynn and Adam returned, then it was the right thing to do.

Yesterday she'd packed up her few possessions and the bags sat in the boot of the medical centre's car. The key to Kat's flat was back under the flowerpot on the top step, her contact details written on a pad inside in case she'd left anything behind. Now all she had to do was drive to the surgery to dump the car and be on her way.

But she turned the car in the direction of Marie's house. 'One last cuddle with Jacob.' So much for leaving unobtrusively. But she couldn't bring herself to turn away yet.

Marie opened her front door before Ally had time to knock. 'Hey, you're out and about early.'

'Yeah, thought I'd see everything's okay with you.'

'Come in. Want a coffee?' Marie headed for the kitchen. 'Jacob's just gone down.'

'Then I probably should carry on.'

There was already a mug of steaming coffee on the bench and Marie poured another without waiting to see if Ally wanted it. 'We had a good night. Jacob only woke four times.' She grinned.

'How do you manage to look so good after that?' Ally paced back and forth.

'Mark's coming home today.' Marie slid the mug in Ally's direction. 'Excuse me for being blunt but *you* look terrible. What's up?'

'Nothing.' She tried to shrug, but her shoulders were too heavy.

'Ally, I don't know you well, but something's not right. Has Flynn done something wrong?'

'No. Not at all.' She'd gone and fallen in love with him, but that didn't make him a bad man. She was the fool.

'Good, I'd have been surprised. He thinks the world of you and would do anything for you. Apart from that hiccup the day Jacob was born.'

Coming here had been a mistake. 'I'd better go. I've to be somewhere. Thanks for the coffee.' Which she hadn't even tried. 'I'll see myself out.'

'Don't go,' Marie called.

Ally shut the door behind herself and ran to the car.

A taxi dropped her off at the ferry terminal half an hour later. Once on board she found an empty seat out of the way of the happy hordes and pushed her earbuds in, turned up the music on her music player and pretended all was right with her world. Except it wasn't, as proved by the onset of deep sobs that began racking her body as the ferry pulled out. Her fingers dug into the palms of her hands and she squeezed her eyes tight against the cascade of tears.

Someone tapped her knee. 'Here. Have these.' An older woman sitting opposite handed her a pack of tissues.

'Th-thanks,' she managed, before the next wave of despair overtook her.

Flynn. I love you so much it's painful.

Flynn. What I wouldn't give to feel your arms around me one more time.

Flynn. I had to go. It wouldn't have worked.

For every wipe at her face more tears came, drenching the front of her jersey. 'I love you, Flynn Reynolds,' she whispered. Shudders racked her body from her shoulders all the way down to her feet.

This was terrible. The last time she'd cried when moving on had been the day she'd left her favourite foster-family—the Bartletts.

The woman opposite stirred. 'We're docking.'

Ally blew her nose and swiped her eyes once more, drew a breath and looked up. 'Thank you again.'

'You'll be all right?'

'Yes, of course.' Never again. With one last sniff she inched forward in the queue to disembark and headed for her real life; the one she'd worked hard to make happen and that now seemed lonely and cold.

Flynn felt a chill settle over him the moment he turned into his street. Ally's car was gone. Somehow he wasn't surprised but, damn it, he was hurt. How hard would it have been to say goodbye?

Spinning the steering wheel, he did an about-turn and headed for Kat's flat to say to Ally the goodbye she hadn't been willing to give him.

But it was Marie's car outside Kat's flat, not the one Ally had been using. As soon as Flynn pulled up Marie was at his window. 'Do you know where Ally's gone?'

'I hoped she'd be here.' He was too late.

'She came to my place about an hour ago. She was very upset. I tried to find out why, but she left again. In a hurry, at that. That's why I came around here.'

Flynn's mouth soured. Ally was upset? Why? *Did you want to stay on? With me? No, that was going too far.* 'I'd say she's on the ferry, heading home.' Except she didn't have a home to head to. Just a bed she borrowed on a daily basis.

'Flynn, what's going on? Why's Ally upset? As in looking like she was about to burst into tears?' Marie's voice rose.

Ally and tears didn't mix. He'd never seen her close to crying. *Duh.* There hadn't been any reason for it. His gut clenched. If Ally was crying, then he wanted to be with her, holding her, calming her down and helping sort whatever her problem was. 'She's finished her contract with us, but from what I've learned about her that wouldn't be the reason for her being unhappy.'

Marie clamped her hands on her hips. 'Unhappy? Broken-hearted more like. Downright miserable.' She stared at him. 'A little bit like how you're looking, only more so.'

'I look miserable? Broken-hearted?' Here he'd been thinking he could hide his feelings. But, then, most people didn't know him as well as Marie did.

Marie's stance softened. 'You love her, don't you?'

Ouch. This might not go well, Anna having been Marie's best friend and all. 'You don't pull any punches, do you?'

'Have you told Ally?'

He shook his head.

'What's held you back? Anna? Because if that's the case, you have to let her go. The last thing Anna would've wanted would be for you to be on your own for the rest of your life.'

Flynn growled, 'Since when did you become my therapist?'

She smiled. 'Just being a good friend. So? Spill. Why haven't you talked to Ally about this?'

'All of the above. And Adam. I'm totally focused on giving him everything he needs in life and I don't know if there's room for Ally. But, yes, I love her, so I guess I'll be making space.' Over the past weeks he'd begun to feel comfortable living here, enjoying his work more. Without Ally, life wouldn't be as much fun.

'I hope you come up with a more romantic approach when you tell Ally all this.' Marie leaned in and brushed a kiss over his chin. 'Adam adores Ally, and vice versa. What's more, he needs a mother figure in his life. You're not so hot on the soft, womanly touch.'

'Thank goodness for that.' Flynn felt something give way deep inside and a flood of love and tenderness swamped him. *Ally, love, where are you?* 'She's afraid she isn't mother material.' When astonishment appeared on Marie's face, he hurried to add, 'She's a welfare kid, lived in the system all her childhood.'

'Oh, my God. Now I get it. She was running from you. She doesn't want to make things any worse for you.'

'Yep, and I let her go.' Actually, no, he hadn't. He'd fully expected Ally to be waiting when he and Adam had got back. He should've known better. If he hadn't diverted to the vet's to pick up dog shampoo, would he have been in time to see her before she'd left? 'Marie, thanks, you're a treasure. Now, go home to that baby of yours and tell your mother to leave before Mark gets here.'

'On my way. What are you going to do?'

'Adam and I are taking a trip.'

CHAPTER TWELVE

'THE COFFEE'S ON,' Darcie said as she buzzed Ally into the apartment building.

'Hope it's stronger than tar,' Ally muttered, as she waited for the lift that would take her to the penthouse. She was wiped out. All those tears and that emotional stuff had left her exhausted. No wonder she tried so hard not to get upset.

The apartment door stood wide open as Ally tripped along the carpet to her latest abode, and she felt a temporary safety from the outside world descend.

'Hey, how's things?' Darcie appeared around the corner, took one look at her face and said, 'Not good. Forget coffee. I think this calls for wine.'

A true friend. 'Isn't it a bit early? It's not quite eleven yet.'

'It's got to be afternoon somewhere in the world.'

Good answer. 'I'll dump my bags.' And dip my face under a cold tap. But when Ally looked into the bathroom's gilt-edged mirror she was horrified at the blotchy face staring back at her. 'Who are you?' she whispered.

Cold water made her feel a little more alive but no less sad. She found her make-up and applied a thick layer in a misguided attempt to hide some of the red stains on her cheeks. Quickly brushing her hair and tying it up in a ponytail, she went out to Darcie. 'Sorry about that. I needed to freshen up a bit.'

Darcie immediately handed her a glass of Sauvignon Blanc. 'Let's go out on the deck. The sun's a treat for this time of year.'

She followed, blanking out everything to do with Phillip Island and Flynn, instead trying to focus on what might've been going on at the midwifery centre while she'd been away. 'Tell me all the gossip. Who's gone out with who, who's leaving, or starting.'

Sitting in a cane chair, Darcie sipped her wine and chuckled. 'You won't believe what's happening.'

Ally sprawled out on the cane two-seater, soaked up the sun coming through the plate-glass windows, and tried to relax. Darcie was very understanding. She'd wait to be told what was going on in Ally's life. And if Ally never told her she wouldn't get the hump. A rare quality, that. Exactly what Ally needed right now. 'Great wine.' She raised her glass towards Darcie. 'Cheers.'

At some point Darcie got up and made toasted sandwiches and they carried on talking about the mundane.

It was the perfect antidote to the tumultuous emotions that had been gripping Ally all morning. There was nothing left in her tanks. She'd given it all on Phillip Island, left her heart with Flynn and his boy. Thank goodness she had tomorrow to recover some energy and enthusiasm for work before turning up at the midwifery unit on Monday.

Then Darcie spoilt it all. 'Who's this Flynn you keep mentioning?'

Ally sat up straight. 'I don't.'

Darcie held her hand up, fingers splayed. 'Five times, but I'm not counting.'

I can't have. I would have noticed. 'He's one of the doctors I've been working with.'

'Yet I don't recall you mentioning any of the others. Guess this Flynn made an impact on you.'

You could say that. 'Okay, I'll fess up and admit to having a couple of meals with him and his wee boy.'

Darcie said nothing for so long Ally thought she'd got away with it and started to go back to her relaxed state.

Until, 'Ally, what else do you do when you're not being a midwife?'

That had her spine cracking as she straightened too fast. 'Isn't that enough? I'm dedicated to my career.' Apart from shopping for high-end clothes and getting in the minimum of groceries once in a while, what else was there to do?

'Your career shouldn't be everything. Don't you ever want a partner? A family? Your own home? Most of us do.'

'I'm not most of you.'

'What about this Flynn? Do you want to see him again?'

Yes. But she wasn't about to admit that. 'No,' she muttered, hating herself as she lied.

'You haven't fallen in love with him, have you?'

And if I have? Ally raised her eyes to Darcie and when she went to deny that suggestion she couldn't find the words. Not a single one.

'I see. That bad, huh?' Darcie leaned back in her seat. 'I don't know what's gone on in your life, Ally, and I'm not asking.' She paused, stared around her beautiful apartment before returning her gaze to Ally. 'Sometimes we have to take chances.'

Ally shook her head. 'Not on love,' she managed to croak.

'Loving someone can hurt as much as denying that love. But there's always a chance of having something wonderful if you accept it.'

There really wasn't anything she could say to that so she kept quiet.

The buzzer sounded throughout the apartment, its screech jarring. Darcie stood up. 'That's probably Mary from the ward. We're heading out to St Kilda for a few hours. Want to join us?'

Ally shook her head. 'Thanks, but, no, thanks. I've got a couple of chores to do and then I'm going to blob out right here. But with coffee, not wine.'

She tipped her head back and closed her eyes, pulled off the band from her ponytail and shook her hair free. Her hand kneaded the knots in her neck. What was Flynn doing? Had he taken Adam around to see Jacob? Her heart squeezed. *I miss you guys already.*

'Hello, Ally.'

She jerked upright. 'Flynn?' Couldn't be. Her imagination had to be working overtime.

'Ally, we came to see you.' No mistaking that excited shriek. Or the arms that reached for her and held tight.

Not her imagination, then. Adam was here. *Flynn* was here. Meaning what? Lifting her head, she stared at the man who'd stolen her heart when it was supposed to be locked away. The man she'd walked away from only hours ago without a word of goodbye or a glance over her shoulder—because any of those actions would've nailed her to the floor of his home and she'd still be on Phillip Island.

Adam tightened his hold. 'I'm missing you, Ally. You didn't wait for us.' Out of the mouths of babes—came the truth.

Her head dropped so her chin rested on Adam's head. 'Adam, sweetheart.' Then her throat dried and she couldn't say a word. Finally, after a long moment of trying not to think what this was about, she raised her eyes to find Flynn gazing at her like a thirsty man would a glass of cold water on a hot day. The same emotions she'd been dealing with all day were glittering out from her favourite blue eyes. 'Flynn,' she managed.

'Hey.' He took a step closer. 'The house didn't feel the same when we got back from our walk. Kind of empty.' Flynn didn't sound angry with her, but he should. She had done a runner.

She owed him. 'I'm really sorry but I couldn't wait.' *If I did I'd never have left.* Her heart seemed to have increased its rate to such a level it hurt. 'It's an old habit. Get out quick. Don't look back.'

Bleakness filled his gaze, his tongue did a lap of his lips. 'I see.'

Adam wriggled free of her arms and sat on the floor beside her.

Flynn didn't move, just kept watching her.

Suddenly Ally became very aware that this was the defining moment in her life. Everything she'd faced, battled, conquered, yearned for—it all came down to now and how she handled the situation. She loved Flynn. Before— *Gulp.* Before she told him—if she found the courage—she had to explain. 'It's an ingrained habit because of all those shifts I made as a child. I learned not to stare out the back window of the car as my social worker took me away from my latest family to place me in the midst of more strangers.'

Flynn crossed to sit in the chair Darcie had been using earlier. He still didn't say a word, just let her take her time.

Her chest rose and fell as she spoke. 'I know it's not the same as what I did today, that you do care about me and never promised me anything that you haven't already delivered, but I come pre-conditioned. I'm sorry.'

'You were waiting for one of those families to adopt you.' Flynn looked so sad it nearly brought on her tears.

Adam, who shouldn't be taking the slightest notice of this conversation, stared up at her and asked, 'What's adopt mean?'

'Oh, sweetheart. It's when people give someone else a place in their family, share everything they've got, including, and most importantly of all, their hearts.'

'Don't you have a family?' He'd understood far too much.

'No, Adam, I don't.'

'We can adopt you. Can't we, Dad?'

Ally's mouth dropped open. Her stomach tightened in on itself. Her hands clenched on her thighs. What? No. Not possible. He didn't understand. It wasn't that simple.

She leapt up and charged across to the floor-to-ceiling window showcasing Melbourne city. Her heart was thudding hard, and the tears that should've run out hours ago started again.

'Ally.' A familiar hand gripped her shoulder.

She gasped. 'You've taken your ring off.' Could she start believing?

He tugged gently until she gave in and turned around.

But she couldn't look up, couldn't face the denial of Adam's silly statement if it was staring at her out of Flynn's eyes. 'Ally, look at me. Please.'

Slowly she raised her head, her eyes downcast, noting the expanse of chest she'd come to know over the last month, the Adam's apple that moved as Flynn swallowed, that gorgeous mouth that had woken every part of her body and could kiss like no other man she'd known. Expelling all the air in her lungs, she finally met Flynn's gaze. There was no apology there, no *It's been nice knowing you but we don't want to know you any more*. All she found was love. Genuine love, deep love that spelled a bond and a future if she dared take it.

'Flynn,' she whispered. 'I have to tell you something.' The breath lodged painfully in her chest, but if she was going to gamble, then she had to start by being honest. 'Today was different. For the first time ever I didn't want to go. That's why I ran.' Tremors rippled through her. This was way too hard. But there was a lot to lose—or gain. A deep breath and she continued. 'I've fallen in love with you. Both of you.' And then she couldn't utter another word as tears clogged her throat.

His arms came around her, held her loosely so he could still watch her face. 'This is the last time you're walking away. You're not on your own any more. You have me, us. We are your family.' His mouth grazed hers.

'You want to adopt me?' she croaked against his lips, being flippant because she was afraid to acknowledge what he'd said for fear his words would vaporise in a flash.

'Try amalgamate. We want to bring you in with us, make us a threesome, a family.'

'Amalgamate? Sounds like a business deal.' But the

warmth lacing his voice was beginning to nudge the chill out of her bones. 'I'll bring two bags of clothes and my music player and you'll supply a home.' She smiled to show she wasn't having a poke at him. Then she gasped and dashed to her bag to pull out the dogs. 'Plus these two. I take them everywhere. This time when I put them on the shelf they'll stay there so long they'll gather dust.'

Flynn looked ready to cry. 'That's the closest you've got to owning a pet?' His arms came around her again.

'Bonkers, eh?'

He stepped back, shoved his hand through his hair. 'You have no idea how much I mean every word. I love you so much it hurts sometimes.'

She gasped. Had Flynn said he loved her?

He hadn't finished. 'I could've told you that days ago, but I got cold feet. I put Adam before everything else. Which I have to do, but I used him as an excuse not to let you know where my feelings for you were headed. I didn't want you to leave, yet I didn't know how to tell you that. I think I was kind of hoping you'd just hang around and that would solve my dilemma.'

She stared at him as a smile began breaking out across her lips, banishing the sadness that had dominated all day. 'You said you love me.'

'Yes, Ally, I did. I mean it. I love you.'

'No one's ever told me that before.' Oh, my goodness. Flynn loved her. But it wouldn't feel so warm and thrilling and wonderful if she didn't love him back. '*I've* never loved anyone before.' There hadn't been anyone to bestow that gift on. 'This love is for real, I promise.'

'Hey, I can see it in your eyes. It's been there for days if only I'd known what to look for.'

'Adam, look away. I'm going to kiss your father.'

'Why?'

'Because I love him.'

'Do you love me?'

'Absolutely.' She bent down to press a kiss on his forehead. 'Yes.' When she straightened Flynn was waiting for her, his arms outstretched to bring her close. His head lowered and his mouth claimed hers.

This kiss was like no other they'd shared. This was full of promises and love and life.

'How long are you going to kiss Dad?' Adam tapped her waist.

'For ever,' she murmured against Flynn's mouth, before reluctantly pulling away. She was afraid to let him go. She needed to keep reassuring herself he'd always be there.

Flynn took her hand and laced their fingers together. 'Want to come home with us for the rest of the weekend?'

'I can't think of anything I'd rather do.'

'Thank goodness.' Until he'd relaxed she hadn't realised how tense he'd become.

'I have to be back here on Monday.'

He nodded. 'But now you have a home to go to when you're not on a job.'

Her heart turned over. 'You're not expecting me to give up working for the midwifery unit, then?'

'You'll do that when you're good and ready. We've got all the time in the world to learn to live together and for you to feel right at home on the island. I won't be rushing you, sweetheart.' Then he really stole her heart with, 'When I say I love you, I mean through the best times and the worst, through summer, winter and Christmas and birthdays. I'm here for you, with you, Ally, for ever.'

'But what if I fail? This will be new for me.'

'You won't fail, Ally. You'll make mistakes.'

'Fine. What happens when I make these mistakes?' she asked, her heart in her mouth.

'We sort them and we move on. Together.'

Her heart cracked completely open. Could she do this? 'Can I do this? Really?' She locked her eyes on the man who'd turned her world on its head.

'Your call, sweetheart. But I believe you can do anything you set your mind to.'

Was Flynn not as scared as she was? For all his understanding, maybe he didn't get it. But looking into those eyes she'd come to trust, she saw nothing but his confidence in her. He trusted her to look out for Adam to the best of her ability, even if that ability needed fine-tuning along the way. He trusted her to love him as much as she'd declared. Her mouth was dry. Finally she managed to croak, 'Let's go home.'

'Yes.' Adam jumped up and down, then ran circles around the lounge. 'Yes, Ally's coming back home with us.'

Flynn reached for her, his smile wobbly with relief. 'Home. Our home. The three of us.' Then his smile strengthened. 'And the dogs.'

Eighteen months later...

Ally laid baby Charlotte over her shoulder and rubbed her tiny back. 'Bring up the wind, sweetheart, and you'll feel so much better.'

Flynn grinned. 'Look at you. Anyone would think you'd been burping babies for ever. Charlotte is completely relaxed lying there.'

Ally's heart swelled with pride and happiness. 'Seems I got the mothering gene after all.'

Flynn's grin became a warm, loving smile. 'Ally, I was never in doubt about that. I've seen you with Jacob, with Chrissie's Xavier and half the other new babies on the island. You're a natural when it comes to making babies happy.'

She blinked back a threatening tear at his belief in her. That belief had helped her through the doubts that had reared up throughout her pregnancy, had meant he hadn't hovered as she'd learned to feed and bath and love her baby. And Adam. Well. 'Adam's been complaining this morning. Apparently I should've made a boy so he had a brother to play football with.'

'He'll have to wait a year or two.'

'We're having more?'

'Why not?'

She blinked. That told her how much he believed in her. In her chest her heart swelled even larger.

The bed tipped as Flynn sat down beside her and reached for his daughter. 'Hello, gorgeous.' He laid Charlotte over his shoulder and held her with one hand.

'Hello,' said Ally, her tongue in her cheek.

He leaned over and kissed her. 'Hello, gorgeous number one. Did you get any sleep last night?'

'An hour maybe.' Charlotte had had colic and nothing had settled her. But Ally had been happy, pacing up and down the house, cuddling her precious bundle, kissing and caressing. Just plain loving her baby. She'd known what to do, hadn't had any moments of doubt when Charlotte wouldn't settle. And this morning she was being rewarded with a contented baby.

Yep, she did have the right instincts. When Charlotte

had been born three weeks ago she'd been stunned at the instant love and connection she'd felt for her baby. It had been blinding in its strength. For the first time ever, Ally realised how hard it must have been for her mother to give her up. She might have desperately wanted to keep her baby but had been too scared, troubled or unable to support herself. Now, as a mother, Ally knew it wasn't a decision any woman would make lightly. She'd never know the reason her mother had left her on that doorstep. But now at last, with Flynn by her side, she was moving on, making a loving life for her family and herself.

'Flynn.' She wrapped her hands around his free one. 'I love you so much. I'm so lucky.'

'You and me both, sweetheart.'

'Let's get married.' She hadn't thought about it. The words had just popped out, but she certainly didn't want to retract them.

His eyes widened and that delicious mouth tipped up into a big smile. 'That's the best idea you've had since we decided to get pregnant.'

'I thought so.' Her lips kissed the palm of his hand, and then his fingers. Life couldn't get any better.

* * * * *

HIS BEST FRIEND'S BABY

BY

SUSAN CARLISLE

Published in Great Britain 2015
by Mills & Boon, an imprint of Harlequin (UK) Limited,
Eton House, 18-24 Paradise Road, Richmond, Surrey, TW9 1SR

Special thanks and acknowledgement are given to Susan Carlisle for her contribution to the *Midwives On-Call* series

ISBN: 978-0-263-24711-4

Harlequin (UK) Limited's policy is to use papers that are natural, renewable and recyclable products and made from wood grown in sustainable forests. The logging and manufacturing processes conform to the legal environmental regulations of the country of origin.

Printed and bound in Spain
by CPI, Barcelona

Dear Reader,

A number of years ago my mother and I visited Australia. It was a beautiful and amazing country and I fell in love with it. I often speak of my visit to this day. When I was asked to join a group of world-class authors in writing the ***Midwives On-Call*** continuity, which was to be set in Australia, I jumped at the chance.

Ryan and Phoebe's story is set in Melbourne—one of the many places I had the pleasure of visiting. While in the area, my mother and I drove to the coast. On our way we visited a farm with a café much as Ryan and Phoebe do. We also went to see the Little Penguins come home. It's one of the most memorable things I've ever done. Like my characters, I had a lesson on what even the smallest of animals will do to take care of their young.

I'd be remiss if I didn't thank Fiona Lowe, one of my sister authors, who helped me—along with making me laugh—to work out the differences between the way Aussies and Americans speak. She was also wonderful in answering my questions about the area around Melbourne.

I hope you enjoy reading Ryan and Phoebe's love story. I like to hear from my readers. You can reach me at SusanCarlisle.com

Susan

Susan Carlisle's love affair with books began when she made a bad grade in maths in the sixth grade. Not allowed to watch TV until she'd brought the grade up, she filled her time with books and became a voracious romance reader. She still has 'keepers' on the shelf to prove it. Because she loved the genre so much she decided to try her hand at creating her own romantic worlds. She still loves a good happily-ever-after story.

When not writing Susan doubles as a high school substitute teacher, which she has been doing for sixteen years. Susan lives in Georgia with her husband of twenty-eight years and has four grown children. She loves castles, travelling, cross-stitching, hats, James Bond and hearing from her readers.

Books by Susan Carlisle

Mills & Boon® Medical Romance™

Heart of Mississippi

The Maverick Who Ruled Her Heart
The Doctor Who Made Her Love Again

The Doctor's Redemption
Snowbound with Dr Delectable
NYC Angels: The Wallflower's Secret
Hot-Shot Doc Comes to Town
The Nurse He Shouldn't Notice
Heart Surgeon, Hero...Husband?

Visit the author profile page at millsandboon.co.uk for more titles

Joseph.
Thanks for being a great tool.

CHAPTER ONE

What am I doing here? Phoebe Taylor asked herself for the hundredth time, pulling her light coat closer. She could no longer get it to meet in the middle. Bowing her head against a gust of Melbourne, Australia, wind, she walked on. It would rain soon.

She looked at the name on the street sign. Morris Lane. This was the correct place. Phoebe didn't even have to check the paper in her hand that was shoved into her pocket. She had it memorized. She'd read it often during the past few weeks.

When had she turned into such a pathetic and needy person?

It had happened slowly, over the last eight months as her middle had expanded. She'd always heard that a baby changed you. She'd had no idea how true those words were until it had happened to her. She was even more fearful of the changes she faced in the weeks ahead. The fact she'd be handling them all on her own, had no one to rely on, frightened her.

She started down the cobblestone street lined with town houses. Joshua had written that if she needed anything she could contact Ryan Matthews. But who was she to him? An old army buddy's wife. People said those types of things all the time but few meant them. But she had no one else to turn to. There were teachers she worked with, but they all had their own lives, husbands and children. They didn't have time to hold her hand. There were plenty of acquaintances but none that she would call on. She'd take this chance because Joshua had said to. And this was Joshua's baby.

But would this guy Ryan help her? Be there for her during the delivery afterwards? Take Joshua's place at the birthing suite? *Yeah, right.* She didn't see any man agreeing to that job. Who took on someone else's widow and unborn child? She could never ask that of him. Would she want to? She didn't know this man outside of Joshua saying he was an upstanding mate.

When the walls of reality had started closing in on her and panic had arrived, she'd been unable to think of where to turn. Joshua's letter had called to her. Seemed to offer her salvation. Phoebe inhaled and released a breath. She'd come this far. She wouldn't turn back now. What was the worst Ryan Matthews could do? Send her away? Act like he'd never heard of her?

What she was sure of was she didn't want to feel alone anymore. She wanted someone to lean on. Be near a person who had a connection to Joshua. Hear a story or two that she could tell her son or daughter about their father. Joshua and Ryan had been brothers in arms. Been there for each other. Joshua had assured her in his last letter seven months ago that if she needed anything, *anything*, Ryan was the person to find. Desperate, she was going to his house to see if that was true.

Phoebe located the house number. It was painted above the door in black against the white frame of the Victorian house. The car traveling down the street drew her attention for a second. She pulled the paper out and looked at the address again, then at the entrance once more. Studying the steps to the door, she hesitated. Now she was stalling.

What was she going to say to this guy?

She'd been rehearsing her speech for days and still didn't know if she could get it out. On the tram coming across town she'd practiced again but couldn't seem to get it right. Everything she'd planned made her sound crazy. Maybe she was. But she had to say something, give some explanation as to why she'd turned up on his doorstep.

Hi, I'm Phoebe Taylor. You were a friend of my husband's. He said if I ever needed anything to come see you. So here I am.

That should get his attention. She placed a hand on her protruding middle and chuckled dryly. *His first thought will probably be I'm here to accuse him of being the father.*

The wind gusted again as she mounted the steps. There were no potted plants lining them, like most of the other houses. Holding the handrail, she all but pulled her way up to the stoop. Could she get any bigger? Her midwife Sophia had assured her she could, and would.

After catching her breath, Phoebe knocked on the door. She waited. Thankfully, the small alcove afforded her some shelter from the wind.

When there was no answer, she rapped again. Seconds went by and still no one came. She refused to go back home without speaking to Ryan. It had taken her months to muster the courage to come in the first place. It was getting late, surely he'd be home soon.

To the right side of the door was a small wooden bench. She'd just wait for a while to see if he showed up.

Bracing a hand against the wall, she eased herself down. She chuckled humorously at the picture she must make. Like a beach ball sitting on top of a flowerpot.

She needed to rest anyway. Everything fatigued her these days. Trying to keep up with twenty grade fivers wore her out but she loved her job. At least her students kept her mind off the fact that she was having a baby soon. Alone.

Phoebe never made a habit of feeling sorry for herself, had prided herself on being strong, facing life head-on. She'd always managed to sound encouraging and supportive when Joshua had prepared to leave on tour again and again. When they'd married, she'd been aware of what she was getting into. So why was the idea of having this baby alone making her come emotionally undone?

Pulling her coat tighter and leaning her head into the corner of the veranda, she closed her eyes. She'd just rest a few minutes.

It was just after dark when Ryan Matthews pulled his sporty compact car into his usual parking spot along the street. It had been drizzling during his entire drive from the hospital. Street lamps lit the area. The trees cast shadows along the sidewalk and even across the steps leading to homes.

He'd had a long day that had involved more than one baby delivery and one of those a tough one. Nothing had seemed to go as planned. Not one but two of the babies had been breech. Regardless, the babies had joined the world kicking and screaming. He was grateful. All the other difficulties seemed to disappear the second he heard a healthy cry. He'd take welcoming a life over dealing with death any day.

Stepping out of the car, he reached behind the driver's seat and grabbed his duffel bag stuffed with his street clothes. Too exhausted to change, he still wore his hospital uniform. As much as he loved his job, thirty-six hours straight was plenty. He was looking forward to a hot shower, bed and the next day off. It would be his first chance in over two weeks to spend time in his workshop. A half-finished chair, along with a table he'd promised to repair for a friend, waited. He wanted to think of nothing and just enjoy the process of creating something with his hands.

Duffel in hand, a wad of dirty uniforms under his arm, he climbed the steps. The light remained on over his door as he'd left it. Halfway up the steps he halted. There was an obviously pregnant woman asleep on his porch. He saw pregnant women regularly in his job as a midwife at Melbourne Victoria Hospital's maternity unit. Today more than he'd wanted to. As if he didn't have a full load at the hospital, they were now showing up on his doorstep.

By the blue tint of the woman's lips and the way she was huddled into a ball, she'd been there for some time. Why was she out in the cold? She should be taking better care of herself, especially at this stage in her pregnancy. Her arms rested on her protruding middle. She wore a fashionable knit cap that covered the top of her head. Strawberry-blond hair twisted around her face and across her shoulders. With the rain and the temperature dropping, she must be uncomfortable.

Taking a resigned breath, Ryan moved farther up the steps. As he reached the top the mysterious woman roused and her eyes popped open. They were large and a dark sable brown with flecks of gold. He'd never seen more mesmerizing or sad ones in his life.

His first instinct was to protect her. He faltered. That wasn't a feeling he experienced often. He made it his practice not to become involved with anyone. Not to care too deeply. He tamped the feeling down. Being tired was all there was to it. "Can I help you?"

The woman slowly straightened. She tugged the not-heavy-enough-for-the-weather coat closer as she stared at him.

When she didn't answer right away he asked in a weary voice, "Do you need help?"

"Are you Ryan Matthews?" Her soft Aussie accent carried in the evening air.

His eyes widened and he stepped back half a pace, stopping before tumbling. Did he know her? She was such a tiny thing she couldn't be more than a girl. Something about her looked familiar. Could he have seen her in the waiting room sometime?

Ryan glanced at her middle again. He'd always made it a practice to use birth control. Plus, this female was far too young for him. She must be seeking medical help.

"Yes."

"I'm Phoebe Taylor."

Was that supposed to mean something to him? He squinted, studying her face in the dim light. "Have we met before?"

"I should go." She reached out to touch the wall as if she planned to use it as support in order to stand. When she did, a slip of paper fluttered to the stoop.

Ryan picked it up. In blue pen was written his name, address and phone number. Had she been given it at the clinic?

He glared at her. "Where did you get this?"

"I think I had better go." She made a movement toward the steps. "I'm sorry. I shouldn't have come. I'll go."

"I'm afraid I don't understand."

"I don't know for sure what I wanted. I need to go." Her words came out high-pitched and shaky.

He put out a hand as if she were a skittish animal he was trying to reassure. "Think of the baby." That must be what this was all about.

Her eyes widened, taking on a hysterical look. She jerked away from him. "I've done nothing but think of this baby. I have to go. I'm sorry I shouldn't have come." She sniffled. "I don't know..." another louder sniffle "...what I was thinking. You don't know me." Her head went into her hands and she started to cry in earnest. "I'll go. This is..." she sucked in air "...too embarrassing. You must think I'm mad."

He began to think she was. Who acted this way?

She struggled to stand. Ryan took her elbow and helped her.

"I've never done anything...like this before. I need to go."

Ryan could only make out a few of her garbled words through her weeping. He glanced around. If she continued to carry on like this his neighbors would be calling the law.

She shivered. What had she said her name was? Phoebe?

"You need to calm down. Being so upset isn't good for the baby. It's getting cold out and dark. Come in. Let your jacket dry." He needed to get her off the street so he could figure out what this was all about. This wasn't what he had planned for his evening.

"No, I've already embarrassed myself enough. I think I'd better go."

Thankfully the crying had stopped but it had left her eyes large and luminous.

She looked up at him with those eyes laced with something close to pain, and said in a low voice, "You knew my husband."

"Your husband?"

"Joshua Taylor."

Ryan cringed. Air quit moving to his lungs. JT was part of his past. The piece of his life he had put behind him. Ryan hadn't heard JT's name in seven months. Not since he'd had word that he had been killed when his convoy had been bombed.

Why was his wife here? Ryan didn't want to think of the war, or JT. He'd moved on.

They had been buddies while they'd been in Iraq. Ryan had been devastated when he'd heard JT had been killed. He'd been one more in a long list of men Ryan had cared about, shared his life with, had considered family. Now that was gone, all gone. He wasn't going to let himself feel that pain ever again. When he'd left the service he'd promised himself never to let anyone matter that much. He wasn't dragging those ugly memories up for anyone's wife, not even JT's.

Ryan had known there was a wife, had even seen her picture fixed to Joshua's CHU or containerized housing unit room. That had been over five years ago, before he'd left the service. This was his friend's widow?

He studied her. Yes, she did bear a resemblance to the young, bright-faced girl in the pictures. Except that spark of life that had fascinated him back then had left her eyes.

"You need to come in and get warm, then I'll see you get home." He used his midwife-telling-the-mother-to-push voice.

She made a couple of soft sniffling sounds but said no more.

Ryan unlocked the door. Pushing it back, he offered her space to enter before him. She accepted the invitation. She stopped in the middle of the room as if unsure what to do next. He turned on the light and dropped his bag and dirty clothes in the usual spot on top of all the other dirty clothes lying next to the door.

For the first time, he noted what sparse living conditions he maintained. He had a sofa, a chair, a TV that sat on a wooden crate and was rarely turned on. Not a single picture hung on the walls. He didn't care about any of that. It wasn't important. All he was interested in was bringing babies safely into the world and the saws in his workshop.

"Have a seat. I'll get you some tea," he said in a gruff voice.

Bracing on the arm of the sofa, she lowered herself to the cushion. She pulled the knit cap from her head and her hair fell around her shoulders.

Ryan watched, stunned by the sight. The urge to touch those glowing tresses caught him by surprise. His fingers tingled to test the texture, to see if it was as soft and silky as it looked.

Her gaze lifted, meeting his. Her cheekbones were high and a touch of pink from the cold made the fairness of her skin more noticeable. Her chin trembled. The sudden fear that she might start crying again went through him. He cleared his throat. "I'll get you that tea."

* * *

Phoebe watched as the rather stoic American man walked out of the room. Why had he looked at her that way? Where was all that compassion and caring that Joshua had written about in his letter? Ryan obviously wanted her gone as soon as possible. He wasn't at all what she'd expected. Nothing like Joshua had described him. She shivered, the cold and damp seeping through her jacket. What had she been thinking? This wasn't the warm and welcoming guy that Joshua had said he would be. He hadn't even reacted to her mentioning Joshua.

He was tall, extremely tall. He ducked slightly to go through the doorway. Joshua had been five feet eleven. Ryan Matthews was far taller, with shoulders that went with that height.

Though he was an attractive man with high cheekbones and a straight nose, his eyes held a melancholy gaze. As if he'd seen things and had had to do things he never wanted to remember, much less talk about.

A few minutes later Ryan handed her a mug with a teabag string hanging over the side. He hadn't even bothered to ask her what she wanted to drink. Did he treat everybody he met with such disinterest?

"I'm a coffee drinker myself. An associate left the tea here or I wouldn't have had it."

She bet it was a female friend. He struck her as the type of man who had women around him all the time. "You are an American."

"Yes."

"Joshua never said that you weren't Australian."

He took a seat in the lone chair in the room. "I guess he didn't notice after a while."

She looked around. Whatever women he brought here

didn't stay around long. His place showed nothing of the feminine touch. In fact, it was only just a step above unlivable. If she had to guess, there was nothing but a bed and a carton for a table in the bedroom.

Phoebe watched him drink the coffee, the smell of which wafted her way as she took a sip of her tea.

Quiet minutes later he asked, "How long were you on my doorstep?'

"I don't know. I left home around four."

"It's after seven now." His tone was incredulous. "You've been waiting that long?"

"I fell asleep."

The tension left his face. "That's pretty easy to do in your condition."

"I can't seem to make it without a nap after teaching all day."

"Teaching?"

"I teach at Fillmore Primary School. Grade Five."

He seemed as if he was trying to remember something. "That's right. JT said you were going to school to be a teacher."

At the mention of Joshua they both looked away.

He spoke more to his coffee cup than to her. "I was sorry to hear about Joshua."

"Me, too." He and Joshua were supposed to have been best buddies and that was all he had to say. This guy was so distant he acted as if he'd barely known Joshua. She wouldn't be getting any help or friendship from him.

He looked at her then as if he was unsure about what he might have heard. "Is there something you need from me?"

Phoebe flinched at his directness. Not anymore. She needed to look elsewhere. She wasn't sure what she'd expected from him but this wasn't it. Joshua's letter had assured her that Ryan Matthews would do anything to help her but this man's attitude indicated he wasn't interested in getting involved.

"To tell you the truth, I'm not sure. You were a friend of Joshua's and I just thought..."

"And what did you think? Do you need money?"

"Mr. Matthews, I don't need your money. I have a good job and Joshua's widow and orphans' pension."

"Then I can't imagine what I can do for you, unless you need someone to deliver your baby?"

"Why would I come to you for that?"

"Because I'm a midwife."

"I thought he said you were a medic."

"I was in the army but now I work as a midwife. I still don't understand why you're here. If you need someone to deliver your baby you need to come to the Prenatal Clinic during office hours."

"I already have one. Sophia Toulson."

His brows drew together. "She's leaving soon. Did she send you here?"

She lowered her head.

Had he heard her say, "I just needed a friend, I guess."

A friend?

He couldn't believe that statement. What kind of person showed up at a stranger's house, asking them to be their friend? Surely she had family and friends in town. Why would she come looking for him now? After all this time. She said she didn't need money so what did she want from him?

"Where's the father of the baby?"

Phoebe sat straighter and looked him directly in the eyes. "Joshua is the father of the baby."

"When...?"

"When he was last home on leave. I wrote to him about the baby but he was..." she swallowed hard "...gone by then." She placed the cup in the crack between the cushions, unable to bend down far enough to put it on the floor. Pushing herself to a standing position, she said, "I think I'd better go."

He glanced out the window. The rain had picked up and the wind was blowing stronger. He huffed as he unfolded from the chair. "I'll drive you home."

"That's not necessary. I can catch the tram."

"Yeah, but you'll get wet getting there and from it to your house. I'll drive you. Where's home?"

Despite his tough exterior, she liked his voice. It was slow, deep and rich. Maybe a Texan or Georgian drawl. "I live in Box Hill."

"That's out toward Ferntree Gully, isn't it?"

"Yes."

"Okay. Let's go."

He sounded resigned to driving her instead of being helpful. This Ryan Matthews didn't seem to care one way or another. Had Joshua gotten him wrong or had Ryan changed?

"If you insist."

"I do." He was already heading toward the door.

"Then thank you."

This trip to see Ryan had been a mistake on a number of levels. But she had learned one thing. She was definitely alone in the world.

Forty-five minutes later, Ryan pulled onto a tree-lined street with California bungalow-style houses. The lights glowing in the homes screamed warmth, caring and permanency, all the things that he didn't have in his life, didn't want or deserve.

Since they'd left his place Phoebe hadn't tried to make conversation. She'd only spoken when giving him directions. He was no closer than he'd been earlier to knowing what she wanted.

"Next left," she said in a monotone.

He turned there she indicated.

"Last house on the right. The one with the veranda light on."

Ryan pulled his car to the curb. He looked at her house. It appeared well cared-for. A rosebush grew abundantly in the front yard. An archway indicated the main door. The only light shining was the one over it.

"Is anyone expecting you?"

"No."

"You live by yourself?"

"Yes. Did you think I lived with my parents?"

"I just thought since Joshua was gone and you were having a baby, someone would be nearby. Especially as close as you're obviously getting to the due date."

"No, there's no one. My parents were killed in an auto accident the year before I married. My only brother had moved to England two years before that. We were never really close. There is a pretty large age difference between us." The words were matter-of-fact but she sounded lost.

"Surely someone from Joshua's family is planning to help out?"

"No."

"Really? Why not?"

"If you must know, they didn't want him to marry me. They had someone else picked out. Now that he's gone, they want nothing more to do with me."

"That must have been hard to hear."

"Yeah. It hurt." Her tone said she still was having a hard time dealing with that knowledge. He couldn't imagine someone not wanting to have anything to do with their grandchild.

"Not even the baby?"

She placed her hand on her belly. "Not even the baby. They told me it would be too hard to look at him or her and know Joshua wasn't here."

"You've got to be kidding!" Ryan's hands tightened on the steering wheel.

"No. That isn't something that I would kid about."

"I'm sorry."

"So am I. But I just think of it as their loss. If that's the way they feel, then it wouldn't ever be healthy for the baby to be around them. We'll be better off without them."

Ryan looked at the house one more time. By its appearance, the baby would be well cared for and loved. "I'll see you to the door."

"That's not necessary." She opened the car door.

He climbed out and hurried around the automobile. She'd started to her feet. He held out a hand. After a second she accepted it. His larger one swallowed her smaller one. Hers was soft and smooth, very feminine. So very different from his. A few seconds later she seemed to gather strength. She removed her hand from his and stood taller.

"Come on, I'll see you to the door." Even to his own ears it sounded as if he was ready to get rid of her.

"I'll be fine. You've already helped enough by driving me home." She started up the walk lined with flowers and stopped, then looked back at him. "I'm sorry to have bothered you."

Ryan waited to see if she would turn around again, but she didn't. When the light went out on the porch he pulled away from the curb.

Phoebe closed the door behind her with a soft click. Through the small window she saw the lights of Ryan's car as he drove off.

What had she expected? That he would immediately say, "I'll take care of you, I'll be there for you"? She moved through the house without turning any lights on. She knew where every piece of furniture and every lamp was located. With the exception of the few times that Joshua had been home during their marriage, no one had lived with her. Nothing was ever moved unless she did it.

Their marriage had consisted mostly of them living apart. They had met when she was eighteen and fresh out of school. The tall, dark man dressed in a uniform had taken her breath away. Joshua had made it clear what it would be like, being married to a serviceman, and she had been willing to take on that life. She was strong and could deal with it.

It hurt terribly that his parents had said they wouldn't be around to help her with the baby. He or she needed grandparents in their life. With her parents gone they were the only ones. She'd been devastated when she'd received the letter stating they would not be coming around. They had sent some money. Phoebe had thought about returning it but had decided to start a fund at the bank for the baby instead. Not knowing their grandchild would be their loss.

For her the baby was about having a small part of Joshua still in her life. Her hope was that Joshua's parents might change their minds. Either way, right now she was on her own. Not a feeling she enjoyed. In a moment of weakness she'd gone to Ryan's house, but she didn't plan to let him know how bone deep the hurt was that Joshua's parents wanted nothing to do with her. How lonely she was for someone who'd known and loved Joshua.

She turned on the lamp beside her bed and glanced at the picture of her and Joshua smiling. They'd been married eight years but had spent maybe a year together in total. That had been a week or two here, or a month there. They had always laughed that their marriage was like being on vacation instead of the day in, day out experience of living together. Even their jobs had been vastly different. Joshua had found his place in the service more than with her. She'd found contentment in teaching. It had given her the normalcy and stability that being married to a husband who popped in and out hadn't.

Each time Joshua had come home it had been like the first heart-pounding, whirlwind and all-consuming first love that had soon died out and become the regular thud of everyday life. They'd had to relearn each other and getting in the groove had seemed harder to achieve. As they'd grown older they'd both seemed to pull away. She'd had her set life and routine and Joshua had invaded it when he'd returned.

Removing her clothes, she laid them over a chair and pulled her pj's out of the chest of drawers. She groaned. The large T-shirt reminded her of a tent that she and Joshua had camped in just after they'd married. The shirt was huge and still she almost filled it.

Pulling it over her head, she rubbed her belly. The baby had been a complete surprise. She'd given up on ever having children. She and Joshua had decided not to have them since he hadn't been home often enough. She wasn't sure whether or not she'd cared when they'd married or if she'd believed he would leave the army and come home to stay. The idea of having a family had been pushed far into the future. It had become easier just not to consider it. So when she'd come up pregnant it had been a shock.

Her fingers went to her middle, then to her eye, pushing the moisture away. She'd grown up with the dream of having a family one day. Now she was starting a family but with half of it missing.

She pulled the covers back on the bed and climbed in between the cool sheets. Bringing the blanket up around her, she turned on her side, stuffing an extra pillow between the mattress and her tummy. The baby kicked. She laid her hand over the area, feeling the tiny heel that pushed against her side.

The last time Joshua had been home they'd even talked of separating. They'd spent so little time together she'd felt like she hadn't even known her husband anymore. She not only carried Joshua's baby but the guilt that he'd died believing she no longer cared. Friendship had been there but not the intense love that she should have had for a husband.

CHAPTER TWO

THE NEXT MORNING Ryan flipped on the light switch that lit the stairs that led down to his workshop. He'd picked out this town house because of this particular space. Because it was underground it helped block the noise of the saws from the neighbors. The area was also close to the hospital, which made it nice when he had to be there quickly.

Going down the stairs, he scanned the area. A band saw filled one corner, while stationed in the center of the room was a table saw. The area Ryan was most interested in right now was the workbench against the far wall. There lay the half-made chair that he had every intention of finishing today. He would still have to spend another few days staining it.

Picking up a square piece of sandpaper, he began running it up and down one of the curved rockers. He'd made a couple of rockers when the nursery of the hospital had needed new ones. A number of the nurses had been so impressed they'd wanted one of their own. Since then he'd been busy filling orders in his spare time.

Outside the moments when a baby was born and offered its first spirited view of the new world with a shout, being in his shop was the place he was the most happy. Far better than his life in the military.

When he could stand it no longer, he'd resigned his commission. He'd had enough of torn bodies. He ran his hand along the expanse of the wood. It was level but not quite smooth enough. Now he was doing something he loved. But thoughts of Phoebe kept intruding.

He couldn't believe that had been Joshua's wife at his home the night before. Ryan had been living in Melbourne for five years. Joshua had always let him know when he was home, but in all that time he'd never met his wife. It had seemed like his friend's visits had come at the busiest times, and even though the two of them had managed to have a drink together, Ryan had never seen her. Now all of a sudden she had turned up on his doorstep.

Even after he'd gotten her calmed down he hadn't been sure what she'd wanted. It didn't matter. Still, he owed Joshua. He should check on her. But first he'd see what Sophia could tell him.

The next morning, at the clinic, Ryan flipped through his schedule for the day. He had a number of patients to see but none had babies due any time soon. Maybe he would get a few days' reprieve before things got wild again.

"You look deep in thought."

He recognized Sophia's voice and looked up. "Not that deep. You're just the person I wanted to talk to."

The slim woman took one of the functional office chairs in front of his desk. "What can I do for you?"

"I was just wondering what you know about Phoebe Taylor."

"Trying to steal my patients now?" Her eyes twinkled as she asked.

Ryan gave her a dubious look.

She grinned. "She's due in about five weeks. What's happened?"

"She was waiting for me when I got home yesterday. At first I thought she'd gotten my name and address from you. That you were sending her to me because you would be on your honeymoon when it was time to deliver."

Sophia shook her dark-haired head. "Oh, no, it wasn't me. But I remember she mentioned you at one of her appointments and said she had your address."

"I thought maybe she was looking for a midwife. She later told me she was the wife of an army buddy of mine."

"Yes, she told me that you were good friends with her husband. Did she seem okay?"

"Not really. It was all rather confusing and she was quite emotional. I let her get warm, gave her something to drink and took her home."

"She's usually steady as a rock. I'll find out what's going on at her next appointment."

"Thanks, Sophia. I owe her husband."

"I understand. You are coming to my wedding, aren't you?"

Sophia was marrying Aiden Harrison in a few weeks and she wanted everyone there for the event. Ryan wasn't into weddings. He'd never been so close to someone he'd felt like marrying them. After his years in the military he was well aware of how short life could be. Too young to really understand that kind of love when he'd entered the army, he'd soon realized he didn't want to put someone through what Phoebe Taylor had been experiencing.

He didn't understand that type of love. Knew how fleeting it could be. His parents sure hadn't known how to show love. His foster-parents had been poor examples of that also. They had taken care of his physical needs but he'd always been aware that they hadn't really cared about him. The army had given him purpose that had filled that void, for a while. That had lasted for years until the hundreds of faces of death had become heavier with every day. He well understood that losses lasted a lifetime. Even delivering babies and seeing the happiness on families' faces didn't change that. Those men he'd served with were gone. Yet, like JT, they were always with him.

He smiled at Sophia. "I plan to be there. I'll even dust off my suit for the occasion."

"That's great. See you later."

Ryan had seen his last patient for the day and was headed out the glass doors of the Prenatal Clinic in the hospital. A woman was coming in. He stopped to hold the door for her, then glanced up. It was Phoebe Taylor.

"Ah, hey."

"Hello." Her gaze flicked up at him and then away.

Phoebe must have been coming here for months. How many times had he passed her without having any idea who she was? She looked far less disheveled than she had two days ago. Her hair lay along her shoulders. Dressed in a brown, tan and blue dotted top over brown slacks and low-heeled shoes, she looked professional, classy and fragile.

"Are you looking for me?" Ryan asked.

"I'm here for my appointment with Sophia."

Another mother-to-be came up behind Phoebe. She moved back and out of the way, allowing the woman to go past her. Ryan held the door wide, moving out into the hall. He said to Phoebe, "May I speak to you for a minute?"

A terrified look flicked in her eyes before she gave him a resigned nod. He had the impression that if she could forget they had already met, she'd gladly do so.

Before he could say anything she started, "About the other evening. I'm sorry. I shouldn't have put you on the spot. I had no right to do that."

Here she was the one apologizing and he was the one who should be. "Not a problem. I should have visited you after Joshua died."

Her look was earnest. "That's all right. I understand. Well, I have to get to my appointment."

Apparently whatever she'd needed had been resolved. "It was nice to meet you, Phoebe."

"You, too." She walked by him, opened the door and went through it. With a soft swish it closed behind her.

Why did he feel as if he needed to say or do more?

Ryan made it as far as his car before curiosity and a nagging guilt caused him to return to the clinic. He waited until Phoebe was finished with her appointment. Phoebe might not agree to him taking her to dinner, but he was going to try. He needed to know why she'd come to see him and even more if there was some way he could help her.

Now that she had contacted him he felt like he owed Joshua that.

On the way to his office he passed a nurse and asked that she let him know when Mrs. Taylor was finished.

Thirty minutes later the nurse popped her head in the door and said Phoebe was on her way out.

Ryan hurried to the waiting room and spotted her as she reached the door. When he called her name she stopped and turned. Her eyes widened in astonishment, then filled with wariness.

"I thought you had left." Phoebe sounded as if she had hoped not to see him again. After his behavior the other night he shouldn't be surprised.

"I came back. I wanted to ask you something."

She raised her brows.

Phoebe wasn't opening the door wide for him. She wouldn't be making this easy.

Thankfully this late in the day the waiting room was empty. "I wondered if I could buy you dinner?"

Phoebe turned her head slightly, as if both studying and judging him. He must have really put her off the other evening. He prided himself on his rapport with people, especially pregnant women and their families. He had let this one down. The guilt he'd felt doubled in size.

"Please. I'd like to make up for how I acted the other night."

"You don't owe me any apologies. I'm the one who showed up on your doorstep unannounced."

"Why don't we both stop taking blame and agree to start again?"

Her eyes became less unsure. "I guess we could do that."

"Then why don't we start by having a burger together?"

"Okay." She agreed with less enthusiasm than he would have liked.

"I know a place just down the street that serves good food. Andrew's Burgers."

"I've heard of it but never been there."

"Great. Do you mind walking?"

"No, I haven't had my exercise today."

Ryan looked at her. If it hadn't been for the baby, she would have been a slim woman. With her coloring she was an eye-catcher, pregnant or not. Her soft, lilting voice was what really caught his attention.

"If you'll wait I'd like to lock up my office."

She nodded. When he returned she was sitting in one of the reclining chairs in the waiting room with her hands resting on the baby.

"I'm ready."

Phoebe looked at him. She pushed against the chair arm to support herself as she stood. "I think this baby is going to be a giant."

"Every mother-to-be that I see thinks that about this time."

As they made their way down the hall to the elevators, Ryan asked, "So how're you and the baby doing?"

A soft smile came to her lips. "Sophia says we're both doing great. I'll have to start coming to clinic every week soon. I just hate that I'm losing her as my midwife. I've become very attached."

"You are getting close."

"I am."

There was depression in her tone that he didn't understand. He knew little about her, but she struck him as someone who would be ecstatic about holding a new life in her hands and caring for someone. Yet he sensed a need in her that he couldn't put a finger on.

They went down the six floors to the lobby of the art deco building and out into the sunlight. The restaurant was a few blocks from the hospital.

"Let's cross the street. I know a shortcut through the park."

She followed him without question. A few minutes later they exited the park and were once again walking along the sidewalk. A couple of times they had to work themselves around other people walking briskly in the opposite direction. Ryan matched his stride to her shorter one and ran interference when someone looked as if they might bump into her.

"I can walk without help, you know."

He glanced at her. She was small but she gave off an air of confidence. It was in complete contrast to her actions that night at his house. Something was going on with her. "I know, but I wouldn't want you to accidentally fall and Sophia would have my head for it."

"I think they gave up chopping off heads in Australia a long time ago," she said in a dry tone.

"Still, I'm kind of scared of Sophia. I don't know if I could face her if I let you get hurt."

That got a smile out of her. "Here we are," Ryan said as he pulled the glass door of the restaurant open and allowed Phoebe to enter ahead of him.

She wasn't sure sharing a meal with Ryan was such a good idea. He'd asked nicely enough and she hadn't eaten out in so long she hadn't had the heart to say no. She suspected either his curiosity or some kind of obligation he felt toward Joshua had made him ask. No way had he changed overnight into being the emotional support she'd naively hoped he might be. A nice meal shared with someone was all she expected to get out of the next hour.

When Ryan was asked if they wanted a booth or table he glanced at her middle and grinned. He had a wide smile and nice even teeth. "I guess we'd better go for a table."

They were directed to one. The restaurant was decorated in a 1950s diner style, all chrome, red-covered chairs and white tile on the floor. Lighting hung over each booth and table. It was still early for the dinner crowd so it wasn't noisy. Phoebe wasn't sure if she considered that good or bad.

She took a seat. Ryan sat in the chair across the table from her.

"So I need to order a hamburger, I'm thinking." Phoebe took the menu out of the metal rack on the table.

"They have good ones. But there are also other things just as good."

The waitress arrived and took their drink order. Phoebe opened a menu but Ryan didn't. When the waitress returned with their glasses, she asked what they would like to order. Phoebe decided on the burger without onions and Ryan ordered his with everything.

The waitress left and Ryan asked, "No onions?"

"They don't agree with me."

"That's typical. I know a mother who said she couldn't cook bacon the entire first three months of her pregnancy."

"Smells used to bother me but that has become better."

Ryan crossed his arms and leaned on the table. "So do you know if it's a boy or a girl?"

"I don't know."

"Really?"

Phoebe almost laughed at his look of shock. "Don't want to know. I like surprises."

"That's pretty amazing in this day and age where everyone is wanting to know the sex and you don't. I wouldn't want to know, either. One of my favorite moments during a delivery is the look on the parents' faces when they discover the sex."

Phoebe got the impression that she'd gone up a notch in his estimation.

"You know, I don't know any other male midwife."

"There are only a few of us around. More in Australia than in the US."

"So why did you become one?"

"I wanted to do something that made me smile." He picked up his drink. "I was tired of watching people's lives being destroyed or lost when I was in the service. I wanted to do something that involved medicine but had a happy ending. What's better than bringing a life into the world?"

He was right. What was better than that?

The waitress brought their meals. They didn't speak for a while.

It fascinated Phoebe that they were virtual strangers but seem to be content sharing a meal together. This evening stood in sharp contrast to when they had met. Being around this Ryan put her at ease for some reason. After their first meeting she would have sworn that couldn't be possible.

She ate half her burger and chips before pushing them aside.

"You're eating for two, you know," Ryan said with a raised brow.

"The problem is that when this baby comes I don't want to look like I ate for three." She wiped her mouth with her napkin and placed it on the table.

"How's your weight gain?"

Phoebe leaned back in her chair. "That's certainly a personal question."

"I'm a midwife. I ask that question all the time."

"Yes, but you aren't my midwife."

He pushed his empty plate away. "I'll concede that. But I'm only asking out of concern."

"If it'll make you feel better my weight is just fine. I'm within the guidelines."

"Good. You look like you're taking care of yourself."

"I try to eat right and get some exercise every day." She looked pointedly at her plate. "Not that this burger was on the healthy chart."

He shrugged. "No, it probably isn't, but every once in a while it's okay."

They lapsed into silence again as the waitress refilled their glasses and took away their plates.

A few minutes later Phoebe said, "I know this might be tough but I was wondering if you might be willing to tell me some stories about Joshua. Something I could tell the baby. Something about him outside of just what I remember."

Ryan's lips tightened and he didn't meet her gaze.

"You don't have to if you don't want to."

After a moment he met her look. "What would you like to know?"

"I guess anything. I feel like you knew him better than me. You spent far more time together than we did. I was wondering how you met?"

Ryan's gray eyes took on a faraway look. "The Aussie and the US troops didn't always hit it off, but JT and I did. We didn't usually work together, but I was asked to go out on patrol with his platoon. Their medic was on leave and the replacement hadn't made it in yet. My commander agreed. It was supposed to be an easy in and out of a village under our control. All went well until we were headed out, then all hell broke loose. The Iraqis had us pinned down and we couldn't expect help until the next morning.

"A couple of JT's men were seriously injured. While

we spent long hours hunkered down together we got to know each other pretty well. He told me about you, and I told him about growing up in Texas.

"When I told him that I was tired of having to patch up people that another human had destroyed, he encouraged me to do something different. Even suggested I move to Australia for a new start. He joked that if he ever left the army he'd use his skills to become a police officer."

Phoebe had never heard Joshua say anything about wanting to do that. He had told Ryan things he either hadn't wanted to share with her or couldn't. It made her sad and angry at the same time. She and Joshua had just not been as close as a married couple should have been.

"After that kind of night you know each other pretty well. We started getting together for drinks whenever we had leave at the same time." His eyes didn't meet hers. "JT found out that I didn't get much mail so he shared his letters with me."

For seconds Phoebe panicked, trying to remember what she had said in her letters. Misery overtook the panic. During the last few years of their marriage her letters had been less about them personally and more about what was happening with her students, how Melbourne was changing, what she was doing at the house. It had been as if she'd been writing to a friend instead of her husband.

"I always looked forward to your letters. They were full of news and I liked to hear about your class. The letters your students wrote were the best. There was something about them that helped make all the ugliness disappear for a while."

"I'm glad they helped. My students liked writing them.

Thank you for telling me about Joshua. I guess I just wanted to talk about him. This is his baby and he isn't around. Just hearing about him makes him seem a little closer. But it's time for me to go." She needed to think about what Ryan had told her. The fact that someone had known her husband better than she had made her feel heartsick.

Ryan stood and Phoebe did also. She led the way to the door. Outside Ryan turned in the direction of the hospital.

"I need to go this way to catch the tram. Thanks for dinner." She turned toward the left.

"I'll give you a ride home," Ryan said.

"I don't want you to drive all the way out to my house."

"I don't mind and you don't need to be so late getting home. Don't you own a car?"

"No, I can take the tram to almost anything I need."

"But you're making two-hour round trips to see Sophia. In America we can't live without a car. There isn't public transportation everywhere."

"Yes, but that's only once a month and it's worth it to have Sophia as my midwife. I wish she was going to be there for the delivery."

"I realize that I live in Australia, but I can't get used to prenatal care being called antenatal. It took me forever to tell the mothers I saw that they needed to come to the antenatal clinic. I just think prenatal."

"The ideas and ways we grow up with are hard to change."

"Yes, once an idea gets fixed in my head it's hard to make me budge. And with that thought, not to make you feel bad, but you look like you could use some rest. I'm driving you home."

"I am tired and I know now that you won't change your mind. I'm going to accept the ride."

"Good."

Ryan escorted Phoebe back to the hospital and to his car. The sidewalk wasn't near as busy as it had been earlier. It had been a long time since he'd done something as simple as stroll through a park with a woman. He couldn't remember ever doing so with one who was expecting. People smiled and greeted Phoebe. She returned them. A number of times they turned to him and offered their congratulations. The first time he began to explain but soon realized it was a waste of time. Instead, he nodded noncommittally.

"I'm sorry," Phoebe said after the first incident.

"Not your fault. You can't help what they think."

He had hardly pulled out of the parking area before Phoebe had closed her eyes. She was tired.

Ryan got a number of reactions when he told someone he was a midwife. He'd gotten used to it. But the one thing he couldn't get used to was not being able to understand all the nuances of the female body when a baby was growing inside it. The sudden ability to go to sleep anywhere and in any position was one of those. It must be like being in the army. He had learned to sleep anywhere at any time.

Phoebe blinked with the small jolt of the car stopping. She'd fallen asleep again. It was getting embarrassing.

"I'm sorry. I didn't mean to go to sleep."

"Not a problem. You're not the first woman I've put to sleep."

Phoebe gave him a questioning look. She bet she

wasn't. What had her thinking of Ryan in that suggestive way?

"I'm the one sorry this time. I didn't mean it like that."

"Like what?" She gave him her best innocent look.

"You know, like..."

Phoebe enjoyed his flustered expression and the pinkness that began to work its way up his neck.

She rested her hands on each side of her belly. "I'm well aware of the facts of life and how a man can satisfy a woman."

He grinned. "You're laughing at me now."

Phoebe chuckled. "I guess I am." She opened her car door. "Thanks for the burger and the ride. Also thanks for telling me about Joshua. You have no idea how much it means to me."

"Hey, wait a minute."

Before she could get completely out of the car Ryan had come round and was standing on the path, reaching to help her. His hand went to her elbow and he supported her as she stood. He pushed the door closed behind her and it made a thud.

"Listen, if there's anything that I can do for you..."

He sounded sincere. "I appreciate it... Uh, there is one thing I could use some help with."

"What's that?"

His voice held an eager tone as if he was looking for a chance to atone for his earlier behavior. She hated to ask him but couldn't think of another way to get it done before the baby came. "I had a bed for the baby delivered but it needs to be put together. I would pay you."

Ryan looked as if she had slapped him. "You will not. How about I come by Saturday afternoon? If I have to work I'll call and let you know, otherwise I'll be here on Saturday."

"Thank you, that would be wonderful." And she meant it. She'd spent more than one night worrying over how she was going to get that baby bed assembled.

"Not a problem. Do you have tools or do I need to bring mine?"

"You might want to bring yours. I have a few but only necessities like a hammer and screwdriver."

"Then it's a plan. Why don't you give me your number?" Ryan took out his cellphone and punched in the numbers she told him.

"I'll be here after lunch on Saturday, unless you hear differently from me."

"Thank you."

"No worries. Furniture I can do."

Something about Ryan made her believe that he had many talents if he was just willing to show them.

"Come on. I'll walk you to your door."

Phoebe didn't argue this time.

"See you Saturday." With that he turned and left her to enter her home.

She was putting her key in the lock when she noticed the curtain of her neighbor's house flutter. Mrs. Rosenheim had been watching. She would no doubt be over the next afternoon to get all the particulars about who Ryan was and how Phoebe knew him.

Ryan was as good as his word. He was there on Saturday just after lunchtime with a tool bag in his hand. Mrs. Rosenheim was sitting at Phoebe's kitchen table when the knock came at the door.

"I won't stay but I am going to check this boy out before I go."

Phoebe would have argued but it wouldn't have done her any good. Despite the fact that Mrs. Rosenheim was probably older than Phoebe's grandmother would be, she was a commanding presence and was only concerned for Phoebe's welfare. They had started taking care of each other two years ago when Phoebe had moved in.

Joshua had only been home once since she'd been living there. He'd not been impressed with Mrs. Rosenheim, calling her the "old busybody bird." Phoebe had learned to appreciate her concern. If nothing else, she knew someone would miss her if she didn't come home.

She opened the door for Ryan. "Come in."

"How're you doing?"

The question sounded like he was making pleasant conversation, but he was also looking at her with a trained eye. He smelled of sawdust with a hint of citrus. It made her want to step closer. Take a deeper breath.

"I'm feeling fine." She smiled and he nodded.

"Good. I told Sophia that I would check."

Mrs. Rosenheim shuffled into the room.

Ryan looked from her to Phoebe. "Ryan, this is my neighbor, Mrs. Rosenheim."

He sat his tool bag on the floor at his feet and extended a hand. "Nice to meet you."

"You're American."

"Yes, ma'am. Texan."

Mrs. Rosenheim made a noncommittal sound low in her throat. Ryan gave Phoebe a questioning look. She shrugged her shoulders.

"So you knew Mr. Taylor."

A guarded look came over Ryan's face. "Yes, JT and I served in Iraq together."

"Bad thing, leaving Phoebe here all by herself all the time. A man should want to be at home with his wife. She needs someone to watch over her. Help her."

Phoebe didn't miss the color wash out of Ryan's face.

"It was his job. The army," Phoebe said quietly.

"I know, sweetie. But a woman not only wants a man to help put a roof over her head but to be around when the times are hard." She directed the last few words at Ryan.

"Uh, Mrs. Rosenheim, I think we need to let Ryan get started on the bed. I'm sure he has other places he needs to go today." Phoebe shook her head at him when she started to say something.

"I'm next door if you need me." Mrs. Rosenheim made her way out with a last glance at Ryan.

"Formidable lady," Ryan said with a grin.

"Yes. She and Joshua didn't like each other on sight, but she's been good to me. She was with the men who came from the military department to tell me about Joshua. I don't know what I would have done without her shoulder to cry on. She's also the one who realized I was pregnant when I started being sick."

Phoebe suddenly needed to focus on something else. She shook away the memories. Ryan was the first male to have come into her home in over a year. He seemed to take up the entire space. "Anyway, let me show you where the bed is."

Ryan followed Phoebe down a hallway that had four doors leading off of it. She stopped at the next to last one and nudged the door open.

Against one wall was a large brown box that Ryan

guessed was the baby bed. That didn't surprise him. What did were the piles of books stacked around the room and the desk painted in a folk art style with a chair of the same kind sitting in one corner. The walls were painted a dark gray. Two cans of paint sat in another corner. He fully expected to see a room decorated in all the frills and with toys waiting for a baby. He'd listened to enough mothers talk about what they had done in the baby's room or were going to do to know that Phoebe was far behind in her preparations.

She placed her hand on the box. "This is the bed."

"Great. I'll get it put together."

Walking to the door, she looked back at him. "You didn't have to agree to this, but I really appreciate you doing it."

"Not a problem."

He'd been working for an hour when Phoebe returned to stand in the doorway. His back was to her but he felt her presence.

"I brought you something to drink." She moved to the desk and placed the drink on it.

Ryan stood from where he'd been tightening a screw on the back of the bed. He picked up the glass, took a long swallow of water and put it back on the desk again.

Phoebe had an odd look on her face that quickly disappeared.

Ryan said, "I guess I'm doing pretty well. I don't think I'm going to have but two screws and one thingamajig left over."

She laughed.

Had he ever heard anything more beautiful? It was almost musical. He vowed then to give her a reason to laugh often.

"My father always said that if you didn't have parts left over then you didn't put it together correctly."

"Where did you grow up?"

"In a small town about fifty miles from here."

"Is that where you met JT?"

"Yeah. We had a military base nearby. I worked at a local restaurant and Joshua and some of his mates came in for dinner one night and sat at my table."

"And, as they say, the rest was history."

"Yes, it was. I was wondering if…uh, you might like to stay for dinner? I do most of my cooking on the weekends so that I don't have to stand up any more than necessary during the week. How do grilled lamb chops with three vegetables sound?"

When had been the last time he'd eaten a home-cooked meal? Ryan couldn't remember. He grabbed what he did eat from the hospital cafeteria or from a fast-food place. The thought of sitting down to a real meal was more than he could resist. "That sounds great."

"Good. Then I'll go finish up."

She'd already moved to leave when he said, "Phoebe, I couldn't help but notice that you don't have this room set up for a baby."

Making a slow turn, she faced him. "I don't need you to make me feel ashamed. I bet you think I sank so far into feeling sorry for myself that I didn't pay attention to getting ready for the baby. I was still in shock over Joshua when I found out I was pregnant. I just couldn't bring myself to do anything for a while. Anyway, it has been pushed back. Maybe I'll have time to do something after the baby comes."

That wasn't going to happen. Ryan had also heard the new mothers talking about how they never got anything done any more. "I didn't mean to make you feel ashamed or defensive. I was thinking I could help. I see you have paint. How about letting me do the walls for you? I could also move this desk and chair to where you want it and the books."

"I hate to have you do all that."

"I don't mind. All you'd have to do is tell me where to put everything."

She rested her hand on her middle. A wistful look came to her eyes. "It would be nice to have the room ready for the baby. I had planned to buy some stuff for the walls."

"We could do that together." It was the least he could do for Joshua. This was practical stuff that needed doing. He had a strong back and could take care of them. He couldn't fix the fact she was having this baby all by herself but he could help with the everyday aspects of adding a new person to her household.

"That sounds like I'm asking too much."

"You're not asking. I volunteered. I'd like to do it. If JT were here, he'd be doing it. This will be my way of helping him out, like he did me."

Her eyes darkened for a second and then she nodded. "Then thanks. I'll gladly accept your help, but I'm going to warn you that you may wish you hadn't."

"How's that?"

"I have so many ideas for this room you'll get tired of me telling you what to do."

"We'll see. I'll be through here in about ten minutes, then I'd like to get started on the painting. Do you have any paint supplies?"

"They're in the shed in the backyard. When you get done, come to the kitchen and I'll take you out and show you where they are."

"Will do."

He watched her leave. Even with the bulk she carried she had a graceful stride. What had possessed him to get this caught up in doing a baby's room? He made a practice of not getting involved.

Guilt, pure and simple.

CHAPTER THREE

PHOEBE HAD SPENT so much time without a man or his help it made her nervous to have Ryan in her house. While he'd been putting together the bed, she'd been in the kitchen, cooking. Still, she'd been aware of every clatter or thump that had come from the direction of the bedroom. On occasion she'd heard a swear word. She smiled. More than once her father had bloodied his knuckles, putting a toy together for her or her brother.

It was nice to have someone in the house. She'd considered getting a dog or cat a couple of times just so there would be a living, breathing thing around. She'd decided to wait because she didn't want the poor animal alone in the house all day.

Ryan came around the corner. "All done. Come see what you think."

She put the plate on the table and headed down the hall, well aware of him following her. He'd pushed the bed up against the wall across from the window. It looked like the perfect place for it. She ran her hand along the railing. "It looks wonderful."

"Do you have a mattress for it?"

"Yes, it's in the other bedroom."

"I'll get it."

He soon returned with a mattress covered in protective plastic. Together they worked to remove it. Ryan lifted the bedding and dropped it into place.

"It almost makes it real," she said with a note of wonder.

"What?"

"A baby coming."

He chuckled. "I would think that large mound you're sporting out front would make it seem pretty real."

"It does but the bed is something tangible."

"What about a rocker or any other furniture?"

She shrugged. "I'll have to go buy something. I was hoping I could find some pieces at a garage sale that I could redo. I wanted to paint it bright and add animals and plants, that sort of thing."

"You mean like the other folk art you have in the living room?"

She looked at him with a brightness that said they were talking about a passion of hers. "You know about folk art?"

"Only what it is. I'm more a straight paint and stain kind of guy. Fancy painting isn't my thing. So, if you'll show me where you want these books, I'll start moving them."

"They go in my bedroom."

She went out the doorway and turned toward the end of the hall, then went through an open doorway. Ryan followed more slowly. Why did it bother him that he had just been invited into his buddy's wife's bedroom? She hadn't even thought about what she was saying. When she looked back he was standing in the doorway.

"They go on this bookshelf. If you'll bring them to me, I can shelve them."

Ryan returned with an armload of books. She'd taken a seat on the floor in front of the shelving while he'd been gone.

He stacked the books on the floor and she went to work, putting them in place.

Ryan looked down at Phoebe. He saw pregnant women day in and day out, but there was something almost angelic about the way her golden hair covered a portion of her face and her small hands put the books so neatly into their spots.

He shook his head and strode toward the door. Had he been spending too much time in his shop alone? The sawdust was filling his brain.

Fifteen minutes later he had all the books moved. Phoebe hadn't worked as fast as he so she was still shelving books. Not wanting to sit on her bed, he stood near the door until she was finished.

"Thanks for doing this. I've been dreading it for weeks. That's why it hasn't been done." She continued to work.

Ryan's cell phone rang and he pulled it out of his pocket. "I have to get this."

She nodded.

"Ryan Matthews."

"It's Julie Habershire. My waters just broke."

"Okay. No need to panic. We talked about what to do if this happens. I'll meet you at the hospital. Drive safe."

"Ryan, the baby will be all right, won't it? It's early."

"The baby should be fine. Not so early it shouldn't be perfect. See you soon."

He touched the phone to disconnect the call. Phoebe looked at him with a slight smile on her face. "Are you always that calm and reassuring with your patients?"

"I try to be."

"That's a special gift."

"I just know that people are scared when they have never experienced something before, especially if it has to do with their bodies. I learned a long time ago if I don't sound upset, then they're more likely not to get upset."

"You must be good at your job."

He slipped the phone back into his pocket. "I hope my patients think so. Anyway, I've got to go. I hate to miss out on that meal, but babies don't wait."

"I understand."

"Would it be all right if I come back tomorrow and get started on that painting? Maybe get in on leftovers?"

"That sounds fine to me. After lunch?"

"Then it's a plan. See you then." He turned to head out the door and stopped. Coming back, he offered her his hand. "If I don't help you up, I'm afraid you might still be on the floor when I return tomorrow."

"Are you implying that I'm so big that I can't get up off the floor by myself?" She accepted his hand. He helped her rise. She did it with grace.

With her on her feet, he put up his hands as if defending himself. "Hey, I work with pregnant women every day and I know better than to do that. Have to go. See you later."

Her soft laugh followed him down the hall. He went out the front door with a grin on his face, something he'd done more in the last few days than he had in years.

The next afternoon Phoebe wasn't sure what was happening but she was going to take Ryan's help while it was being offered. She'd sat around for too long with no direction. Well aware that she needed to be getting the baby's room together, she hadn't had the heart to do so. It was just too sad to work on it by herself. Having the bed assembled made her want to do more. It needed sheets, blankets. There should be other pieces of furniture, pictures on the walls.

Next weekend she'd go to some garage sales and see if she could find a few items. She smiled. For once she was feeling some excitement over the prospect of being a mother. For now she'd be satisfied with just having the room painted.

She'd hardly finished her lunch sandwich when there was a knock at the door. Ryan stood there. Dressed in cargo pants and a white T-shirt that hugged his well-defined physique, he was a fine-looking man. Mrs. Rosenheim had made a point to tell Phoebe the same thing that morning. Ryan proved that just because she was pregnant it didn't mean that she couldn't be affected by a man. It took her time to draw enough breath to say hello.

"Hey," he said in that drawl that left her feeling like she was sitting beside a cool stream on a hot summer day. "How about showing me the paint supplies? If I need anything I'll still have time to go to the store before it closes."

"Okay. It's this way." This was the first time he hadn't taken time to ask her how she was doing. He seemed focused on the project. She kind of liked the fact that he didn't see her as only a pregnant woman.

At the shed, she started to raise the roll-top door. Ryan stopped her by placing his hand over hers. His hand wasn't smooth, like she had expected for a midwife. Instead, it had a coarseness to it that spoke of a man who did more than wear gloves all the time.

"Hey, you don't need to be doing that. Let me get it."

What would have taken her great effort seemed as easy for him as lifting a blind.

"The paint stuff is stacked up over there." She pointed to the right and toward the back of the shed.

"I see it." He leaned over some gardening pots to gather the items, while at the same time presenting her with a nice view of his behind.

"Would you mind carrying a couple of things?"

It took her a second to answer. "No."

Ryan looked over his shoulder and gave her a speculative look. "Here." He handed her a few brushes and a package of rollers, then came out holding an armload of drop cloths and a paint tray. "I think this is everything I need."

They walked back to the house. Phoebe held the door open for him to enter. He was laying supplies on the floor of the baby's room by the time she entered. He took what she carried from her and added them to the pile.

Scanning the room, he said, "Is the desk staying in here?"

She looked at it. Ryan's drive to get things done was surpassing what she had thought through. "I had planned to put it in the living room. But I'll need to move a few things around so it'll have a place. Give me a minute and I'll see what I can do."

"You're not moving anything by yourself."

Phoebe faced him with her hands on her hips. "I appreciate your help. Really I do, but up until a few days ago I had no help. No one telling me what I should and shouldn't do. I am fully capable of moving a few things. If it's too large for me to do so, I'll call you."

Ryan's look met hers. He pursed his lips. She'd got his attention.

"I'm sorry. I stepped over the line, didn't I?"

She nodded. "Yes. Just a little bit."

"Then please let me know if and when you need help." He bowed slightly.

"Thank you. I will." She left the room with her head held high. She was grateful for Ryan's help but she wasn't needy, despite what her behavior at his house had implied.

In the living room, she began moving small items off an end table. Ryan's soft whistle drifted up the hall. It was nice to have someone around. Her smile grew. It would be nice to have a baby in the house.

She had reached to move the end table when behind her came, "I knew I couldn't trust you."

Jerking to a standing position, she looked around to find Ryan standing with his shoulder leaning against the wall.

"Are you checking up on me?"

"Do you need to be checked up on?"

"No." The word didn't come out as confidently as she would have liked.

He came toward her. "I think you might." He placed his hands on the table and looked at her. "Where do you want this?"

She pointed to the other end of the sofa, where she'd cleared a space by moving a floor lamp.

Ryan moved the table into the spot. He ran a finger over a painted swirl on it. "This type of artwork is interesting."

"Thank you."

He looked at her. "You did this?"

"Don't act so surprised."

"I didn't mean it like that." He looked around the room. "You did all of this?"

She stood straighter. "I did, even down to making the cushions and curtains."

"I'm impressed. I like it."

She chuckled dryly. "Now I'm surprised. Joshua hated this type of decorating. He said it made us look like we couldn't afford better. I put most of it away when he came home. Pulled it out again when he had gone again."

Ryan looked at her for a long moment. "Well, I like it. It's you."

She didn't think anyone had said anything nicer to her in a long time. "Thank you. I appreciate that."

"You're welcome. Now, if I go paint another wall, can I trust you to behave?"

Phoebe glared at him. "Yes, I'll put our supper on to warm. Will that make you happy?"

"Yes." With that, he went off whistling down the hall.

Half an hour later Phoebe went to check on Ryan's progress. He was getting ready to start on the last wall. The others were already a pale yellow. A cheerful and happy color.

The room was small but he seemed very efficient. She watched as he bent to apply paint to the roller in the tray. The muscles on his back rippled. He reached up and brought the roller down along the wall. His biceps flexed and released.

Phoebe shook her head. She had been without a man for far too long and yet was far too pregnant to consider having a relationship with one now. Still, she was alive…

Ryan turned. By the look in his eyes and the way he watched her like a cat after a bird, he knew what she'd been doing. She'd never been much of a blusher but she felt the heat rising to her face.

"So what do you think?"

Thankfully he hadn't made a comment about her staring. "It looks beautiful."

"The paint goes on great."

She stepped farther into the room. "This isn't your first time to do this."

"No. My foster-father was a painter. I started working with him when I was fourteen." He moved back to filling the roller again.

Phoebe wasn't sure she should ask but she was too curious not to. "You were a foster-child?"

"Yeah. I never knew my father and my mother was a drug addict. I was five when I was taken away from her."

Her heart hurt for that little boy. "Oh, Ryan."

He shrugged. "It was tough but it was a long time ago."

Something about his attitude told her it still affected him. His focus turned to refilling the roller again.

"So your foster-father let you go to work with him?"

"It was more like made me go. I was a difficult teen and he thought it would help keep me in line. Something about idle hands leaving room for trouble."

"And did it keep you in line?"

"Not really. I ended up going into the army the day after I graduated from high school. It made my foster-parents happy, and me, too."

"Even your foster-mother?"

He glanced back at her. "She didn't mind, either. She was so exhausted from dealing with the smaller kids and my behavior she was glad to see me go. I should be finished here in about thirty minutes. Any chance I could get something to eat?"

He was apparently through discussing his childhood. She would see to it that her child felt loved and wanted. "It'll be ready."

* * *

Ryan washed up in the hall bathroom. Splashing water on his face, he looked into the mirror. What was he doing? He could feel himself getting in too deep. He'd enjoyed the afternoon more than he would have ever imagined. He spent most of his off hours in his shop and he found he rather liked being out in the daylight, spending time with someone.

He entered the kitchen. There he found more of the same decor as the rest of the house. The table had four chairs, each painted a different color yet they seem to complement each other. The eclectic look seemed to suit Phoebe.

The table was set. When was the last time he'd eaten dinner off something other than a takeout plate?

"You may sit there." Phoebe pointed to the chair closest to him and turned back to the oven. She pulled out a casserole pan and placed it in the center of the table.

Ryan leaned in close and inhaled. "Smells wonderful."

He didn't miss her pleased smile. Phoebe would make a great mother. She found pleasure in doing for others.

She handed him a serving spoon. "Help yourself."

Ryan didn't need to be told twice. He scooped two large helpings onto his plate. Phoebe took one. When she picked up her fork, he did also.

"I see you were taught manners. Not eating until everyone else does."

"My foster-mother was a real stickler about them." He put a forkful into his mouth. It was the best thing he'd eaten in years. "This is good. Real good."

"Thank you. It's my grandmother's chicken casserole recipe."

He ate a plateful and one more before he sat back and

looked at Phoebe. She had only eaten about half of what she'd put on her plate.

"You need to eat more."

She looked down at her middle. "I don't think I need to get any bigger."

"You look wonderful."

"You are feeding me compliments now."

Ryan chuckled. "That wasn't my intent. But I guess I am."

"I'll take them any way I can get them." It was nice to be noticed by a male on any level.

Ryan pushed his chair back. "I guess I'd better get the paint supplies cleaned up."

He left and she cleared the table. When done, she went to see if she could help Ryan. He was in the process of moving the desk.

"That's heavy. Let me help you."

Ryan jerked around. "You will not."

"There's no way you can move that desk by yourself."

"It's all in the technique." He gripped it by each side and began walking it from one corner to the other until he'd moved it to the doorway.

"Do you have an old towel I can use?" Ryan asked.

"Just a second." Phoebe went into the bathroom and brought back the largest one she could find. She handed it to Ryan.

"You stay out here." He moved the desk out into the hall. Taking the towel, he laid it on the floor in front of the desk. Lifting one end he asked, "Can you put the towel under the desk as far as possible?"

Glad she could be of some help she did as he requested.

He then lowered the desk. "Perfect." Gathering the

corners of the towel into his hands he slowly pulled the desk over the wooden flooring and down the hall.

Phoebe stepped into the doorway, letting him pass. When he was by, she stepped out and began to push.

Coming to a stop, Ryan growled, "What're you doing?"

"Helping."

"You shouldn't—"

"Stop telling me what to do. I'm not really doing much."

A grunt of disbelief came from his direction but the desk started moving again. She continued to help maneuver it, seeing that it didn't nick the walls or hit any other furniture. When the desk quit moving, she looked over it. Her gaze met Ryan's. For a second his intense gray gaze held hers. Warmth washed over her. Could he see things she'd rather keep hidden?

"Why did you stop?"

His mouth quirked. "I don't know where you want this."

Phoebe tried to squeeze through the space between the desk and the wall.

"Hold on a sec and let me move it." Ryan grabbed the desk and shifted it so she could join him.

"I want it put over there." She pointed to the space she had cleared under a window.

"Okay." He began walking and shifting the desk until it was in place. "I'll go get the chair." He left.

The desk really needed to be centered under the window. Phoebe placed one hip against the side and pushed. It only moved a few centimeters.

"I can't leave you alone for a minute." Ryan's deep voice came from behind her.

"It needs to be centered under the window."

"Then why didn't you say something?"

He put his hands on her waist or what had once been her waist. Her breath caught. Ryan gently directed her out of the way, then quickly put space between them. "I'm sorry. I shouldn't have done that."

Ryan acted as if he'd been too personal with her. "It's okay," she said.

"Stand over there, out of the way, and tell me when I have it where you want it."

"You do know I'm just pregnant, not an invalid."

He gave her a pointed look. "I'm well aware of that but some things you shouldn't be doing, whether you're pregnant or not. This is one of them. Now, tell me where you want it."

Shifting the desk an inch, he looked at her for confirmation. It still wasn't where she wanted it. "Move it to the right just a little."

Had he muttered "Women" under his breath?

"That's it. Perfect. Thank you."

He stood and rubbed his lower back.

She stepped closer. "Did you hurt yourself?"

He grinned. "No. I was just afraid that you might ask me to move something else."

"Hey, you're the one who volunteered."

"That I did. I might ought to think about it before I do that again." He continued stretching.

"Might ought to?" She liked his accent.

"Ought to. Texas. Southern. Ought to go. Ought to get."

Phoebe laughed. "I'll have to remember that. Use it sometime."

"I think you ought not make fun of me."

"And I think you ought not be so sensitive."

They both laughed.

It was the first real laugh she'd shared with someone in a long time. It felt good.

"Well, I guess I had better go. It's getting late."

"I really appreciate all your work today. The baby's room looks wonderful. I can hardly wait to go to some garage sales and look for a chest of drawers."

"And how do you plan to get something like that home?"

"I'll worry about that if I find one. Some people are willing to deliver if I ask."

"I don't have any mothers due for a couple of weeks so why don't I go with you on Saturday?"

She like the idea but didn't want to take advantage of him. "I hate to take up another one of your weekends."

"I'd like to go. I've got a buddy who has a truck and lets me borrow it sometimes."

The truck was a plus and it would be nice to have company. "I won't turn that down."

"Great. I'll be here early Saturday to pick you up."

Ryan headed out the front door. "See you then."

"Bye." Phoebe watched from the veranda as Ryan drove away. She could get used to having him around. Seeing him on Saturday gave her something to look forward to. Of course she appreciated his help but more than that she liked him. There was an easy way about him that made life seem like fun. She was far too attracted to him already. Joshua had been right about him. Maybe she had found someone she could depend on.

Warmth lingered where Ryan had touched her. A ripple of awareness had gone up her spine. What was she thinking? Joshua had been dead for less than a year and she had a baby on the way, and here she was mooning over Ryan.

Still, Saturday couldn't come soon enough.

CHAPTER FOUR

RYAN PULLED THE truck to the curb in front of Phoebe's house just as the sun became warm.

What was he doing? The question kept rotating through his mind like a revolving door. He was too interested in Phoebe. But it was hard not to be. Those large, vulnerable eyes drew him in. Still, he admired the way she had stood up to him when he'd stepped over the line to bossing her around. The brief moments he'd touched her waist had told him that he could want more than just to help her. That wasn't going to happen. Still, he'd looked forward to spending the day with her.

Phoebe met him halfway up the walk. She wore jeans and a simple white shirt. Her eyes sparkled and for a woman of her size she walked with a peppy step. A smile covered her face. She reminded him of springtime. A fresh start.

If he'd seen any woman look more alluring, he couldn't remember when. "Mornin'."

"Hi. You ready to go? We need to get going. You know the early bird gets the worm." She carried a newspaper and passed him on the way to the truck, leaving the smell of flowers swirling in the air. He was tempted to breathe deeply. Let his mind commit it to memory.

"Uh…yeah. I'm ready." Ryan wasn't able to keep the astonishment out of his voice. He hurried to join her. Phoebe was a woman on a mission.

She had climbed into the passenger seat and closed the door before he reached the truck. He took his place behind the wheel. "So where's the fire?"

"What?" She looked up from the open paper.

"What's the hurry?"

"I think they have just what I need at a sale and I don't want it to get bought up before we get there."

"Why didn't you call me? I could have come earlier."

"I didn't know for sure until I phoned a few minutes ago. They wouldn't promise to hold it for me so we've got to go."

Ryan grinned as he pulled away from the curb. There was nothing like a woman looking for a deal. "So where are we headed?"

"South. It's about forty minutes away." Phoebe gave him directions.

"South it is."

They traveled in silence until they were out of the city and he was driving along a two-lane highway.

"Do you have an address for the place we're going?"

Phoebe read it to him out of the paper.

"I have no idea where that is." Ryan kept his eyes on the road as a delivery truck whizzed by them.

"It's another half hour down this road, then we have to turn off."

"Have you always redone furniture?" It was ironic that she enjoyed something that was so similar to his passion.

"I've been doing it for a few years. I found I needed to fill the time when Joshua was away."

"You were lonely, weren't you?"

Phoebe didn't immediately answer. "It wasn't so hard at first. But it got more so as time went on."

Her melancholy tone implied that something more than loneliness had pushed her toward finding a hobby.

"Joshua didn't care for my painting taking up my time when he was home so I always put things away then."

He remembered what she'd said before about putting away her painted furniture because Joshua hadn't like it. That had surprised him. It didn't sound like the Joshua he'd known. Maybe he had changed since they'd known each other in the service. Ryan needed to find a safer subject. "Looks like it's going to be a pretty day."

"Yes, it does. I'm glad. I don't want anything I buy to get wet."

"I brought a covering in case we need it."

She gave him a smile of admiration.

The feeling of being a conquering hero went through him. What was happening to him? He smiled back. "Glad I could be of help."

"You're going to need to take a left turn in a couple of miles."

"You know this area well."

"This isn't the first time I've been down this way to garage sales."

They lapsed into silence until Phoebe began giving him directions regularly. They turned off the main road onto a dirt road that led up to a farmhouse with a steep metal roof and a porch circling it on three sides. A large barn with its doors opened wide stood off to the side. Two other cars were parked nearby.

"They keep the stuff they're selling in the barn," Phoebe said, with the door already open.

She hurried to the barn and Ryan joined her halfway

there. They entered the dim interior. In an unused stall tables had been set up that contained all types of bottles, kitchen utensils, purses and other small items. On the other side were the larger items. Phoebe headed to them. She studied a cabinet that came up to his chest. It was much too high for her to make good use of it.

Phoebe pulled the drawers out and pushed them back in. "Would you mind tipping it forward so I can look at the back's construction?"

He had to give her credit for being knowledgeable and thorough. Ryan did as she requested.

She knocked against the wood and made a sound in her throat. Her hair curtained her face so he couldn't see what she was thinking. Running a hand over the edge and back again, she made another sound. Whether it was positive or negative he couldn't tell. It didn't matter. He was enthralled just watching her.

"You can let it down now."

Ryan lowered it to the ground.

She stepped back and studied it. "I think it'll do."

"May I make a suggestion?"

She looked at him as if she'd almost forgotten he was there. He didn't like that idea. That he could that easily disappear from her thoughts. Raising her chin and cocking her head, she gave him a questioning look. "Yes?"

"I think this chest is too tall for you. You can't even see over it."

Her eyes widened. She turned to face the chest. "You know, I can't. I hadn't thought about that."

"You need one where you can use all the space. You couldn't even find the baby powder if it got pushed to the back on this one."

"You're right. I guess now that I'm in the baby mood

I'm getting in a panic to buy, afraid that time is running out. That I won't get it all done."

"We have all day. You have more places on your list, don't you?"

"Yes."

"Then let's go see what they have. Maybe we can find just the right one."

He offered his hand.

She looked at it for a moment and then placed hers in his. Her fingers were soft and cool. He closed his around them. It was as if they had chosen to face a problem together and see it overcome. Somehow this relationship had gone from less about getting a piece of furniture to having an emotional attachment. He didn't release her hand when she gave his a nudge.

Together, side by side this time, they walked back to the truck.

They visited two more places and didn't find what Phoebe was looking for.

"I don't know about you but I need something to eat," Ryan said, when he saw a sign for a café and ice-cream parlor.

"I am, too, but we might miss out on my chest."

"Then there'll be another one."

"Okay," Phoebe said, but her heart didn't sound like it was in it.

He pulled into a drive much like the one at the first house they had visited. As he came to the end of it he found a house with a restaurant attached to the back. "Come on. We'll have a sandwich, maybe some ice cream and plan our attack. Bring the paper and the map."

She didn't argue and had them in her hand when he came around the truck to meet her.

Ryan held the door for her to enter the café, then directed her to one of the small square tables in the room. Phoebe took a seat in one of the wooden chairs. He sat beside her.

She looked around the space. "I like this. It's my style."

"It does look like your type of decor."

The tables were covered in floral-print cloths. The chairs were mismatched, like hers.

A young man brought them a menu. He and Phoebe studied it for a moment.

"What're you going to have?" Ryan laid the menu on the table.

"A ham sandwich and lemonade."

"I think I'll have the same."

The waiter returned and Ryan gave him their order. When they were alone again, Ryan said, "Hand me that map, then read out the places you want to visit."

Phoebe did as he asked and he circled the places on the map. "Okay, is that it?"

"Yes."

"All right. Show me on the map your first and second, then third choice."

Phoebe pointed them out. He drew a line from one to the other to the other. "This is our game plan. We'll visit these. If we don't find what you want today, then we'll try again next weekend or whenever we can. Agreed?"

"Agreed."

The waiter brought their meals.

"Now let's eat. I'm starved."

She smiled. "You're always hungry."

Her soft chuckle made his heart catch. He was becoming hungry for more time with her.

* * *

Phoebe had always enjoyed junking but never as much as she had today. It turned out that Ryan was not only efficient but also a fun person to have around. She hadn't smiled or laughed as much as she had in the last few weeks. She'd almost forgotten what it was like to have a companion or to just appreciate male company.

Even so, there seemed to be a part of Ryan that he kept to himself. Something locked up that he wouldn't or couldn't share with the world or her.

After they had finished their lunch they climbed back into the truck and headed down the road. This time Ryan was not only driving but navigating as well. It didn't take them long to reach their first stop.

"It looks like they have a lot of furniture," Ryan said as they walked toward a shed.

"Maybe they'll have just the right thing."

A man met them at the shed door but let them wander around and look in peace.

Phoebe had been studying a chest. She turned to speak to Ryan but found he was in another area, looking at a rocker. "What have you found?"

She joined him and watched as he lovingly ran a hand down the arm of the chair. Now that she was closer she could tell it sat lopsided. There was a rocker missing.

"There was a woman who lived next to my foster-family who had a rocker like this. She and only she sat in it. She said it was the best seat in the house."

"She was nice to you."

"Yeah. Her house was where I would go if things got too hard for me at the Henrys'." She could only imagine the little boy who had needed someone on his side. "It's beautiful. I like that high-back style. Gives you someplace to lean your head."

Ryan moved another chair and a small table so that he could pull the rocker out. When he had plenty of space he tipped it over.

Phoebe admired the careful way he took in handling it. Despite his size, he was a gentle man.

"I think I can fix this. The structure is sound. All that's missing is the one rocker. Would you like to have it for the baby's room? I can fix it. You can paint it or I'll stain it."

"You don't need to buy me anything."

He looked at her. "I wasn't buying you anything. I was getting something for the baby."

Before she could argue that it was the same thing, he walked away and had soon agreed a price with the owner.

She didn't find a chest of drawers there but they left with the rocker tied down in the back of the truck. At the next place she found nothing she liked.

As Ryan drove away she looked out the window. "I don't think we're going to find what I need today."

"Don't give up yet. We still have one more place on our list."

She studied his strong profile for a minute. He had a long jaw that spoke of determination but there were small laugh lines around his eyes. His forehead was high and a lock of hair had fallen across it as if to rebel against control. Much like the man himself.

"Do you always approach everything you do with such determination?"

"I guess old habits die hard. Being in the service will do that to you."

"Tell me what it was like being in the service. Joshua would never talk about it. He always said he didn't want me to worry."

This was the last subject Ryan wished to discuss. He wanted those days long gone and forgotten. Without his heart in it, he asked, "What do you want to know?"

"Was it as bad as the news makes it out to be?"

"Worse."

"I'm sorry."

"It's war. Few people understand. War is never pretty. It's all death and destruction. Until you have looked into someone's eyes and watched life leave them, no one can ever grasp that."

"That happened to you?"

His glance held disbelief. "Yeah, more than once."

At her gasp he couldn't decide if he was pleased he'd shocked her or disgusted with himself for doing so. "I'm sorry. I shouldn't have said it like that."

"Yes, you should have. You have experienced horrible, unspeakable things while I've been here safe in my home." A second later she asked, "How did you deal with it?"

Ryan gripped the steering wheel and kept his eyes on the road. He wasn't sure he had or was. "I did what I had to and tried not to think about how lives were being shattered."

She laid a hand on his shoulder. Even that small gesture eased the flames of painful memories. Suddenly he wanted her to understand. "There was this one guy in my unit who had lost half his face. He cried and he kept repeating 'I'm going to scare my kids, I'm going to scare my kids.' How do you reassure someone in that kind of shape that he won't?"

As if a dam had broken he couldn't stop talking. "There was another guy who had tried to kill himself because he'd received a Dear John letter. We were in a war zone and we had our own guys trying to kill themselves."

"That had to be hard to deal with."

"Yeah, more than anyone should have to deal with. We lived in metal shipping containers that had been divided into two small rooms by thin wooden walls. We showered in bath houses, ate in the same mess hall. It's hard not to get involved in each other's lives."

"I imagine you do."

"Even though we had R and R time, you never truly got away from it. We could go to the rec building, call our families or use the internet, but the minute we stepped out of the building the fence and sentries told us we weren't at home."

He'd confessed more than he'd ever told anyone about his time in the service. Had he terrified her? He glanced her direction. A single tear rested on her cheek.

His hand found hers. "I'm sorry. I shouldn't have told you all that."

"I'm glad you did. This baby deserves to know about his daddy and what he did. What life was like for him before he died. Thank you for telling me."

Ryan went back to looking at the road. "Joshua was a strong leader. I saw more than one man panic in the kind of situation we were in in that village. He held it together. Because of him I'm alive and so are a lot of other men. You can tell the baby that his father was a good soldier and a hero."

It was a relief to see the turnoff to their next stop. The

conversation had gone in a direction he'd not expected or really wanted to continue. He made the turn into the road leading to the farmhouse. He released Phoebe's hand. The feeling of loss was immediate. "I have a good feeling about this place."

"I hope you're right."

Phoebe's voice held a sad note that he'd like to have disappear. He hadn't intended to bring what had been a nice day to a standstill. Even so, he had to admit it was a relief to get some of what he felt about the war off his chest. He'd carried that heaviness too long. It was strange that Phoebe, the wife of an army buddy, was the one person he had felt comfortable enough with to do so. He had never even told his coworkers as much as he'd just told Phoebe.

The house they were looking for came into view. He pulled to a stop in the drive.

"Doesn't look like we're at the right place. Let me double-check the address." Phoebe opened the newspaper.

A woman came around the corner of the house.

Ryan stepped out of the truck. "Excuse me, ma'am, but is this the place where the yard sale is?" he asked.

"Yes, but it has been over for an hour. We've put everything away."

Phoebe joined them. "Do you still have any furniture? I'm looking for a chest of drawers for my baby's room."

"I'm sorry but we had very little furniture and what we did have is all gone."

Ryan looked at Phoebe. He hated seeing that defeated look on her face. "We'll just have to try again on another weekend."

They were on their way back to the truck when the woman called, "Hey, I do have a chest of drawers out in the old smoke house that my husband says has to go. It was my mother's. It's missing a leg and a drawer, though."

Ryan looked at Phoebe. "I could fix those things. It wouldn't hurt to look."

Phoebe shrugged. "I guess so."

She didn't sound too confident. He gave her an encouraging smile. "Come on. You might be in for a surprise."

He certainly knew about them. Phoebe had been one of those in his life.

"It's back this way." The woman headed around the house. She led them to a wooden building that looked ready to fall down and opened a door.

Ryan looked into the dark space. All types of farming equipment, big and small, was crammed into it.

"You're gonna have to move some of that stuff around if you want to get to it," the woman said from behind him.

Glancing back over the woman's shoulder to where Phoebe stood, he saw her look of anticipation. Not wanting to disappoint her, he didn't have any choice but to start moving rakes, hoes, carts and even larger gardening implements. He definitely didn't want her to do that.

Picking up things and shifting them aside to make a narrow path, he could see a chest leaning against a wall. In the dim light provided by the slits in the boards it looked the right height. His heart beat faster. It might be just what Phoebe was looking for.

He made his way to it by squeezing between a stack of boxes and a tall piece of farming equipment that he couldn't put a name to. Pulling the chest away from the wall, he leaned it forward to look at the back.

"Doesn't it look perfect? It's just right."

His head jerked toward the voice. "Phoebe! What're

you doing back here?" He shouldn't have been surprised. She managed to dumbfound him regularly.

"I wanted to see."

"You should have waited until I brought it out."

"What if you had done all that work and I wasn't interested? I didn't have any problem getting back here, except for between the boxes and that piece of equipment. I'm certainly no larger than you."

He eased the cabinet back against the wall. "What's that supposed to mean?"

"You're no little guy, with your broad shoulders and height."

He wasn't and he liked that she had noticed.

She circled around him, as if wanting to get a closer look at the chest. She pulled each drawer out and examined the slot where the missing drawer went. "What do you think?"

"What?" Ryan was so absorbed with watching her he'd missed her question.

"What do you think?" she asked in an impatient tone. "Can it be fixed?"

"Yes. It has sturdy construction. With a new drawer and a leg you would be in business."

She looked at him and grinned. Had he just been punched in the stomach?

"In business?"

"What kind of business would that be?"

"The baby business," he quipped back.

"I think I'll like that kind of business." Her smile was of pure happiness.

He returned it. "And I think you'll be good at it. So do you want the chest?"

"Yes, I do."

For a second there he wanted her to say that about him. He shook the thought away. Those were not ones he should be having. He and Phoebe were just friends. That was all they could be or should be.

"If you'll slide your way back out, then I'll bring this."

"I could help—"

Ryan leaned down until his nose almost touched hers. "No. You. Will. Not."

She giggled. "I thought that's what you might say." She gave him a quick kiss on the cheek and started for the path. "Thanks. You've been wonderful."

All he could do was stand there with a silly grin on his face. What was he, ten again?

With a groan, he began manipulating the chest through the maze. With less muscle than patience, he managed to get it outside. Before he could hardly stand the cabinet against the side of the building, Phoebe began studying it with a critical eye. She pulled each of the drawers out and pushed them in again.

"What do you want for it?" Phoebe glanced at the lady.

Heck, now that he'd worked to bring it into the light of day it didn't matter what the woman wanted. He'd pay her price just to not have to put it back.

"One hundred dollars," the woman stated.

"It has a leg and a drawer missing. How about thirty?" Phoebe came back with.

"Make it eighty, then."

Ryan watched, his look going from one woman to the other like at a tennis match.

"I don't think so. There's too much work to be done. Thanks anyway." Phoebe started toward the truck.

Ryan stood there in disbelief. She was going to leave after all the looking they had done today and the trouble he'd gone to get the chest out of the cluttered building? After she'd found what she wanted?

He gave her a pointed look. She winked. He was so stunned he couldn't say anything.

"How about we make it fifty?" the woman called after her.

Phoebe made almost a ballerina turn and had a smile on her face when she faced the woman. "Deal." Phoebe opened up her purse and handed the woman some bills.

He had to give Phoebe credit, she was an excellent bargainer.

She looked at him and grinned in pure satisfaction. What would it be like to have her look at him that way because of something he'd done? Heaven.

Clearing his head, he asked, "Ma'am, do you mind if I pull the truck closer to load this up?"

"Sure, that's fine."

Twenty minutes later, Phoebe was waving bye to the woman like they were long-lost friends.

"That was some dickering you did back there."

"Dickering?"

"Bargaining."

"Thanks."

"The next time I have to buy a car I'm taking you with me."

Phoebe smiled.

"Where did you learn to do that?"

"I don't know. I just know that it usually works. And it's always worth a try."

"There for a few minutes I was afraid that I was going to have to wrestle that chest back into that building."

"I wouldn't have let that happen. I wanted it too badly. I would have paid the hundred."

"Well, I'm glad to know that."

A few minutes later he pulled out onto the main highway that would take them to the larger road leading to Melbourne.

"Oh, the little penguins. I haven't seen them since I was young," Phoebe remarked as they passed a billboard.

"Penguins?"

"You don't know about the penguins? At Phillip Island?"

"No."

"They come in every night. It's amazing to watch. They go out every morning and hunt for food and bring it back for their babies. They're about a foot tall."

"How far away is this?"

"On the coast. About thirty minutes from here."

"Do you want to go?"

"They don't come in until the sun is going down. It would be late when we got home."

She sounded so wistful that he didn't have the heart to say no.

"Tell me which way to go."

"Surely you have something to do tonight. A date?"

"Why, Phoebe, are you fishing to find out about my love life?"

She rewarded him with a blush. "No."

"I have no plans. I'd like to see these tuxedo-wearing birds."

"Then you need to turn around and head the other direction."

"Yes, ma'am."

CHAPTER FIVE

PHOEBE HADN'T BEEN to Phillip Island in years. She still had the picture her father had taken of her standing next to the penguin mascot. The area had changed. The building had been expanded and more parking added.

Ryan found a space and pulled into it. "I'm glad we ate when we did. I haven't seen any place to do so in miles."

"I was hungry, too."

Inside the welcome center they were directed outside. In another hour it would be dark. They followed the paved path that zigged and zagged down toward the beach. Other people mingled along the way.

"What's that noise?" Ryan asked.

"That's the baby chicks."

He looked around. "Where are they?"

Phoebe placed a hand on his arm. She pointed with the other at a hole in the grass embankment. "They're in there. Watch for a second and you'll catch a glimpse of them."

A grin came to Ryan's lips. "I see one."

"The penguin's mother and father leave the nest in the morning and spend all day hunting food. They return each night to feed the young and do it all over again the next day. Fifty kilometers or farther."

"Every day?" Ryan asked in an incredulous tone.

"Yes. The ocean is overfished so they have to go farther and farther. It's pretty amazing what parents will do for their children."

Ryan looked at her. "Are you scared?"

"Some. At first I was shocked, frightened, mad, then protective. It has been better here lately." She left off *because of you.*

"So it takes both parents to find enough food?"

"They are partners for life."

Ryan looked off toward the ocean and didn't say anything.

Had she made him nervous? Made it sound like she expected something from him? "I think I'm most scared that I won't be enough for the baby. That I can't be both mother and father."

"I think you'll do just fine. Your baby will grow up happy and loved. Let's head on down."

Phoebe didn't immediately move. Did he think she expected him to offer to help? That she thought he'd be around when the baby came? Would take Joshua's place? She wouldn't force commitment on any man. She was looking for someone who wanted to spend time with her. Who would put her first, over everything. Someone that would willingly be there for her and her baby.

She started walking but at a slower pace.

They walked in silence around a couple of turns before Ryan said, "Whew, the smell is something."

"There are thousands of small chicks living in this bank."

"Really?" Ryan leaned over the rail and peered down. "I don't see them."

"Most are asleep right now. When they wake up you

can see their heads stick out. There is one small nest after another."

"Everywhere."

Phoebe chuckled. It was fun to be around when Ryan experienced something new. He seemed to get such enjoyment and wonderment from it. It made her see it the same way. "Yes, they are everywhere."

"If you had told me about this I wouldn't have believed it."

"You haven't seen the best yet. Come on, let's get a good seat."

"Seat for what?"

"To watch mum and dad come home." She took his hand and pulled him along the walk.

When she tried to let his hand go he hung on tighter. She relaxed and reveled in the feeling of having someone close. Ryan seemed to like having contact with her.

"What do you mean?"

"We have to go down to the beach. There are grandstands."

"Like bleachers?"

"Come on, I'll show you."

As they continued on Ryan pulled her to a halt every once in a while to peer into the bank. "I can't believe all these little birds here."

She just smiled. They finally made it down to the sand. She was glad to have Ryan's help as she crossed it and they found a seat on an aluminum bench.

Ryan looked around. "This many people will be here?"

"Yes, the three sets of bleachers will be full and there will be people standing along the rails."

"I wonder why I've never heard about this."

"I don't know but I do think it's the best-kept secret about Australia."

The bleachers filled as the sun began to set. Minutes later the crowd around them quieted.

"Look," Phoebe whispered and pointed out toward the water. "Here they come."

Emerging from the surf was a small penguin, and behind it another until there was a group of ten to twelve. They hurried up the beach and into the grassy areas.

A loud chirping rose as their chicks realized dinner had arrived. Soon after the first group, another one came out of the water. Then another. Occasionally the group would be as many as twenty.

Ryan leaned close. There was a smell to him that was all Ryan with a hint of the sea. Phoebe liked the combination.

"Why do they come out in groups?"

"For protection from predators. If they all come at once, then they all could be killed. They come out in groups and in waves. That way there will be someone left to take care of the chicks if something happens to them."

Who would take care of her child if something happened to her? She wasn't going to think about that. Glancing at Ryan, she saw that he was looking out at the water. Was he thinking about what she'd said?

As they watched the penguins, the sun went down and floodlights came on. Phoebe shivered as a breeze came off the water. Ryan put an arm around her and pulled her in close. She didn't resist his warmth. Instead, she snuggled into his side.

As they watched, a cluster came out of the water and quickly returned.

"See, that group was frightened by something. Watch for a minute and they will try it again."

Out of the water they came. Ryan gave her a little squeeze.

"You know, I expected the penguins to have black coats but they are really a dark navy."

"That was my biggest surprise the first time I saw them. Aren't they cute?"

"I have to admit they are."

They watched for the next hour. As they did so the penguins continued to come out in waves and the noise from the nests rose to almost a point to where Ryan and Phoebe couldn't hear each other.

Finally they sat there for another ten minutes and no more birds arrived. The crowd started moving toward the walkway.

"Is that it?" Ryan sounded disappointed.

"That's it for tonight."

"Amazing."

When they passed a park ranger, Ryan asked, "How many penguins are there?"

"Two thousand two hundred and fifty-one tonight."

"How do you know that?"

"We count them. There are rangers stationed in sections along the beach."

Ryan's arm supported her as they climbed the hill on the way back to the welcome center. He didn't remove it as they walked to the truck.

As they left the car park he said, "Thanks for bringing me. I'll be doing this again."

"I'm glad you had a good time."

"I did. I bet you are beat." He grinned. "You didn't even fall asleep on me today."

"I'm sorry. I can't help it."

"I'm just teasing you."

They talked about their day for a few minutes. It was the best one she'd had in a long time. Even before Joshua had died. Ryan had proved he could be fun and willing to try new things. She had more than enjoyed his company. Unfortunately, she feared she might crave it. Her eyelids became heavy and a strong arm pulled her against a firm cushion.

Ryan hated to wake Phoebe but they were in front of her house. He had given thought to just sitting in the truck and holding her all night.

Visiting the penguins had been wonderful. He'd especially enjoyed the look on Phoebe's face when the first bird had waddled out of the water. It was pure pleasure. He'd like the chance to put a look on her face like that.

That was a place he shouldn't go. He'd been more than uncomfortable when the discussion had turned to how parents protected their young. He couldn't be that person in Phoebe's life and the baby's. That devotion those tiny birds had to their young wasn't in him. He couldn't let Phoebe start believing that it was. He wouldn't be around for the long haul. That required a level of emotion that he wasn't willing to give.

Still, she felt right in his arms. Too right.

He pushed those thoughts away and settled for practicality and what was best for Phoebe. She would be sore from sleeping in the truck and he would ache for other reasons. He smirked. Plus he was liable to end up in jail when her neighbor called the police.

"Phoebe." He shook her gently. "Phoebe. We're home."

Her eyes fluttered open. "Mmm...?"

"We're at your house."

"Oh." She tried to sit up but it wasn't happening quickly.

"I'm sorry, I didn't mean to fall asleep on you, literally and figuratively."

"Not a problem." And it hadn't been.

Ryan opened his door and got out before helping her out. He walked her to the door.

"What about my chest of drawers?"

"I need to fix the leg and build a drawer before you can do much with it anyway. I'll just take it home with me. You could come to my house and work on it. I'll do the paint stripping anyway. You don't need to be around those fumes."

"You've already done so much."

Ryan put a hand under her chin and lifted it. "Hey, today was no hardship for me."

She smiled. "I enjoyed it, too."

With reluctance he stepped back. "You need to get to bed."

"And you still have a drive ahead."

"I do. I'll see you in clinic Wednesday afternoon. Plan to come to my place afterward. I should have the leg on and the drawer done by then."

"Okay."

He liked the fact that she readily agreed.

"See you then."

Phoebe made her way into the hospital and up to the clinic waiting room. She hadn't been this nervous since her first visit. Her name was called and she was directed to an examination room. She was told to remove her trousers, sit on the exam table and place the sheet over her. Soon

Sophia entered. "Well, have you made a decision on who you want to replace me?"

"Not yet. I hate to lose you. Are you sure you can't put off the wedding until after this baby is born?"

"I don't think Aiden will agree to that. You're going to have to make a decision soon."

"I know."

"I'm sorry that I can't be there to deliver." Sophia's smile grew. "But love doesn't wait."

"I understand. I wish you the best."

"So how's it going between you and Ryan? I know your first meeting was a little rocky."

Phoebe smiled. "That would be an understatement. It turns out he's a great guy. He's been helping me get the baby's room together. I asked him to put the baby bed together and he volunteered to paint the room."

"I'm not surprised. He's the kind of person who keeps to himself and quietly goes about helping people."

A few minutes later Sophia had left and Phoebe had just finished dressing when there was a knock on the door. "Come in."

Ryan entered. "Hey."

"Hi." She sounded shy even to herself. She'd never been timid in her life.

"So how're you feeling?"

"Fine."

"Great. No aches or pains after our adventure on Saturday?"

She appreciated his friendly manner. "I was tired but no more than I'm sure you were."

"I have to admit it was a long day. You mind waiting on me in the waiting room? I have one more patient to see."

"Sure."

She hadn't been waiting long when he came out of the office area.

"You ready?"

She stood. "Ryan, I have to work tomorrow. I can't be out late. Maybe I should just come by this weekend."

"Don't you want to see what I've done with the chest?"

Ryan sounded like a kid wanting to show off his new toy. He opened the door leading to the main hall. She went out and he followed.

"Sure I do, but I also have to get to bed at a decent hour."

"I'll drive you home."

"I don't want you to have to do that."

He looked at her. Worry darkened his eyes to a granite color. "Is something wrong? Did I do something wrong?"

"No, of course not."

"Then stop arguing and come on. I'll get you home for your regular bedtime. We'll go to my place and then walk down to a café for dinner. Then I'll take you home."

"Okay. If you insist."

"I do."

Twenty minutes later Ryan unlocked the front door to his home. She followed him in. The place looked no different than it had the last time she had been there yet everything had changed. She felt welcomed where she hadn't before.

Ryan dropped his clothes in a pile next to the door just as he had done before. "Are you thirsty?" he called from the kitchen area.

"No, but I would like to use the bathroom."

"That's right. Pregnant women and their bladders. You'll find it off my bedroom. Sorry it isn't cleaner."

"I'll try not to look."

Phoebe walked to the only doorway she'd never been through. She stopped in shock. The most perfect bedroom suite she'd ever seen filled the room. The furnishing here was nothing like what was in the rest of the house. There was such a contrast it was like being in two different worlds. She went to the sleigh-style bed and ran her hand along the footboard, then turned to study the large dresser. The workmanship was old world with a twist of the modern. She'd never seen any like it. She'd give anything to have furniture like this.

"Hey, Phoebe—" Ryan walked into the room.

"These are beautiful pieces. Where did you get them?" She walked around the end of the bed to the bedside table. She couldn't stop herself from touching it.

"I made it."

She pivoted. "You did? It's amazing. If you ever give up being a midwife, you could become a millionaire, making furniture. It's just beautiful."

A hint of redness crept up his throat.

"Thank you. I don't think it's that good. But I'm glad you like it. You ready to go downstairs?"

"Downstairs?"

"That's where my workshop is."

"I haven't made it to the bathroom yet."

"You go. The door to the basement is in the kitchen. I'll leave it open."

A few minutes later Phoebe gingerly descended the stairs. She was half way down when Ryan rushed over.

"Give me your hand and I'll help you. I forget how steep the steps are."

"I think I've got it." She took the last three steps, then looked around. The area was immaculate. There was equipment spaced around the room that she couldn't put a name to but there wasn't a speck of sawdust on the floor. It was in marked contrast to his living area upstairs. He obviously loved and spent a lot of time down here.

Her cabinet stood near a wooden workbench. Ryan walked over to it. There was a look of anticipation on his face. As if it really mattered to him what she thought. He moved from one foot to the other. The man was worried about her reaction.

"So what do you think?"

"About what?"

"The chest."

"I know what you're talking about, silly. I'm just teasing you. It looks wonderful."

As if he'd been awarded a prize, his chest puffed out. She would have never thought that this self-assured man would be that concerned about her opinion.

"I couldn't find a leg that matched the others so I bought four new ones that were as close to the original as I could find."

"They look great. The drawer looks like it was made with it. I'm not surprised after I saw your bedroom furniture. Thank you, Ryan. It's perfect."

"I managed to strip some of the paint but it still needs more work. I was going to do some of it tonight but I promised to get you home."

"You know I'd rather have that finished so I can work on it than go out for a meal. Why don't I go down to the café and get takeout—?"

"While I work?" Ryan finished with a grin. "I think you could be a slave driver for a little bit."

"You're the one that said I shouldn't be stripping it. I

would have put it out in the backyard where there was plenty of ventilation."

He propped his hands on his hips. "And just how were you planning to move it out of the weather?"

"I would have found a way. Ms. Rosenheim could help me."

"That would have been a sight worth watching."

She glared at him. "You don't think we could do it?"

He threw up his hands. "I don't think I would put anything past you two."

"Good. You need to remember that. Now, I'm going to get us something to eat and you'd better get busy."

"Yes, ma'am."

His chuckle followed her up the stairs.

Ryan was aware of Phoebe returning. Her soft footfalls crossed overhead. As she moved around in the kitchen, something about the sound made him feel good inside. When her eyes lit up at the sight of the chest of drawers he felt like he could carry the world on his shoulders. For so long he'd only seen the look in eyes of those in pain or life slipping away. He could do nothing to change it but this time he'd been able to help someone and see pure joy. It was the same feeling he had when he delivered a baby.

Taking the can of paint stripper off the bench, he poured it into an empty food can. Using a brush, he applied it to the wood of the chest.

He liked too many things about Phoebe. The way her hair hid her face like a curtain and then when it was drawn away discovering she'd hidden a smile from him. The way she insisted on helping. Phoebe was no shrinking violet. She was a survivor. JT's baby was lucky. JT's baby!

What was happening to him? Phoebe was JT's wife. *Was*. It didn't matter how attracted to her he was, she would always belong to JT. There was the bro code. You don't take your best friend's girl.

Ryan picked up the putty knife and began to scrape the paint off in thin sheets.

No matter how much you might want to.

A board creaked above him.

It didn't matter. Phoebe didn't feel that way about him. She'd been alone during a hard time in her life and she was searching for a connection to JT. All *he* meant to her was someone who had known the father of her baby. He would be her friend and nothing more.

Still, it was as if he saw the world as a better place when he was around her. Like his wounds were finally closing. That life could be good. Not black-and-white. Living or dying. But happy, healthy and hopeful.

"Hey, down there, your dinner is served." There was a cheerful tone to her voice, like someone calling another they cared about.

Ryan's heart thumped hard against his chest. Wouldn't it be nice to be called to every meal that way? Even those little things improved life.

Phoebe was filling their glasses when Ryan's footsteps drew her attention to the door of the basement. It had been over a year since she had called someone to dinner and here she was doing it twice in less than two weeks. She liked it. There was something about it that made her feel like all was as it should be in her world.

"Smells good."

"You do know that all I did was pick it up, don't you?" she said, putting the pitcher back on the corner.

"Yes, but you did a good job with that."

He looked at the table. She had set their places with what little she could find in Ryan's woefully low-stocked kitchen. Passing a shop, she'd impulsively bought a handful of flowers. She hoped he didn't think she was suggesting that this was more than a friendly meal.

He nodded toward them. "Nice touch."

She smiled. "I like fresh flowers. I couldn't resist them."

"I'll have to remember that. Let me wash my hands."

Ryan went to the sink. With his back to her she had a chance for a good look. What would it be like to run her hands across these wide shoulders? To cup what must be a firm butt?

She didn't need to be thinking like that. But she was pregnant, not dead.

"What's wrong? You feeling okay? You have an odd look on your face."

She'd been caught ogling him. "No, no, I feel fine."

A slow smile stole over his face and his eyes twinkled, pushing the worry away. "Okay, let's eat. I'm hungry."

Had he figured out what she'd been thinking?

They each took one of the two chairs at the table.

"I didn't know what you liked so I got two kinds of soups and two sandwiches, hoping you liked at least one of each."

"It all looks good."

"I didn't move your mail off the table. I thought you might not be able to find it if I did." She pushed it toward him. Ryan's hand brushed hers when he reached for it.

The flutter in her middle had nothing to do with the baby moving. She jerked her hand back.

"Is that a valid comment on my housekeeping skills?"

"Not really, but now that you mention it I've not really seen any of those skills outside your shop."

He laughed. "I deserve that. I'm not here much and when I am I go downstairs. As for my mail, I usually let it stack up and then open anything that isn't bills when I get around to it." He glanced through the pile and pulled an envelope out, tearing it open. Slipping a card out, he studied it a moment, then laid it on the table. "It's an invitation to Sophia's wedding next weekend."

"You weren't kidding. That had to have come weeks ago."

He gave her a sheepish look. "I'm sure it did."

"I'm happy for her but I hate it she isn't going to be there to deliver this baby. I've become attached to her. It's hard to give her up. I don't want just anyone to deliver. But I've got to make a choice soon."

There was a long pause before Ryan leaned forward and said, "I'd like to do it."

Phoebe sucked in a breath. "You want to do what?"

"Be your midwife. Would you let me take over from Sophia?"

She wasn't sure it was a good idea but she didn't want to hurt his feelings by saying no immediately. She'd been looking for emotional support, not medical help. Ryan being her midwife sounded far too personal. "Ooh, I don't know if I'm comfortable with that."

"You need a midwife and I'm one."

"Yes, but isn't there something about not delivering people you know?"

His gaze held hers. "I don't see it as being a problem. And I'd rather be the one there if there's a complication than wishing I had been."

She nodded.

"Phoebe, I'd like to be a part of bringing Joshua's baby into the world."

Wasn't this what she'd been looking for? Someone to support her? Be there for her? She loved Sophia but she wasn't available. Why shouldn't Ryan be the one? Because she had feelings for him that had nothing to do with the baby.

He shifted forward in his chair. "I didn't mean to put you on the spot."

"No, no. It's okay. I'm just not sure what to say. Let me think about it."

"Take all the time you need."

She didn't have much time. He had proved more than once he was the guy Joshua had said he was. What she knew was that she didn't feel as alone as she had only a few weeks ago. Ryan had been tender and caring with her so why wouldn't he be a good midwife? Right now what she needed to do was change the subject. "Where's Sophia getting married?"

"I forget women are always interested in a wedding." He slid the card toward her.

Phoebe picked it up. It was a classic embossed invitation. "They're getting married at Overnewton. It'll be a beautiful wedding. That's an amazing place."

Ryan gazed at her over his soup spoon.

"What wedding doesn't a woman think is beautiful?"

"Mine wasn't. We got married at the registry office."

"Oh?"

"It was time for Joshua to ship out and we decided to just do it. I wore my best dress and he his dress uniform. And we did it."

"Do you wish you'd had a fancier wedding?"

"Sometimes. But that was us back then. Fast in love,

fast to the altar. It seemed exciting. My parents were gone. My brother showed up and one of Joshua's friends from school was there. We all went out to eat lunch afterward. The next day Joshua was gone."

"No honeymoon?"

"We took a trip into the mountains, camping, when he came home nine months later. Those were good times."

It was nice to talk about Joshua. People were hesitant to ask about him. They were always afraid it would make her cry. What they didn't understand was that she wanted to talk about the husband she'd lost. Wanted to remember. She and Joshua had had some fun times. It was a shame they had grown apart there at the end. She'd wanted better for him. For him to think of her positively.

She picked up her sandwich. "How about you? Ever been married?"

"No."

"Not even close?"

"Nope. Never found the right one."

"I bet there have been women who thought you were the right one."

He shrugged.

"So you've been a 'love them and leave them' guy?"

Ryan looked at her. "I wouldn't say that. It's more like it's better not to get involved unless your heart is fully in it. Mine never has been."

His eyes held a dark look, despite the effortlessness of the words. There was more to it than that but she didn't know him well enough to probe further. "I guess that's fair."

"You know, Joshua used to talk about you all the time. It was Phoebe this and Phoebe that."

"Really?" She'd always thought she'd been more like a

toy that he'd come home to play with and then left behind to pick up again during the next holiday. Would things have been different between them if Joshua had not been gone so much?

"He talked about how you liked to camp and hike. What a good sport you were. I liked to hear stories about places you went, things you did."

Guilt washed through her. And the last time Joshua had been home they'd done nothing special. Instead, they'd talked about getting a divorce. How had their relationship deteriorated so much? Would anyone ever love her like she needed to be loved? Want to come home to her every night? Have a family? She put down her half-eaten sandwich and pushed back her chair. "I need to get this cleaned up and get home. It's getting late."

"Do you mind if I finish my sandwich before we go?"

"I'm sorry. I didn't mean to be rude." She settled in her chair again.

"It's okay."

Phoebe watched as Ryan finished his meal. As soon as he had she started removing their plates and glasses.

"I need to put a cover over a few things before we leave." Ryan went down the stairs.

Ten minutes later she called through the door to the basement, "I'm ready to go when you are."

"I'll be right up."

Coming from Ryan, she could depend on it happening.

CHAPTER SIX

JUST UNDER AN hour later Ryan joined Phoebe on the sidewalk in front of her house.

"Thanks for the ride home."

"When are you planning to come to my house and work on the cabinet? This weekend? I'll have it ready for you by then."

"I hadn't thought about that. I guess I need to get busy. I'll bring my paints and be there early on Saturday morning."

"I can come get you—"

"No, I'll take the tram." She started up the walk.

"I don't mind."

She looked at him. "Ryan, please."

"Okay, okay. Have it your way. Come on, you're tired." He took her elbow and they started toward the door.

Phoebe stopped walking.

Ryan jerked to a stop. "What—?"

She kicked off her shoes and picked them up by two fingers. "My feet are killing me."

They continued to the door. Phoebe unlocked it, pushing it open.

"If you soak and massage your feet it would help," Ryan said behind her.

"I don't do feet." She dropped her shoes inside the door.

Ryan followed her in and closed the door behind him. "That's all right, because I do. You get a bath and come back here. Bring a bottle of your favorite lotion with you. I'll be waiting."

"It's late. We've both had a long day."

"It won't take long and I promise you'll like it. So stop complaining and go on."

Phoebe gave him a dubious look but went off toward her bedroom.

While she was gone Ryan found a cook pot and put water on to heat. Looking under the sink, he pulled out a wash pan. He added a little dish soap to it. He searched the cabinets for a container of salt and, finding it, he added a generous amount to the soap. When the water started to steam he poured it into the pan.

Going to the bathroom in the hallway, he pulled a towel off the rack. Returning to the living room, he placed the towel on the floor in front of the most comfortable-looking chair. He then went for the pan of water.

"What's all this?" Phoebe asked. She wore a gown and a housecoat that covered her breasts but not her belly. Her hair flowed around her shoulders and her cheeks were rosy. Ryan had never seen a more captivating sight.

Gathering his wits and settling his male libido, he took her hand and led her toward the chair. "I'm going to help make those feet feel better. You sit here."

She lowered herself into the chair.

"Now, slowly put your feet into the water. It may be too hot."

"This feels wonderful." She sighed, lowering her feet into the water.

He left her to get a chair from the kitchen, returned and placed it in front of her.

"What're you planning now?"

Taking a seat, he faced her. "I'm going to massage your feet."

"I'm not letting you do that!"

"Why not? You ticklish?"

Phoebe didn't look at him. "No."

"I think you're lying to me. Did you bring the lotion?"

She shifted to her right and put her hand in her housecoat pocket. She pulled out a bottle and handed it to him. Without even opening the bottle he recognized the scent he thought of as hers. He reached down, his hand wrapping her calf and lifting it to rest on his thigh.

"I'm getting you wet." She tried to pull her foot away.

He held it in place. "If it isn't bothering me, then don't let it bother you. Lean back and relax. Close your eyes."

He squirted a liberal amount of lotion into his palm and began rubbing Phoebe's foot. At the first touch she flinched and her eyes popped open. Their gazes met as he began to massage her skin. Seconds later, her eyes closed and she relaxed. As he worked the tissue on the bottom of her foot she let out a soft moan.

"Where did you learn this?" she asked almost with a sigh.

"In the army. The men in the hospital always seemed to respond and became calmer if they had a massage of some kind."

"I can understand that."

His hands moved to her ankle and then along her calf, kneading the muscles.

"I'm sorry if I put you in a difficult position when I

asked to be your midwife." He squeezed more lotion into his hand and started at her toes again and pushed upward.

"It was sweet of you to ask."

He wasn't sure that Phoebe thinking of him as sweet was to his liking.

"Well, something that was said seemed to upset you." He gently pulled on one of her toes.

"It wasn't what you said as much as something I remembered."

"I guess it wasn't a good one." His fingers continued to work her toes.

"No. When Joshua was home the last time, we talked about separating."

"That's tough." He moved up to her knee and started down again.

"We had grown apart. I had my life and he had his. We just didn't make sense anymore." A tone of pain surrounded every word.

"I'm sorry to hear that. It must really have been difficult to deal with when you realized you were pregnant."

"That would be an understatement. How about an ocean of guilt?"

Ryan could more than understand that feeling. He placed her foot back into the pan and picked up the other one. He gave the second one the same attention as he had the first.

Phoebe leaned back and neither one of them spoke for the next few minutes. Ryan was content to watch the expression of pleasure on her face.

"You sure know the way to a woman's heart."

His hands faltered on her calf. He didn't want her heart. Having someone's heart meant they expected some emotion in return. He didn't get that involved with anyone.

Her eyes opened and met his look. There was a realization in them of what she'd said. Regardless of what his mind told him, his body recognized and reacted to the longing in her eyes. His hands moved to massage her knee and above, just as he had done before, but this time the movements requested more. Unable to resist, his fingers brushed the tender tissue of her inner thigh.

Phoebe was no longer thinking about her feet. This gorgeous, intelligent hunk of man in front of her wanted her. She couldn't remember the last time she'd felt desired. If it had ever felt this compelling.

Ryan's gaze captured hers. His eyes were storm-cloud gray. He held her leg with one hand and slowly trailed a finger upward past her knee to tease her thigh again before bring it down. It was no longer a massaging motion but a caress. With what looked like regret in his eyes, he lowered her foot into the water.

With his gaze still fixed on her, he offered both of his hands.

She took them. He gently pulled her closer and closer until she was in an upright position. Leaning forward, his mouth drew near. "I may be making a huge mistake but I can't help myself."

Ryan's lips were firm, full and sure as they rested on hers. He pressed deeper.

Phoebe wanted more but wasn't sure what that was or if she should want it. This was the first kiss she'd had since Joshua's parting one. She pulled away, their lips losing contact. Her eyes lifted and her look met Ryan's. He didn't hold it. Without a word, he scooped her up into his arms. She wrapped her hands around his neck.

"What?"

"Just be quiet." The words were a low growl. He carried her down the hall to her bedroom and stood her on her feet next to her bed. "Get in."

His tone was gruff. She didn't question, instead doing as he asked. He tucked the extra pillow under her middle and pulled the covers over her shoulders before he turned off the light and left the room. "Good night, Phoebe."

Had he been as affected by the kiss as she had? She still trembled inside. Ryan's lips meeting hers had been wonderful and shocking at the same time. He had surprised her. Everything had remained on a friendly level until his hand had moved up her leg. She'd wanted his kiss but hadn't been sure what to do when she'd got it.

Those days of schoolgirl insecurity had returned. She was soon going to be a mother. Did he feel sorry for her because of the baby? Joshua? Or just because he thought she needed the attention at the moment? The doubts had made her pull away. Now she regretted doing so. Her body longed for him. But it couldn't be. She wouldn't have Ryan feel obligated to her because of her situation. She'd put him on the spot when she'd shown up at his house and she had no intention of doing that to him again. It was best for them just to remain friends.

A few minutes later the front door was opened and closed. Ryan had gone. She didn't have to wonder if the pan and chair had been put away or the front door secured. Ryan would have taken care of that just like she knew she could rely on him to be there for her.

Ryan couldn't sleep and any time he couldn't do that he went to his workshop. What had he been thinking when he'd kissed Phoebe? That was the problem. He hadn't been thinking but feeling. Something he couldn't remember doing in a long time. The need to do more than touch her had pulled at him to the point he'd been unable to stand it any longer. When she'd raised those large questioning eyes…

How could he have done it? He had kissed his dead best friend's wife. Someone who had trusted him. Could there be a greater betrayal? He'd stepped over the line. Way over. Both personally and professionally. It wouldn't happen again. He could put his personal feelings aside and concentrate on the professional. That was enough of those thoughts.

He had the chest of drawers to finish and sand, and there was also the rocking chair to repair. Phoebe would be here in two days ready to work on them. Soon that baby's room would be complete and the baby here. Then he could back out of Phoebe's life. He would have done then what he could do to honor JT. Phoebe would no longer need him.

Had he seen a cradle at Phoebe's? She would need a cradle for the first few months to keep the newborn close. He'd been given some pink silkwood by an associate who was moving out of town. It had been stored away for a special project. This was it.

Would he have time to get it done before the baby came? If he worked on it every chance he had, he might make it. He'd finish the chest and then start on the cradle. If he worked on the rocker while Phoebe was busy painting, he could keep the cradle a surprise.

He had plenty to do so there wouldn't be time to think about Phoebe. The feel of her lips. The desire in her eyes. The need that was growing in him. With his mind and hands busy he wouldn't be tempted to kiss her again. He had to get control of his emotions. In Iraq he'd been the king of control. He needed to summon some of that now. Compartmentalize when he was around Phoebe. Keep that door she was pushing open firmly closed.

On Saturday morning Ryan came home as the sun was coming up. He'd been gone all night, delivering a baby. Phoebe would be there in a few hours. He wanted to get some sleep before she arrived. Taking a quick bath, he crawled into bed.

He woke with a start. Something wasn't right. The room was too bright. He groaned. He'd slept longer than he'd planned. But something else was off.

Music. His workshop. He had a radio there. Had he left it on?

Wearing only his boxer shorts, he headed for the kitchen. The music grew louder. The basement door stood wide open and a humming mixed with the song playing drifted up the stairs. He moved slowly down the steps, being careful not to make a noise. Halfway down, he bent over to see who was there.

Phoebe. She sat on a stool with her back to him, painting a side of the chest. She'd been smart enough to open the outside door to let out any fumes. Ryan trod on the next step hard enough that she would hear it. He didn't want to scare her by calling her name.

She twisted around. "Hey."

There was a tentative sound to her voice. Was she thinking about what had happened the last time they had seen each other? Was she worried he might try to kiss her again? He needed to put her at ease. "Hey, yourself. You're not afraid of being hurt when you come into someone's house while they're sleeping?"

"I knocked and knocked. I tried the front door and it

was open. I came in and saw you were sleeping. I figured you'd had a late night and had left it open for me."

He nodded. Some of that was true, except he had planned to be up when she arrived. "I had a delivery early this morning."

"How's the mother and baby?"

He moved down the stairs going to stand beside her. "Great. Beautiful girl named Margaret."

"Nice. What do you think?" She indicated the work she'd been doing.

Phoebe had left the wood a natural color and was painting a vine with flowers down the side. "Looks great. What're your plans for the rest of it?"

"I'm going to paint the drawers different colors and paint the other side like this one."

"Sounds nice. Well, I'm going up and see if I can find some breakfast. Then I'll be back down."

He was headed up the stairs when Phoebe said in a bright voice, "Hey, Ryan. I like those boxers. Very sexy."

There was the straightforward Phoebe he'd come to appreciate. Ryan glanced down and shook his head. He'd forgotten all about what he was wearing. "Thanks. I do try."

Phoebe laughed. Ryan did have a good sense of humor. She liked that about him. In fact, she liked too much. He was sexy man and a good kisser, as well. He hadn't mention the kiss or even acted as if he would try again. She couldn't let that happen. Her life was already too complicated. She wouldn't add another emotional turn to it. If he didn't say something, she would have to.

A harsh word filled the air.

She heaved herself off the stool and walked to the door. Another harsh word and pounding on the floor filled the air. She climbed the stairs.

Ryan stood at the sink with the water running.

She moved to his side. "What happened?"

"I burned my finger."

Phoebe smirked at his whiny tone. She went to the refrigerator and opened the freezer compartment. Taking out an ice cube, she handed it to him. "Here, hold this over it."

With a chagrined twist to his mouth he took it. Phoebe looked around the kitchen, found a napkin from a fast-food restaurant and handed that to him, as well. He placed the ice in it and put it on his finger.

"Nothing like the big strong medic needing a medic."

"Hey, taking care of someone hurt is different than being hurt yourself."

She grinned. "Or cooking. Looks like you were having eggs and bacon."

Phoebe pulled the pan that looked as if it had been hastily pushed to the back burner forward and turned on the stove. The bacon was half-cooked.

"I didn't mean for you to come up and cook for me. I'm interrupting your painting."

"It can wait."

She picked up the two eggs sitting on the counter. Cracking them, she let them drop into the pan. There was a *ding*. The toast popped up.

Ryan pulled the slices out and placed them on a plate. "See, I can make toast without hurting myself."

"You get a gold star for that."

"Is that what you give your students when they're good?"

"Fifth years are too old for that sort of thing. Mostly they are happy to get to be first in line to lunch."

He stood nearer than she was comfortable with, but

there was nowhere for her to go and still see what she was cooking. It made her body hum just to have him close. This was not what she'd told herself should happen.

"JT was very proud of the fact you're a teacher."

"Really? I always felt like he resented me having to go to work when he was home." Phoebe lifted the bacon, then the two fried eggs out of the pan, placing them beside the toast. She put the frying pan on the back burner and turned off the stove.

Ryan took the plate and sat down at the table. "Maybe that was because he wanted to spend as much normal time with you as possible. Nothing was normal where we were. People thought differently, ate differently, dressed differently. Everything was different. When I had leave I just wanted as much normalcy as I could get."

She slid into the chair across from him. "Then why did he always look forward to going back?"

"I don't know if I can really answer that question. Because it was his job. Because you feel like you're doing something bigger than yourself, something important. You're helping people who can't help themselves. Then there's the excitement. The adrenaline rush can be addictive.

"What I do know is that JT was good at his job. He was good to his men, protected them at any cost, even to himself."

She nodded. Some of the ache over their last words left her. "Thanks for telling me. Now I better understand why he always seemed so eager to return. Sometimes I worried it was more to get away from me. If you think you can finish up your breakfast without injuring yourself, I'll go and work on the chest."

Half an hour later Ryan went down the stairs. "I'm just going to work over here, out of your way."

"You're not going to be in my way."

Over the next hour they said little to each other as they both concentrated on their own projects. Every once in a while she glanced at Ryan. It appeared as if he was drawing off a pattern onto a plank of wood once when she looked. Another time he looked like he was studying a pattern he had spread across the workbench. There was something easy and comfortable about the two of them doing their own things together. It was the companionship she had been missing in her marriage.

Phoebe rubbed her hand over the baby as she looked at the painting she'd just completed. The world would be a good place for him or her. She felt more confident about that now. Glancing at Ryan, she found him with his butt leaning against the bench looking at her.

"Is something wrong?"

"No, I was just enjoying watching you."

Warmth flooded her. She had to stop this now or their new-found friendship might be damaged. She needed it too much to let that happen. "Uh, Ryan, about the other night..."

Ryan tensed slightly, as if he was unsure what she was going to say next.

"Why did you kiss me?"

"Because I wanted to." His eyes never wavered. Ryan was being just as direct.

She shifted on the stool. "That's nice but it can't happen again."

"Why not? We're both adults. I'm attracted to you. I believe you like me. So why not?"

"Because I don't think I can handle any more emotional baggage right now. I've lost a husband who died thinking I no longer loved him. Finding out I was expecting his baby was a shock of a lifetime. Realizing I'm going to have to raise a baby on my own is all I can handle right now. I can't take on more upheaval. I just think it would be easier if we remain friends and friends only."

He nodded. "I understand." Then he turned back to his work at the bench.

Phoebe believed he did. But she hadn't missed that he'd made no promises. She pressed her lips together. Did she really want him to?

Ryan opened the door to the examination room at the clinic the next Wednesday afternoon. To his shock, Phoebe was his next patient. He hadn't seen her since Saturday around noon when he'd had to leave her to deliver a baby. He'd told her she could stay as long as she wished and just to close up before she left as he doubted he'd be home before she was ready to leave.

Hours later he'd arrived home to a neat and tidy house. His bed had been made and his kitchen spotless. Even his pile of dirty clothes had gone. They were neatly folded on his bed. He'd had to admit it was nice to be cared for. It would be easy to get used to.

He'd been astonished at how much he'd missed Phoebe in the next few days and how much he was looking forward to seeing her again. After her statement about nothing more happening between them he didn't want to push her further away. Still, the thought of kissing her kept running through his mind. He'd be tempted when he saw her, but instead he would put on his professional hat and control himself.

"Hi, Phoebe," he said, as he stepped into the room and

to the end of the table she was sitting on so he could face her. "This is a surprise."

She smiled. "Hey."

"Thanks for cleaning my house. You shouldn't have but I'm glad you did."

"It was nothing. It gave me something to do while I waited for the paint to dry. I saw the rocker. It looks great. You have a real talent."

"Thanks. Did you ask to see me for some reason?"

"I did. I'd like you to deliver my baby."

She had his complete attention.

"That is, if you still want to."

Ryan did. He owed it to JT. For not only his life when they had been pinned down, but because he had made a new start because of him. He had left the army, become a midwife and moved to Australia. Death was no longer a daily event. Ryan had been afraid that if he'd continued to be a medic that he would have never seen another side of life. Would have gone deeper into depression. He'd needed a change and JT had helped him see that.

That was what it had been about when he'd first asked but now, if he was truthful with himself, he wanted to be there for Phoebe and baby. They had started to matter more than he would have ever believed. "I'd be honored."

"I can't think of anyone I'd rather have."

"Thanks. So for your first official visit with me I'm going to listen to the baby's heartbeat, check your blood pressure, measure the size of the baby and check the position by feeling your belly."

"I understand." She said this more to the floor than him.

"Hey, Phoebe." She met his gaze. "Are you sure you're good with me taking over?"

"I do want you to do the delivery, it's just that this exam stuff the first time is a little…awkward."

"For both of us. So what do you say that we get it over with and go have some dinner? Why don't you lie down on the table and tell me what else you have planned for the baby's room?"

Ryan enjoyed her nervous chatter. He didn't blame her. More than once he reminded his hands not to tremble as he placed his hand on her skin and felt for the baby's position. "Well, you and the baby are doing great. You get dressed and we'll get that dinner."

"Do you invite all your patients out to eat?" she asked in a saucy tone.

"No, I do not. I save that for very special ones."

Less than half an hour later they were ordering their dinner at a café a few blocks from the hospital.

"I would have been glad to cook."

"You've done enough of that for me."

"As compared to all you have done for me?" Phoebe glared at him.

"Okay, let's not fight over who has done more." Ryan grinned back at her. "So how have you been?"

"I'm feeling fine. Just ready for this baby to get here and tired of people treating me like I can't do anything for myself. I was moving a box across the floor in my classroom the other day. It wasn't heavy but the janitor rushed to help me. On the tram on the way in a woman offered to hold my schoolbag. She said, 'Honey, isn't that too heavy for you?' I know she was just being nice but I'd like to go somewhere and enjoy being me instead of a pregnant woman."

"People are just naturally helpful when someone is carrying a baby."

The waiter brought their dinner.

"I know. But besides the baby, there's also Phoebe Taylor in here." She pointed to her chest.

He knew that too well. The sweet taste of her kiss still lingered in his memory like the fragrance of fresh-cut wood. Still, he shouldn't have stepped over that line. He owed her an apology but he couldn't bring himself to utter the words. Nothing in him regretted kissing her, not even for a second. Maybe he could show her he'd honor her decision in another way. He would show her he could be a gentleman. That she had nothing to fear on that level from him.

"Sophia really wants me at her wedding Friday evening. Would you like to go with me? We could dance the night away. I'll promise not to treat you like a pregnant woman." That was a promise he already knew he would break. He was far too attracted to her. The pregnancy hadn't even entered his mind when he'd kissed her. Still he would work not to go beyond that barrier Phoebe had erected.

At her skeptical look, he said, "No touching outside of dancing. Just friends."

"I don't know."

"Come on, Phoebe, you know you want to. Dinner and dancing. You don't want me to show up dateless, now, do you?"

She smiled at that. "I don't think you would have any trouble getting a date if you wanted one."

"It seems I'm having to work pretty hard right now to get one."

Phoebe smirked. "Okay, but only because you sound so pitiful. My dancing may be more like swaying."

"I don't mind. We'll just go and enjoy ourselves."

"All right. It may be a long time before I get to do something like that again."

"Well, every man wants to hear that kind of enthusiasm when he asks someone out."

"I didn't mean for it to sound like that. Thanks for inviting me."

The waiter stopped by the table and refilled their glasses.

"That was much better. Why don't I bring the chest of drawers and the rocker out when I come to pick you up? That's if you don't mind me dressing at your place."

"That sounds fine. I can hardly wait to see what they look like in the baby's room."

The wedding suddenly didn't seem like the drudgery that Ryan had thought it would be.

They finishing their meal talking about movies they'd enjoyed and places they would one day like to visit.

On Friday, Phoebe wasn't sure which she was looking forward to more, seeing the furniture installed in the baby's room or the evening of dancing with Ryan. Thankfully it was a school holiday so she didn't have to lose any of her leave time by being off that day.

Ryan had said she was special. She liked being special to someone and especially to him. But it wasn't something she was going to let go any further.

Ryan had taken over her care. As odd as it was, it seemed right to let him be there when the baby was born. In the last couple of weeks he had more than proved himself the compassionate and understanding person Joshua had promised he would be. She couldn't have asked for better help. And it had been cheerfully given. She liked

Ryan too much. Appreciated his support. She could use all those attributes when she delivered.

He was as good as his word. Which she had learned Ryan always was. He pulled up in front of her house at three o'clock.

She stepped out onto the veranda when she saw a sports car followed by a red truck she recognized pull to the curb. Ryan stepped out of the car and waved. She strolled down the path toward him. A man almost as tall as Ryan climbed out of the truck.

"Phoebe, this is Mike. He came along to help me move the chest in."

"Hi, Mike, thanks for going out of your way to do this."

"Nice to meet you. No worries. Ryan has given me a hand a few times."

She looked at Ryan but he gave no explanation. Knowing him, he'd gone out of his way more than once to help people, yet he had no one special in his life. It was as if he was all about deeds but not about becoming emotionally involved. Did he feel the same way about her?

"Let's get these in. Phoebe and I have a wedding to attend," he said to Mike.

The two men undid the straps securing the chest and rocker in the truck bed. They carried the chest into the house.

"Show us where you want it," Ryan said to her. She followed them down the hall and into the baby's room.

She had them place it against the wall opposite the bed. "Perfect."

Ryan grinned. "I'll get the rocker."

"Thank you for your help," Phoebe told Ryan's friend as he followed Ryan out the door.

He waved an arm. "No problem, mate."

She waited there for Ryan to return.

Doing a back-and-forth maneuver, he brought the rocker through the doorway. "Where do you want it?"

"Next to the bed, I think."

He placed it where she'd suggested.

She gave the top of the chair a nudge and watched it rock.

"Aren't you going to try it?"

"Yes, I am." She promptly took a seat, placing her hands on the ends of the arms. Moving back and forth a couple of times, she looked up at him and said in a reverent tone, "It's wonderful. Just wonderful."

"I'm glad you like it."

"I do." She continued to rock and rub the arms with her hands.

"I hate to mention this but we need to get a move on or we'll be late to Sophia's wedding."

"I know. All I need to do is slip on my dress. It shouldn't take long." She pushed out of the chair with obvious reluctance.

"My suit is in the car. Mind if I change in the other bedroom?"

"Make yourself at home," Phoebe said, as she walked out of the room. She stopped and faced him. "Ryan, it's really nice to have you around. You have been a good friend the last few weeks. I really needed one."

A lump came to Ryan's throat he couldn't clear. His heart thumped in his chest. All he could do was look at her. Before he could speak she was gone. With those few words from her he received the same high he did when he delivered a baby. That the world could be a good and kind place. Her happiness was starting to matter too much.

What had he gotten himself into? As hard as he'd worked to keep their relationship centered on helping her get ready for the baby, he'd still grown to care for the fascinating and fabulous woman that was the mother. If he wasn't careful he could become far too involved with Phoebe. Start to care too much. Did he have that in him?

He'd dressed and was waiting in the living room for Phoebe when she entered, carrying her shoes. She wore a modest sleeveless pale blue dress that had pleats in front. Her hair was down but she had pulled one side of it away from her face. It was held in place with a sparkling clasp. She was beautiful in her simplicity.

"I hate to ask this but could you help me buckle my shoes? I've been working for five minutes to figure out how to do it around this baby and it's just not working."

Ryan smiled. "Have a seat and I'll give it a try."

She sat on the sofa and Ryan went down on one knee.

"You look like Prince Charming, dressed in your suit."

"More like a shoe salesman."

They both laughed.

She handed him a shoe and he lifted her foot and put it on.

Working with the small buckle, he said, "No wonder you were having such a hard time. This would be difficult for an aerospace engineer."

"Yes, but they look good."

Ryan rolled his eyes.

"Let's get the other one on. Man went to the moon with less effort than I'm putting into this."

She gave his shoulder a playful slap. "Remind me not to ask you for help again."

He gave her a pointed look. "And your plan for getting these off is?"

She smiled. "You are now acting like a shoe salesman and not Prince Charming."

He finished the task and stood. "Just so you'll recognize it, this is the part where I am Prince Charming." He reached out both hands.

Phoebe put hers in his and he pulled her up until she stood. Ryan continued to hold her hands as he stepped back and studied her. "You look beautiful."

She blinked and a dreamy smile spread across her face. "Thank you. That was very Prince Charming-ish. You look very dashing yourself."

He chuckled. A ripple of pride went through him at her praise. "I do try."

She removed her hands from his and went across the room to where a shawl and purse lay in the chair nearest the front door. "We should go."

"Yes, we should. It's an hour's drive and I've not been there before."

"I know how to get there. I've been by Overnewton Castle many times. I've always wanted to go there for afternoon tea but never have been in."

"Well, princess, this is your chance." Ryan opened the door.

As she went out onto the veranda she said, "Yeah, like I look like a princess. More like a duck."

Not to me.

CHAPTER SEVEN

PHOEBE HAD HEARD that Overnewton Castle was gorgeous but she'd never imagined it was anything like this magnificent. As Ryan drove up the tree-lined drive, the Victorian Tudor-style house came into view. It resembled a castle with its textured masonry, steep roofs and turrets. The multiple stories of corners and angles covered in ivy made it look even more impressive. The expanse of rolling hills and river below created a view that was breathtaking. It was a fairy-tale spot to hold a wedding or a princess for the evening.

"Wow, what a place," Ryan said, as he pulled into the car park that was secluded by trees. "After getting engaged in a hot-air balloon, I shouldn't be surprised that Sophia and Aiden would pick a place like this to marry."

"You don't like it?"

"Sure. It's just a little over the top for me."

"I love it." She did rather feel like a princess, being out with Ryan with the beautiful house as a backdrop.

He came around and helped her out. "I'm more like a beside-the-creek kind of guy but I have to admit this is a nice place."

"Getting married beside a creek, with the water washing over the rock, does sound nice." She pulled the shawl closer around her. When she had trouble adjusting it Ryan removed it, untwisted it and placed it across her shoulders once more. His hands lingered warm and heavy on her shoulders for a second. She missed his touch the instant it was gone.

"I think it's more about making a commitment and less about having a wedding."

Worry entered her voice. "You don't think Sophia and Aiden will last?"

"I'm not saying that. I think they'll do fine. It's just that I was in the service with too many guys whose wives had to have these big weddings and the marriages didn't last two years." He took her arm and placed it through his, putting his other hand over hers. She felt protected. Something that had been missing in her life for too long. They walked in the direction of the house.

"I had no idea you were such a cynic."

Ryan shrugged. "Maybe I am, but I just know what I've seen."

Her foot faltered on the stone path and he steadied her by pulling her against him. They continued down the path until it opened into a grassy area where white chairs had been arranged for the ceremony. Surrounding the area were trees, green foliage and brightly blooming flowers. It was a cozy place for a garden wedding.

"This must be the place." Ryan led her through the hedge opening.

Men and women stood in small groups between the house and the ceremony area. Phoebe recognized a few staff members from the hospital. An unsure feeling washed over her. Should she be here?

"Something wrong?" Ryan asked, as they made their way across the garden.

He always seemed to know when she was disturbed. She pulled away from him. "Are you sure you should have brought me? These are the people you work with and I'm not one of them."

"Look at me, Phoebe." She did. His gaze was intense. "I wanted you here with me." He took her hand. "I want to introduce you to some people I work with."

With Ryan beside her she was capable of facing anything. Phoebe had no doubt that he would remain beside her. She could rely on him. What it all came back to was that she could trust him. He would be there for her. This was the kind of relationship she'd been looking for, dreamed of. A man who would stand beside her. She glanced at his profile, and smiled.

Phoebe recognized a number of the guests from their pictures on the wall of the clinic but there was no reason that they would know her. She had only been a patient of Sophia, and now Ryan. Still, were they surprised to see him show up with a pregnant date?

She pulled on Ryan's hand, bringing him to a stop. "In that case, we both need to look our best. Let me straighten your tie."

"What's wrong with my tie?"

"It just needs an adjustment." Phoebe stepped so close that the baby brushed against him as she reached up to move his tie a centimeter to the left. "Now it's perfect."

Their gazes met.

"No, *you're* perfect." She blinked. His low raspy voice sent a ripple of awareness through her.

"Thank you," she said softly, "and thanks for this evening. It's already been wonderful." She meant that with all her heart.

His brow arched. "We haven't done anything yet."

"I know, but it was nice just to be invited out." *And to be treated as someone special.*

The group opened up as they approached to include them. Ryan went around the circle, introducing everyone. His hand came to rest on the curve of her back. "And this is my friend, Phoebe Taylor."

She noticed that Ryan had presented her as a friend when he'd only introduced the people he worked with as his colleagues. It seemed as if he didn't have many people he considered friends. Yet he and she had formed what she would call a friendship. Why didn't he have more of them?

Ryan was acting nothing like he had the day she had met him. Was he hiding from the world for some reason? What had happened?

She smiled and listened to the conversation and banter between the members of the group. Ryan wasn't left out. He was obviously liked so why didn't he consider any of them his friends?

A few minutes later the notes from a harp sounded to announce it was time for the ceremony to begin. People started taking their seats.

"Sophia has pulled out all the stops for this wedding. I don't believe I've ever been to one with someone playing the harp," Ryan whispered. His breath brushed her neck as they stood in line, waiting for the usher to seat them.

Shivers ran down her spine. Thankfully her reaction went unnoticed because a tuxedo-wearing groomsman approached. He offered his arm and escorted her down the aisle, with Ryan following.

As they took their seats Ryan spoke to a couple of women sitting behind them. One he introduced as Isla, the head midwife in the maternity unit, and her husband,

Dr. Alessandro Manos, who was one of the doctors there. Phoebe recognized Isla from visits to the clinic. A number of times Phoebe had seen her in the hallway. She was also very familiar with the prominent Delamere name. It appeared often in the society pages. She and Isla had something in common. Isla was pregnant as well but not as far along as she was. The other woman was Dr. Darcie Green. Phoebe was told she was a visiting obstetrician from London but she didn't catch her date's name.

After they were settled in their chairs she glanced at Ryan. He wore a stoic look. She leaned toward him. "This really isn't your favorite thing to do, is it?"

His shoulder touched hers. They must have looked like two lovers whispering. What would it be like to be loved by Ryan? Amazing would be her guess. She'd sworn to herself she wouldn't cross the line, had made Ryan pledge the same, but she wasn't sure she wanted it that way any longer.

"Do you know a man that enjoys this?"

She paused. "No, I guess not. We don't have to stay."

"I promised dinner and dancing and I don't plan to disappoint you." Ryan moved closer, putting his mouth to her ear. The intimacy made her grow warm. "*Men* do like food and holding women."

Was he looking forward to dancing with her as much as she was look forward to spending time in his arms? Thankfully, a woman stood in front and began to sing a hymn, leaving Phoebe no more time to contemplate the anticipation of having Ryan hold her. She wasn't sure she could have commented if she'd had a chance. Minutes later the parents of the bride and groom were seated. The harpist played again. The groom and groomsmen stepped to the altar, which was defined by a white metal arch.

Phoebe straightened her back as far as she could to see over the heads of those sitting in front of them. The men wore black tuxedos, making them look not only dashing but sophisticated. She glanced at Ryan and imagined what he would look like in a tux. Very handsome, no doubt. She could only see the top of the best man's head. He was in a wheelchair.

Ryan put his arm across the back of her chair and whispered, "That's Aiden's brother, Nathan, in the chair."

Phoebe nodded.

The harpist continued to play as the bridesmaids came down the aisle. They were dressed in bright yellow knee-length dresses of various styles. Each carried a bouquet of white daisies. As they joined the men, they made a striking combination against the backdrop of trees and plants.

A breeze picked up and Phoebe pulled her wrap closer. She felt Ryan adjusting the wrap to cover her right arm completely. His hand rested on her shoulder. There was something reassuring about the possessive way he touched her.

She looked at him and smiled.

It was time for Sophia to come down the aisle. At the first note of the traditional wedding march everyone stood. Phoebe went up on her toes to catch a glimpse of the bride going by.

"Move so I can see." She nudged Ryan back a step so she could peer around him.

He gave her an indulgent smile and complied.

What little she could observe of Sophia looked beautiful. When she reached Aiden all the guests sat.

Ryan's hand came to rest on her shoulder again. He nudged her close. "You really do like this stuff."

"Shush," Phoebe hissed.

He chuckled softly.

It wasn't long until Sophia and Aiden were coming back down the aisle as man and wife.

Ryan took Phoebe's hand as they filed out of their row. He continued to hold it while they walked across the garden toward the house where the reception would be held. They entered the main hall through glass doors. Cocktails and hors d'oeuvres were being served there. Phoebe gasped at the beauty of the majestic circular staircase before them. It and the dark wood paneling were all the decoration required.

"Come over here," Ryan said, placing his hand on her waist. "If you plan to dance the night away, I think you need to get off your feet and rest while you can."

For once she accepted his concern and consideration. She'd gone so many years doing everything for herself that having someone think of her was fabulous. This evening she was going to enjoy being pampered. Having it done by Ryan would be even nicer.

There were high-backed chairs sitting along the wall and she took one of them. Ryan stood beside her. When the waiter carrying drinks came by they both requested something nonalcoholic, she because she was pregnant and he because he said he would be driving. She liked it that he was acting responsibly. Now that she was having a baby it seemed she thought about that more.

A number of people stopped and spoke to Ryan. While he talked to them, his fingers lightly rested against the top of her shoulder. It would be clear to everyone that she was with him. He never failed to introduce her. A few people gave her belly a searching look and then grinned at them. They must have thought they were a couple.

"Why, hello, Ryan. I never took you for a wedding

kind of guy. I've never even seen you at a Christmas party." The words were delivered in a teasing tone by a woman who joined them.

Phoebe looked up at Ryan and he seemed to take the comment in stride.

"Hello, Vera. It's nice to see you, too. Sophia twisted my arm on this one. Couldn't get out of it. I'd like you to meet Phoebe Taylor." He directed the next statement to Phoebe. "Vera is the hospital's chief anesthetist."

"Hi." Phoebe smiled at Vera.

"Nice to meet you." Vera's attention went back to Ryan. "I had no idea you were expecting a baby."

"It's not mine."

"Oh." She made the word carry a mountain of suggestions and questions.

"Phoebe was a wife of a friend of mine in the service. He was killed eight months ago."

Vera looked down at Phoebe. "I'm sorry."

"Thank you." Somehow the pain of Joshua not being there had eased over the last few weeks.

"So when's the baby due?"

"In just a few weeks," Phoebe said.

"You're being followed at Victoria antenatal?" Vera showed true interest.

"You mean prenatal," Ryan quipped.

She glared at him. "I wished you'd get away from calling it that. I have to think twice when you do."

"And I have to think when you called it antenatal. Old habits die hard."

"I guess they do. Well, I'd better mingle. Nice to meet you, Phoebe."

"Bye." Once again Ryan had proved that he was well

liked and respected. So why didn't he socialize with his colleagues?

A few minutes later the guests were called to dinner. On a table outside the room was a place card with Ryan's name on it and a table number. He picked it up and led the way.

The room was stunning. Round tables with white tablecloths covering them to the floor filled it. Chairs were also covered in white with matching bows on the back. At the front of the room, facing the guests, was one long table for the bridal party.

By the time they arrived at their table, Isla and Darcie, the two women who had sat behind them during the ceremony, were already there. Ryan took the chair next to Darcie, and Phoebe sat on his other side. Another couple who knew Isla joined them and took the last seats. Everyone introduced themselves. Most of Phoebe's time was spent talking to the woman beside her. Occasionally, someone across the table would ask a question but hearing was difficult with the amount of chatter in the room.

The bridal party was introduced and Sophia and Aiden took their places before the meal was served. The noise dropped as people ate.

"So, Phoebe," Isla asked from directly across the table, "when's your baby due?"

That was the most popular question of the evening. "In a couple of weeks."

"Are you being seen in the MMU?"

"I am. Sophia was my midwife but she thought falling in love was more important." Phoebe smiled.

"That does happen. Who's following you now?"

"That would be me," Ryan announced. There was a note of pride in his voice.

A hush came over the table. Phoebe didn't miss the looks of shock on the two women's faces. Was something wrong? She glanced at Ryan. It wasn't a secret. Why should it be?

"Phoebe needed someone and I volunteered," Ryan offered, as he picked up his water glass and took a sip.

Both women looked from him, then back to her and back again. Ryan didn't seem fazed by their reaction.

Finally Isla said, "Ryan's one of the best. You'll be happy with his care."

After they had eaten their meal, Ryan watched Phoebe make her way to the restroom. His attention was drawn away from her when Isla sat down in Phoebe's place.

Isla leaned close and hissed, "Just what do you think you're doing?"

He sat back, surprised by her aggression. "Doing?"

Darcie moved in from the other side, sandwiching him in. "You're dating a patient!"

"I am not."

"What do you call it when you bring the woman you're going to deliver for to a wedding as your date?" Isla asked.

"I call it dating," Darcie quipped.

"Look, Phoebe is the widow of a service buddy of mine. All I'm trying to do is be her friend. She doesn't have anyone else."

"That wasn't a friendly arm around her at the ceremony. Or a friendly look just a second ago when she walked away," Isla stated, as if she were giving a lecture to a first-year student.

"Or when you were looking at her as she fixed your tie," Darcie added.

"You saw that?" Ryan was amazed. They had seen

what he'd believed he'd been covering well—his attraction to Phoebe.

"Yes, we…" Darcie indicated her date "…went past you and you didn't even see us, you were so engrossed."

"I was not."

"You can deny it all you want but I'm telling you what I saw. The point here is that you shouldn't be dating a patient. It's bad form and if someone wanted to make a big deal of it you might lose your job." Isla looked around as if she was checking to see if anyone was listening.

Ryan chuckled. "You're overreacting to two friends spending an evening together."

"I still say you better be careful. You're stepping over the line with this one," Isla said.

Darcie nodded her agreement.

He leaned back and looked at one then the other. "Well, are either one of you going to report me?"

The two women looked at each other. Both shook their heads.

"Thank you. I asked Phoebe to come with me because she's had a rough year, finding out her husband was killed and then that she was pregnant. This was her big night out before the baby comes. In any case, all of that about me delivering the baby will be a moot point in a few weeks. So, ladies, I appreciate your concern but I'm going to show Phoebe a pleasant evening and if that looks bad to you I'm sorry."

They grinned at each other.

"You were right, Isla. He does care about her." Darcie smirked.

Isla patted him on the shoulder. "Good luck."

Ryan wasn't sure what that meant but it was better

than being reprimanded for something he didn't believe was a problem.

Phoebe returned, and Isla moved back to her chair and kissed her husband on the cheek as she sat down. She smiled at Phoebe.

After Phoebe sat she leaned over and whispered, "Is everything all right?"

He took her hand beneath the table, gave it a squeeze and held it. "Everything is great."

Dessert had been served by the time the bride and groom started around the room, greeting their guests. When they reached Phoebe and Ryan's table Sophia hugged each person in turn until she worked her way to Ryan.

"Well, I'm glad to see you. I wasn't sure you'd be here."

Ryan hugged Sophia in return. "O ye of little faith."

She laughed and turned to Phoebe. For a second there was a look of astonishment on Sophia's face when she saw her but it soon disappeared. "Phoebe, I'm so glad to see you. I'd like you to meet my husband, Aiden."

While Phoebe spoke to Aiden, Ryan didn't miss the look that passed between Sophia, Isla and Darcie.

Did his feelings for Phoebe really show that much? They must if they were that obvious to the three women. How had he let it happen? He glanced at Phoebe. The devil of it was, he hadn't. All it took was just being around Phoebe to make him care. And that he did far too much.

She giggled at something Sophia said. He wanted her too much. There was little that was professional about his feelings. How would she take it when he told her that he could no longer be her midwife?

* * *

The strains of an orchestra tuning up came from somewhere in the house.

Sophia's father asked everyone to join them for dancing and a toast to the bride and groom in the solarium. Ryan took her hand as they made their way there. It was as if he didn't want to break the contact with her. She didn't want to, either.

Phoebe had been sure that what she'd already seen of the castle couldn't be surpassed, but she'd been wrong. Two-thirds of the solarium consisted of glass walls and glass ceiling. It had turned dark and small lights above created a magical place.

Ryan directed her to one of the café-size tables stationed around the room. They sat and watched the bride and groom dance their first dance. The staff saw to it that everyone had a glass of champagne to toast the couple. Ryan smiled as he tapped her glass. Phoebe took the smallest sip and set the glass down. His joined hers on the table. The orchestra began to play again.

Ryan stood and offered his hand. "It's time I made good on my promise. Would you care to dance?"

"Why, sir, I think I would." Phoebe smiled at him and placed her hand in his.

"I'll have to tell you that I'm not a very good dancer," Ryan said, as he led her out on to the floor.

She laughed. "Have you looked at me lately? I'm not very graceful so I don't think it'll matter if you're a good dancer or not."

"Then I guess we're the perfect match."

Were they really?

Ryan took her into his arms, holding her close as they moved around the floor. He'd touched her before but had never put his arms completely around her. It was lovely to have him so close. He smelled like a warm forest after a spring rain. She leaned in and inhaled. Wonderful.

The overhead lights were turned low and the tiny ones became more brilliant. They slowly swayed to the music. Did fairy tales really come true? Phoebe had no idea if they were with the beat or not. It didn't matter. The next song was a faster one and they separated. She felt the loss of Ryan's warmth immediately and her body waited impatiently to have it returned. Not allowing her to completely lose contact, he continued to hold one of her hands. As soon as the faster dance was over, he brought her back into his embrace. Her fingers rested on his shoulders and his found her waist. As they moved slowly, they looked into each other's eyes. Something was occurring here that she'd never planned, never thought would happen. She was falling in love.

"Does dancing with me make you think of that game you might have played in gym class where you had to keep a ball between you and your partner without using your hands?"

He stopped moving. "How's that?"

"Dancing with the baby between us."

Ryan laughed. "I had skill at that game. Always won." He pulled her closer. "You're the best partner I've ever had."

Her hand cupped his face. "You're a nice guy."

Ryan's eyes grew intense and he cleared his throat. "It's warm in here. Why don't we go outside for a few minutes?"

She nodded. He led her through a half-hidden glass door that looked like part of the wall, onto a brick patio.

"It feels good out here." Phoebe breathed in the cold

evening air. The music from inside drifted around them. It was painfully romantic. Was Ryan feeling the same need?

"It does." Ryan stood a couple of steps away, just out of touching distance.

She wanted his touch. Wanted to feel desired. It had been too long. Even with Joshua the last time she hadn't felt desire. Sex had become more of an obligation, expectation than anything else. There should be more than that in a relationship. There was with Ryan. Would he think she was too forward if she reached for him?

A wide set of steps led to a pond below. Surrounding it was an extensive grassy area. The lights of the solarium reflected off the water, making the view even more dreamlike. Phoebe started down the steps.

"Where're you going?" Ryan asked.

"I thought I'd stand in the garden and admire the solarium." She was already watching the others dance when Ryan joined her.

"It reminds me of a carousel music box I once had as a child. As it played, horses with people riding them went by in shadow. It was like watching something magical. I could look at it for hours. I loved it," she whispered, as much to herself as to him.

"You are a romantic." He now stood close enough that his arm brushed hers as their fingers intertwined.

"Because I think there can be fairy tales?"

He didn't say anything for a while. "I haven't believed in fairy tales for a long time, but somehow when I'm around you they do seem possible."

"I know you've lived through some horrible things you can't seem to leave behind, but you need to know there's good in life, too. Happy times that can replace the bad.

Like this baby. Joshua is gone, yet in a way he's bringing new life into the world. Something good for me."

"Good can be hard to find."

His fingers tightened. Phoebe glanced at him. He stood rigid, as if the discussion was painful for him. His gaze met hers and she said, "It can be. And it can come from unexpected places, too."

"Like you?"

"I like to think so but I wasn't talking about me so much as from friends and family. Finding people that matter to you. Letting them know they are important to you."

"I can't do that."

She stepped closer, her body touching his. "I think you can. In fact, I know you can. You've been a friend to me these last few weeks."

They continued to stand there, not saying a word. It wasn't until the doors were opened wide by the Overnewton staff members that the spell was broken and they broke apart. The crowd poured out of the solarium and began lining up along the steps.

"I guess it's time for Sophia and Aiden to leave," Phoebe murmured.

"We should join everyone." Ryan didn't sound like he really wanted to. Had their conversation put a dampener on the evening? She would hate that to happen. Had she ever enjoyed a wedding more?

As they stood at the bottom of the steps, a gust of wind caught her shawl. She shivered and pulled it closer.

"You're cold." Ryan removed his jacket and placed it over her shoulders. It still held his body heat. His scent. She pulled it tighter around her.

Someone near passed them each a small container of

bird seed. As Sophia and Aiden descended the steps they were showered with the seed for good luck. When they reached Phoebe and Ryan, Aiden whisked Sophia into his arms and carried her to a waiting car.

Phoebe looked down at her expanded middle. "I'd like to see someone whisk me up like that."

Suddenly her feet were in the air and she was being held against a hard chest. "Oh."

Her arms went around Ryan's neck. He swung her around a few times. She giggled.

Ryan put her on her feet again. "I didn't see it as a problem."

As he smiled down at her, a tingle grew low within her from the warmth she saw in his eyes. She glanced around. Some of the crowd was watching them. She didn't care. What she wanted was to help make Ryan see that fairy tales could come true. He had the biggest heart of anyone she knew, loyal, caring and generous. With a wicked sense of humor that only made her love him more. That's what she felt. Love for him. She'd fallen under his spell. He wasn't going to leave her. More than once he'd proved he'd be there when she needed him. She could depend on him.

Phoebe's hands remained about his neck. She looked up into his eyes and smiled. "That was fun."

"I think it's time for us to go." He looked down at her, his voice coming out soft and raspy.

Ryan walked Phoebe to her door. She'd been quiet on their drive home. Had she been thinking about those moments when they had looked into each other's eyes? He'd known then there was no going back. He wanted her and she wanted him. It had been there in her crystal clear look of assurance.

As he'd pulled out onto the main road, he'd taken her hand and rested it on his thigh. She hadn't resisted. For once she hadn't fallen asleep during the drive. Had she been as keyed up as he'd been? He wanted her but he couldn't lead her on. Have her believe there was more than just a physical attraction between them.

Her hand had remained in his the entire way back to Box Hill. She had asked for his help with her shoes when they'd arrived at his car. He had obliged. When they'd arrived at her house she'd stepped out of the car carrying them by two fingers.

They walked to her front porch. "It was a perfect evening, Ryan. Thank you so much for inviting me."

"I'm glad you had a good time. Mine wouldn't have been near as nice if you'd not gone with me."

She fumbled with her purse.

"Hand those to me." Ryan indicated the shoes. She found her keys and unlocked the door, pushing it open. Ryan followed her in.

"Would you like some coffee?" Phoebe dropped her shoes beside the door.

"I thought you didn't drink coffee."

She turned to look at him. "I don't. I bought it for you."

"Then, yes, I would." It had been a long time since someone had bought anything especially for him. It meant she thought about him even when he wasn't around. That idea he liked far too much.

He followed her to the kitchen. He leaned against the door frame and watched as Phoebe put a kettle of water on a burner. He was fascinated by the combination of her in a beautiful dress with bare feet, preparing coffee. There was something so domestic about the picture that it made him want to run as far away from there as he could get while at the same time it pulled him in, making him wish for more, had him longing for someone special in his life.

Phoebe stood on her toes to reach the bag of coffee. Her dress rose enough that he had a view of the backs of her knees and thighs. An impulse to run a hand along all that skin and under her dress made his pants tighten. Heaven help him, he wanted her so badly. Right here, right now. The entire evening had been leading up to this moment. From the time he'd was on his knee, helping her put her shoes on, until now he'd known he had to have her.

He should walk away. Go out the door without a word said. The gentleman in him, the professional, screamed for him to leave. But he wouldn't. The temptation to kiss her was too great. Unable to resist, he closed the small distance between them. Pushing her hair away, he kissed her neck. He pressed his front to her back, letting his desire be known. "I know what I agreed to, but I can't stop myself. I want you."

Before he could say more, she pushed back against him, gaining enough room to face him. She wrapped her hands around his waist and lifted her face. Her eyes were clear and confident. The quiver of her lips gave him a hint of what this boldness was costing her. Still, she was offering.

Slowly his mouth met hers.

A flood of disappointment went through him when she pulled away seconds later but quickly turned into a storm of longing as Phoebe's lips met his again. They were soft and mobile. Small cushions of bliss. This was better than he remembered. He wanted more.

Ryan reached around her and turned off the burner,

then pulled her closer. He brought his lips more fully against hers.

Phoebe's hands moved to grip his biceps. She shifted, pressing her breasts to his chest.

The arousal he felt at the first touch of her lips grew, lengthened. Hardened. His mouth released hers and moved across her cheek. He left a trail of butterfly kisses on his way to the sweet spot behind her ear. Phoebe moaned, then tilted her head so that he could better reach her neck. She snuggled against him.

The desire to have her made his muscles draw tight. He wanted her here. Now. His hands caressed her back and settled low on her hips. He gathered her dress in his hands and pulled her against his throbbing need.

"Phoebe, you'll have to stop us because I can't," he murmured as his mouth pressed down on hers, begging her for entrance.

Her hands went to the nape of his neck in an eager movement, pulling his lips more firmly to hers. She opened her mouth, and his tongue didn't hesitate to gain entrance. Hers met his to tease and tantalize. It was a duel of pleasure that he didn't want to win.

His body hummed with a need that only Phoebe could ease.

She pulled her mouth away.

"Aw. What's wrong?"

"The baby kicked."

Damn. He'd forgotten all about the baby. How could he? Because he was so focused on his hunger for Phoebe. He stepped back far enough that he was no longer touching her.

"I'm sorry. I didn't mean to hurt you."

"Silly, you weren't hurting me." She took a predatory step toward him. "Babies kick."

"I shouldn't, we shouldn't..."

"Come on, Ryan. We're adults. I'm certainly aware of the facts of life, and I'm sure you are, too. So we both know that what we were doing wouldn't hurt the baby. I want this. I want you. From what I could tell, you wanted me."

That would be an understatement.

"I'm going to my bedroom. I hope you join me. If not, please lock up on your way out."

She went up on the tips of her toes, kissed him and left the kitchen. Ryan stood there with his manhood aching and the choice of a lifetime to make.

How like Phoebe to be so direct. If he joined her, could he remain emotionally detached? He already cared more than he should and certainly more than he was comfortable with. But if he didn't, he would never know the heaven of being with Phoebe. There was no decision. A beautiful, desirable woman that he wanted was offering him the world. There was no question of whether or not to accept.

CHAPTER EIGHT

PHOEBE SAT ON the edge of the bed in her room. A lone lamp burned on her bedside table. She'd never been so brazen in her life. But how else was she going to get through to Ryan? She wanted him desperately. Needed his calm caring, his reliability and assurance in her life. It was so quiet in the house that she feared he'd slipped out and gone home. Seconds later her heart thumped against her ribs at the sound of footfalls in the hallway.

He'd stayed.

Ryan hesitated at the door. Their gazes met, held. He removed his tie and jacket and dropped them over the chair, then he stalked across the floor and pulled her to her feet and into his arms.

This was where she belonged.

His mouth met hers. She opened for him. Their tongues mated in a frenzied battle of touch and retreat. Heat flowed through her, strong and sure, pooling low in her. Ryan's lips left hers and he buried his face in her neck. He nipped at her skin. The desire that flickered in her blazed.

He gathered her dress along one leg, sliding a hand under the fabric. She hissed as his fingers touched her skin. His hand glided around her leg until it found the inside of her thigh and squeezed lightly. She shivered.

Ryan removed his hand. He met her gaze. Placing his hands on her shoulders, he turned her around.

"What…?"

"Shush," he all but growled. He gathered her hair, running his fingers through it. "Beautiful," he murmured, before placing it over a shoulder.

There was a tug at the top of her dress. He opened the zipper. The tug ended and his lips found the skin between her shoulder blades. A shudder traveled down her spine. His mouth skimmed over each vertebra to her waist. There he spent some time kissing and touching with the tip of his tongue the curve of her back.

She began to move but he said, "Not yet."

Ryan's fingertip followed the same path upward, then his palms until he brushed her dress off her shoulders. She crossed her arms, preventing the dress from falling away from her breasts.

He kissed the length of the ridge between her neck and arm. "So silky."

Phoebe sighed. This was too wonderful. "Let me turn off the lamp."

He guided her to face him. "Phoebe, look at me."

Her eyes rose to meet his gaze.

"You're beautiful." He placed his hands on either side of the baby. "That's a new life you're carrying. There's nothing more amazing or natural than that. Please don't hide it from me."

If she could have melted she would have. "You're sure?"

"Honey, I'm more than sure." Ryan moved closer to bring his taught length against her belly, leaving her in no doubt of his desire.

It was an empowering thought to know that was all for her.

Stepping back, he took both her hands and opened her arms. The dress fell away, leaving her breasts visible, cupped in a lacy pink bra. Her dress gathered on her belly. Ryan gave it a gentle tug at the seams and the dress pooled around her feet on the floor.

His gaze fixed on her breasts. He sucked in a breath and she crossed her arms again.

"Please, don't. You're amazing. I want to admire you."

"They're so large." She couldn't look at him.

Ryan lifted her chin with a finger until her gaze met his. "I don't know a man in the world who doesn't love large breasts. Especially if they are his to admire."

The heat building in her grew. Ryan knew how to make her feel beautiful.

He removed her arms. Using a finger, he followed the cleft of her cleavage. Her nipples pushed against her bra as they swelled. A tingle zipped through her breasts. His finger traced the line of her bra first over one mound and then the other. She swayed and Ryan slipped an arm around her.

With a deft movement of his fingers he unclipped her bra. He slipped it off one arm. His tongue followed the same path as his finger. On the return trip, he veered off. At the same time his free hand lifted her right breast, his mouth captured her nipple.

Her womb contracted. "Ryan…" she muttered. She wasn't sure if she was begging for him to stop or to continue.

Ryan supported her as she leaned back, offering herself completely to him. Her hands went to his shoulders in the hope she could steady her body and her emotions. His mouth slid to the other nipple. Her fingertips bit into his shoulders.

Ryan's hand traced the line of her undies until he reached her center. It brushed her mound and retreated. Her center throbbed with the need for him to return. Using the arm around her waist, he pulled her toward him until she was no longer leaning back. His hand swept the other strap of her bra off and down her arm, letting the undergarment drop to the floor.

She looked at him. Ryan's gaze was fixed on her breasts. His hand reached up and stopped millimeters from her nipple. It had the slightest tremor to it. She would have missed it if she hadn't been watching. They both understood the facts of life well and still these moments of passion were overwhelming. He touched the tip of her nipple with the end of his finger.

Something similar to lightning shot through her.

"So responsive," Ryan murmured in a note of satisfaction as he ran a finger gently over her skin. It was as if a breeze had come through. He did the same to the other breast.

Phoebe quaked all over. There was something erotic about watching Ryan touch her. Her nerve endings tingled. She had to touch him. See his reaction.

He moved back and lifted both her breasts, kissing each one in turn. Taking a nipple in his mouth, he traced it with his tongue and tugged. She bucked against him.

"Clothes." The word came out as a strangled sound. "I want to see you."

A noise came low in his throat. Leaving a kiss on the curve of her breast, he stepped back. Undoing his tie, he jerked it from his collar and began unbuttoning his shirt.

While he did that she released his belt. She ran the back of her hand down the bulge of his manhood. His body's reaction to hers was stimulating. It gave her a boldness she'd never had before. She backed away until her legs found the side of the bed and she sat. Looking up at Ryan, she caught his gaze. "Come here. It's my turn."

His shirt fluttered to the floor. He stepped close enough for her to touch him. Finding his zipper, she slowly lowered it. Her hand moved to touch him but he stopped her by capturing her hand and bringing it to his lips. "Don't." The word sounded harsh with tension. "I don't think I can control myself if you do."

Phoebe pulled her hand from his. Sliding her hands between the waist of his pants and his hips, she pushed. His trousers fell to the floor. He wore red plaid boxers that didn't disguise his size. Ryan was no small man anywhere.

He kicked off his shoes, then finished removing his slacks. Leaning over, he jerked off his socks.

Phoebe reached out and ran her hand through his hair. Her fingers itched to gather the mass and pull him to her. Had she ever been this turned on? She wanted Ryan beside her, on her and in her like she'd never wanted before. Her hands slowly slipped from his hair and Ryan looked at her. He nudged her back on the bed and came down beside her.

"I want to touch you like you did me." Phoebe rolled to her side.

He faced her.

Her heart leaped at his unspoken agreement. The lovemaking between Joshua and her had always been fast and desperate, never slow and passionate, as she was experiencing now.

* * *

Ryan wasn't sure he could stand much more of Phoebe's administering. As it was, he gritted his teeth to control his need to dive into her.

Her index finger traced the line of his lips. He captured the end and drew it into his mouth and sucked. Her eyes darkened. She slowly removed her finger. His manhood flinched. Did she have any idea how erotic she was?

Phoebe's small hand ran down the side of his neck in a gentle motion. It glided over his shoulder. She placed a kiss there. Her hair hid her face as it flowed over his skin like silk. He couldn't resist touching it, watching it move through his fingers. Pushing it away from her face, he cupped her cheek and brought her lips to his. She eagerly accepted. Her hands fluttered across his chest, moving up to the nape of his neck.

When he leaned over to take the kiss deeper, Phoebe pushed against his shoulders, breaking the connection. One hand at his neck dropped lower to run across his chest. She took an infinite amount of time tracing each of his ribs. As if she was trying to commit each curve, dip and rise of him to memory. His muscles quivered from the attention.

Her hand went lower, a finger dipping into his belly button. At his sharp inhalation she giggled. He loved the sound. Her hand moved to his side and rubbed up and down it to return to his stomach. She smoothed her fingers over his hip. The tips slipped under the elastic band of his boxers and retreated just as quickly.

Phoebe rose enough to accommodate the baby and kissed the center of his chest. At the same time her fingers went deeper under his boxers than before, touching the tip of his manhood.

Only with a force of control he hadn't known he possessed did he manage not to lose it.

Pulling her back, he gathered her to him and kissed her with a depth of need he was afraid to examine. She clung to him as if she never wanted to let him go.

"Phoebe, I need you now."

"I'm here."

Ryan scooted off the bed and removed his boxers. Phoebe's intake of breath made his manhood rise. He held out his hand and she took it, standing. His hands found the waistband of her undies and slipped them down her legs. She stepped out of them. He flipped the covers back to the end of the bed. Phoebe climbed in and seconds later he had her in his arms again.

"I don't want to hurt you. Or the baby."

She met his direct look with one of her own. "You would never do that."

The confidence she had in him shook him to the core. This wouldn't just be a physical joining but an emotional one, as well. He'd never intended to care but he did.

Ryan shifted to the center of the bed, then brought her over him until she straddled his waist. On her knees above him, her beautiful full breasts hung down like juicy melons, tempting him to feast. He wasted no time in doing so. As he savored all that was offered, Phoebe shifted so that her entrance teased his length. It ached in anticipation of finding home.

Phoebe kissed him as he lifted her hips and positioned her on him. He slid into her and they became one. He held his breath. It wasn't he but she who moved first. He joined her. Using his hands, he helped control their movements. At her frustrated sound he eased his grip and she settled farther down on him.

His hands remained lightly on her as he guided her up and down again and again. She was a beauty with her golden hair hanging down, her eyes closed and her head thrown back. With a shudder and a hiss of pleasure, she looked at him and gave him a dreamy smile.

Yes, he was the king of the world.

He kissed her deeply and flexed his hips against hers. After two powerful thrusts he found his own bliss.

Phoebe rolled off Ryan. Her head came to rest on his arm, a hand on his chest, her baby between them. She wished it would always be this way. She loved Ryan. He cared for her. She had no doubt of that. His lovemaking proved it. But would he ever admit it to himself or her that he might want something lasting? It didn't matter, it wouldn't change how she felt.

She yawned. "I'm tired."

Ryan grinned. "Me, too. For a pregnant lady you sure can be rough on a man."

"So what you're saying is that you're not man enough for me."

Ryan pulled her to him for a kiss that curled her toes. His already growing manhood pushed against her leg.

"You need me to prove I'm man enough?"

"No, I think you did that just fine a few minutes ago. Right now, I need to rest. Too much dining, dancing and man." Her eyes closed to the feel of Ryan's hand rubbing her back.

Phoebe woke to the sun streaming through the bedroom window. She was alone. Panic filled her. Had Ryan left?

A clang came from the direction of the kitchen. She'd woken once during the night. Her back had been against his solid chest and his hand had cupped her right breast. It had been a perfect night. She wanted more of them.

He'd said nothing about how he felt. He had been an attentive and caring lover. She had never felt more desired. Still, she might be reading more into his actions than there was.

"Hey, I was hoping you were still asleep." Ryan walked into the room with a smile on his face and carrying a tray.

Phoebe pulled the sheet up to cover her chest. "Good morning to you, too. What do you have there?"

"It's supposed to be your breakfast in bed."

She'd never had anyone feed her in bed. Sitting up, she peered at the tray. "Really? That sounds nice."

He didn't seem to feel any morning-after awkwardness. She would be happy to follow his lead. Her biggest fear the night before had been that she would be a disappointment because of her size. The second fear had been that there would be unease between them this morning. Ryan had made it clear he wasn't turned off by her body. By his actions so far this morning, he was the same Ryan he had been last night.

He sat the tray at the end of the bed. She recognized it as one off the table in her living room. On it was sliced apples, two bowls of cereal and two glasses of orange juice.

"Lean forward."

Phoebe did as he asked. Ryan stuffed pillows behind her and she settled back. He joined her on the bed.

"No bacon and eggs?" She added a mock pout. "Afraid you'd burn yourself?

"You're so funny. I did what I was capable of doing. We can have something more substantial later."

"This looks wonderful to me."

She kissed him on the cheek.

"That wasn't much of a thank-you kiss. I think you can do better." His lips found hers. Seconds later Phoebe wanted to forget about their breakfast and concentrate on nothing but Ryan. Her arms went around his neck and she pulled him closer.

Ryan broke the kiss. "We need to be careful or we'll have juice and cereal everywhere. As much as I'd like to go on kissing you, I know you need nutrition."

"That sounded very midwife-ish."

He lowered his chin and gave her a serious look. "Well, that's what I am."

"And you are mine."

He was hers. Ryan liked the sound of that but he could never be what she needed. He couldn't commit to being hers, like she deserved. He wasn't who she thought he was. She should have someone who could love her wholeheartedly, holding nothing back. He had to see to it that their relationship remained light and easy. But after what had happened between them last night, that might be impossible.

"As your medical professional, I say eat."

"Can I put something on first?"

"I don't mind you the way you are." He grinned.

"That's sweet of you to say but I think I'd be less self-conscious with my gown on. After all, you have your underwear on."

Ryan stood. "Okay, if it'll get you to eat something, tell me where your gowns are."

She pointed to a chest. "Second drawer."

He didn't make a habit of going through a woman's personal things and found it almost too much like they were in a lifelong relationship to do so in Phoebe's. As quickly as he could, he pulled out a light blue gown. Returning to her, he helped her slip it over her head. Sitting on the edge of the bed, he asked, "Satisfied now?"

"Yes, I'm not used to breakfast in bed and I'm sure not used to sharing it with someone when I have no clothes on."

"I like you naked."

"Even with this beach ball of a belly?" She touched her middle.

He kissed her. "Women are at their prettiest when they are expecting. You glow."

She gathered her hair and pulled it over one shoulder. Her chin went up and she batted her eyelashes. "I glow? I like that."

"Yes, you glow but you would be brighter if you'd eat something." Ryan pulled the tray closer and handed her a glass of juice.

They spent the next few minutes discussing the wedding, the weather and what other plans she had for the baby's room.

When they had finished eating Ryan stood, took the tray and was on his way out the door when Phoebe's squeak stopped him. He wheeled to look at her. Concern washed over him. Was something wrong? Should he take her to the hospital? "Are you okay?"

"Yes, just the baby making its presence known." She grinned. "I did have a little more activity last night than I normally do."

Relief flooded him. He needed to calm down, not overreact. Being a midwife, he should know better, but this was Phoebe. He cared for his patients but on no level did that came close to what he felt for Phoebe. How was he going to remain professional when he delivered the baby? Maybe it would be better if someone else did. "I'm sorry."

"I should hope not! Because I'm sure not."

"Thanks. My ego would have been damaged otherwise."

"I wouldn't want that to happen." She winced and shifted in the bed. "This baby is getting his morning exercise."

Ryan grinned. "I have an idea to help with those aches and pains. You stay there while I take this to the kitchen. I'll be right back. Don't move."

The anticipation of being in Ryan's arms again was enough to have Phoebe's blood humming. He soon returned with the bottle of lotion in his hand he had used the other night during her foot massage.

"Oh, I'm going to get another foot massage." She couldn't keep the eagerness out of her voice and started moving toward the edge of the bed.

"No. Stay where you are. Just move forward some." He put the lotion on the bedside table.

Her brow wrinkled but she did as he asked. What did he have planned this time?

Ryan climbed in bed behind her, putting a leg on each side of her hips so that she now sat between his.

"What're you doing?"

There was all kind of movement behind her until Ryan's arms came around her and pulled her back against his chest. "I was having a hard time getting the pillows to stay in place. Pull your gown up."

"What is this? Some special pregnant woman's sex position?"

He chuckled behind her. “Is that all you think about? Sex?”

“When you’re around, yes.”

He kissed her neck. “Thank you for the nice compliment but right now I have something else in mind. Now pull your gown up.”

She did as he said until it was gathered under her breasts then adjusted the sheet over her thighs, giving her some modesty.

Ryan reached around her neck.

“Hey, is this a fancy way of choking me?”

“You sure are making it hard for me to be nice to you.”

Cold hit her bare middle, making her jerk. “Ooh.”

“That’ll teach you not to have such a smart mouth,” Ryan said in a teasing tone. His hands began to glide over her middle. “You’re all tense. Lie back and enjoy.”

She did, settling against his chest and closing her eyes. Ryan’s hands made slow circles over her middle.

“This is wonderful. Did you learn to do this in the service, too?”

“No. But I did deliver my first baby there.”

“Will you tell me about it?”

Ryan’s body tensed behind her. He was quiet so long she wasn’t sure he would say anything more.

“One weekend we were invited to a local celebration. I’m still not sure what it was for, but anyway some of the unit went along. We ate the food. Played with the kids.

“You know, kids are the same wherever you go. All they want is their parents there for them and to play and be happy. Every child deserves that.” Ryan’s hands drifted to the sides of her belly. His palms pressed lightly against her. “Especially this one.”

Phoebe placed her hand over one of his. "He or she will have that. I promise."

It would be wonderful if Ryan would be a part of helping her make that come true. But he said nothing that indicated he wanted that kind of involvement in their lives.

"After the celebration we were going back to the base but had to stop because there was mechanical trouble with one of the trucks. There happened to be three or four huts that locals lived in nearby. There was a loud scream from that direction. A couple of the men went to investigate. It turned out that there was a woman having a baby. She was in trouble. They returned for me.

"I don't think I've even been in a house that had less. It was made of mud bricks, with a grass roof and dirt floor. Water was drawn from a barely running creek half a mile away. The kitchen consisted of a pot over a fire. In this horrible war-torn country, in this nothing shelter was a woman trying to give birth. The only people around were a couple of children about the ages of six and eight."

His hands stopped moving but continued to rest on her.

"I had the interpreter ask her if she would like me to help. Her culture dictated that she shouldn't agree but she was in so much pain she wouldn't tell me no. I had seen a baby delivered once. I'm not sure who was more scared, me or her. I sent everyone out but the interpreter. It took some explaining on the interpreter's part to get her to understand I needed to examine her. Finally she relented. The baby's shoulder was hung. I was thankful it wasn't breech, which was what I'd expected. It was work but I managed to help bring the baby into the world. It was exhilarating. The baby had a healthy cry and the mother a smile on her face when I left. Imagine living like that and still smiling. I knew then that it was far better than patching up men who had been shot or torn apart by landmines. As soon as I returned to camp I put in my papers to get out of the army."

"Did you ever see the baby again?"

"No. I never wanted to. I was afraid of what I might find. Children have a hard life in Iraq. You know, this conversation has suddenly taken a negative turn. Not what I intended. How about you tell me what you have planned for this week."

His fingers started moving over her skin again.

"I think I forgot to tell you that some of the teachers at school are giving me a shower on Monday after classes. I hope now I'll have some baby clothes to fill the drawers of the chest. I also hope to buy a few pictures for the walls. If I do, would you hang them for me?"

"As long as someone doesn't go into labor, I don't see why not."

She twisted to look at him. "Could you come out to dinner one night?"

Ryan's fingertips fluttered over her middle. "Sounds great to me. Sit up. I want to massage your lower back."

She did so and he pushed her gown up to her shoulders. He put more lotion in his hands and began to rub her lower back firmly.

"For a little bit you could get a permanent job doing that."

Ryan's hands faltered a second, then started moving again. Had she said the wrong thing?

"Well, I've done all I can to make you comfortable."

"It was wonderful. Feel free to stop by and do that anytime. If I got a foot massage and body rub on the same day, I might melt away."

"I wouldn't want you to do that. I like knowing you're around." Ryan moved out from behind her. "As much as I would enjoy staying in bed with you all day, I promised to cover for Sophia this afternoon and tomorrow until the new midwife takes over on Monday."

She hated to see this time with Ryan end.

"Mind if I get a quick shower?" he asked.

"Of course not," she said, pulling her gown back into place.

"Why don't you stay in bed, take it easy today?" Ryan suggested, as he picked up his clothes off the floor.

"Are you afraid you were too rough on me last night?"

His grin was devilish. "Are you kidding? It was more like you being rough on me. I had no idea a pregnant woman could be so aggressive."

She threw a pillow at him. "I'll show you aggressive."

Ryan's deep laughter filled the room even after he'd closed the bathroom door behind him.

Phoebe was in the kitchen when he came in to say goodbye. His shirtsleeves were rolled halfway up his forearms. He had his jacket over his arm and his tie in his hand. A couple of damp locks of hair fell over his forehead. She had never seen anyone look more desirable.

She resisted the urge to grab his hand and beg him not to leave. When he went out the door she was afraid that fragile fairy-tale bubble they had been living in since yesterday afternoon would burst. Could she ever get it back again?

Phoebe stood with her back to the counter. "I'll be in town on Thursday for my next checkup."

"I'll see you then if not before. I have to go."

"I know. There are babies to deliver."

He grinned. "And they don't wait."

"I sure hope not. I'm ready now for this one to come." She looked at a picture on the wall instead of him, scared he might see her sadness. There had never been this type of emotion when Joshua had left and she'd known she wouldn't see him for months. She had it bad for Ryan.

Phoebe walked with him out to the veranda. At the steps he wrapped her in his arms and pulled her tightly against him, giving her a kiss. Letting her go, he hurried down the steps.

"A little overdressed for a Saturday morning, aren't you, dear?"

Phoebe smiled as Ryan threw up a hand and continued down the path. "Good morning, Mrs. Rosenheim. Beautiful day, isn't it?"

Phoebe waved as he pulled away.

"I see you found a young man who'll be around for you." Mrs. Rosenheim's voice carried across the gardens.

Phoebe waved and called, "I hope I have."

Ryan pulled up in front of his house, turned off the engine and banged his head against the steering wheel a couple of times.

What had he done? He knew the answer and didn't like it one bit. He'd spent the night with his best friend's wife. Crossed the professional line and, worse, he'd started to think of Phoebe as more than a friend. She was his lover. How low could he go?

He'd even spent most of the morning playing house with her. He had nothing emotionally to offer Phoebe. She needed someone to rely on, to love her and the baby. He wasn't that guy. He didn't commit to anybody. There wasn't even a cat or a dog in his life.

He had no intention of pledging himself to a woman

with a child. Or to any woman, for that matter. He wouldn't be any good at it. Worse, didn't even want to try. He wouldn't take the chance on heartache. Fun while it lasted was all he'd ever wanted. He'd had all the pain he was willing to live with. He'd see to the practical things, like getting the baby's room ready and even delivering the baby, but then he was backing out.

Some other man would take his place. Phoebe was an attractive woman. No, that wasn't strong enough. She was beautiful and smart, funny, with a quick wit, and someone far better than him would come along. He was afraid he would hurt her, but over time she would get over it. Someone would enter her life and give her what she deserved. Maybe in time she'd forgive him.

He sat up and stared out the window. His hands tightened on the wheel. Someone else would share her bed. The thought made him sick. But it was the way things should be. For her sake and the baby's.

Ryan opened the door of the car and climbed out. There was a light mist, just as there had been the evening he'd found Phoebe on his doorstep. Would he always think of her when it rained? No, he couldn't let things go any further, but he worried they had already gone too far. He'd enjoyed her body too much, liked having someone to laugh with, eat with, to look forward to seeing. He'd never had trouble keeping himself shut off but now he couldn't seem to get past his feelings for Phoebe.

He needed to get into his shop, work. Push her out of his mind. He groaned. The project he was working on was the cradle. He wasn't even safe from her in his only sanctuary. How had she invaded his life so completely in such a short time? Why had he let her? Because he'd fallen for her. Cared about her more than he had anyone since JT. How ironic was that?

Disgusted with himself, he climbed out of his car and slammed the door before heading for his front door.

Maybe when he finished the cradle and Phoebe delivered, he would be able to get her out of his mind. A nagging voice kept telling him that wasn't going to happen.

CHAPTER NINE

PHOEBE WALKED THROUGH the archway entrance of the hospital on Thursday afternoon on her way to her appointment. Her soft-soled shoes made squeaking sounds as she crossed the tiles on the floor of the lobby. At the lift, she pushed the button for the sixth floor. She could hardly contain her excitement over seeing Ryan.

Despite their plans, she'd not seen him since he'd left her house on Saturday morning. She'd only heard from him once. That had been a quick phone call to say that he couldn't make it to dinner. It was a full moon and he'd been busy. He needed to remain near the hospital.

She understood. When it was her turn to deliver she would want to know he was close. He had asked how she was doing but otherwise the call had been short and to the point. Still, she had to remember that he worked odd hours and had no control over when those would be.

The doors to the lift whooshed open and she entered. Would he kiss her? Probably not. That would be very unprofessional during an antenatal visit. Maybe he would take her out to eat or, better yet, home. She had missed his touch but more than that she missed talking and laughing with him.

She was acting like a silly schoolgirl with her first crush. Here she was almost a mother and giddy over a man.

The lift doors opened again and Phoebe stepped out and walked toward the clinic. Inside, she signed in at the window. She took a chair and looked at the pictures of the medical staff lining the wall. They included Ryan. He looked handsome but far too serious in his picture. Nothing like the man with the good sense of humor that she knew. Besides him there were a number of people she'd met or recognized from the wedding.

"Phoebe."

It was Ryan's voice. She would have known it anywhere. Every night she heard it in her dreams. Her head jerked up and their gazes met. There was a flicker of delight in his before it turned guarded. Wasn't he glad to see her?

Phoebe smiled. "Hi."

He cleared his throat and said, "Hello. Are you ready to come back?"

She moved to stand. It took her a second more than she would have liked but Ryan hadn't moved from his position at the door. A few days ago he would have hurried to offer her help. "Yes, I'm ready."

"Come this way."

What was going on? Maybe he didn't want anyone to see him touch her or overhear them. Still, this was a little much. She'd always spoken in a friendly manner to Sophia. That was part of the appeal of having a midwife—it was more like having a friend there to help deliver her.

"Follow me," he said, and led her down the hallway to an exam room. Once she'd entered he closed the door.

She sat on the exam table.

"So how have you been?" Ryan asked, as if speaking to someone he'd just met.

Phoebe gave him a questioning look. Ryan couldn't see it because his focus was on the computer. Other than those few seconds when their eyes had met after he'd called her name he hadn't looked at her again.

"Any pains?"

Just in her heart all of a sudden. "No."

"Well, it won't be long now."

Why was he talking to her like that? As if he didn't really know her? Was he afraid someone might walk in on them? "No, it won't. Next week is my due date."

He finally looked up but his focus was over her right shoulder. "You know that the chance of a baby coming on a due date is slim. A first baby is almost always late."

"I know." This all business attitude was getting old. "How are you, Ryan? I've missed you this week."

He went back to studying the computer screen. "I've been busy. Sophia being out makes things a little complicated."

Apparently their relationship was included in that.

"Any chance we could get something to eat this evening?"

"I have a mother in labor on her way in. I'm going to the unit as soon as I'm finished here."

Phoebe had never received the brush-off before but she recognized it when she heard it. *I won't cry, I won't cry.* She clenched her teeth.

Ryan was acting as if they'd never been intimate. But they were at the clinic and he should act professionally. But he was overdoing it.

He left without giving her another look.

What had happened between now and Saturday

morning that had made him so distant? He was acting like the guy she'd met that first night. When he returned she was going to find out what was going on.

She was prepared and waiting on the table when he returned. He wasn't by himself. A woman in her mid-twenties followed him into the room.

"Phoebe, this is Stacy. She's the new midwife who has joined our group. Would you be willing to let her do the exam?"

She looked at him in disbelief. He wouldn't meet her gaze. Now he didn't even want to touch her.

"All right." Phoebe drew the words out.

Stacy stepped to the table. "Phoebe, may I check the position of the baby? I promise I have gentle hands."

Phoebe said nothing. She knew gentle hands and those belonged to Ryan.

As Stacy's hand moved over her expanded middle, she rattled off some numbers while Ryan typed on the computer.

"Well, you're doing fine. Everything is as it should be. I don't see why you won't have an uneventful delivery," Stacy gushed. "I look forward to being there."

"What?" Phoebe looked at Ryan. Nothing was as it should be.

He looked over her head as he spoke. "Stacy is going to step in for me. My, uh, caseload is heavy and she's taking some of my patients."

Stacy was all smiles when she said, "I'll see you here next week for your appointment or at the delivery, whichever comes first. Do you have any questions for us?"

Yes, she had a pile of questions but none that she could ask in front of Stacy.

"No" came out sounding weak.

"Okay, then. I'll see you next week," Stacy said, without seeming to notice the tension between her and Ryan.

He opened the door and left without even looking at her. Stacy followed.

Phoebe sat in silence. Stunned. Never had she felt so used. She'd shared her body with Ryan. Opened her heart. Believed that she meant something to him. Now he was treating her like she was nothing. What a jerk. He didn't even have the backbone to tell her that he no longer wanted to help deliver the baby.

She climbed off the table and dressed. Had she ever felt more humiliated? Discarded?

Ryan was there four hours later when a new life entered the world. This time he missed the amazement he usually felt. All he could think about was Phoebe's large sad eyes when he'd left the exam room. What must she think of him? Probably the same as he was thinking of himself.

He had called to check on her a few days earlier, using all his self-control to wait as long as he had before he'd picked up the phone. Justifying the call, he'd told himself he was after all her midwife. But that hadn't been the real reason he'd done it. He'd been desperate to hear her voice. He'd done some difficult things in his life but acting as if he didn't care about Phoebe in front of her had been the hardest. It had been even more challenging not to touch her. She'd looked so dejected when he'd walked out of the room. The devil of it all was that he cared about Phoebe more than anyone else in the world.

The irony was that he had treated her the way he had because he couldn't deal with the depth of his feelings for her and his inability to handle the mountain of guilt for how he had treated someone who had been important to JT. He was so messed up he had no business being involved with anyone. Until Phoebe, he had managed to keep everyone at bay, but she had slipped past his defenses.

The dark of the night mirrored his emotions as he drove home hours later. For once in his life he wished someone was there to come home to. He let himself into his house and dropped his clothes on the floor. That was a habit that he and Phoebe shared. They both dropped things as soon as they came in the door. He his clothes and she her shoes.

Going to his bedroom, he flipped on the light. When he looked at his bed all he could see was the way Phoebe had lovingly admired his work. He'd never shared his workshop with anyone before. Even the few times female company had stayed over he'd never taken them down there. It had taken one sunny day of driving Phoebe around to garage sales to open it to her.

How quickly she had found a way into his home, his shop and his heart. But none of that mattered. He would never be able to be there for her as she needed. She deserved someone who could open his heart completely. Hold nothing back. Be there for her for the long haul. He wouldn't invest in people that way after he had he'd lost so many of them. He couldn't take the chance of going there again. It was better to let her go now.

Ryan turned off the light, removed his clothes but didn't bother to pull the covers back before he lay on the bed. He squeezed his eyes shut and put his arm over his eyes. All he could see was the confusion, then disappointment and pain in Phoebe's eyes.

Had he ever been happier than he had been in the last few weeks? When had he last thought about even being happy? It certainly hadn't been for a long time. He could remember that emotion. A few times when he'd been a kid. But he'd recognized happiness when Phoebe had kissed him on the cheek. Or when they had watched the little penguins waddle out of the water to take care of their chicks, or the look on Phoebe's face when she'd looked down at him as they'd become one. Because of her he'd known true happiness.

He hadn't realized how he'd shut out the world until she had shown up on his doorstep, leaving him no choice but to rejoin it again. He'd carried the pain of war, the agony of trying to help men and women whose lives would never be the same, bottled up until Phoebe had started asking questions. He'd talked more about his time in the war in the last few weeks than he'd done in the last ten years. The more he'd told her the easier it had become to talk about those times. Now it felt like a weight had been lifted off his chest. After he'd returned from a difficult mission, he'd been required to talk to the shrink. He'd never thought it useful. Thanks to Phoebe, he was starting to see a value in not holding those memories in.

All this didn't matter anyway. He'd hurt Phoebe so badly today that even if he tried to have a relationship with her she would close the door in his face. No, it was better this way.

Phoebe leaned her head against the glass window of the tram. The clack of the cars made a rhythm that would have lulled her to sleep if her emotions hadn't been jumping like balls in a pinball machine. She fluctuated between disbelief and anger.

How had she let Ryan matter so much? Worse, how had she been misled by him?

He had made her believe he cared. It hadn't only been his lovemaking but the way he'd thought of little things to help her. Painting the baby's room, going with her to garage sales, massaging her feet. Her back. In just a few weeks he had done more for her and with her than Joshua had done during their entire marriage.

So what had happened to make Ryan do such an about-face?

Had she pushed too hard? Assumed things she shouldn't? Had making plans for them to eat together, see each other scared him off?

When she heard her stop called she prepared to get off. She still had a few blocks to walk before she made it home. She was tired. Didn't even plan to eat anything before going to bed. If Ryan knew he would scold her. Maybe not, after what she'd experienced today.

Slipping her key into the lock a few minutes later, she opened the door. She entered and turned on the light. How different this homecoming had been from the one she had imagined. She'd hoped that Ryan would bring her home and stay the night. That bubble had been completely popped.

Phoebe kicked her shoes off. She chuckled dryly. The action made her think of Ryan dropping his clothes inside his door. Making her way to her bedroom, she turned on her bedside lamp, then undressed. She slid between the sheets and leaned over to turn the light off. The picture of her and Joshua caught her attention.

Had the fact that she was carrying Joshua's baby been the reason Ryan had suddenly slammed the door between them? Was the baby too much of a reminder that she would always be tied to Joshua? Or was it that they represented the painful loss of Joshua? Or the other men that

Ryan had seen die. In some way they must be part of the past he worked so hard to shut out or forget.

Sliding the drawer out of the bedside table, Phoebe pulled out the crumpled letter Joshua had sent her. Opening it, she smoothed it out on the bed before reading it. Had Joshua known he wasn't coming home when he had written it? Had he known he was leaving on a dangerous patrol like Ryan had described? Even after they had discussed separating, had he wanted her to be happy, to find someone else? Had he thought Ryan might be that person?

Whatever it was, she'd done as Joshua had said and gone to Ryan. Joshua had been right. There she'd found the piece of her life that had been missing all these years. Moisture filled her eyes. But Ryan didn't want her. Once again she was on her own. Would she ever find a real partner in life?

Turning off the light, she curled around her baby. At least this little one would be someone to love who would return it.

Sunday afternoon there was a knock at the door.

Her heart leaped. Was it Ryan?

Phoebe answered it to find Mrs. Rosenheim waiting on the veranda. Phoebe's spirits dropped like a person falling off a bridge. Had she really expected it to be Ryan?

"Hello, dear. I was just checking on you. I've not seen you all weekend. Didn't want you to have that baby and me not know about it."

"I'm right here. No baby yet." She didn't want any company. How could she get rid of her neighbor gracefully?

"From the sound and look of you, something else is

going on." Mrs. Rosenheim brushed past Phoebe into the living room.

Phoebe really didn't feel up to dealing with the older woman. She wanted to wallow in her misery alone.

"I haven't seen that nice young man around."

That was all it took for Phoebe to burst into tears.

"My goodness, it's all that bad?" Mrs. Rosenheim patted her on the arm. "Why don't you fix us some tea and tell me all about it?"

Phoebe swiped at her cheek, then nodded. Maybe it would be good to tell someone about what had happened.

As she put the kettle on and prepared the cups, Phoebe told Mrs. Rosenheim about how she'd met Ryan.

"Well, at least that absent husband of yours did one thing to show he cared," Mrs. Rosenheim murmured.

"Joshua cared—"

Mrs. Rosenheim waved her hand. "Let's not argue about that. So, what put you in this tizzy about Ryan?"

Phoebe placed a teacup in front of Mrs. Rosenheim and one in front of the chair across from her. She wouldn't sit in Ryan's chair. How quickly he had become a central part of her life.

Phoebe told her about how Ryan had acted during her clinic visit. During the entire explanation Mrs. Rosenheim sipped her tea and nodded.

"Sounds scared to me. So what do you plan to do?"

"Do? What can I do?"

"Yes, do. You're getting ready to have a baby. Do you want to bring a baby into the world feeling that kind of discord? Go and make Ryan explain himself. Tell him how you feel."

Phoebe sighed. "You're right. I need to talk him. Get

the air cleared. I was so shocked and hurt by his actions that I've not been able to think."

"Then I suggest that you make yourself presentable and give that man a piece of your mind."

Ryan already had her heart, he might as well get part of her mind. If things stayed the way they were, she would lose him. To move on she needed answers, and those could only come from Ryan.

Phoebe bowed her head against the wind that was picking up as she walked along Ryan's street. Like the first time she had visited him, she had practiced what she was going to say on the tram ride there. She was going to demand answers. More than that, she was going to get answers.

Would Ryan be home? She'd thought of calling first but had been afraid that he would make some excuse as to why she couldn't see him. She would have none of that.

She had accepted Joshua's decisions. Knowing what he did was important hadn't disguised the fact he'd been more interested in fighting wars than being with her. She wouldn't let Ryan put her to the side. She'd stay at his place until she knew what was going on.

Phoebe walked past Ryan's car. He was home. She climbed the steps to his door and groaned. Her back was killing her. The baby had grown so large.

She hesitated. Would Ryan answer if he realized it was her? It didn't matter. She was staying until she found out what his problem was, even if she had to sleep on his veranda all night. That wouldn't happen. No matter how hard Ryan was trying to push her out of his life, he was too kind and tenderhearted to leave her out in the elements.

To come all this way and not knock was ridiculous.

She was no longer the woman she'd been when she'd shown up on his doorstep last month. With or without him, she would have this baby and the two of them would make it. It would be wonderful to have Ryan in their lives, but if not, she and the baby would still survive. That much she did know.

Lifting her hand, she boldly knocked on the door. Seconds went by with no answer. There was no sound from inside. Again she knocked. Nothing. Maybe Ryan was in the basement and couldn't hear her. She turned to descend the steps and search for a way around back when the door opened.

Ryan looked as if he hadn't slept in days. There were dark circles under his eyes. His hair stood on end. He was still wearing his hospital uniform and it was rumpled, as if he'd been too distracted to change. Her heart went out to him for a second and then she reminded herself of why she was there. Life hadn't been kind to her since last Thursday, either.

CHAPTER TEN

Phoebe.

Ryan's heart skidded to a halt then picked up the pace double-time. What was she doing here?

How like her to show up unannounced on his doorstep. Was that how they had started out?

She looked wonderful, irritated and determined all at the same time. He had missed her. There had never been another time in his life when he'd longed for someone like he had for Phoebe.

"What're are you doing here?"

"We need to talk." She stepped forward, leaving him no choice but to move and let her in.

"Talk?"

She whirled to face him with surprising agility. "You mean after your performance the other day you don't think we need to talk?"

Ryan closed the door. He really didn't want to do this. "Performance?"

"Really, Ryan? You don't think you owe me an explanation for your behavior at the clinic?"

"I did my job."

"Job? Was it your job to take pity on the poor widow woman and go to bed with her?"

Ryan flinched. That hurt. Yes, she was hitting below the belt but he deserved it.

"What I don't understand is why I let you get away with acting like there was nothing between us. Or why I've given you so many days to explain yourself. I didn't expect a public display at the clinic but I did expect you to act as if I had some importance."

"Stacy was there—"

"That's your excuse for going AWOL on me and not hearing from you? You know, I would never have taken you for a coward."

Ryan winced. That's what he had been. If he ran, then he wouldn't have to face what he'd done and how he felt about Phoebe. He sat in his chair. Phoebe's glare bore down on him. "Look, you don't understand."

"Oh, I understand. This is all about you hiding from the world, the things you saw in Iraq and your feelings. If you don't let someone in, then you don't have to worry about them dying, like your friends did. Like Joshua.

"You live mechanically. You just go through the days. Look at this place." She swung her arm around, indicating the room. "You just exist here. No pictures, no rugs, a sofa and a chair. Your bedroom is a step better only because of your woodwork. It shows some warmth. The one place where you actually look like you're living is ironically in your shop, and it's underground. You come up and do what you have to do and then disappear again like a mole that's afraid of the light, but in your case you're afraid of feeling anything for someone. You care more about that furniture downstairs than you do people. In fact, those inanimate objects in your bedroom have received more love than you show the rest of the people in your life."

She was right. There was nothing he could say to defend himself.

"You're afraid that if you care too much you'll lose part of yourself. But you'll never be happy that way. You have to let people in. Let them see the person I see. The warm and caring person. The fun and humorous one. The person who gives despite any pain to himself."

Ryan raised a hand with his index finger up. "Hey, don't be putting me on a pedestal. I'm not one of your fairy-tale knights on a white horse, riding in to save the day."

Phoebe looked at him. Was he right? Had she tried to make more of their relationship than there was? Had she been so desperate that she had clung to Ryan? Needed anyone to rely on? To fill the void of loneliness?

"I haven't." Her remark sounded weak even to her own ears.

"Haven't what? Become self-contained, built your own perfect little world where Joshua came home as the hero, loved you and left to return again? Where you were willing to accept a small piece of his life just so you could have someone to share that perfect life? Except it wasn't all that perfect, was it? You wanted more. A family, but you couldn't or wouldn't tell him that it was time to think of you."

She cringed. Was that what she had been doing? "You're wrong."

"Really? Did you ever once ask JT to take an assignment that would bring him home for longer than three months? Did you ever ask him to choose you over the army?"

She hadn't.

"I can see you didn't. What were you afraid of? That

he would leave you all together? As strong as you act on the outside, you're a marshmallow of self-doubt on the inside. You don't understand why you weren't good enough to make JT want to stay at home. You feel sorry for yourself but cover it with acting as if you can handle everything on your own. No matter how hard I might try, I could never fix those for you. That's something you have to recognize and do for yourself."

All Ryan's accusations hit home. A number of them she didn't want to face.

"Phoebe, I can't be someone that I'm not. Seeing what humans can do to each other makes you stop and think before you get involved. I cared then and what did it get me? All I wanted was out." He spoke to the floor, then looked at her.

"That's understandable. But look at you now." She lowered her voice. "You help bring life into the world. You sure picked a funny occupation to not care about anyone."

"That was part of the appeal of being a midwife. I'm only involved in a patient's life for a short time. After the baby comes I'm done."

"How sad. You know you brought warmth and joy into my world. I came to your doorstep lonely, sad and afraid. For heaven's sake, I was weeks away from having a baby and I didn't even have a room ready. I was going through the motions, just like you, until we met. It was far past time for us both to start living our lives again."

"I have lived like that. I've had friends. Joshua was a friend and look what happened to him. You say that I'm afraid but you are afraid of something, too, and that is being alone. You've lost your parents, you brother is nowhere around, Joshua is gone, his parents are jerks and now you're clinging to me. People leave and die, it's a part of life."

Phoebe stepped forward. "I'm well aware of that. The question is, are you? People die. Do you think I don't understand that? He was my husband. My parents are gone. Even my brother is halfway across the world from me."

Ryan jumped up. Phoebe stepped backward. He move forward and glared at her. With his hands balled at his sides, he barked, "And I'm the man who slept with his best friend's wife."

Phoebe blinked and stumbled backwards. She quickly righted herself. That was what all of this was about? Some male idea of solidarity to his best friend. Ryan thought he'd betrayed Joshua.

He made a sound of disgust and turned away. His shoulders were tense. She wanted to reach out and touch him. Reassure him that he'd done nothing wrong. If she did, she feared he'd reject her forever. She had to reason with him, get through to him. Reaching into her pocket, she pulled out Joshua's letter. Maybe with Joshua's help she could.

"Ryan, Joshua is dead."

He jerked slightly.

"We're alive." She kept her voice low. "He doesn't stand between us. He's gone. You did nothing wrong. In fact, it was very right. Here, I think you should read this." She stepped around him and handed him the letter. "I'm going to leave you to read it."

Walking to the bedroom, she went into the bathroom. Her back was aching. Maybe the baby was just pressing against something it shouldn't. Would Joshua's letter help Ryan let go or would it only make things worse? She hoped with all her heart it made him see the truth.

* * *

Ryan opened the crumpled pages. Why had Phoebe given him something to read? He scanned the page and saw JT's name at the end. Guilt churned in his stomach. With his heart bumping against his chest wall and his hands shaking, he let his focus move to the top of the page.

Phoebe—

I know I've not always written like I should. For that I'm sorry. Especially when you have been so good about it. I know now that when we married you didn't bargain on us spending so much time apart. For that I'm sorry also. When we parted a few weeks ago I knew things had changed between us. We have spent too much time living separate lives to the point where our relationship has slipped into one of friendship instead of one that we both wish it could be. I have done you an injustice. You have such a large capacity to love that it was never fair of me to deny you that.

I wish for you a happy life. If you ever need anything and don't know where to turn I want you to find my friend, Ryan Matthews. He will help you. We are buddies from his army days. I trust him with my life and you can with yours. He lives in Melbourne. He will take care of you. Believe in him, he won't let you down. I think you will like him. I hope you do.

Take care, Phoebe. Have a good life.

Joshua

JT had sent Phoebe to him. As if he'd known they would needed each other. Had it been JT's way of giving his blessing to their relationship? He looked at the letter. How long had Phoebe had this? Why hadn't she said something sooner?

Ryan went into his room. Phoebe must have purposely taken her time in the bathroom because she was coming toward him. She stopped and stared at the cradle sitting in a corner. She must have missed it on her way to the bathroom because the closet door stood open, obscuring it.

It was his finest piece of work to date. He didn't know if he would ever do better. It was as if his heart and soul had been emptied into it. It sat low to the floor with a high front and sides that wrapped around slightly. It looked like one that would be handed down in a wealthy family. It was as much like one he'd seen in a history museum back home as he could make it.

Going over to the cradle, Phoebe ran her hand along the smooth lip of one side. She pushed it and watched the slow movement back and forth.

"It's for the baby." The emotion in his voice made it come out as a croak.

She glanced at him. "It's the most beautiful thing I've ever seen."

He raised his hand with Joshua's letter in it. "This is why you came here that first night."

She nodded.

"Why didn't you tell me?"

"At first because you acted all cold and unwelcoming and I wasn't sure Joshua had been right about you."

His lips formed a tight line. "I wasn't at my best. I'm sorry. So why not later?"

She shrugged. "I started to trust you. You agreed to deliver the baby. I wanted you to and the letter didn't matter anymore. I had started to care about you. I had hoped you cared about me. Thought you did until I saw you on Thursday."

"I'm sorry I hurt you. I hated doing so but I didn't know how else to handle it. The night we made love was the most wonderful of my life but on my way home I thought of Joshua, of how I was not the best man for you. I knew we couldn't continue." He looked at the letter. "But after reading his letter, I wonder..."

"If it was Joshua's way of telling us both to move on? That we would need each other? I don't know if he thought this..." she pointed to him and then herself "...would happen, but I think he knew we could help each other. We were the two people he knew best in the world. I don't think what's between us is wrong. I think we honor him by caring about each other and living well. I love you, Ryan, and want you in my and this baby's life. By the way, you could have talked to me on Thursday, just like you are doing now."

His chest tightened. He'd rather die than not be the person Phoebe needed him to be. "I don't know if I can give what you and the baby should have."

Her look met his. "I don't think either one of us knows that for sure. Yes, there're risks but that's what love is all about. Think with your heart, not your head. I know you care." She touched her chest. "I feel it here. That was part of the reason I came." She grinned. "And because I was so mad. But everything you do proves you care. For example..." she touched the cradle "...you messed up with this. It shows your true feelings. You care. There's no doubt that you do, you're just scared of doing so.

"I've been waiting most of my life to have someone love me, really love me, want to be with me. I thought it was Joshua but I soon learned we didn't want the same things. I wanted the rocker on the veranda and watching the sunset and he wanted to always be going off somewhere. Don't get me wrong, what he was doing was important but that didn't bring me any closer to my dreams.

"I love you, Ryan. I don't want you doing anything for me out of obligation to Joshua any more. I want you to care about me for me."

Could he be a part of that? He wasn't sure. But he had been for the last six weeks. He'd never been happier. Had he found the place he belonged? The place where all the ugliness in life disappeared? When had the last time been he'd thought of the war? He'd already realized that talking to Phoebe had eased the past. Now, could he grasp what she was offering and hang on to it?

There was a silence between them. The air between them was heavy with tension.

"I guess I should be going."

She sounded defeated.

"I've said what I came to say. Found out what I needed to know." She moved past him and headed for the door.

Fear flooded him that surpassed any he'd ever felt before. Even when bullets had been flying over his head. If he let her go out the door he might lose her forever. He couldn't let that happen. His fingers wrapped around her forearm, stopping her.

Her gaze came up to meet his. There was a question there, along with hope.

"I don't want you to leave."

Her hand came up to cup his cheek. "I don't want to go."

The band around his chest popped, letting all the love he'd held back flow. He gathered her to him and brought his mouth to hers. Phoebe melted against him.

Deep kisses, small sweet ones, filled his world until they broke apart.

"Can you stay the night?" Ryan looked down at her.

"Yes. My maternity leave starts tomorrow. No due babies?"

"Only this one." Ryan placed his hand on her belly. "And I intend to keep a close eye on him or her. Not let the mother out of my sight or out of my arms."

Phoebe smiled, one that reached her eyes. "That sounds perfect to me. I promise to be willing to accept life isn't about fairy tales if you're willing to believe they are a possibility."

"Agreed." Ryan kissed her again.

She broke away. "Augh." She reached behind her and rubbed her lower back.

"What's wrong?"

"My back aches."

He gave her an intense look. "When did it start?"

"On my way here."

He grinned. "You may be in labor."

"Really?" Her hands went to her belly and a dreamy look covered her face.

"We'll see what happens in the next few hours. It still might be Braxton-Hicks contractions or, in other words, false labor pains. Come with me. I have something we can do to keep your mind off them." He took her hand and led her toward the bath.

"Can we do that if I'm in labor?"

Ryan chuckled. "No, but there are plenty of other things that we can do that are almost as satisfying."

"Like a foot massage?"

"That could be arranged. But I have some new ideas in mind. Like starting with a nice warm shower."

Inside the bathroom, he reached in the tub area. Turning the water on, seconds later the shower sprayed water. Ryan turned back to her and began removing her clothes.

"I can do that."

"But I want to." He carefully worked each button out of its hole. Soon she was naked. He didn't touch her but he took his time looking.

"You're embarrassing me."

"Because I enjoy admiring you? I think you're the most amazing woman I know." With a look of regret he pulled the curtain back and offered her his hand. "Be careful. We don't need you slipping."

Phoebe took it and stepped under the steaming water. A few minutes later the curtain was pulled back and Ryan joined her. His manhood stood tall between them. He was dazzling. "Oh, I wasn't expecting you."

"I need a bath, too. Saves water to share. Turn around and let me massage your back."

Phoebe did as he instructed. He made slow circles with the pads of his thumbs pressing but not too hard.

"That feels great."

Ryan continued to ease the ache for a few more minutes before his hands moved around to make wide circular motions over her belly. He pulled her back against him. His length pressed against her butt. He didn't move but said close to her ear, "Hand me the soap."

She took it out of the holder and placed it in his hand. He stepped back and began to run the soap across her shoulders, then down her back. "Turn around."

Phoebe did. His hands traveled to her breasts. She watched the tension grow in his face. A muscle jumped in his jaw. He continued his ministrations. Her nipples grew and tingled. His hand moved on to her belly and down to do her legs. As he stood he kissed the baby.

Her breath caught and her lips quivered. She put her hands on both sides of Ryan's face and brought his mouth to hers. He returned her kiss, then set her away.

"You need to get out before the water turns cold."

"What about you?"

"I think I'll stay for a while."

Phoebe stepped out of the shower with a smile on her face. It was nice, being desired. She dried off. "Ryan, I don't have any more clothes. Do you have a large shirt I can wear?"

"You don't need any clothes. Just climb into bed. Is your back still hurting?"

"A little. It comes and goes."

A few minutes later Ryan came out of the bathroom in all his naked glory. He was all man. Leaving the room, he returned with a fat candle and a pack of matches. He set the candle on the bedside table and lit it before he turned off the overhead light.

"Move over." He climbed in next to her. "Face me, Phoebe."

She rolled to her side and he did also. Ryan's hand started rubbing her belly and moving around to her back and forward again. He looked into her eyes.

A few minutes later he cleared his throat. "I loved the aggressive way you pushed your way in here tonight and made me see reason. JT and I could have used you on patrol with us a couple of times."

She snickered. "I actually learned that maneuver from Mrs. Rosenheim. She's been using it on me for a few years now. In fact, she did so this afternoon. She's the one who encouraged me to come and see you."

"Well, remind me to give her a kiss when I see her again."

Phoebe placed her hand on his chest. "You might not want to do that because she could expect it every time you see her."

"I think it'll be worth taking the chance." He captured her hand and held it against him.

"Ryan, I want you to know that I'm not going to push you for more than you can give or do. Ooh..." Phoebe tensed.

He looked at her closely. "Stronger?"

"A little."

"Why don't you try to get some sleep? You may need it later. I'll be right here." Ryan rolled to his back and pulled her closer. His length lay firm against her hip. Regardless of his obvious need, he made no move to do anything but care for her. She drifted off to sleep knowing she and the baby were in good hands. A sharp pain radiating around her waist woke her. The candle had burned low.

"How're you doing?"

"That pain was stronger."

Ryan set up in bed. "Then we need to start timing them. Let me know when you feel the next one."

She lifted one corner of her mouth and gave him a look. "I don't think you'll have to be told. I'm a wimp when it comes to pain. You'll hear me."

He chuckled. "I'll keep that in mind as this goes on. Do I need to call in someone else so they can lose their hearing?"

"You've already done that with Stacy."

Ryan had the good grace to look repentant. "I'm sorry

about that. I'll try to make up for that by doing what I can to help make you comfortable. Do you need anything? Need more support on your back?"

"I'm fine right now but I do love to have my back rubbed."

"Then a back rub is what you'll get." He climbed out of bed.

"Where're you going?"

"I'm just going around to the other side."

"But I liked you here." She watched him walk by the end of the bed. Even in labor he turned her on.

"I appreciate the compliment but I can do a better job over here. Less distractions." His hands moved across her back.

"Like what?"

"Your beautiful face. When your pains get to twenty minutes apart we'll need to call Stacy and go to the hospital."

"Do we have to? I want you to deliver," she said in a melancholy tone.

"No, I guess we don't have to. Do you want to deliver at your house? If you do, we need to get moving."

"I'd like to have the baby here. In this beautiful bed. Just you and me."

Did he realize that if he agreed it would be a sign of commitment? He was giving her and the baby permission to enter his personal space. To share his home and bed for a significant event.

Ryan's hands stopped moving for a second then started again. "I would like that."

She smiled, then winced.

"I take it that was another pain. Try to breathe through them. It'll make it easier. Remember your lessons."

"Is this the moment that you morph into a midwife?"

"It's time. I'm going to get my bag and put on some pants. You stay put."

"You're going to put on clothes when I'm not wearing any?"

"It's a long shot that something might go wrong. If I have to call for help I don't want to get caught with my pants down, so to speak."

Phoebe laughed.

He gave her a reprimanding look. "You go on and make fun but it would be hard for me to live that one down."

She enjoyed the sight of Ryan's backside as he search a drawer. He pulled out some boxers and stepped into them. Going to the wardrobe, he came out wearing a pair of athletic shorts. He then left the room and returned with a backpack. Ryan flipped the bedside lamp on and blew out the candle.

"I liked it better the other way." Phoebe rolled toward him.

"I did, too, but I need to see." Ryan unzipped the backpack and removed a stethoscope. He placed it on her belly, then listened to her chest and back. Finished, he put the stethoscope on the table. "Sounds good."

"I'm scared" slipped out before she knew it.

Ryan pushed her hair away from her forehead and kissed her. "There's nothing to be afraid of. I'll be right here with you all the way. This is a natural process."

"That's coming from a man who never had a baby."

"That's true, but I've been there when a lot of them have been born. I'll give you an example of how natural it is. My great-great-grandmother had twelve babies. They all lived. While she was in labor she would fix breakfast for the family and get everyone off to the fields. They were farmers in north Alabama. She would lie on the floor and have the baby, then tie the cord off with a thread from a flour sack because it was thin enough to cut the cord. She would clean herself and the baby up, then get into bed. At the end of the day when everyone came in from the field there would be a new baby to greet."

"Are you expecting me to do that?" Her voice rose.

Ryan took her hand and squeezed it. "No, I'm not. What I'm trying to say is that if my grandmother can do it by herself twelve times, then the two of us can certainly do it together once without any problem."

"I think I can do anything as long as I have you to help me."

Ryan leaned over and gave her a leisurely kiss. "I feel the same way, honey."

Another pain gripped her. She clutched Ryan's hand.

When it had passed he said, "Why don't you walk around some? It would help with the pain and get the labor moving along."

"I'm not going to walk around your place with no clothes on, in labor or not."

"Okay, let me see if I can find something comfortable for you to wear." Ryan went to his wardrobe. The sound of hangers being pushed across a rod came out of the space. "This should do it."

He returned to the bed with a button-up shirt in his hand. "Swing your feet over the side and I'll help you get this on."

She did and he held the shirt while she slipped her arms into it. The sleeves fell well past her hands. Ryan buttoned it for her, then rolled the sleeves up to the middle of her forearms.

He reached out and wiggled his fingers. "Let me help you stand."

Phoebe took them and let him pull her to her feet.

Ryan stepped back and looked at her. "Cute. I do believe I like you wearing my shirt."

Phoebe pushed at her hair, trying to bring it to some kind of order. "Thanks. I just hope I don't mess it up."

"Not a problem. It'll be for a good cause.

"Okay, let's do some walking. There isn't as much space here as there is at the hospital but we'll just make do."

Ryan stayed by her side as they made a pass round the living room through the kitchen and back to the bedroom. "Let's do it again," he encouraged as she looked wistfully at the bed. With each contraction Ryan checked his watch, which he had slipped on his wrist before they'd started out of his bedroom.

"They're getting closer."

After one particularly lengthy pain he said, "Tell me about your shower at school."

It was his sly way of keeping her mind off what was going on with her body. She was grateful for his efforts. "It was wonderful. I received all kinds of cute baby things."

He touched her arm to encourage her to keep walking. "Did you get some baby clothes, like you were hoping?"

"I did. I filled a drawer and have some hanging in the wardrobe."

"You must have had a lot of people there."

They continued the slow pace around the house.

"I was surprised. Most of the teachers came. Those who didn't sent presents by others. Everyone was very generous."

"Why were you surprised? Haven't you been working there for some time?"

"I have but they have all seemed to be a little standoffish since Joshua was killed. It became worse when I told them I was pregnant. It was as if they didn't know what to say or do so they did nothing."

"I'm sorry you were so alone for so long. You should have come to me sooner."

She stopped and looked at him.

He put up a hand. "I know, I know. I wasn't very approachable at first. For that I'm sorry."

She smiled. "But you came around very nicely, so I'm happy." But he hadn't said anything about loving her. Even when she had confessed her love for him. She could wait. Ryan showed he cared in so many other ways. He was someone she could count on. Even if she couldn't, she had learned she could depend on herself. "Oh."

"Breathe. Don't hold your breath." Ryan showed her how.

They made small swooshing sounds together.

"I think it's time to get you settled in. I also need to check and see where that baby is."

Ryan led her toward the bedroom.

"How much longer?" As she went by the footboard, she let her fingers trail over the surface of the wood.

"Let me examine you, then I'll have an idea."

She sat on the edge of the bed while he prepared it.

"You're not going to make me lie on the floor like your great-great-grandmother did?"

"I hadn't planned to, but I can." He shook out a blanket as if getting ready to place it on the floor.

"I was kidding."

He smiled. "I'm glad to hear that. I was worried about my back hurting when I bent over to help deliver."

"What kind of midwife are you? Being more worried about your comfort than mine?"

Ryan put a hand down on the mattress on each side of her. His face was inches away from hers. "Honey, I care too much about you to let you be uncomfortable." Ryan kissed her deeply and moved away. He helped her settle into the center of the bed and then he did the exam.

"You're well on your way. Dilated five centimeters. When you get to ten you'll be ready to have a baby."

Another pain cramped her back and radiated around to her sides. She grabbed Ryan's hand. He rode it out with her, all the time whispering sweet encouragement.

Ryan had seen countless husbands in the delivery suite when their wives had been giving birth. Some handled the process with aplomb while others were just a step above worthless. Ryan knew what was going to happen and still waves the size of a tsunami rolled through his stomach because this time it was Phoebe having the baby and he was that significant other helping. He felt more like that guy who was useless.

She had taken over his life, captured his heart and made him a ball of nerves in a situation where he usually had all the confidence. Even with all his reassurances, he worried that something might not go right during the birth. If she died or the baby did, he didn't know what he would do. He'd survived other deaths but he didn't think he could live without Phoebe.

"You look worried all of a sudden. Is something wrong?" Phoebe asked.

"No, everything is fine. You're doing wonderfully. Keep up the good work."

"I need to go to the bathroom?"

"Sure." Ryan stood and helped her up. "I'll leave the door open. If you need me I'll be right out here."

While Phoebe was in the bathroom Ryan pulled out his cellphone and called the hospital to let them know that he was in the process of delivering Phoebe's baby. He wanted them aware so that if there was a problem someone could be here to help in minutes.

"Ryan!"

"Yes?" He hurried toward the bathroom.

"My waters just broke."

"Well, this baby is getting ready to make a showing. Stay put and I'll help you get cleaned up. I'll find you something dry to wear."

He left to search for another shirt. This time he went to the chest of drawers and found a T-shirt. It might not fit over all of her middle but at least it would cover her lovely breasts so that he could concentrate on delivering the baby. He went back to Phoebe.

"You're going to run out of clothes." She pushed a button through a hole.

"If I do, I won't mind. I like you better naked anyway."

Moisture filled her eyes and she gave him a wry smile. "Thanks. You really are being wonderful."

"Not a problem." A delivery had always been a matter-of-fact event for him. A job with a happy ending most of the time. But with Phoebe it was much more. This was an event to cherish.

He helped her pull the T-shirt over her head.

"This doesn't cover much," she complained.

"I need to see your belly and you can pull the sheet up to cover yourself if you must. I don't know why you're being so modest. I've seen all of you and there isn't anything or anyone more stunning. Now, come on and get into bed. We have a baby to welcome into the world."

Another pain shot through her.

"Let's get you settled and I'm going to have another look." He help her move to the center of the bed.

"I'm feeling pressure."

"Good, then you're almost ready. Bend your legs."

Ryan placed her feet in the correct spot so he could see. He put on plastic gloves and checked her. "You're almost there."

"Here comes another one." Phoebe gritted her teeth.

"Look at me," Ryan demanded.

She did.

"Now, let's breathe together."

Phoebe followed his lead.

With the contraction over, Ryan lightly trailed his fingers over her middle until the tension left her and she lay back.

"I need to get a few things out of the bathroom and find something soft to swaddle the baby in. You should have let me know you were planning this tonight and I could have been better prepared."

"You're a funny man, Ryan Matthews."

"I thought you could use some humor right about now." He found the things he needed and placed them at the foot of the bed within arm's length.

Another pain took Phoebe and she met his look. They went through it together. This was one time he didn't mind looking into the pain in someone's eyes.

"I feel pressure. I need to push."

"Hold on just a second."

"This baby isn't waiting for you," she growled.

Ryan examined her. "The head has crowned." He

moved to the end of the bed and leaned over the footboard. "Phoebe—" his voice was low "—I want you to look at me. On the next contraction I want you to push."

Her gaze met his between her knees. They didn't have to wait long. "Push."

Ryan reached for the baby's head and supported it. His look went to Phoebe again. "You're doing beautifully."

Another contraction hit. His gaze held hers. He wished he could hold her hand and comfort her but he couldn't be at two places at once. "Push, honey."

Ryan glanced down. The baby's shoulders slid out and the rest of the tiny human followed. He saw birth all the time but none had been more amazing.

Exhausted, Phoebe fall back on the bed.

"It's a boy," Ryan announced. He tied off the umbilical cord before cutting it and laid the baby on Phoebe's stomach.

She reached a hand up to touch the tiny head.

At the baby's squeaking sound, Ryan came around to the bedside table and reached for the suction bubble. He cleaned the air passages and mouth. Grabbing a clean towel, he wiped the newborn.

The sight before him was more beautiful than any he'd ever witnessed. His heart swelled. For once he could understand the feeling new parents had when their child was born.

"He's perfect, Phoebe." Ryan couldn't keep the reverence out of his voice.

She looked at him with a tired smile. "He is, isn't he?"

Ryan leaned down and kissed her on the forehead. "No more perfect than you. I'm going to lay him beside you and go get a washcloth and finish washing him up. You and I still have some work to do." He took a towel from the end of the bed. Wrapping the baby in it, he placed him beside her.

Phoebe secured him with her arm.

"Don't move." Quickly he went to the bathroom and prepared a warm washcloth. Returning to Phoebe, he cleaned the baby boy, swaddled him in a sheet and placed him in the cradle.

Going to the end of the bed, Ryan said, "Okay, Phoebe, I need a couple of big pushes and we'll be done here. Then you can rest."

Half an hour later Ryan had Phoebe settled with the baby at her breast. He stood at the end of the bed and watched them. He was so full of emotion all he could do was stare. It had been an honor to be a part of such a special event. Phoebe's eyelids lifted.

They were full of love that extended to him.

"What's your middle name?"

"James."

Phoebe looked down at the baby. "Joshua James Taylor." She looked back at Ryan. "We'll call him JJ."

Ryan's eyes watered.

"Why don't you join us and get to know your namesake?"

Ryan didn't hesitate to join them on the bed. Phoebe lifted her head and he slipped an arm under her neck. JJ mewed as if he wished the two adults would stop interrupting his sleep. He soon quieted. Ryan ran his palm over JJ's silky head. Despite having delivered hundreds of babies, Ryan had never spent any time enjoying the touch and feel of a newborn. He picked up the tiny hand and JJ wrapped it around Ryan's finger. His heart was captured.

Ryan had spent so much of his life alone and now he wanted more. He would never go back to living closed off from people. His world was right here in his arms and he was going to hold on to it tight.

He looked at Phoebe. Her eyes were clear and confident. "We are yours. All you have to do is accept us."

"I love you, Phoebe. And I love JJ. I want to be a part of your lives if you will let me."

"And we love you. We are family now."

Ryan kissed her tenderly on the lips. When he lifted his mouth from hers Phoebe's eyelids had already closed. He shut his, releasing a sigh of contentment. He'd gone from being a man alone and caring nothing about the future to a man who had everything he could hope for, including a bright future. Life was worth living.

* * * * *

Don't miss the next story in the fabulous
MIDWIVES ON-CALL *series*
UNLOCKING HER SURGEON'S HEART
by Fiona Lowe
Available in July 2015!